T0006965

BY SUSIE DUMOND

Queerly Beloved

Looking for a Sign

LOOKING
for a SIGN

LOOKING
for a SIGN

A NOVEL

Susie Dumond

THE DIAL PRESS

NEW YORK

A Dial Press Trade Paperback Original

Published in the United States by The Dial Press, an imprint of Random House, a division of Penguin Random House LLC, New York.

THE DIAL PRESS is a registered trademark and the colophon is a trademark of Penguin Random House LLC.
DIAL DELIGHTS and colophon are trademarks of Penguin Random House LLC.

LIBRARY OF CONGRESS CATALOGING-IN-PUBLICATION DATA
Names: Dumond, Susie, author.
Title: Looking for a sign : a novel / Susie Dumond.
Description: New York : The Dial Press, 2024.
Identifiers: LCCN 2023052149 (print) | LCCN 2023052150 (ebook) |
ISBN 9780593596272 (trade paperback) | ISBN 9780593596289 (ebook)
Subjects: LCGFT: Lesbian fiction. | Romance fiction. | Novels.
Classification: LCC PS3604.U494 L66 2024 (print) |
LCC PS3604.U494 (ebook) | DDC 813/.6—dc23/eng/20231108
LC record available at https://lccn.loc.gov/2023052149
LC ebook record available at https://lccn.loc.gov/2023052150

Printed in the United States of America on acid-free paper

randomhousebooks.com

2 4 6 8 9 7 5 3 1

Book design by Diane Hobbing

To every starry-eyed wanderer who has texted a parent asking for your exact birth time: Keep looking up.

LOOKING
for a SIGN

One

THE MOMENT GRAY stepped out of her car into the gravelly mud pile that was supposedly her destination, she considered getting right back in, driving another hour back north to New Orleans, and forgetting this whole endeavor. She could probably gain just as much insight and comfort from the bottom of a pint of Ben & Jerry's as from this ridiculous plan. She was sure she'd put the right address into her GPS, but now, surrounded only by trees and mosquitoes, this didn't feel right. Not that she really knew what "right" felt like anymore after the past month. But then she remembered her best friend Cherry's words that convinced her to give it a try: *If you really want to find your soulmate, if you really want your new life to begin, then you need wisdom beyond what traditional measures can provide.* She *did* want to find her soulmate. She *did* want to live her perfect life and create the family of her dreams. So shouldn't she be willing to try something different, even if it was uncomfortable?

Determined, Gray pulled her boots from the muck with a loud squelch and navigated around a gnarled old oak tree, looking for something, anything, that could point her in the right direction. A row of citrus trees to her left wasn't much help, nor the Spanish moss shifting in the wind overhead. The echo of what sounded like women's chatter drew Gray's attention to her right. As she trudged through the swampy ground toward the noise, she discovered a weathered barn and small house with peeling yellow paint. The source of the noise soon revealed itself to be not a group of gossiping ladies but the residents of a wooden chicken coop. One of the birds marched straight up to Gray, made a curious clucking sound, and began pecking at her feet.

"Excuse me!" Gray stepped back from the speckled brown hen. "These boots are new!" And not so much meant for actual outdoor adventuring as a fashionable suggestion that Gray *might* be into such things. She had a tough, devil-may-care lesbian aesthetic to uphold, after all, although she hadn't expected to find herself navigating actual mud and chicken poop when she put them on.

"Petunia, get over here, you rascal." An older woman with a wild poof of blondish-white hair appeared around the corner of the coop, a smaller white hen tucked under her arm. "Ignore her. She thinks she's a guard dog," she said to Gray.

The chicken made a rumbling noise that did sound almost like a dog's growl, puffing up her feathers at Gray as if to make a point.

Gray took a step back from Petunia, still eyeing the chicken nervously. "Sorry to interrupt. I think I'm lost. Do you know if there's a Madame Nouvelle Lune nearby?"

The woman wiped a hand against her worn denim overalls. "You found her. Please, call me Dori."

Gray's head tilted to the side. "You're Madame . . ."

"In the flesh! You're Gray, yeah? Let me get the ladies tucked in for the night and I'll be right with you."

Dori herded the loose chickens into the coop, talking to them along the way like they were old friends. Even though she spoke slowly, it took Gray an extra few seconds to process her words. Her accent was thicker than the humid bayou air. That's why Gray almost missed it when Dori stopped talking to the birds and returned her attention to her appointment.

"I said, you coming this way or staying out here?" Dori yelled over her shoulder, already walking toward the yellow farmhouse.

Gray followed her into a crowded kitchen that smelled strongly of onion, garlic, and Cajun spices. "Leave your shoes by the door and wash your hands over there," Dori commanded as she kicked off her own boots.

Gray followed the instructions, knocking as much dirt as possible off her formerly shiny boots, then turned back to the old woman. "Is now, um, still a good time?"

"Good a time as any. Neptune is in retrograde, but we can work with that. You know how to devein shrimp?"

"I don't think so." Gray ran a hand along the buzzed hair on the left side of her head, flipping the longer dirty-blond hair on top to the other side. "Is that like reading tea leaves or something?"

Dori threw her head back with a squeaking laugh. "Lord, no. I'm just trying to get dinner on the table. How about chopping okra? That's easy as it gets."

Within minutes, Dori and Gray were seated across from each other at the wooden kitchen table, Gray chopping okra on a faded old cutting board as Dori peeled and deveined a pile of shrimp.

"All right, let's get started. Birth date, please."

"Is this how you usually meet with clients?"

Dori looked up at Gray. "Expecting something else? Dark room, crystal balls, velvet curtains, incense?"

Gray looked sheepish.

The older woman returned to her shrimp. "Well, I used to have that right in the French Quarter. Then Katrina hit. That's when I moved out here, where I got plenty of room to commune with the stars, and started moving my astrology business online, since most of my regulars moved outta Louisiana anyway. I only meet in person with special cases, and based on what your friend told me, you're mighty special." Dori popped the head off a shrimp, sending it rolling across the table. "So now, if you don't mind us getting to business rather than talking about it, when's your birthday?"

Gray sat up straighter. "April fourth."

"I need down to the minute. Location too."

"Born in Tulsa, Oklahoma. As for time . . ." Gray pulled out her phone to find the photo of her birth certificate she'd asked her brother to send her after she'd moved out of her parents' home. Turned out having an image of that document was crucial after being disowned at the age of eighteen. She didn't, however, understand its relevance in this situation. Once she found the photo, Gray zoomed in on the exact time and turned the screen to show Dori.

Dori wiped her fingers on a dish towel before pulling a pair of reading glasses from her pocket and poking at a tablet on her lap. "Ah. Okay, okay. *Hmm*. Well, good that you came when you did."

"Sorry?"

"No need to apologize, dear. Saturn return affects us all, long as we're lucky enough to live to see it."

Gray froze, her phone halfway back to her pocket. "Saturn return?"

"That's right. No wonder you're all out of sorts." Dori shifted the reading glasses into her tangle of white hair and resumed peeling shrimp. "See, Saturn is the planet of big life lessons. Its place in your chart is gonna have a lot to do with your sense of purpose, where you're supposed to be, whatever the hell you're on this Earth to do. Every twenty-nine years, Saturn returns to the exact place in the sky where it was the day you were born. So round abouts the ages of twenty-nine, fifty-eight, and eighty-seven, stars willing, you're gonna experience some existential discomfort."

"Existential discomfort," Gray echoed. She'd been trying for months to put her finger on the pressure in her chest, the itchiness in her fingertips, the zings in her brain that all worked together to tell her something had to change. Dori's description fit just right.

"Saturn wants to make sure you're on the right track, and you're due for a big old checkup right about now, turning twenty-nine in a couple months and all. You've probably been feeling Saturn's gaze for the last year or so. That sound right?"

Gray gulped. Ever since she could remember, she'd felt like she should be running faster, pushing herself harder, showing off what she could do. But the last few months had felt different somehow. More urgent, maybe. It's why she'd left the only town she'd ever lived in, moved to Louisiana, and started a challenging new job as a PR manager all in the past three weeks. And most important, it's why she'd ended up at Madame Nouvelle Lune's kitchen table.

Dori placed the tablet aside and swept the cleaned shrimp into a bowl. "As an Aries sun, you're competitive and driven and optimistic. Saturn's probably got you worried about reaching all these life goals you set for yourself, making you feel like you're behind your peers. Feel like the clock's ticking."

The knife slipped in Gray's hand, narrowly missing where her thumb held a piece of okra. Hands shaking, she set the knife down. "Well, that's just a quarter-life crisis. Everybody feels like that, right?"

"Around age twenty-nine, sure enough. Quarter-life crisis, Saturn return, different names for the same celestial thing." Dori rose from the table, grabbing the bowl of shrimp and the cutting board of okra. She lifted the lid of a large pot, releasing a burst of fragrant steam, before tipping the additional ingredients in. "You're a Taurus rising, that's a good balance for the Aries sun. Keeps you grounded, helps make sure your expectations for yourself are reasonable. Also means you value family and a stable home atmosphere. I'm guessing Saturn's brought you some doubts in your love life lately. Maybe you're looking for something different in relationships. Maybe what worked for you in your first twenty-nine years ain't working anymore." Dori paused at the sound of a whimper from across the kitchen and looked up to see Gray's lip trembling and her eyes filling with tears. "Oh, *cher*. It's all right, let it out."

Gray's tough exterior cracked as a whimper turned into a sob and tears rushed down her cheeks. How did she go from distrustful to sobbing in a stranger's kitchen so quickly? "Cherry told you about the breakup, didn't she?" she choked out.

"She just told me you were at a crossroads, unsure which way to go next. I don't like to know too many details before a consultation." Dori returned to the table with a cloth napkin and handed it to Gray. "Lot of relationships end around age twenty-nine or thirty. You'll notice if you look for it. That's 'cause Saturn comes back around, asking folks to take a hard look at where they are and where they want to be. I know it hurts now, but *lâche pas la patate*."

Gray racked her brain for lingering knowledge from her high school French classes. "Don't lick the potato?"

"Don't *drop* the potato," Dori said, graciously not mocking Gray's mistranslation. "It's an expression, meaning don't give up. Things will get better. Saturn may have you feeling a mess right now, but in a year or two you'll look back and realize this moment is putting you on track to just where you need to be. How are you with goats?"

"Is that an expression too?"

Dori chuckled as she strode toward the garage. "Sit tight, I'll be right back."

As much as Gray tried to slow the stream of tears and snot with the cloth napkin, she struggled to pull it together. After worrying she'd made a mistake leaving a chunk of her heart in McKenzie's house in Tulsa, hearing Dori's explanation of Saturn return was the first time Gray truly felt like she'd made the right call, that the end of her relationship was destined. That she hadn't made a massive error by leaving behind the life she'd been building for a decade for the dream of something different.

Dori emerged from the garage with a small fuzzy creature in each arm, one covered in fluffy white fur, the other mostly white with a dark-brown head and legs. "Here, take Disco." She shifted the baby goat into Gray's arms. Finally, Gray's tears dried up as she stared into the wiggling fluff ball's big eyes. Dori returned a moment later with a bottle full of milk, which she pushed into Gray's hand and angled into the goat's mouth. "Poor things. Found 'em crying behind my barn, couldn't have been more than a couple days old, no mother in sight."

The goat suckled happily as Gray looked on, idly wondering if Cherry would let her keep a baby goat in her garage apartment.

Dori sat down at the table with her own baby goat and examined the sappy look on Gray's face. "You're quite the oyster, aren't ya?"

Gray looked up, one eyebrow arched. Was that a regional slur for lesbians?

"Beautiful, smooth, and ice-cold on the outside," Dori said, nodding at Gray's carefully crafted outfit, trendy haircut, sparkling green eyes, and striking bone structure that often caught the glance of strangers of all genders. "But once someone gets past your shell, they'll see you're softer and more delicate than you appear."

So it wasn't a slur, but Gray wasn't sure if it was a compliment either. Still, it resonated with her. "I guess."

"Now let's talk about that Aquarius moon," the astrologer said, getting back to business. "Your moon sign represents your truest inner soul, deeply tied to your emotions and how you treat yourself. Only the people you're closest to get to know your

moon sign. Yours is Aquarius, which means you value your indi-
viduality and freedom. Deep down, you'd rather stand out than
fit in. So at your Saturn return, maybe you're feeling a bit misunderstood, trying to realize the passions and talents and instincts
that make you *you*."

"So I measure myself against my peers and want to keep up
because I'm an Aries, but I also want to be unique because of my
Aquarius moon?"

Dori nodded sagely, stroking a finger across her goat's head.
"Starting to make sense why Saturn has you feeling some kind of
way?" Gray shrugged. "All right, then. Tell me about your relationship that ended. Sounds like that's a good place to dig in."

"I'm sorry I cried like that earlier. I haven't really done that."
Gray wasn't usually much of a crier, even in the midst of an emotional life change, but something about Dori's strange euphe-
misms and the baby goat in her arms made her feel like she was
in an otherworldly but safe place. "It feels weird to be so upset,
since I initiated the breakup. Well, technically, we called it a 'conscious uncoupling.'" She gave the best summary of the breakup
she could manage without leading herself right back into crying
territory. How she'd spent ten years with McKenzie only to realize she wasn't interested in Gray's dreams of kids and family life,
and she couldn't be convinced. How that left Gray feeling like
she was running years behind in starting the family she so deeply
desired.

Dori took in the story silently. When Gray was finished, she
closed her eyes and nodded as if listening for guidance from the
universe. "What's your ex's sign?"

"Also an Aries. March twenty-eighth."

Dori clicked her tongue against the roof of her mouth. "Two
Aries in a relationship, that's a lot of fire sign right there. I'd bet
y'all were always competing over something. One person always
has to win, and the other one's left none too pleased about it."

How could Dori make Gray feel so exposed, knowing so little about her? Every fight with McKenzie felt like a life-or-death battle that ended with one person gloating and one seething with frustration. Their competitive spirits brought a lot of fun to the relationship—and often to the bedroom—but after ten years, Gray was exhausted.

"Not to mention two babies of the zodiac, neither with celestial maturity. Souls as young as Disco and Cha Cha here. Speaking of, it's getting past their bedtime. Hand her over." Dori collected the goat from Gray and disappeared momentarily to the garage. Gray felt strangely cold and empty without Disco in her arms.

When Dori returned, Gray straightened up. "What exactly do you mean by 'babies of the zodiac'?" she asked.

"There are twelve signs, running in order of Aries through Pisces," Dori explained as she stirred the concoction on the stove. "They represent the life cycle of the zodiac, each at its own stage of maturity. Course, you have your own journey and lessons to learn. But the maturity and celestial understanding of your *soul*, that comes from your place in the karmic wheel. As an Aries, you're a newborn, all dewy-eyed and taking in the world with a fresh perspective. Signs get a little more wisdom as you follow the wheel, hitting teenage round abouts Leo, middle age around Capricorn, all the emotional wisdom of end of life in Pisces."

Was this why Gray always felt like a beginner? Like other people just got it more than she did, whatever "it" was? "So shouldn't everyone marry a Pisces, since they're the wisest?"

"Not necessarily." Dori tasted the stew in the crockpot with a spoon, then bustled about the kitchen adding various herbs and spices. "There's something to learn from each sign's stage in life. Curiosity from Geminis. Vulnerability from Cancers. Focus from Virgos. Courage from Sagittariuses. Determination from Capricorns. So on and so forth."

Gray's mouth watered as the scent of Dori's dinner wafted across the kitchen, but she couldn't let her hunger distract her from why she'd come in the first place. "But how do I know which sign I'm supposed to be with? What's most compatible with Aries?"

"Ain't no right or wrong answer to that," Dori said. "The only real way to learn and comprehend the full life cycle of the karmic wheel is to get to know each sign, learn how your souls harmonize together. Let's take another look at your birth chart."

TWO

CHERRY RAISED A spoon of gumbo to her lips, delight written across her face. "Oh my god. I can't believe I'm eating *Madame Nouvelle Lune's* gumbo. She made it with her own hands? You're sure?"

Gray had spent almost two hours at Dori's farmhouse, far longer than she'd expected, and her head was still spinning with sun signs and moon signs and zodiac wheels. "Well, I chopped the okra," she said over her shoulder as she scrubbed her boots with an old toothbrush over the kitchen trash can.

Cherry snorted. "More cooking than you did all of last year." She took another bite of the gumbo, closing her eyes to savor the spicy stew. "You know, I probably could've sold this gumbo on eBay. Madame Nouvelle Lune has fans all over the country. The world, really."

"Yeah, but then you wouldn't get the magical experience of eating it yourself."

"Do you think the Tupperware is worth anything?" Cherry asked, examining the red plastic lid.

"No. Plus I promised Dori I would return it if I went back to see her again."

Cherry sighed. "I can't believe you're on a first-name basis with Madame Nouvelle Lune. I've been wanting to meet her for years."

"Then why don't you?" Gray asked, looking up briefly from her boots. "If she was willing to meet with me, an astrology skeptic who barely knew who she was, surely you'd be welcome."

"It doesn't work like that," Cherry said, her voice low in reverence for the astrologer. "She only takes one-on-one meetings at her house for people at a crucial point in their lives based on the planetary positions and the stars and . . . I don't know, however else she divines the universe. It's not just whoever's been a fan the longest. That's part of why I'm obsessed with her."

Gray hadn't fully realized what a rare opportunity her meeting had been. She supposed it made sense, considering how all of Dori's observations were so eerily on point. Or maybe Cherry, a longtime subscriber to Madame Nouvelle Lune's horoscope newsletter, podcast listener, and member of the paid Celestial Circle club, had more sway than she thought.

"Give your boots a rest and come tell me everything," Cherry demanded.

She dropped her shoes on the doormat and joined Cherry on a barstool at the marble kitchen island. Gray trusted no one more with the intimate knowledge of her birth chart than her oldest and closest friend. Although she wasn't entirely sure how much she bought into astrology, Gray did believe her friendship with Cherry was written in the stars. They'd known each other since the womb, when their mothers had attended the same Sunday school group for expecting mothers at a Tulsa megachurch, and remained friends throughout Cherry's and Gray's childhoods. Born only a couple of months apart, they'd taken just about every life step together, including their literal first steps, as documented on a dusty old VHS tape.

At first, their mothers were thrilled by watching them learn new words and try new foods together as curious toddlers. But by the time they hit their rebellious teen years, their parents realized the monsters they'd created, despite the strict conservative upbringings they'd tried to enforce. At thirteen, the two friends were grounded after their mothers found fiery diatribes against them on the girls' MySpace pages. They were banned from sleepovers for the summer of their fifteenth year for sneaking out past curfew to a Paramore concert. After years of begging to transfer to public school instead of their uptight Christian private school, the girls took any chance to get away from campus once they had their driver's licenses, eventually getting suspended for skipping too many classes. Gray disastrously came out to her parents at age seventeen, and she was especially grateful for Cherry, who took some of the heat off Gray by immediately getting her tongue pierced and threatening to attend an art school for college.

But none of their previous punishments could prepare them for the consequences of getting caught in their greatest scheme of all. After Gray came out, her parents had forced her to attend anti-gay "reparative therapy" at a church in Oklahoma City. Without a car of her own, that meant one of her parents had to spend three hours twice a week driving her to and from sessions. Weeks of scheduling conflicts and annoying traffic finally helped Gray convince them to let Cherry drive her to Oklahoma City after school on Tuesdays and Thursdays. But when they found out Gray was only entering the church long enough to mark her name on an attendance list and then sneaking out to gallivant around the city with Cherry, the two best friends were banned from seeing each other outside of school until they turned eighteen.

But their parents' efforts to break up their friendship had the reverse effect. It brought Cherry and Gray closer together and permanently damaged their relationships with their families. Upon turning eighteen, Gray and Cherry officially changed their birth names—Grace and Charity—to their preferred monikers. Cherry dyed her naturally strawberry blonde hair her now-signature firetruck-red and stopped seeing her parents outside of major holidays. Gray cut ties with her parents entirely, developed a fondness for trendy gay haircuts and faux leather jackets, and found a new family with her girlfriend, McKenzie, and Tulsa's tight-knit queer community.

Through college stress, romantic drama, first jobs, and life milestones, their friendship proved it could weather any storm. Robbie, Cherry's husband, had caused a bit of a tiff when he entered the scene. Gray worried at first that he wasn't good enough for her best friend, and Cherry grew frustrated with Gray for being too tough on him. But Gray eventually learned that Robbie, a lanky, nerdy IT support specialist, had a heart of gold, and he treated Cherry like a respected equal. Plus his gift for troubleshooting spotty wifi networks made even Gray want to ask Robbie out to dinner when her devices got buggy.

By the time Cherry and Robbie got married, Gray was fully on board and gave a legendary toast at their wedding. When Robbie got a job in New Orleans, the best friends promised through teary goodbyes that it wouldn't change a thing. And when Gray was hit by Saturn return or a quarter-life crisis or whatever it is that causes a relationship to fail, they were proved right. Gray packed her things and moved from the two-bedroom midcentury home she shared with McKenzie in Oklahoma to the studio apartment above Cherry's garage in Louisiana, knowing the only thing that could cure what ailed her was being around her chosen sister.

After describing Dori's farmhouse and various animal companions, Gray turned to the astrological advice she'd received, or at least what she could remember of it. At Cherry's insistence, she unrolled the birth chart across the table, pointing out Dori's notes and commentary on her sun, moon, and rising signs. Cherry made the perfect audience, laughing and gasping in all the right places, occasionally nodding sagely and saying things like "Of course, classic fire sign." When Gray shared Dori's explanation of Saturn return, Cherry grabbed her hands and promised they would figure out their Saturn-inspired journeys together.

Robbie lumbered into the kitchen just as Gray pointed out her Mars in Pisces. "River is bathed and down for the night," he said, opening the refrigerator. "I'm starving. Hey, what's that?"

He arrived at the island with one long-legged step, sniffing the Tupperware in Cherry's hands. Cherry offered him her spoon. "Gumbo from, get this, *the* Madame Nouvelle Lune."

"Get out!" Robbie took a bite and nodded. "Tastes like it was made by someone with the wisdom of the universe."

"Didn't realize you were a fan of Madame, Robbie," Gray said, shifting her birth chart away from the dripping spoon.

"Cherry got me into her horoscopes. But of course, as a self-centered Leo, I only care about my own sign. Not as well read on the others as Cherry. Can I have some more of this?"

Cherry pushed the plastic container toward him. "Go for it."

"Cool. I'm gonna play Tears of the Kingdom. If River wakes up, it's your turn." Robbie planted a kiss on Cherry's cheek and plopped a baby monitor on the kitchen island.

"Still trying to beat the Wind Temple?" Gray asked.

Robbie nodded grimly. "I don't know why I'm so stuck. Any tips?"

"The Ultrahand ability and perseverance, my dude," Gray said sagely. "And bring lots of Ice Fruit."

Robbie thanked Gray and exited to the living room.

Cherry twirled a strand of bright-red hair around her fingers. "All right, back to the good stuff. What did she say about dating? Did she tell you what sign you should look for?"

Gray leaned heavily onto the island. "If only it were that easy. Apparently I'm an inexperienced baby when it comes to dating."

"Obviously. You've only ever seriously dated one person."

"Right, but do you know the whole life-cycle-of-the-karmic-wheel thing? Where the signs are different parts of the life cycle or whatever?"

"Oh, yeah!" Cherry said. "I think she had a blog post on it a few years back. As a Gemini, I'm in my terrible twos or something."

"Right! And I'm an Aries newborn. So apparently the best way to understand life and the signs and the universe is to spend time with someone from every sign."

"Like, romantically? Did she say to *date* each sign?" Cherry said, leaning onto the marble island with both elbows.

"I don't know. Maybe? She said a lot. But she definitely thought Saturn return was the time to explore my compatibility with the different signs, if I'm looking for love."

"Then you have to do it!" Cherry jumped up and started pacing the kitchen, her hands flying around her as she thought out loud. "Really, if you think about it, it's perfect. I mean, of course it is. Madame Nouvelle Lune would never lead you astray. If Saturn is telling you the path is to get married and start a family, you've got to get a move on. So you date someone from every sign in order, bingo—you've unlocked the secret of the karmic wheel. You'll know what sign is right for you and your field of potential wives is considerably smaller."

Gray scratched the side of her head, thinking as her fingertips met her buzzed scalp. "I'm not sure, Cherry. I have about zero dating experience and I'm still kind of . . . you know, off-kilter. Can I really just jump into the dating pool like that?"

"Sure you can! You're a total catch. Plus you've got Saturn on your side!" Cherry stopped pacing and flung an arm over Gray's dejected shoulders. "It's going to be tough, especially at first. But if you really want to start a family soon, we don't have a lot of time for you to drag your feet. You've got to put yourself out there! Start meeting people, figure out what it is you want in a partner who isn't McKenzie. Think of these twelve dates as a kind of test for yourself, to see if you're really ready. And as a test for the zodiac, to figure out what sign you should settle down with. It's a challenge. You love those. You're an Aries!"

Gray couldn't help but feel buoyed by Cherry's enthusiasm. "I do love a challenge."

"And if Madame Nouvelle Lune gave you the idea, it has to be part of the universe's plan."

Gray frowned. "I kind of think it was *your* idea more than Madame Nou—"

Cherry strode away, ignoring Gray's correction, and pulled the freezer open. "Hey, would you eat some pizza bagels if I heated them up?"

"Yes!" echoed from the island and the living room as Gray and Robbie replied in unison.

Cherry bustled about the kitchen as she listed the signs she dated before meeting Robbie. She paused in her criticism of a Capricorn suitor, her eyebrows rising close to the strawberry blonde roots peeking out under the red dye at her hairline. "Wait, are you going to sleep with every sign? Did Madame Nouvelle Lune say anything about sex?"

"Definitely not!" Gray blurted. She lowered her voice, looking toward Robbie in the living room before continuing. Robbie likely knew that Gray wasn't as romantically experienced as her edgy, alluring lesbian style suggested, but it was still a bit of a sore subject for Gray. "You know I've only ever slept with McKenzie. I can't just start having sex with everyone I meet. It's like moving to Paris after taking one high school French class."

"Not a fair metaphor," Cherry said as she slid a tray of pizza bagels into the oven. "It's more like going from high school French to an intense, immersive French course to *prepare* you to move to Paris. *Oui?*"

"So Paris is what, my future spouse?" With a heavy sigh, Gray dropped her head into her hands. "I'm overwhelmed at the idea of sleeping with one new person, I can't even think about twelve."

"Well, obviously you should only have sex with someone if you really want to and feel comfortable with it in the moment," Cherry said, backing off after seeing Gray's reaction. "I just think you should be *open* to the idea of sleeping with someone during this experiment, since the whole point is trying new things and figuring out what you like. Don't put any pressure on yourself, but if it feels right, maybe it's worth exploring."

Gray stared intensely at the counter for a moment before she looked back up at Cherry. "I guess I can stay open to it."

"That's my girl!" Cherry said. "An adventurer at heart."

Gray fidgeted with the small silver ring piercing her nostril. "Can I really do this? I don't even know how to ask a stranger on a date, much less have sex with them."

"Oh, you'll be fine. You don't know how dating apps work. Everyone's pretty up-front about what they're looking for. It speeds things up." Cherry spun around, a devilish grin on her face. "Oh my god, wait, this means I get to set up a dating profile for you."

"Hold it right there. You will not be setting up a dating profile for me. *Maybe* I'll consider your advice. But it's a maybe."

"Chill. It's not like I'll put anything on it you hate." Cherry plopped down onto the barstool next to Gray. "But I'm the expert here and you're the novice. Remember when Robbie and I started getting serious, you had to teach me how to be in a long-term relationship? How to settle arguments without blowing up? How to live together without getting on each other's nerves? That's how *you* excel in relationships. But me? I excel at flirting through dating apps."

"Come on, Cherry. Don't you think it's different being queer? Your dating app experience is in the world of dick pics and chauvinism. Mine will be, I don't know, dates at hardware stores and trading Mary Oliver poems."

Undeterred, Cherry dove into a lecture on dating app culture and profile picture best practices. When the oven timer interrupted her stream of thought, Gray was relieved. Her head was swimming with planets and elements and acceptably interesting hobbies. And after promising Cherry that she would take a stab at creating a dating profile that evening, Gray was thrilled to shift the conversation from her Saturn-inspired dating spree to Robbie's adventures in Hyrule. But throughout the evening, the idea of her zodiac dating challenge took shape in the back of her mind.

Only twelve dates until Saturn makes everything clear, she hoped.

Three

ALONE IN HER garage apartment, Gray quickly pulled off her restrictive skinny jeans, dropped into her favorite antique armchair, and turned the TV to reruns of a nineties sitcom to fill the silence. Having Cherry and Robbie only a flight of stairs away was helpful, but she still wasn't exactly sure how to be home alone. Going straight from her college dorm to living with McKenzie meant she'd never really had to sit silently with her own thoughts for very long. Even looking around the small apartment now at her belongings was jarring. She couldn't help but see her furniture where it once sat in her Tulsa home: the bed made up in the guest room with McKenzie's old comforter, the bedside table paired with the matching one left behind, the bookshelf full of McKenzie's cookbooks and mystery novels.

But she definitely wasn't in her three-bedroom midtown Tulsa home. She was in a space clearly added on after the rest of the house was built, one she imagined had previously homed a brooding teenager or college grad who moved back in with their parents. At the top of the staircase between Cherry and Robbie's kitchen and garage sat a simple room painted a bleak off-white color with stained beige carpeting. There was a bathroom by the door that was so cramped Gray couldn't sit on the toilet without bumping her knees against the sink, as well as a shower that was grimy no matter how much she scrubbed. The only upsides to the room were the large window looking out over the driveway and the sizable closet, primarily designed for long-term storage. Well, those things and the exceedingly low cost. Cherry and Robbie refused to take any rent from Gray, although she regularly helped out with River and occasionally chipped in for utilities and groceries.

For the time being, it was home. Gray stroked the floral embroidery of her magenta armchair, remembering when she first spotted it outside a Tulsa antiques store. She'd begged McKenzie to let her bring it home. McKenzie always had more minimalist tastes when it came to design, while Gray liked quirky pieces with character. It was one of the many things Gray should have seen as a sign that their home life was incompatible. Gray wanted a lived-in home, full of bright colors and broken-in furniture and kids and pets running around. Meanwhile, McKenzie wanted sleek lines, neutral colors, and a big, easily cleaned stainless steel kitchen for her culinary experiments. In the case of this particular chair, Gray had won her over by promising to find beige throw pillows to tie it into their living room décor. The rest of their home turf battles hadn't been so easily settled. "At least we've still got each other," Gray murmured to the chair.

Who was Gray to sit around feeling sorry for herself when she was the one who called it off? She got exactly what she wanted: a chance for a fresh start, an opportunity to find someone who fit into her picture of the future, someone who could be the partner and co-parent McKenzie wouldn't be. And at least they'd managed to end things amicably. They hadn't spoken in the month since then, agreeing to give each other space to adjust. Gray believed one day they could be something like friends again.

She'd said goodbye to the person with whom she'd shared her every worry, every bit of good news, every mundane story for ten years. That was the cost of her choice. But she still caught herself craving a spoonful of McKenzie's blueberry jam every once in a while, or wishing she could hear her snarky commentary on the latest reality TV sensation. Gray had unpacked a lightweight spring quilt only a few days prior, and the delicate, lingering scent of McKenzie's favorite perfume had sucker punched her right in the gut.

With a resigned nod, Gray decided to make good on her promise to Cherry and herself and download a dating app. But a scroll through the app store showed her just how out of touch she was. Each app tried to distinguish itself as the only platform to really help you find true love, but Gray couldn't figure out how one was any different from the others in practice. Growing frustrated by the rampant heteronormativity in the various descriptions, Gray turned to her favorite queer blog for help. Their latest ranking of dating apps was a couple years old, but it was immediately more helpful than anything else she'd seen online.

One app on the blog's list caught Gray's eye. According to the blog, Mercurious was by and for queer people. Even better, it offered a multitude of ways to filter potential matches beyond the typical options: by vacation style, favorite book and film genres, "out" status, preferred climate, and most important, astrological sign. Gray happily paid $4.99 to download the app.

Next, Gray waded through a multistep authentication process and endless questions until she finally arrived at the daunting task of choosing a profile picture. It turned out Gray hadn't taken a cute photo of herself alone in at least a year. And the pictures on her phone were a land mine of bittersweet memories with McKenzie. When she'd scrolled all the way back to the Caribbean cruise they'd taken for their eighth anniversary, Gray threw her phone across the room in frustration. Then, of course, she went to confirm she hadn't broken it. Her new job paid well enough, but she couldn't justify throwing a few hundred dollars in the hole.

Did she really want a wife and family so desperately that she was willing to try Cherry's foolhardy plan? Gray wondered. Would it even work if she did?

Gray dropped onto her bed, massaging her aching forehead

with the heels of her palms. Yes, of *course* she wanted a family. She wouldn't have blown up her life in Tulsa if she didn't.

When Gray thought about her dream family, one moment always came to mind. It was back when she was around ten or eleven, when she played on a youth softball team called the Tulsa Twisters. A Sunday afternoon game got rained out shortly after it began, but Gray couldn't get in touch with her parents, who were at a church function. She normally would have caught a ride home with Cherry, also on the Twisters, but she was home sick. The lesbian moms of one of Gray's teammates took pity on her and invited her back to their home until her parents could pick her up.

"I'm, uh, not supposed to go to anyone's house without my parents' permission," Gray had said, although it wasn't technically true. It was specifically *their* home Gray's mom had told her not to visit. In fact, Gray's mother had demanded that she keep her distance from her teammate Alyssa *and* her two moms.

"That's all right," one of them said kindly, Alyssa's younger brother clinging to her pants to shelter under her umbrella. "We usually go to Tastee-Freez for ice cream after games anyway. It's not far from here, and we can call your mom to let her know where to find you. Surely she'd prefer that to you standing in the rain alone."

There it was: a loophole. Gray's mother hadn't said anything about Tastee-Freez. It was a chance to feed her endless curiosity about Alyssa's family, only made more irresistible thanks to the rule against getting to know them. Although she hadn't known it at the time, it was that half hour in a vinyl booth over ice-cream cones that cleared a path for Gray to grow into the person she was today, and a path to the person she hoped to be in the future. The conversation hadn't been anything radical; Alyssa's moms asked Gray about school, the softball team, and her summer plans. But simply seeing the two women together, one's arm draped around the shoulders of the other, trading tastes of ice cream, caringly wiping chocolate from their son's chin, reminding Alyssa to say "please" and "thank you" to the cashier, exchanging whispered words and meaningful glances . . . Well, it changed everything for Gray. For the first time, she could imagine herself growing up, an adulthood that wouldn't feel like trying on someone else's itchy, too-big clothes. Even now, when she pictured her future, she saw herself out for ice cream after a softball game with her wife and children.

It was that mental image that gave Gray the courage to open Mercurious again and finish her first dating profile. Maybe that's what it took to build a family like Alyssa's. Even all these years later, Gray didn't know their names. Alyssa had quit softball the following year. But she would do anything to give herself what they had.

THE NEXT MORNING, Gray stumbled down the garage stairs in a hoodie and sweatpants to join Cherry, Robbie, and River for their regular Sunday brunch. But by the time Gray had topped her waffles, poured her coffee, and settled at the table, Cherry's plate was empty. Gray thought back to the days when Cherry would be so absorbed in conversation that she'd spend hours working her way through a meal. That was before she became a mom. Now she usually finished eating before Gray could take her first bite.

"All right, show me your dating profile," Cherry said, jumping right over any pleasantries.

Gray took a heartening chug of coffee, then unlocked her phone and slid it across the table to Cherry. "Completed, as promised," she said.

Cherry scrolled through the profile with one hand while passing a slice of strawberry to River with the other. "Ew, these pictures are awful. Is McKenzie in this one? Not to worry, we'll fix that. Hobbies could use a little work too. Everyone says 'travel.' It's predictable and boring. And 'videogames' makes you sound like a nerd."

"But what if I am a nerd?" Gray muttered into her waffles.

"Dating profiles aren't about showing your true self, they're about creating an illusion."

"Wait, are you saying I swiped right on an illusion?" Robbie said, scrambled eggs dropping from his fork.

"Of course, dear," Cherry said, batting her eyelashes. "You wouldn't have asked me out if my profile said I was a five-foot-two living troll doll with a weak chin and an astrology obsession."

Robbie snorted. "Oh my god. The hair. The belly ring. You really are a troll doll! Why have I never thought of that before?"

"Because I'm a *master illusionist,* babe. Now, about this profile." Cherry wiped River's mouth with a napkin before turning her full attention to Gray's phone. "Mm, that won't do . . . Here . . ." she mumbled while speed-typing. After only a couple minutes, Cherry set down the phone and looked Gray up and down. "Now," she said, "a quick photo shoot."

"Back up a second," Gray said. "What about the pictures I chose?"

"Do you mean the one where you look sickeningly happy with your ex, the one where you can't tell which of the seven people in the photo you are, or the one where you're literally sneezing?" Cherry rolled her eyes. "I seriously don't understand how someone so hot can look so terrible on camera. It's a travesty."

"Maybe my dates will be pleasantly surprised when they see me in person, then," Gray said.

"Go upstairs and change," Cherry said, ignoring her. "Then meet me in the backyard."

———

AN HOUR LATER, back at the kitchen table, Cherry presented Gray with her brand-new profile.

"I don't know, Cherry," Gray said, scanning through Cherry's draft. There were benefits to having a best friend's perspective on why someone would make a good date. Cherry's answers to Mercurious's questions made it clear she knew Gray better than she knew herself: She loved vacations where she could hit the beach and still explore a city full of historical character, her favorite books and movies all involved rooting for an underdog, and fall was her best season because she could wear her most fashionable jackets. But still, she felt a little itchy, a reaction to dishonesty that had developed when she was a kid in Sunday school, where Gray was told God always knew when she lied and added it to a list of her sins. Even though she no longer believed in God, at least not as a man in the clouds who added a tally to his stone tablet enumerating all of Gray's faults, the itching discomfort was harder to kick. "This profile makes it look like I've really got my shit together," Gray elaborated. "Like I'm some suave, eligible lesbian bachelor, instead of a nerd in the middle of a quarter-life crisis who lives above her best friend's garage."

"Stop scratching!" Cherry swatted at Gray's hand. "Both things can be true. This is how the game is played, okay? Just like you put your best foot forward on a date, you put your best foot forward on a dating app. Anyway, you can always edit your profile later. We've got to get a move on if you're going to get through all the signs before your birthday."

"Before my birthday? When did that become the rule? That's only in . . . six weeks!" Gray calculated, feeling her twenties wilting away before her eyes.

Cherry gave Gray a stern look. "Saturn return. Keep up. When Saturn hits the exact spot where it was at the moment you were born, don't you want to be ready? Don't you want to have this under your belt so you're prepared to meet your true love?"

Her true love. Someone she could sit beside as they cheered on their kids at softball, then exchange loving looks over postgame ice cream. The first step toward the family she'd always wanted. Gray's vision for the future was more traditional than people might guess based on her alternative haircut and nose ring, but she could see it shining in the distance, calling to her. "Yeah," she said. "I'm ready."

"Great. Then let's lay out some ground rules." Cherry placed her clasped hands on the table in front of her with utmost seriousness. "Rule number one: No talking about your ex. There's no good way to do it. You'll sound either bitter or still hung up on her."

"McKenzie and I were together for a third of my life. How do I talk about myself without her coming up?" Gray asked.

"Avoid stories with her in them as much as possible," Cherry said. "If you get stuck or it's awkward to leave her out, fill in someone else. Me or another friend or a fake cousin or something." Gray raised a skeptical eyebrow. "It's only one date with each person. Make it work, okay?"

"Fine. What's the next rule?"

"Rule number two: Don't talk about the zodiac dating challenge."

"How very *Fight Club* of you," Gray joked.

Cherry looked up, her eyes more serious than Gray expected. "You're about to find out that first dates are scary. Putting yourself out there to a total stranger, risking rejection and humiliation and, at least with straight dudes, potential murder? It's terrifying. And making anyone brave enough to put themselves out there feel like part of a game, or a science experiment? Massively not cool. This is an interesting challenge for you, but when you walk in the door, you need to meet them on equal ground."

"This is starting to sound a lot harder than I thought," Gray confessed, wiping her palms on her pants.

"This will make it easier," Cherry said. "Rule number three: Don't fall in love."

"Oh my god, Cherry, that's so cliché."

"The whole point of this experiment is to go on a date with each sign with an open mind to see what vibes best with you, right? If you fall in love with the first Aries you meet, as you've done before, *cough cough McKenzie,* you won't be able to finish the challenge, at least not in the spirit of the whole thing. You'll just be going through the motions." Cherry traced an invisible path on the wooden table in front of her as if mapping out a plan of attack. "And going into a date knowing you're experimenting and having fun will make it less scary. As long as you are still vulnerable and don't let the other person know you're just trying their sign on for the night, i.e., rule number two, you're free to enjoy yourself and let the night take you where it will. Capeesh?"

Gray breathed in and out, then nodded. "I accept your terms."

"Excellent. Then let's get your match parameters set and get this show on the road." Standing and coming around the table, Cherry looked at Gray's phone over her shoulder. "I would recommend keeping them pretty wide, since limiting it to an individual sign is already going to make it a small pool."

"Roger that."

As Gray began checking boxes of genders she wanted in her matches, Cherry made a surprised *hmm.* "I figured you would just mark women."

"I've only been in a relationship with a woman, sure. But I would date a trans man, or a trans woman, or a gender nonconforming person. I guess I would date"—Gray looked at the only unchecked box on the list—"everyone but cis men, apparently."

"So are you vibing in the pansexual lane these days, then?" Cherry asked.

Gray shrugged. "Kind of?" she said. "I still like the word 'lesbian' though. I think I can be a lesbian and still date people of all genders."

Cherry nodded. "Totally. Fuck gender essentialism. Maybe put some age limits on there though," she advised. Gray slid the age bar to between twenty-five and thirty-two. "A little broader. You don't want your search to come up empty," Cherry said, reaching across Gray to widen the age limits to twenty-one to forty.

Gray marked the Aries box under astrology, then hovered over the View Matches button. She froze, memories of the past and visions of her future comingling in her head. This was it: the moment her life would change. Even if it was a failed project and didn't get her any closer to finding her life partner, it was the moment she left her old relationship behind and started working toward a life without McKenzie in it. Was she ready?

Although Gray hadn't spoken her thoughts aloud, Cherry knew exactly what was going through her head. Best friends always do. She placed a hand on Gray's tense shoulder and squeezed. "You've got this, Gray. And even if you don't, I'll be right here."

Gray took a deep breath in and out, then with a small nod, pressed the button. A rainbow loading wheel gave way to a short list.

"Wow, that's not many options," Cherry said, squinting over Gray's shoulder. "Must be the sign filter."

"I like it. Did you know research shows that people are happier with their choices when given fewer options?" Gray scrolled down the short page. "Plus this one's really cute."

Gray clicked on someone named Carmen's profile, which listed her pronouns (she/her), age (twenty-four), hometown (Tuscaloosa, Alabama), and distance from Gray's current location (seven miles). The first photo of Carmen showed a woman with an infectious smile and a stylish platinum blonde wavy bob holding an armful of stuffed prizes from a carnival booth over her left shoulder. The next photo showed Carmen smiling in hiking gear atop a rocky cliff, and in the last, she was leaping above a trampoline, arms and legs stretched fully out into space. Beneath the pictures was an About Me box, which read: "Always looking for the next mountain to climb. Perfect match must love dogs, trying new things, and heated debates."

The description spoke straight to Gray's Aries heart. Maybe this wouldn't be so scary after all. "Carmen seems cool. What do I do now? Message her?"

"God, teaching you to navigate dating apps is like potty training River. No sense of direction. You can't message any old stranger! Otherwise it's a haunted house of unsolicited dick pics." Cherry leaned closer to Gray's phone. "You have to like her profile first. Try that Star button there."

Clicking the Star button whisked Carmen's profile away, leaving another in its place. This one showed someone in khaki waders holding up what appeared to be a large catfish. But before Gray could finish reading the new page, a banner notification popped up: "You've got a new match!"

Gray gasped, clasping a hand to her chest. "Cherry, I've got a match!"

Cherry squealed and clapped. "They grow up so fast! All right, I thought we'd have more time to prepare for icebreakers, but it looks like you're a hot commodity. What's your first question going to be?"

"Question? Can't I just say hi?"

"Absolutely not. That's the number one most common and number one most boring way people start conversations on these apps. You've got to start with a question because people love talking about themselves."

"What's your job?" Gray suggested.

Cherry held a hand to her heart as if mortally offended. "This isn't a networking event."

Gray chewed her bottom lip, racking her brain. "Um, what's your favorite color?"

"Gween!" River chirped from Robbie's lap in the living room, reminding them both that he was listening to more than they realized.

Cherry grimaced. "Great question for an almost two-year-old. Not so much for a twenty-four-year-old. Try again."

"Uh . . . What's your five-year plan?"

"How do your suggestions keep getting worse? Something more lighthearted, unique, personal but not too personal." Cherry paced the kitchen. "This is all about astrology, so let's look to the stars! Aries, as you know, are fiery, competitive, and driven, and like to be entertained. What kind of question would hook you? What sparks those qualities in you?"

"What's your favorite videogame?" Gray offered.

"How about board game? A little broader appeal." The sound of a small crash and then a cry from River drew Cherry's attention. "Robbie? Everything okay in there?"

"Only if you weren't too attached to that flower vase on the end table," Robbie's voice called from the other room.

"Shit," Cherry said under her breath. "Gray, you've got this! I'll be back in a bit."

Once Cherry exited, Gray took a deep breath, trying to shift her nerves into something more optimistic. This was it! She was taking her future into her own hands, putting herself out there, as common wisdom advised. At best, she would learn about what she wanted in a partner. At worst, she'd meet some new people and see more of her new city. Gray had always been a bit of a flirt, and now she could test her charm without worrying about it starting a fight with McKenzie afterward. What did she have to lose? Only time. Six weeks was a short window in which to identify and meet twelve different people for dates. No time for dillydallying.

Pumped up from her own pep talk, Gray clicked the chat bubble to contact Carmen. She typed out, "Hey Carmen! Nice to connect. What's your favorite board game?" Her thumb was hovering over the Send button when her phone vibrated with an incoming message.

CARMEN: Are you good at trivia?

Okay, a little lacking in niceties, but that was as good of an entrance as any. Gray deleted her draft message and started again.

GRAY: I'm pretty good! At least based on the weekly trivia nights at my old neighborhood queer bar. Are you a trivia fan?
CARMEN: What are you doing tonight at 9?
GRAY: I don't have plans.
CARMEN: You do now! Trivia at Cat O'Connor's Pub. Better be on your game! ;)

Wow, this Aries was really getting straight to the point. If Gray wasn't in such a rush herself, she might have been put off by having so little time to get to know each other before making plans. But with an intimidating challenge ahead, Gray was grateful that her first date practically fell into her lap. Carmen's invitation felt a bit more perfunctory than come-hither, but if she was being honest, Gray wasn't ready to dive into spicy romance with perfect strangers yet anyway. A casual trivia night sounded like just what she needed to kick off her astrological challenge. Maybe the planets really were on her side.

Four

$\mathscr{I}$T TOOK GRAY'S EYES a moment to adjust to the dark interior of Cat O'Connor's Pub once the heavy wooden door closed behind her, cutting off the brassy sound of the jazz band playing on the street outside. She didn't spot Carmen during her glance around the crowded room, so Gray made her way to the corner of the long bar.

"What are you having?" a bartender asked without lifting his eyes from the martini he was pouring.

Gray scanned the chalkboard menu behind him. Spending most of the afternoon trying on various outfits and practicing icebreakers in the bathroom mirror had only served to increase her nerves. A cocktail sounded like just what she needed. "What's in the Alligator Tears Punch?"

"Vodka, pineapple juice, Midori, and sweet and sour," the bartender rattled off.

It sounded too sweet for Gray's taste. "Just a whiskey Coke, please," she requested instead.

After grabbing her drink, Gray turned around to look again for her date and noticed someone waving at her from a booth near the door. Gray walked hesitantly toward the booth, speeding up as she recognized Carmen's face.

"Hey. Carmen, right? I'm Gray," she said, extending her arm for a handshake and, second-thinking the overly formal move halfway through, transitioning to something between a wave and a salute.

"Just in time!" Carmen said, sitting up straighter. "Miguel

just came around for team sign-ups, so he'll get started in a few minutes." She nodded at a tall man at the bar in a backward baseball hat with a clipboard in hand.

"Cool." Gray realized she was still standing as a group of four tried to squeeze past her. "Um, mind if I join you?"

Carmen smirked. "Wouldn't be much of a date if you didn't."

Gray laughed stiffly, then slid into the booth across from Carmen. With an arm slung across the back cushion, a cropped sweatshirt showing a glimpse of her midriff, and her blond beachy waves falling across one eye, Carmen looked effortlessly cool. Gray knew this was where she should pull out one of those icebreakers she'd tested earlier, but the only one she could think of now was *What was your high school mascot?* What was she, a robot helping Carmen reset an online password? Would she ask her to identify photos of fire hydrants next? Gray pinched her thigh under cover of the table in a desperate attempt to get over her nerves. What was *wrong* with her? She had had no trouble charming strangers when she was with McKenzie! Maybe there was something freeing about flirting when she was in a relationship. The stakes were lower since it wouldn't lead anywhere. Talking to dates while single was turning out to be a whole different ball game.

Luckily, Carmen seemed oblivious to Gray's internal struggle. "We're team Lez Get Information, by the way."

"Was 'Put Your Freakum Guess On' taken?" Gray said. *Ugh.* Why were puns the only thing her brain could produce in awkward moments?

"No, but I like where your head's at," Carmen said. "We have a legacy to uphold. We've finished in the top two teams for the past forty-nine consecutive weeks, and I'll be damned if we don't make it to week fifty."

Gray's eyes shifted toward the rest of the room. "Are there, uh, more people joining our team?"

"Not this week," Carmen said with a sigh. "Trina is sick, the Sophies had to leave town for a funeral, and none of our backups were available."

"The Sophies?"

"My friends, a couple, both named Sophie. Classic lesbian shit." Carmen took a sip from the bright-green drink in front of her. "Anyway, that's where you come in. What are your strongest trivia knowledge bases? Mine are sports, especially the Olympics and geography, and I've been working on U.S. presidential history. Oh, and I'm fluent in Spanish and Portuguese."

Gray was suddenly thankful to have a structured activity for her first date. Sure, trivia wasn't a particularly sexy choice, and she was getting more friendly teammate vibes from Carmen than a romantic spark. But actually, that was perfect. She had plenty of time to try out the sexier side of dating on her next eleven dates. For now, Gray just needed to get her feet wet.

She took another sip of her drink as she considered her own trivia strengths. "Um, I'm pretty good on movies and music, especially the nineties forward. Videogames too. I work in PR, so I'm pretty good on national brands and Fortune 500 companies. And food, since . . ." Gray trailed off. She knew food because she'd tasted so many of McKenzie's culinary experiments, not to mention the hours of cooking shows and YouTube videos she'd heard in the background while she played Halo. But if she wanted to follow Cherry's rules, no ex talk was allowed. "Just because, I guess."

"That's good," Carmen said, nodding. "We may only be a team of two, but that's a nice spread of topics. Fifty weeks, here we come!" She clinked her hurricane glass against Gray's whiskey Coke, then chugged the last of the green liquid inside. "Can I buy you a drink? The Alligator Tears Punch is to die for."

Gray's first drink was still half-full, and the cocktail had sounded too sweet before, but it seemed uncouth to turn down Carmen's recommendation. "Sure," she said. "Thanks!"

Carmen wandered off with her empty glass and Gray took the opportunity to text Cherry that everything was going great, along with a couple of thumbs-up emojis. The pub around her was cramped, due both to the sizable crowd and the beer signage, old tap handles, and Irish flags covering every inch of the red-brick interior walls. She couldn't help but think that McKenzie would have hated this place, its overly decorated walls, its in-your-face vibe, although she would have loved the trivia part. McKenzie and Gray were always at their best when they were on the same team in a competition. Gray was craning her neck to examine the high shelves along the top of the walls, which seemed to be filled with some kind of dusty collectibles, when Carmen returned with two violently green drinks in hand.

"Checking out the Pub Club pint glasses?" Carmen asked as she set a hurricane glass in front of Gray.

"Is that what they are?"

"Well, kind of." Carmen slid into the opposite side of the booth from Gray. "Once you've joined the Pub Club and tried one hundred unique draft beers, you get to pick a pint glass to put on the wall up there. But there was a bit of a debate about what counted as a pint glass and what didn't, so they finally landed on a very broad definition: anything that can hold a pint of beer and fit on the shelf." She turned to look at the ledge running along the opposite wall from their booth. "See, there are plenty of traditional pint glasses, a bunch of antique glassware, a whole section of beer steins over there. But also"—Carmen began pointing around the shelf at some of her favorites—"a baby bottle, a conch shell, a rain boot, and that up there? That's a water gun."

Gray examined the strange assortment. "Do you have a pint glass up there?"

"Yep! It's . . ." Carmen scooted to the end of the booth farthest from the wall and pointed at the shelf above them. "That brown ceramic one there? It's an antique ram's head tiki glass. I found it at some vintage store in the Garden District and figured it was perfect, since I'm an Aries."

"Me too!" Gray said, almost forgetting the whole reason they'd connected on Mercurious in the first place. "Are you, uh, into astrology?"

Carmen took a slurp of her drink and swallowed. "Yeah, who isn't?"

"Right." Gray paused. She didn't really know much about astrology, at least not beyond what she'd recently learned from Madame Nouvelle Lune. Was she the last queer person on Earth to jump on the astrology bandwagon? Unless she wanted to talk about her astrological dating challenge, which was decidedly against the rules, Gray needed to change the subject. She cleared her throat and took a chug of the Alligator Tears Punch, then immediately cringed.

"Strong, yeah?" Carmen asked, somewhat misinterpreting Gray's expression.

"Mm-hmm," Gray said, swallowing again to clear the syrupy taste from her mouth. It felt rude to criticize Carmen's favorite drink so early in the date, especially when she'd bought it for her. Determined to keep the evening on track, Gray took another long chug. At least she could get it over with quickly.

A short, high-pitched screech sounded from the pub's speaker system. Gray and Carmen turned to see someone with a microphone in hand at a tall table near the front of the room. "Hello, everyone, and welcome to Sunday night trivia at Cat O'Connor's! I'm Miguel. If you haven't signed up and you want to play, you've got about thirty seconds to hustle up to this clipboard and get your team name on it." He waved the clipboard in the air before stepping away from his microphone to place it on the bar. "All right, let me hit you with the rules."

Miguel dove into a description of what to expect, clearly using the same memorized script from many weeks of trivia. The game would consist of five categories, each worth twenty points, for a total possible score of one hundred. It would start with a jack-of-all-categories round, followed by ten questions on a theme, then an image-driven round, another theme, and finally a music round.

Gray's head was swimming with all of the information Miguel was so quickly sharing, but Carmen seemed completely unfazed as she scribbled "Lez Get Information" across the top of the first-round answer sheet that seemed to have appeared at their table out of nowhere.

"Get your pens ready, it's time for the jack-of-all-categories round! Question one: Which three U.S. presidents were quadrilingual, or fluent in four different languages? You get one point for each president you get right."

"Dang, that's hard," Gray said, but before she could finish, Carmen was already writing down an answer on the first line of the answer sheet.

"Jefferson for sure, he was known for being into languages." Carmen stopped writing and tapped the end of the pen against her chin. So far, she'd seemed to have a certain air of nonchalance, but Gray noticed that there was an intensity to her now that the questions had begun. This was Carmen in her element. "I'm pretty sure John Quincy Adams is right too, since he did a bunch of diplomatic work and translated stuff for fun. Weird guy, that JQA. But the third one, that's where I'm stuck."

"Doesn't Obama speak Indonesian or something?" Gray asked quietly.

Carmen shook her head. "Conversationally, and no other languages."

Gray held up her hands, admitting defeat. "This one's all yours." She settled back into the booth, tousling her dirty-blond hair in a way she hoped looked devastatingly handsome since she couldn't actually make herself useful.

"I'm thinking it's one of the older presidents," Carmen continued, musing under her breath, "unless it's a Roosevelt, but I think they both just knew English, French, and German. No, probably someone who knew Latin and ancient Greek or some other dead language. Van Buren spoke Dutch as his first language, maybe him?"

"Moving on to question two," Miguel's voice rang through the speaker system.

Carmen quickly jotted down "John Quincy Adams" and "Martin Van Buren" as the next question was announced. The round flew by with Carmen taking the lead and Gray hardly fitting in a suggestion edgewise. Before Gray could blink, Miguel was collecting answer sheets and Carmen was leaning back in the booth, confidently sipping her Alligator Tears Punch.

Feeling intimidated by Carmen's trivia prowess, Gray nervously sucked down the last of her own punch and then cleared her throat. "So you're from Alabama, huh?"

"Tuscaloosa," Carmen answered. "My parents are still there. I went to Vanderbilt for undergrad, then moved here to get my MBA at Tulane."

"Go back often to visit?" Gray asked, attempting to ride the conversational wave.

"Few times a year. It's not too long of a drive. What about you?"

Gray swirled the half-melted ice cubes in the bottom of her hurricane glass. "Oklahoma. Tulsa, to be exact."

"What brought you to New Orleans?"

"Oh, you know . . . friends in the area, work, good timing?" Gray rambled, trying to find an explanation that didn't send her down a rabbit hole directly toward her life-changing breakup.

"Cool, cool." Carmen paused for a moment, and Gray noticed the intensity return to her eyes. She leaned in conspiratori-ally. "Okay, so I feel pretty good about round one. We'll know for sure in a few minutes. But I think we got at *least* fifteen points, hopefully more like eighteen."

Gray nodded, feeling like she was little more than window dressing for their trivia team.

"But between that presidents question and that one about South American rivers, I think we've got a leg up on Smartacus."

"On who?"

Carmen jerked her head toward a tall table where six people were laughing and chatting over pint glasses of beer. "Our com-petition."

Gray didn't have a chance to size them up, as Miguel inter-rupted to read out the correct answers. Carmen had gotten a near-perfect score; her only mistake was naming Martin Van Buren instead of James Madison on question one.

Miguel reeled off the scores for six teams from the first round. "In third place, we've got team Panic! At the Pub Trivia with fif-teen points. Team I Am Smartacus is in second with eighteen points. Winning by a hair is team Lez Get Information with nine-teen points."

Carmen beamed while team Smartacus exchanged high fives.

"Now, who's ready for round two? I don't know about y'all, but now that March is almost here, I'm feeling a little March Madness. The category is: spring sports seasons."

"Yes!" Carmen cheered under her breath.

Knowing she had little to contribute to the topic, Gray busied herself stirring the watered-down remains of her whiskey Coke with her straw. Miguel read out the first seven questions of the category and Carmen answered them just as quickly without even asking Gray for input. But on the eighth question, Gray's ears perked up.

"How many players are on the field in fast-pitch and slow-pitch softball?" Miguel read from his tablet. "Each correct answer is worth one point."

Carmen held her pen above the answer sheet and began narrating her thought process. "There are nine players per team in baseball, right? So it's probably similar to that."

Gray leaned toward the table. "Nine players in fast-pitch, ten in slow-pitch."

Carmen looked up at Gray for the first time since the round began. "You're sure?"

"One hundred percent. I went to college on a softball scholarship." That scholarship was what had allowed Gray to break off from her parents after a disastrous coming-out process. Plus her ass had looked amazing in the softball uniform pants, as McKenzie had told her more than once.

"All right, then," Carmen said, looking a little impressed. She scribbled down the answer, then looked back up to examine Gray. "Nice one."

That tiny compliment echoed in Gray's head as Miguel asked the last two questions of the round. Sure, she'd done little more than nod her agreement to the rest of Carmen's answers for the round, but it felt good to beat her teammate to one correct response.

With the second round completed, Carmen hopped up to turn in their answer sheet and returned to the booth with two new glasses of Alligator Tears Punch. She slid one across the table to Gray. "Cheers to softball scholarships."

Gray clinked her glass against Carmen's and took a sip. It went down a little easier the second time around. They had another opportunity for a toast a few minutes later, once Miguel revealed the answers, and they found they'd achieved a perfect score. That put team Lez Get Information at thirty-nine points, followed by team I Am Smartacus at thirty-five, and a new team in third, Hoops There It Is, with thirty points.

The third round proved surprisingly lucky for Gray. The category was weapons, something Gray wouldn't have considered a strong point until Miguel started clicking through the images on screens around the bar. As it turned out, most of the weapons from Gray's favorite videogames were inspired by real devices. Carmen quickly realized Gray's advantage on the topic and passed over the answer sheet and pen, which Gray accepted with a sense of great responsibility.

With Gray's confidence boosted and Carmen recognizing Gray as an asset to her team, conversation flowed more naturally. That might have also been thanks to the punch, Gray realized when she stood up and found the room tilting around her. Maybe Carmen was right about it being strong. "Where's the restroom?" she asked, trying to steady herself against the back of the booth.

"See those frosted doors that look like phone booths?" Carmen asked, pointing toward the back right corner of the pub. "Those are the bathrooms. Confusing, I know."

Gray carefully made her way to the faux phone booth doors, returning just as Miguel was beginning the fourth round. Carmen caught Gray up on the score. They'd only missed one weapon, but Smartacus had gotten a perfect score, putting them only three points behind team Lez.

The fourth category was famous museums, and Carmen seemed to grow more tense as their lead shrank, picking apart a cardboard coaster and leaving pieces of it scattered across the table. "We just have to nail the music round. You said you're pretty good at music, right?"

"I'm all right, especially if it's more contemp—"

Gray was cut off by Miguel's voice over the speakers. "Get those final answer sheets ready, because it's time for the music round! Category is: movie musicals."

Carmen made a sour face, then looked hopefully at Gray. Gray shrugged. "I used to really like *Moulin Rouge*?" she said.

Carmen groaned. "Smartacus has a theater nerd on their team. We're toast."

A few songs from jukebox musicals like *Across the Universe* and *Mamma Mia!* proved easy to identify. Both Carmen and Gray were relieved to recognize the opening notes of "The Time Warp" from *The Rocky Horror Picture Show*. But the other show tunes were harder. Even if they recognized it, they couldn't nail down which musical it belonged to. At the end of the round, Carmen delivered their answer sheet and they nervously awaited their final score.

"I'm going to be so pissed if that round broke our streak before we hit fifty weeks," Carmen said, wrapping a strand of blond hair around her finger.

"Well, I looked around at the other teams during that last round, and team Panic! looked totally lost and confused. I think we're a safe bet for second, at least," Gray said, hoping it was true.

"The Sophies will never forgive me," Carmen said, as if she hadn't even heard Gray.

"Hey, I think you did a pretty incredible job, considering you were the only original teammate here to represent," Gray said.

That got a tiny smile from Carmen. Finally, Miguel's voice filled the room, revealing the correct answers. They ticked off their points on their fingers, coming up with twelve to add to their score and bringing them to a grand total of eighty-five.

After announcing the scores of the six teams with the fewest points, Miguel paused, adjusted his backward cap, and allowed the anticipation to build. "In third place, winners of four Cat O'Connor's bottle openers and a hearty pat on the back . . . Panic! At the Pub Trivia!"

The group cheered from the end of the bar, seemingly unbothered that they hadn't managed to snag first place. Gray breathed a small sigh of relief, knowing she hadn't broken Carmen's fifty-week record of being in the top two, but Carmen looked just as on edge as before.

Miguel waited for the applause to subside. "Now, I Am Smartacus and Lez Get Information have been separated by only a few points the entire game, but that last round mixed things up a bit . . ."

"Dammit, they won," Carmen said under her breath, seeming to deflate. Gray reached across the table to grab Carmen's hand, a touch that felt awkward but, Gray hoped, a bit consoling as well.

". . . putting I Am Smartacus and Lez Get Information in a tie at eighty-five points each!"

Carmen and Gray gasped in unison at the news.

"In the event of a tie," Miguel said theatrically, "the teams in first go into a tiebreaker round, where they have thirty seconds to list as many items in a category as possible. I'll bring fresh answer sheets to both teams, then I'll announce the category and start the clock."

The other first-place team was already huddled up and whispering, throwing occasional looks at Gray and Carmen's booth. Gray felt her heart racing. They could still win! She wasn't sure when she'd become so invested, but she was in deep now.

Once Miguel dropped off their answer sheet, Carmen pulled it in front of herself. "I can write. Unless you're, like, a really intense speed writer?"

Gray shrugged. "You go for it."

Miguel returned to the mic stand and fumbled with his phone. "Okay, I've got thirty seconds on the clock here. List as many items as you can from this category: Books of the Bible, Old Testament only. Go!"

Before Carmen could finish saying "fuck," Gray had pulled the pen and answer sheet from her, immediately scribbling down "Genesis," "Exodus," "Leviticus," and "Numbers."

When Carmen saw Gray spelling out "Deuteronomy," she whispered, "Skip the long ones! Write the short ones first!" Gray nodded, penning "Joshua," "Judges," and "Ruth."

"Ten seconds left!" Miguel announced.

Taking Carmen's advice, she skipped to the shortest books she could think of: 1 Kings, 2 Kings, Ezra, Esther, and Job.

"Time's up!" Miguel said.

Carmen swung the paper around to face her. "Barely legible, but still counts." She ticked off the books listed, counting silently, just before Miguel swooped the sheet away from her. "Fourteen," she whispered to Gray across the table. "You're sure they're all right?"

"Absolutely sure."

"Good," Carmen said, nodding. "I'm glad you're here. I would have bombed that category. I've only ever stepped foot in churches for weddings and funerals." She paused, eyeing Gray across the table. "How do *you* know the Old Testament so well?"

"Twelve years of private Christian school," Gray said with a shudder. "I try to forget most of it, but the song they taught us to memorize books of the Bible is actually pretty catchy."

Carmen smirked. "Well, it came in handy tonight." She scooted closer to the wall and patted the booth next to her. "Want to come around on this side for a better view when Miguel tells us who won?"

"Sure!" Gray left her side of the booth and sat down next to Carmen. With their hips brushing against each other, Gray suddenly remembered that this was a date. Not just a fun trivia night with a friend. A *date*. The only first date she'd been on in the past decade. And whether it was the thrill of competition, the buzz from the boozy punch, or actual chemistry with Carmen, Gray was enjoying it. She rested her arm along the back of the booth, her hand grazing Carmen's shoulder, and was pleased that Carmen leaned into her touch instead of backing away.

A rustle of papers drew Gray and Carmen's attention back to the high table by the bar. Miguel held the microphone to his mouth. "All right, we have a winner. Coming in second place and winning twenty-five dollars off their tab tonight, drumroll, please . . ."

Customers around the bar contributed by beating their hands against their tables. Carmen grabbed Gray's knee, and Gray felt something flutter in her stomach.

"I Am Smartacus!"

The competing team groaned as Gray and Carmen looked at each other, realization dawning.

"And coming in first, winning fifty dollars off their tab, with a crucial fourteen books of the Old Testament, Lez Get Information!" Miguel announced.

"*We won!*" Gray and Carmen screamed, throwing their hands in the air as the pub cheered around them.

Before Gray knew what was happening, Carmen had grabbed her face in her hands and pulled her into a passionate victory kiss. Gray's body reacted instinctively, wrapping her arms around Carmen's bare midriff and tasting the essence of Midori on her tongue. Miguel finished off his post-trivia script, but Gray didn't hear a word of it through the sound of her own heartbeat in her ears. Nothing else mattered but the feeling of Carmen's skin and the adrenaline running through her veins.

After a minute, they pulled apart and the look shared between them felt like it might catch the room on fire. Carmen took a jagged breath. "I want you. Now."

An image of sparkling decorative tile and cool mood lighting appeared in Gray's head. "The bathroom."

Carmen all but pushed Gray out of the booth, then grabbed her hand and pulled her through the crowd of people waiting at the bar to close their tabs. Before Gray could blink, they were behind the faux phone booth door and had their hands all over each other. Carmen tugged off Gray's jacket and slung it across the sink. Brushing aside Carmen's hair, Gray sucked at a spot on Carmen's neck, then reached under her cropped sweatshirt to release the clasp on her bra with one hand. The strapless bra tumbled to the ground, and Carmen evened the score by tugging Gray's black V-neck over her head and just as expertly unhooking her bra.

Feeling the cool air of the bathroom against her skin, Gray paused, one hand cupping Carmen's breast under her shirt. "Wait, are you sure you want this?"

"So sure," Carmen panted, unbuttoning Gray's jeans. "You?"

Still riding the wave of their win and certain she would combust if Carmen stopped touching her, Gray nodded. "Very sure."

Their mouths met again, Carmen kissing forcefully enough to push Gray's bare back against the cool tiled wall beside the sink. Carmen unzipped Gray's pants and dove a hand into her boy-cut shorts, already damp with anticipation. With her mouth finding one of Gray's nipples, Carmen stroked a finger down Gray's center, drawing a moan from Gray's lips. Carmen's fingertip circled Gray's clit and Gray closed her eyes and cried out, "Oh god, that's good," forgetting entirely that anyone might be able to hear them. Carmen slid a finger deep into Gray, still rubbing against her clit with the side of her thumb, and it took Gray only a moment longer before she came.

Gray ran a hand through Carmen's hair, then pulled her in for a kiss. With a twist, Gray changed their positions so that Carmen was against the wall. She pulled Carmen's sweatshirt over her head and pressed the heated skin of their torsos together, grabbing Carmen's ass with both hands and then running her palms up her sides until they reached her breasts. Circling her thumbs around Carmen's hard nipples, Gray elicited a shiver from her date. One hand continued caressing Carmen's breast while the other slid into the stretchy waistband of her leggings. Carmen leaned into the touch, pressing eagerly against Gray's fingers.

As Gray met Carmen's need, Carmen pressed her face into Gray's neck, suppressing a moan by biting the tender skin beneath her ear. Within a few minutes, Carmen cried out against Gray's collarbone, tightened her grip on Gray's back, and then released it. They held each other for a moment longer, catching their breath.

Removing her hand from Carmen's leggings with a gentle stroke up her torso, Gray stepped back. "Wow. That was . . . wow."

"I love winning trivia," Carmen said with a devilish grin.

"Same."

A pounding on the door caused them both to jump. "Hello? Anyone in there?" a booming voice said from outside the bathroom.

Jumping into a flurry of motion, Gray called out, "Just a second!" She pulled her T-shirt over her head and buttoned her jeans while bumping against a similarly frenzied Carmen. Gray pulled her jacket from the sink and turned on the faucet. "Just washing my hands!" Carmen and Gray hurried to scrub their hands and adjust their hair and clothes.

Right as Gray reached to unlock the door, Carmen threw out a hand to stop her. "Your bra!" Carmen pulled it from where it had landed above the paper towel dispenser and passed it to Gray, who jammed it into her jacket pocket.

With a grateful nod to Carmen, Gray unlocked the door and stepped into the low-lit pub. Luckily, it seemed their interrupter had found a vacant stall elsewhere, and no one was there to raise an eyebrow at the two of them leaving the bathroom together, hair ruffled, cheeks reddened, and clothes slightly askew. Carmen followed Gray back to their booth by the door, both avoiding eye contact with any nosy patrons.

Carmen eyed their mostly empty glasses still at the table. "Shall we finish our drinks?"

"Sure," Gray said, feeling a bit dizzy from the bathroom rendezvous. She dropped into the booth and sipped the last of the Alligator Tears Punch.

It only took one long slurp for Carmen to empty her glass. "Guess I was thirstier than I thought," she said with a wink. "I don't have class on Mondays, so I'm not in a rush. Do you want another round?"

"Mondays?" Gray said, realization dawning. "Wait. Shit. It's Sunday." She lit up the digital watch on her wrist. "Jesus, it's already almost midnight? Fuck me."

"Again?" Carmen said. "Sure, I'm in."

"I wish," Gray said. "But I've really got to go. I totally lost track of time." She pulled her phone from her pocket to call a rideshare. How had she so completely forgotten that she had work tomorrow? Gray had thought the evening couldn't last more than an hour, two tops. But then she'd gotten so wrapped up in the competition that she hadn't even looked at her watch since the first round of trivia started.

A driver around the block accepted her ride, and Gray looked up at Carmen apologetically. "Sorry I have to run. This was fun. Really fun."

"Thanks for helping me keep team Lez Get Information at the top for another week," Carmen said, seeming unbothered by Gray's swift exit. "Maybe I can text you next time we have another vacancy and need a Bible scholar?"

"I'm sure my Sunday school teacher would be thrilled to hear you call me that." Gray stood and zipped her jacket. "But yeah, text me. Oh, should I close the tab?"

"No need. It's covered since we won."

Gray dug a twenty-dollar bill from her wallet and dropped it on the table. "For the tip, then." She leaned down and pressed a kiss against Carmen's cheekbone. "See you around, Carmen."

Carmen grinned. "Welcome to NOLA, Gray."

Five

GRAY WAS AWAKENED by the toxic combination of a terrible taste in her mouth, a pounding in her skull, and bright sunlight invading her room through the window. With a groan, she pulled the quilt over her eyes, but her brain was already dredging up details from the previous night: the too-sweet cocktails, the frenzied list of Old Testament books, and . . . Wait, did she really have sex in a public restroom?

The idea of having sex with someone besides McKenzie had terrified her in the month since their breakup. But the excitement of winning trivia paired with the spark between Gray and Carmen had made their dalliance feel easy. Even better than easy; it was fun. Maybe, she thought, the astrological dating challenge really could show her new parts of herself. Who knew what the next eleven signs could teach her?

Gray's musings were interrupted by a trill from her phone. She picked it up to see a notification that sent her flying from the bed in a panic: a reminder for a work meeting in fifteen minutes. *Dammit!* How could she have forgotten? She normally wouldn't need to be in the office until 9 A.M., but her introductory meeting for her first major project was scheduled for 8 A.M., and she'd somehow managed to completely forget about it when she crawled into bed after her night out with Carmen. And now she was going to meet her colleague hungover, ill prepared, and, seeing as how the meeting was across town from Cherry's house, late.

When Gray was hired as the PR manager of a prestigious private school with elementary, middle, and high school campuses, she was pleased, but also surprised. She'd been desperate for a job that would get her out of Tulsa, but with her very gay haircut, nose ring, and grungy taste in fashion, Gray didn't really expect St. Charles Collegiate Academy to see her as a good fit. Luckily, Gray was excellent in an interview, and Dr. Timothy Donovan, the harried but well-meaning school superintendent she reported to, seemed to recognize the unique skills that had helped Gray succeed in marketing and promoting a queer-wedding-planning company in conservative Oklahoma. And it didn't hurt that Gray had gone to an academically rigorous private school herself. When it came to getting the austere school board's sign-off on her job offer, well, she looked great on paper, and only Dr. Donovan knew how queer she appeared in person.

As Dr. Donovan had explained on Gray's first day on the job two weeks ago, some of the leaders within St. Charles Collegiate were working to move the school into a more diverse, inclusive, equitable future, a mission he supported. But, predictably, they were meeting backlash from old-money alumni on the school's board of directors and a few angry parents who wanted to ensure that the advantages of an acclaimed SCCA education remained exclusive. Gray's first opportunity to prove herself would be smoothing over some of the conflict around the newly promoted middle school principal—the one she was now late to meet—who was leading efforts to bring in a more diverse group of students and update the curriculum to reflect a changing world. Gray hoped her enthusiasm for the mission would make up for her tardiness.

Gray threw on the first clothes she could find, tossed a random assortment of junk in her bag, brushed her teeth, and hopped into her car to drive to the historic uptown Garden District, where the middle school campus was located. If it weren't for this meeting, Gray would have had an hour to clean up the mess she'd made of herself the previous night. Instead, she hoped a little confidence and a breath mint could disguise a multitude of sins.

It was only thirteen minutes past the scheduled meeting start time of 8 A.M. when Gray's car swerved into a parking spot in front of a regal, ivy-covered redbrick building. As she jogged up the rather imposing steps to the front door, Gray's stomach lurched. She paused for a moment, letting a wave of nausea pass as she wiped a sheen of sweat from her forehead. Was she imagining it, or did she smell like vodka?

With a deep breath, Gray tugged on the front door only to find it locked. She peered through the glass, then knocked to capture the attention of a nearby security guard. The guard looked up at Gray, then stood, stretched, and meandered toward the door at a pace that felt especially glacial. When the door finally cracked open, Gray burst through it.

"Thanks. Which way is . . . uh . . . Principal Taylor's office?" Gray said, consulting the calendar reminder on her phone. In her first two weeks at St. Charles Collegiate, she'd had a chance to tour the elementary and high school campuses, but the middle school was still a mystery to her.

"Hold up, you have to sign in at the attendance office first," the security guard said.

"Oh, I'm not a student. I have a meeting. I'm Gray Young from the superintendent's office. PR manager."

He examined Gray. "Got a badge?"

"Not yet, I just started and I—"

"Then you still gotta sign in." The security guard nodded down the hall to his left.

"I'm running a little late, can I sign in after?" Gray said with a pleading smile.

The guard shook his head. "Rules are rules."

By the time Gray had signed in, handed over her driver's license, gotten a visitor badge, and found the principal's office, her head felt like it might actually explode. She winced at the sound her knuckles made against the door.

"Come in," a voice sounded from inside the office.

Gray smoothed her hair, put on her best colleague-facing smile, and opened the door.

The office had all wooden furniture, several floor-to-ceiling bookshelves, and a big window overlooking a grassy sitting area behind the school. It felt scholarly and intimidating, a stark contrast to Gray's cramped, impersonal space at the administrative office downtown. At the center of the room was a large desk covered in organized stacks of books and file folders, a nameplate that said PRINCIPAL VERONICA TAYLOR (SHE/HER), and a computer, behind which sat a woman whose very presence screamed "stern." Her shiny, chin-length, dark-brown hair looked so precise that it gave the impression she'd had it trimmed that morning. Her black suit was pressed within an inch of its life.

"Good morning!" Gray said as brightly as she could manage. She was having déjà vu from visits to her own high school principal's office during her teenage years. They'd been frequent.

Principal Taylor looked up at Gray, arching a thin eyebrow over her thick-framed glasses, then turned back to her computer screen. "Art teacher interviews are down the hall in room one twenty-six," she said, her voice cold.

"Oh, I'm not an art teacher," Gray said, suddenly self-conscious about her wrinkled blue button-down shirt and bomber jacket from the previous night. "I'm Gray Young, the new PR manager for SCCA, here for our meeting."

"And what time is it now, new PR manager Gray Young?" the principal asked without looking up.

Gray looked at her watch, her cheeks burning, to see she was over twenty minutes late. "I'm so sorry. I didn't realize the sign-in process would take—"

"I tell my students that if you're not fifteen minutes early, you're late," Principal Taylor said, her eyes turning again to Gray. "And if I don't tolerate lateness from middle schoolers, why exactly should I tolerate it from you, a presumably responsible adult?"

Gray felt as if she were shrinking into her twelve-year-old form underneath her clothes. She tucked a hand in her jacket pocket, where she felt . . . was that her bra from last night? *Yikes.* Hoping to put herself back on equal footing, she said, "I sincerely apologize, Veronica. Can I call you Veronica?"

"I'd rather you didn't."

Gray gulped. "Right. Principal Taylor. I see that my lateness has started us off on the wrong foot, and I'm sorry about that. I hope that as we start working together, you'll see that I am a hardworking, reliable, trustworthy professional, and I don't plan to let you down again."

Principal Taylor abruptly stood, her hands tensed on the desk in front of her. "I've already told you I don't tolerate tardiness, and I don't believe in second chances. Showing up late, in clothes that look like they time traveled from a nineties rave, covered in hickeys, is incredibly unprofessional."

Gray's humiliation was overwhelming. Hickeys? Had she even looked in the mirror before she left this morning? She tugged at the collar of her shirt, not even certain which part of her neck to hide.

"Please leave my office," the principal continued. "I'll be in touch with Dr. Donovan shortly to let him know that this arrangement won't work out, as you can't seem to keep your commitments."

"Whoa, wait, please," Gray said, her heart beginning to race. "I know I made a mistake, but I promise I can make it up to you."

"And how exactly do you plan to do that?" Principal Taylor said abruptly. "Do you have sway with the local papers that keep airing the school's dirty laundry to the city at large? Have you figured out how to stop the board from banning all the books in our updated curriculums? Are there binders full of brilliant ideas to get every disruptive member of the faculty and staff on board with my agenda in that pin-covered messenger bag?"

Gray gripped her bag closer, suddenly conscious of both its unprofessional exterior and the lack of prepared materials in its interior. "I was under the impression that this was an introductory meeting, a chance to meet each other and start discussions on the work ahead of us," Gray said weakly.

"I'll take that as a no," Principal Taylor said, turning away from Gray as if her case was closed.

Gray usually wouldn't have done much to prepare for a first meeting with a colleague. But because she knew the job was slightly out of her depth and wanted to prove she could make it in her new city, Gray had actually spent some time diving into the school's digital archive. She gathered her courage. "I've done my research," she said firmly. "I've briefed myself on you and your plans for the middle school. I'm totally supportive of your DEI initiatives—"

Principal Taylor scoffed. "I'm sure. There are plenty of people who are *totally supportive* of my *little DEI initiatives* until actual changes start taking place."

Seeing she'd poked a sore spot, Gray backtracked. "I'm truly sorry that's been your experience. But I promise you that I'm not a fair-weather partner in this. From everything I've read, I know your plans aren't about optics or some kind of progressive brownie points. I can tell how much work and care you've put into creating an action plan that will give a more diverse student body a better chance at academic and future career success. Even more, you're working to give all of your students a more well-rounded education that recognizes the impact women and people of color have made on every field in ways that too often go ignored. I can tell this matters to you by the way you've talked and written about it. And it matters to me too."

Principal Taylor raised an eyebrow.

"You see, I went to an elite private school myself, in Oklahoma," Gray continued, bolstered by the fact that the principal hadn't thrown her out yet. "It wasn't as prestigious as SCCA, and definitely more religiously affiliated. But I came from a privileged background, and that afforded me a ton of benefits when it came to education. Even with those advantages, I was a queer kid with a rebellious streak, and I always knew I wasn't the kind of person the other students, the teachers, or the administrators wanted around. I never want another kid to feel like doors are closing in their face the way they closed in mine."

Principal Taylor's eyebrow remained raised. Gray took that as a sign to keep going.

"I've also done my research on what you're up against. I've read the articles in the papers and local blogs. I've read the board meeting minutes. More important, I know what it's like inside some of these alumni families. I know the rhetoric they use to justify excluding kids who don't fit their idea of 'deserving.' I have an insider perspective for the kind of work you want to do, for pushing back against the board's closed-minded leadership. I know what it takes to change their minds, or if that's not possible, I can at least stop them from blocking your work at every turn."

Principal Taylor didn't say anything, but she was looking at Gray a little differently now.

"I'm really sorry that I showed up late today. It was disrespectful, and it's a mistake I won't repeat. I know we've only just met, but"—Gray ran a hand across the buzzed side of her head, her fingers shaking—"I want to be your biggest ally on this. Your right-hand man. I want to show you that, on days when I've had my morning coffee, I'm unstoppable. And I want us—your students, this school—to be unstoppable together."

Principal Taylor removed her glasses and polished them with a blue cloth from her desk drawer. "I've seen your résumé. Not a single school or educational institution in your employment history. In fact, you worked for a wedding company, correct?"

"You're right. I haven't worked for a school before," Gray said. "But I *did* take a tiny queer-wedding-planning startup in ultraconservative Oklahoma and helped grow it into the most prominent queer-wedding-planning company in the entire region. What you're trying to do here may seem close to impossible right now, but I've faced impossible odds before, and I've beat them."

Principal Taylor put her glasses back on and examined Gray over the top of the frames for one more moment, her lips pursed, before speaking. "Fine. I'll give you another chance. But only one more, and not today. You've already wasted enough of my time, and I have a faculty meeting at nine." She leaned over to flip through a planner on her desk. "Does 8:30 A.M. on Friday work for you?"

"Yes, Friday morning is great," Gray said, feeling a rush of relief. "Thank you so much."

"I'll see you then," Principal Taylor said. "And Young?"

Gray paused, her hand already grabbing the doorknob. "Yes?"

The principal arched one eyebrow atop her glasses. "Don't forget your coffee next time."

Six

GRAY BURST THROUGH the kitchen door, dropping her bag next to a pile of shoes before dramatically collapsing into a chair. Across the table, River banged together a toy boat and his favorite stuffed unicorn.

"That bad?" Cherry said over the sound of running water as she scrubbed dishes.

"Worse," Gray said, sore from hours spent hunched over her computer at her office in the Central Business District, trying to piece together a PR strategy that might win Principal Taylor's favor. "Totally shit day."

"Sit day!" River said with a delighted giggle, narrowly missing the curse word Gray had dropped in front of him. He started singing a made-up tune to his toys with the words: "Sit day, sit day, shhhh . . . shhhhhhii . . ."

"Ship!" Gray course corrected. "It's another word for boat."

"Boat!" River said, showing Gray his toy. She nodded encouragingly.

Across the kitchen, Cherry turned off the faucet and pulled her rubber gloves from her hands, then joined Gray and River at the table. "So tell me about your day. Lots of boats?"

"Well, I woke up hungover as . . . ship," Gray said. "Headache, nauseous, and late to my first meeting with the middle school principal, who turned out to be a total hard-ass and threatened to have me *fired*."

"Yikes," Cherry said sympathetically.

"Yeah, big-time yikes," Gray said, reaching her hands behind her head to massage her shoulders. Maybe it was time for her to get a standing desk for her office. "My day never really recovered from there, and I still feel like I got run over by a truck."

Cherry leaned in, looking at Gray's neck. "And you've got the bruises to prove it. Are those *hickeys*?"

Gray swatted her away with one hand, covering her neck with the other. "Geez, does everybody feel like they have to point it out?"

"I'm taking this as a sign your first date went well," Cherry said, wiggling her eyebrows.

"Actually, yeah," Gray said, a genuine smile reaching her lips for the first time all day. "It was, uh . . . spicier than I expected."

Cherry squealed, then hopped out of her seat to grab an iPad and toddler-sized headphones from the living room. Once she'd covered River's ears and turned on a video of dancing robots, she turned back to Gray. "Tell. Me. Everything."

Gray shared a rundown of the date, from the trivia to the sticky-sweet cocktails to the steamy moment in the bathroom. When she finished, Cherry clapped her hands and danced in her seat. "You lesbian Casanova, you! You put yourself *out* there! Do you think you'll see Carmen again?"

"Isn't that kind of the point of this whole astrology dating project, that I get through all twelve before taking anything further? Wasn't that *your* rule?" Gray asked.

"Oh yeah, that. You know I suck at following rules," Cherry said. "Well, maybe when you're through with the project, then. It does seem like you're pretty compatible with other Aries. And you can still be friends in the meantime, right?"

"Well, I'm starting to rethink the whole thing, to be honest," Gray said, eliciting an outraged look from Cherry. "I was hungover and pissed off my colleague this morning—hell, I could have even lost my job—because I got so distracted by the date last night. If finishing this challenge means getting fired, it doesn't really seem worth it."

"First off, this isn't just some fun TikTok challenge, it's about finding your *life partner* and starting a *family*." Cherry flipped her bright-red hair over her shoulder and leaned in. "Second, they're not mutually exclusive. Of *course* two Aries got all caught up in their fire sign passion and made some unwise decisions. But they won't all be like that. And you'll be smarter, right? You'll, like, actually check your calendar before you bang some girl in a pub bathroom again."

"I guess that's true." Gray looked over to confirm that River was still thoroughly absorbed in his iPad, then turned sideways in her chair toward Cherry. "Speaking of, you can go ahead and congratulate me now on losing my non-McKenzie virginity."

"Super proud of you, my brave little ho." Cherry leaned in conspiratorially. "And since you got over the sexy-times fear . . . do you think you'll sleep with every sign now?"

"I mean, it was pretty spontaneous. I still don't think I could pull that off twelve times in a row." Gray stretched her arms upward and clasped her hands behind her head. "But you know? Maybe it will happen again here and there. For compatibility research purposes."

"Of course, for science." Cherry chewed on her lip thoughtfully for a moment, then clapped her hands together in delight. "Oh, I've got an idea! What if you sleep with one of every element? A fire sign, an earth sign, an air sign, a water sign. It's enough to give you a taste of each element, but still some flexibility on who you do and don't feel comfortable getting groovy with."

"Big *Avatar* energy too." Gray nodded as she considered the concept, feeling an extra dose of confidence from her success on date one. "So if there are four elements, then I choose one of three signs in each element? Is that math?"

"Exactly. Pick one of the three for a sexy rendezvous if you're feeling it," Cherry said. "And you can already mark fire sign off your list."

"You know, I think that could actually work." Gray tapped her fingers against the back of her head in silence for a moment, deciding she had the nerve to go for it at least three more times. "Yeah. Consider it officially part of the challenge."

Cherry grinned. "I'm loving this more every day. Have you found a Taurus yet?"

"Not yet."

"You better get on it," Cherry said. "Tauruses are earth signs. Slow-moving, deliberate. It might take a while to get one to commit to a date. And I've got the perfect icebreaker for this one: favorite national park. They love being one with nature or what-ever."

Gray whipped out her phone and pulled up Mercurious. "Okay, I'll get started. But once I find a good prospect, I *have* to spend some time researching ideas for the middle school fiasco. I'm not letting that principal make me feel like a delinquent twelve-year-old again."

"You got this, G," Cherry said. "Just don't be too flirty with the earth signs. It freaks them out."

"Noted," Gray said, already scrolling through a list of profiles and feeling surprisingly optimistic about her next date.

Seven

As cherry had predicted, wooing a Taurus proved tricky. After several false starts, Gray finally zeroed in on Riley, a thirty-four-year-old lesbian born and raised in New Orleans. She seemed to take herself pretty seriously, based on all the jokes Gray had unsuccessfully tried to crack in their Mercurious chat, and was a bit more masc than the people Gray usually found herself crushing on. But wasn't the point of this whole experiment for Gray to think outside of her dating box? Who knew what her type was anyway, besides the one person she'd dated for a decade?

The national parks question, while good in theory, hadn't been as productive as Gray hoped. She'd given her own lengthy answer about Carlsbad Caverns in New Mexico, where she'd assisted in planning a wedding for a couple of outdoorsy lesbians a couple years ago. All of the permits and noise restrictions and complicated rules had been a headache, but the stunning beauty of the caverns and surrounding desert had made it all worth it. Meanwhile, Riley had given a dispassionate answer of New Orleans Jazz National Historical Park because it was closest to where she grew up. But after a few days of casual chatting, Riley seemed to crack open a bit more, sharing her passion for coffee and espresso. She'd spent years working at the same coffee chain, moving her way up to manager and later being tapped to help open new locations and train staff. Recently, she'd left the chain to start her own shop, which was slated to officially open in a couple of weeks. Gray had responded with enthusiastic support, impressed by the kind of determination that led Riley from barista to entrepreneur. And that conversation had guided them to what Gray truly sought: a chance at a date.

Riding high on the thrill of a recently delivered espresso machine, Riley invited Gray to the shop early on Friday morning for a test run. Gray knew she was testing fate by scheduling a date right before her makeup meeting at St. Charles Collegiate Academy, but this date was entirely different. It was for coffee, not potent cocktails. Even better, the caffeine combined with the early start time would ensure Gray was awake and alert before her meeting with Principal Taylor. That is, as long as she didn't get carried away with any surprise bathroom rendezvous.

Still remembering Principal Taylor's eyes raking over her informal outfit on Monday morning, Gray veered on the side of overdressed on Friday. Most of her work at the queer-wedding-planning business in Tulsa had been away from the altar—advertising, budgeting, business planning, et cetera. Still, she had a few nice suits for ceremonies and receptions that required all hands on deck. She'd picked out one of her favorites for her date with Riley: a deep-forest-green suit paired with a crisp white button-down and silky white pocket square. To complete the look, she'd matched her shiniest brown oxfords with a belt and briefcase, then slicked the longer part of her hair back in a style that was undoubtedly dapper. No one could mistake her for a middle school art teacher in this outfit.

The sun was just beginning to peek over the horizon when Gray arrived at Riley's coffee shop. It was a cozy space on the street level of a new condo building in the trendy Warehouse District. When she'd moved to New Orleans, Gray had pictured the whole city looking something like the French Quarter. She'd quickly been proved wrong by neighborhoods like the Warehouse District, which blended eclectic Southern architecture with sleek modern design. Despite its seemingly mismatched styles, the whole city was tied together seamlessly by the grand oaks, Spanish moss, and Big Easy attitude.

Riley greeted Gray at the door with a firm, if somewhat formal, handshake and an inspection of her outfit. "Nice suit. Tom Ford?"

"Yeah, actually. Thanks," Gray said, pulling on the hem of her jacket. "I like your glasses."

"Thanks. Gucci." Riley adjusted her boxy tortoiseshell glasses, then ran a hand over her braids to where they met in a bun at the back of her head.

A moment of silence ensued, neither sure where to take the conversation next. God, why was Gray so awkward on dates? Talking to strangers was never as difficult when she was doing it in a professional capacity, excluding her introduction to Principal Taylor. She looked around the shop, trying to shake her nerves. "So, this is the new place?"

"Yes! Here, let me take you on the tour." Riley opened the glass door into a small space with chairs and café tables pushed to one side and a pile of boxes to the other. "This is Demitasse Café, or at least it will be by the time it opens in a couple weeks. Tables will be spread around here. I ordered some carpeting to show where the line goes around this wall." Riley pointed out a path along the white subway tile from the door to the counter.

"I love the flooring! Really makes the dark wood of the tables and chairs pop," Gray said, following Riley toward the counter.

"Thanks! I had my eye on this nice white-and-gray marble, but it would have blown the budget. And I was saving for this baby," Riley said, arriving at an enormous copper espresso maker.

"Damn," Gray said, stepping back to admire the machine. "That looks intense."

"It is!" With her hands gently running along the top of the espresso maker, Riley dropped her chill distance and glowed with enthusiasm. "Semiautomatic brass heat-exchange boiler for temperature stability, three-way solenoid valve to keep the shots coming . . . It doesn't get better than this, my dude."

Gray nodded, feeling a bit like they were two bros bonding at a car show. "It's, uh, very shiny."

"Copper is great at conducting and retaining heat, and it's antimicrobial," Riley said, gazing fondly at the machine. "Shall we fire it up?"

"For sure!"

"What's your drink of choice?" Riley asked, already twisting and pushing the various controls on the espresso maker.

"Caramel latte," Gray said, bewitched by the sounds and smells emanating from the machine.

"Sorry, no caramel syrup."

"Oh. Vanilla latte?" Gray tried.

"Actually, I don't have any flavorings," Riley said, twirling a dial that caused a burst of steam to appear. "I've had way too much of the cookie-dough-butterscotch-toffee-nut madness. Now that I'm in charge, I'm getting back to basics. Enjoying the perfect simplicity of the coffee bean."

"Right," Gray said, feeling a bit embarrassed by her pedestrian coffee preferences. "Then . . . I don't know, whatever you're having."

Riley grinned. "Two macchiatos, coming right up."

Watching Riley work the espresso maker was like being in the audience for performance art. She was masterful with the copper beast, her capable hands making it seem like she'd spent a lifetime with the machine instead of only a day. After a few minutes, Riley came around the counter with two ceramic mugs and placed them on a café table, then gestured for Gray to sit.

Once they were both seated, Gray felt the pressing weight of being on a date. She took a sip of the drink in front of her, wincing as it seared the roof of her mouth. "Delicious," she said, lisping to avoid exacerbating the burn.

"Thanks," Riley said, then held her mug up to blow across the steaming surface.

"So, uh . . . Tell me about yourself," Gray said, still struggling to get her feet under her at such an early hour.

Riley shrugged. "Not much to tell. Born and raised in New Orleans. Into coffee, obviously." She sipped her espresso. "What about you?"

The answer didn't reveal anything Gray didn't already know. "Born and raised in Tulsa. Just moved to New Orleans. Into . . . public relations, I guess? God, that sounds boring."

"No, not boring at all," Riley said. "I feel like I've been trying to learn PR and marketing on the fly for the past few weeks and I'm way out of my depth."

"Really? It's not so hard." Gray crossed an ankle over her knee, settling in. "I mean, we've all had commercials and sales pitches shoved down our throats our whole lives. The best ones just don't feel like it."

"I haven't thought of it like that. You make it sound so easy."

"It *is* easy most of the time. You just think about what would make you want to buy something, or one of your friends or family if they're more of the market," Gray said, now fully in her lane. "Don't tell my boss I said that. Us PR professionals have a big con going where we pretend it's not common sense ninety percent of the time."

Riley laughed. "Your secret is safe with me."

"Tell me more about the coffee shop," Gray said. "Maybe I can hit you with some ideas."

Riley's eyes lit up beneath her tortoiseshell glasses as she shared her plans for Demitasse Café. Before long, Gray was struggling to keep up with the descriptions of single-source organic coffee beans and steeping methods and sustainable supply chain politics. Riley's passion for her work was so palpable that Gray couldn't help but get excited too. When Riley shared her plans to promote the store leading up to opening, Gray's mind came alive. Now that she felt the caffeine from her macchiato lifting her out of the morning fog, she dove into her ideas for advertising on local blogs and positioning the café as socially and environmentally conscious. Riley whipped out a pad and pencil, taking notes as Gray suggested offering catering services to local offices to drum up attention in the neighborhood, partnering with organic food co-ops, and leaning into the space's retro vibe by decorating with antique photos of famous people drinking coffee.

Their brainstorming session was interrupted by an alarm on Gray's phone. Gray silenced it, then took the last sip of her drink. "Sorry to interrupt, but I have a meeting to get to. This was really cool though. I love the shop."

"Thanks, man," Riley said, rising from her chair and collecting both of their mugs. "Hey, I believe in being up-front whenever possible, and I know that often comes off as harsh, but . . ." She paused, pushing her chair against the table. "I'm not feeling much of a romantic vibe here. Nothing personal, just want to be real with you."

Gray let out a relieved laugh. "Totally on the same page. Way more of a friend vibe, right?"

"Exactly!" Riley said with a genuine smile. "And, like, maybe a business partner vibe? Your advertising ideas could be huge for me. I can't afford a PR consultant or whatever just yet, but if things go well . . ."

"Absolutely!" Maybe Gray had veered a little too far into professional networking territory. She'd be more cautious of that on future dates. But in this case, it had helped her break the ice, and she genuinely enjoyed talking shop with Riley. Gray pulled a business card from her briefcase and, seeing Riley's hands still full with the mugs, dropped it on the table. "Happy to chat whenever. I hope this place blows everyone away. The coffee was fantastic." She looked at her watch. "And actually . . . any chance I could buy a macchiato for the road?"

Riley returned to the shining espresso machine and placed the mugs beside it. "After all the advice you just gave me pro bono? It's on the house."

Having allowed ample time to park, sign in, and navigate the winding middle school hallways, Gray knocked on Principal Taylor's office door fifteen minutes before their scheduled meeting time.

"Come in," the principal's voice sounded through the thick wooden door.

Gray strode into the office and Principal Taylor looked up over the rim of her glasses, taking in Gray's pressed suit, polished shoes, and carefully styled hair, and then looked at the clock. "Right on time," she said smoothly. "I take it you've had your coffee this morning."

"I have," Gray said, walking toward the large desk at the center of the room. "In fact, I brought some for you too. A macchiato from Demitasse Café. Organic, fair-trade, ethically sourced, and delicious."

Principal Taylor accepted the cardboard cup from Gray with an approving nod and . . . was that a bit of a smile? She pointed to the chair across from her. "Have a seat."

Eight

ONCE SHE'D GAINED enough respect from Principal Taylor to finally get to work, Gray found the forward-thinking initiatives at St. Charles Collegiate Academy to be a fascinating first challenge in her new job. Initially, Gray had struggled to reconcile the stuffy, strict principal she met with the progressive ideas she'd learned about from the superintendent and board meeting minutes. But the more Gray worked with her, the more she saw what an impressive visionary Principal Taylor was for the prestigious old school. Since she'd taken the helm at the beginning of the school year, she'd done a lot of incredible work to welcome a more diverse student body, hire more people of color as teachers and staff, make the campus more accessible for students with different abilities, and shake up the curriculum to include thoughtful discussions of prejudice and equity throughout subject areas. But she couldn't escape pushback from school board members, wealthy alumni donors, parents, and even some teachers whose vision of SCCA was stuck in the past.

That's where Gray came in. Her brain lit up with ideas during her makeup meeting with Principal Taylor. She may have been new in town, but she wasn't afraid to put herself out there to support the school's mission. Gray had found a couple of networking events with local journalists and PR professionals to attend so she could start charming her way into the papers and blogs writing less than favorably about SCCA. But she didn't just want to run damage control; Gray wanted to get ahead of Principal Taylor's opponents by giving the middle school's public image a big boost. Overhauling the school website with a more modern and accessible design, finding new community partnerships, reaching out to companies to sponsor scholarships and student events, getting positive press coverage of their updated priorities . . . Gray talked a mile a minute about everything she wanted to do. It was a gift to have a project at her new job that she could throw herself into wholeheartedly. Although the principal hadn't fully forgiven her for their first meeting—she'd shot down nearly all of Gray's initial ideas and seemed skeptical of the ones she hadn't downright rejected—there was enough of an opening for Gray to eventually prove she was capable of quality work.

And now that her work life was back on track, Gray had no qualms about moving forward with her astrology dating challenge. With her steamy rendezvous with Carmen and her friendly morning with Riley fresh in her mind, Gray returned to Mercurious in search of the next sign in the zodiac: a Gemini.

As a Gemini herself, Cherry was overly invested in Gray finding the perfect third date. "Your first air sign! It's the element that makes the most sense for you," Cherry said over pizza on Friday night after Gray caught her and Robbie up on her morning with Riley. "We all knew Taurus was a long shot, so honestly, I'm glad you got along as friends. Gemini though, this could be the one."

After dinner that night, Gray scrolled through a page of single Geminis on Mercurious while Cherry shot down anyone she thought might give her sign a bad name. It didn't take too long for Gray to find a match on which they could agree. Jackson was a nonbinary Gemini who, based on their profile and early conversations with Gray, was charming, clever, and cute. Even better, they were a concierge at a boutique hotel downtown, so when Gray mentioned that she was new to town, Jackson dove into a list of their favorite things to do in New Orleans.

Gray felt an immediate sense of ease with Jackson, quickly falling into a fun rapport and set of their own inside jokes. In fact, they spent the better part of Friday night exchanging puns on iconic New Orleans food and discussing astrology, a subject about which Jackson was very knowledgeable. By the time they said good night, it was well past 3 A.M. and Gray was bleary-eyed from the hours of flirtatious banter. But most important, they'd settled on a date for the following evening.

WITH SO MUCH EXCITEMENT about the evening ahead of her, Gray found it difficult to relax. She spent most of the day entertaining River while Cherry and Robbie tried to catch up on chores. Since Gray couldn't convince Cherry and Robbie to take any rent money, she volunteered to help care for River to make up for it, like on Thursdays, when Gray watched River for a few hours after work so Cherry and Robbie could have a regular weekly date night.

Gray enjoyed practicing a bit of parenting on River. And watching him grow into toddlerhood with all his own personality and quirks was a delight. She especially loved how Cherry and Robbie were raising him without the same gendered expectations Gray's parents had placed on her and her brother. If Gray's brother had declared a unicorn was his favorite animal, as River had recently done, her parents would have pushed him toward something more traditionally boyish like dinosaurs. But River was free to carry his stuffed unicorn toy wherever he wanted, to prance around the playground holding his pointer finger on his forehead like a horn, to use a sparkly pink throw blanket as a cape. Gray wasn't necessarily rooting for River to be queer when he grew up; she simply wanted him to grow up to love what (and who) he loved as unabashedly as he adored unicorns at this moment, on the precipice of turning two. Being River's godparent, his beloved "Aunt Gay," was healing parts of Gray's childhood trauma in beautiful ways she'd never expected.

But this Saturday, no matter how much she enjoyed time with her godson, the promise of an intriguing date ahead of her made the minutes tick by at an excruciatingly slow pace. She pushed River on the backyard tire swing again and again and again, occasionally sneaking a glance at her phone to see if Jackson had sent a new message.

Once Robbie came home to relieve Gray, she raced upstairs to change into her fashionably ripped jeans, a vintage Grateful Dead T-shirt, and her favorite faux leather jacket and set off. With help from their concierge connections, Jackson had scored two free tickets for a ghost tour of haunted pubs and bars in the French Quarter. Gray was to meet Jackson at the first stop on the tour, Lafitte's Blacksmith Shop, but first she had to make her way through a thick crowd of incredibly drunk tourists getting an early start on Mardi Gras and the many jazz and zydeco bands playing for extra holiday tips. The French Quarter was absolutely packed a few days ahead of the coming festival despite the drizzly, overcast weather. This was precisely the atmosphere Gray had expected when she moved to New Orleans, although she'd come to find that, like any city, it also had its quieter neighborhoods, trendy shopping areas, and office-building-filled business district. But the Mardi Gras crowd in all its noisy, raucous, bacchanalian glory was indeed a sight to behold.

Spotting an old brick building with a slate roof, Gray squeezed her way through the crush of bodies into the packed blacksmith shop turned pub and elbowed her way to the bar. Gray had just handed over cash in exchange for her beer when she heard a breathy voice in her ear.

"Arrrgh, me ghostly boooo-ty!"

Gray jumped a little, then turned to find Jackson grinning back at her. They laughed at Gray's surprise, then tucked a strand of shoulder-length auburn hair behind their ear. "Sorry, couldn't resist. Pirate ghosts are the most fun. I'm Jackson, it's nice to meet you in person." They presented a hand with glittery black and silver nail polish and a variety of rings with colorful gemstones.

Maybe Cherry was onto something when she said a Gemini would be Gray's ideal match. Jackson already struck Gray as incredibly cool. "Nice to meet you," she yelled over the noisy pub, struggling to turn around to face her date without bumping into the strangers around her. "It's packed in here. It didn't even occur to me that Mardi Gras would get started this early."

Jackson laughed, a warm full-body chuckle. "Around here, Mardi Gras gets started sometime around New Year's and runs through, oh, Halloween?" they said. "It's more a state of mind than a day."

Jackson pointed out their tour guide and gave her an idea of what to expect from the neighborhood spirits. As they chatted, Gray felt something like a charge in the air between them. Was it a ghost? Or relationship potential?

Just as the bartender handed Jackson their daiquiri, the tour guide's voice, amplified by a headset connected to a Bluetooth speaker, sounded over the noise of the crowd. "Hello to the living, the dead, and those in between. I am Céline, interdimensional medium and tour guide with Ethereal Walking Tours. If you're scheduled for the six forty-five ghost pub crawl, please order your drinks in a plastic to-go cup and join me on this side of the room in five minutes."

People throughout the bar shuffled toward Céline's corner. Jackson and Gray followed and found a space to linger near the wall.

"This is really cool," Gray said, one hand in her jacket pocket and the other grasping her plastic cup of beer. "Thanks again for getting us tickets. Do you know much about New Orleans ghost stories?"

"Oh, I've been interested in NOLA ghost stories since I've beignet high," Jackson said, holding a hand a few feet from the ground, a smile curving the edge of their lips.

"If I said I wasn't afraid of ghosts, I'd be jambalayin'." Gray winced a little at her own terrible pun, but it only seemed to make Jackson's grin even bigger.

Céline approached them, looking down at her clipboard. "Name?" She looked up at Jackson and her face relaxed. "Oh, hey, Jackson! I don't think I had you on my list tonight."

"Late addition," Jackson said. "You know I can't resist when you're the tour guide."

Céline beamed, then scribbled something on her clipboard. Gray realized that she was much younger than the lacy shawl and heavy eye makeup made her seem, although they did add to her mystical vibe. "Glad you're here," Céline said. "Although it's gonna be a tough one with all the crowds. Mind bringing up the back of the group, making sure nobody gets lost?"

"Anything for you," Jackson said.

"Thanks, hon." Céline looked at Gray for the first time. "You Jackson's date?"

"Yes, Gray Young. Nice to meet you."

Céline looked Gray up and down, wiggled her eyebrows suggestively at Jackson, then made a note on her clipboard. "We'll get started as soon as I get everyone checked in. And remember, don't get cheeky with the spirits! They're extra feisty around the holiday."

She moved on to the next group of tour participants and Gray turned to Jackson. "So you, like, *believe* in ghosts?" Gray asked.

"Yes and no."

"That's a very Gemini answer."

Jackson laughed. "You're right. I'm sure there's plenty of ghostly lore that's entirely false. But mostly, I believe there's a lot that we don't know, don't understand, don't *perceive* as living humans. It's completely possible that the dead walk the Earth with us and we just aren't equipped to see them. But why not try anyway?"

Gray thought over Jackson's argument for a moment. It sounded something like how she approached astrology. Interesting to explore, and maybe there was some truth to it, but it was hard to figure out how much she really bought into it. "I guess that makes sense."

"Do *you* believe in ghosts?" they asked in return.

"Not really, but maybe this tour will change that," Gray said with a wink.

"All right, let's get started!" Céline announced, her voice again amplified by the speaker attached to the strap of her bag. In a perfectly haunting tone, she shared the history of Lafitte's Blacksmith Shop and rumors of its haunting by legendary pirate Jean Lafitte. "If you're looking to encounter Jean Lafitte's spirit," Céline said, "you're most likely to find him staring out of the fireplace with glowing red eyes."

When Gray looked at the large stone fireplace in the center of the room, she felt tiny hairs rise on her arms. Jackson nudged her with a grin, pointing out their own goosebumps.

Céline whipped around toward the door, her voice suddenly much airier and less sinister. "All right, follow me to our next destination."

Jackson and Gray tagged along at the end of the tour group as they walked down Bourbon Street, chatting about the city around them. Their next destination was the Bourbon Orleans Hotel, a stately white building with green shutters and an expansive balcony across the top. With Ramos Gin Fizzes in hand, they gathered at a bar attached to the hotel to hear Céline's description of ghostly dancers lingering from the building's days as a ballroom, and haunting children and nuns who died from yellow fever during its years as a convent and orphanage.

"Nothing creepier than kid ghosts," Gray said to Jackson, a sense of unease creeping across the back of her neck.

They continued on to Pat O'Brien's Bar, famous for its Hurricane cocktails and the Prohibition-era ghosts that still danced the Charleston at the upstairs piano lounge, and an old stone-paved road called Pirates Alley supposedly full of lingering spirits. As the night grew darker, Gray and Jackson found themselves wedged between raucous tourists, artists, and psychics hawking their services on the sidewalks. At one point, Gray narrowly avoided being puked on by a reveler who had clearly overindulged.

"You okay?" Jackson asked, catching Gray's elbow before she could trip on the curb.

"I'm great. Miles ahead of that guy," Gray said, taking another step farther from the splash zone.

After another stop at a restaurant where a ghost had been caught on camera smashing wine bottles behind the bar, the tour group walked to Tujague's Restaurant, which was established when the city was still known as la Nouvelle-Orléans.

"This one's my favorite," Jackson said as they waited at the bar for their Grasshopper cocktails, a drink invented at Tujague's. "And Céline is the only one who does it justice."

Once the group was gathered around her, Céline described three spirits stuck in a dramatic love triangle often heard breaking dishes in the kitchen. "Tujague's is also the post-life home of Julian Eltinge, also known as Vesta Tilley, one of the most famous drag performers in the early 1900s."

Jackson leaned in and whispered, "Total badass. Vesta Tilley had a career on the silent screen *and* their own makeup line. Basically the RuPaul of vaudeville."

Gray raised her eyebrows, impressed. Céline was pointing to a sepia portrait of Julian/Vesta in a large sun hat, gazing slyly at the camera with a lipsticked grin. "Julian gave this signed portrait to the owner of the restaurant in 1917, and it hung on that wall for nearly a century before it was moved to the attic during renovations," Céline said. "But then Julian became restless, causing trouble and appearing in photographs taken in the restaurant for a couple of years until their portrait was returned to its rightful place. They've been pretty quiet since then. Apparently Julian just wanted to be back in the middle of the action."

"Maybe Julian's ghost hasn't made as many appearances lately," Jackson whispered. "But I like to imagine they're still around, putting on a full face of makeup and performing for sold-out crowds beyond the veil." Goosebumps rose again along Gray's arms, but this time they had less to do with supernatural reasons and more because of Jackson's lips lingering only an inch or two from Gray's ear.

Jackson and Gray got lost in conversation about what it must have been like to perform in drag during the height of vaudeville until they arrived at their last stop, the Carousel Bar, an iconic New Orleans location attached to the beautiful Hotel Monteleone. Once inside, Gray looked over the crowd to the room's centerpiece: an enormous spinning merry-go-round-style bar, decorated in ornate circus fashion. Although moving slowly, Gray could see that the people seated at the bar were actually rotating around the room. Jackson grabbed Gray's hand and pulled her onto the platform surrounding the bar to order two Vieux Carré cocktails.

As the room gradually moved around them, Gray realized that this was, without a doubt, a phenomenal date. Maybe it was the joy of the Mardi Gras celebrations and lively street jazz bands, or maybe the delightful combination of history and legend on the tour, but being around Jackson was so easy. They were funny and smart and kind, and really cute to boot. Gray already regretted that she wouldn't be able to schedule a second date with Jackson until she'd gone on nine more dates with strangers. How could any of them measure up to this?

Gray and Jackson tipped Céline and made their way back into the night air. Feeling daring from the drinks she'd nursed throughout the tour, Gray grabbed Jackson's hand. She felt high on first-date butterflies. After her Taurus date, Gray was worried she'd never figure out how to engage in natural small talk without putting on her PR persona or being embarrassingly awkward. But conversation had flowed easily from the minute Jackson found Gray at Lafitte's Blacksmith Shop. Maybe Gray was getting better at this dating thing. Or did the stars have something to do with it?

Gray admired Jackson's profile as they walked hand in hand. "You're a total babe," Gray said in a burst of unabashed honesty. "You've got a killer smile and a sense of fashion I envy, and hanging out with you makes me feel like we've known each other for years."

Gray could see a blush creep across Jackson's cheeks in the streetlights. "You're, like, intimidatingly hot, Gray," Jackson said earnestly. "So hot I figured you'd ghost me."

"What? No!" Gray said. "I came on this date to get ghosted *with* you."

Jackson laughed. "And not only do you have this, like, bad boy look, with cheekbones that could cut glass and green eyes that put emeralds to shame," they continued. "But you've got this off-the-charts energy like confetti is just falling on you all the time. Like when I'm close enough, it falls on me too."

It was Gray's turn to blush. She squeezed Jackson's hand as they continued walking through the crowded street. "Now I'm all paranormaled up with nowhere to go," she said. A purple neon sign along the balcony next to them caught her eye. "Should we go to a psychic?"

"Oh, darling," Jackson said, the pet name awakening a warmth in Gray's chest she hadn't felt in a while. "If you want an authentic psychic, *never* go to the ones with a storefront."

"Really? Where should I go instead?"

Jackson pointed ahead of them. "The square. You find the chillest-looking person sitting in a folding chair at a card table covered with a bunch of scarves. *That's* who you ask to look into your future." Gray looked skeptical, but Jackson only grew firmer in their resolve. "Trust me on this one."

"Then let's go," Gray said, swinging their clasped hands between them.

They followed the flow of the crowd toward Jackson Square, a location Jackson loved so much that they changed their name to it. Along the way, they collected a variety of Mardi Gras beads, saw plenty of people on the street flashing their breasts at strangers on balconies, and avoided the most aggressively inebriated tourists, all while chatting and laughing at the ridiculousness of the French Quarter. Eventually, they found a strip of card tables set up on Chartres Street.

"Looking for a reading, *mon cher*?" said someone in all black, including the scarf covering their hair. The endearment reminded Gray of Madame Nouvelle Lune and the astrology consultation that had led her here in the first place. Maybe it was a sign. Or maybe it was just New Orleans. "Twenty dollars for palm or tarot, thirty for both."

Gray looked questioningly at Jackson, who nodded discreetly. "Sure," Gray said, pulling a bill from her pocket and sitting down across from the psychic. "A palm reading, please." She handed over the cash and held out her hands, palms up. "I'm Gray, by the way."

"I'm Raven Crescent," the psychic said, sliding her left hand under Gray's right. "Please relax your fingers. Right-handed?" Gray nodded. Raven pointed a small flashlight at her palms and squinted, interpreting the lines. "Nice long life line. Very strong head line too. You're firm in your beliefs, determined, maybe a little stubborn."

More than a little, as McKenzie had certainly pointed out in multiple fights. And Gray's mom, who had given her the nickname Bighorn when she was a preteen for her hardheaded tendencies. And Cherry, who had called Gray "ornery" just the night before during a heated match of Super Smash Bros., giving both Gray and Robbie a good laugh. "Some people might say that," Gray admitted.

"Heart line though . . ." continued Raven, "ah. *Ah.* Not so easy, huh? Starts strong, but then peters out and hits a rough crossing with the life line here," she said, pointing to a spot in the center of Gray's palm. "Poor thing. But see, it's even stronger up ahead."

Gray felt a burst of hope in her chest. It was silly to believe in these few words from a total stranger, but after a whole night of embracing the occult, why stop now? She glanced over at Jackson, who smiled encouragingly.

Raven traced a line from under Gray's forefinger to just above her wrist. "Not much connection to your family, I see. Many disturbances on the Mount of Venus. Painful history with your parents?"

The psychic looked up at Gray, who felt her face go red. Was she really such an open book? "Um, yeah." She felt a warm hand on her shoulder, then turned to find Jackson closer than before. Their presence was comforting. Gray looked back at Raven to continue.

Raven tilted Gray's hand to the side, looking at the lines between her forefinger and thumb. "One sibling." She didn't even look up, but Gray nodded anyway, impressed by the accuracy of the reading. "And this fainter line here, that's a presence in your life *like* a sibling, someone with you from a young age for many years."

Cherry's face appeared in Gray's head. Raven was right. She was more of a family member than anyone Gray was actually related to.

Turning Gray's hand the opposite way, Raven examined the side of her hand beneath her pinky. "I see a long relationship here, very meaningful, but see how it forks? Not meant to be. Your paths are not aligned."

Gray gulped, feeling a rush of heat. *McKenzie.* Although she knew, she *knew,* that breaking up with McKenzie was the right thing to do, it felt different to hear it from someone else. Someone with mystical clarity that Gray couldn't understand. She almost said something about McKenzie to Raven but stopped short, remembering Cherry's rule of not bringing up her ex during dates.

"But here, this second line . . ." She traced a dent along the side of Gray's hand. "This one is steady. Lasting love is ahead for you, my dear. Just stick to your path."

She continued pointing out areas of Gray's palm and their various meanings, but Gray hardly absorbed a word. *Lasting love is ahead.* She just had to stick to the path. Her astrology dating project! Maybe she'd find love with one of the signs she met. Maybe even with Jackson.

Once the reading was complete, Gray thanked Raven Crescent for the eerily accurate reading and turned to Jackson. "Your turn?"

"Oh, my palms have been read and reread more than I can count. I'm good, but thank you." Jackson smiled at Raven, then looped an arm through Gray's and started walking toward the river. "This has been a blast, but I've had enough of the French

Quarter for one evening. What do you say we have a nightcap at my place?"

Gray hesitated. She wanted to, actually *really* wanted to. But it also felt too soon. She couldn't go on another date with Jackson for at least a few weeks while she got through the next nine signs, and she might potentially come back to Jackson after finishing her last astrology date and make a real go of it. Those were the rules, right? Only one date with each person until she made it past the Pisces finish line. Getting too attached could ruin the whole thing. And hadn't Raven just told her to stick to the path?

Seeing the changing expressions on Gray's face, Jackson backtracked. "Hey, it's totally fine. You can say no."

"I *hate* to say no though," Gray said earnestly. "It's just . . ." She reached for a decent excuse without breaking Cherry's rule number two for the dating challenge, *no talking about the dating challenge.* "I have to be up early tomorrow for work. In fact, I have a lot of work stuff going on right now and will be super busy, so I'm not sure when I'll be able to see you again. But I . . ." Gray ran a hand along the buzzed side of her head as she remembered Cherry's rule number three: *No falling in love.* "I really like you. Just . . . Can we put a pin in it? For now?"

Jackson smiled kindly. "I get it. If Raven Crescent was right, it seems like you may have some personal stuff to sort out." They leaned forward, planting a soft, sweet kiss on the corner of Gray's lips. "If it's meant to be, we will meet again. But until then, good luck, Gray."

Feeling the spot where they kissed her still tingling with warmth, Gray watched Jackson disappear into the dark, crowded streets of the French Quarter.

Nine

$\mathcal{A}$s GRAY HAD seen firsthand on Saturday, New Orleans residents and visitors were passionate about Mardi Gras. In fact, almost every business and school in town was shut down for Lundi Gras, Fat Tuesday, and Ash Wednesday, including St. Charles Collegiate Academy. But Gray's comment to Jackson about having to wake up early for work on Sunday wasn't technically a lie, as Gray spent the morning drafting a strategic plan for the middle school's prospective-student campaign, then grabbed lunch with a couple of the journalists she'd met during a networking event to catch up on some local newspaper gossip. She spent the rest of the afternoon avoiding the deafening noise of the crowds by tucking herself away in her garage apartment to research companies she could convince to sponsor student scholarships.

On Tuesday, she happily ignored Cherry and Robbie's suggestion that she join the drunken revelers in the French Quarter for her first Mardi Gras in New Orleans, insisting she'd seen enough on her date with Jackson. Instead, Gray joined them and River in a family-friendly celebration at a nearby park. Seeing River delightedly dancing with someone in a purple, green, and gold unicorn costume made Gray even more satisfied with her decision to skip the R-rated celebrations elsewhere in town. Once River was knocked out from the day of fun, the adults stayed up late eating takeout and playing board games. And on Wednesday, she took advantage of the day off to complete her next date in the astrology challenge: Cancer.

With all the tourists in town, Gray had plenty of choices once she filtered Mercurious profiles to Cancers only. But most of them were either looking for a raucous night of debauchery or their one true love, neither of which fit Gray's goals. She'd finally connected with Carolina, a sweet, shy bisexual veterinary technician. They'd bonded over the many animal photos Carolina featured on her profile, but once they'd exhausted that topic, Gray struggled to keep up a flow like she had so easily done with Jackson. Once they hit a lull, Gray remembered to use Cherry's suggested icebreaker: "What's your favorite childhood movie?" This worked wonders. Carolina shared a list of her top-ten favorite Disney movies, with *Toy Story* coming in first due to her nostalgia for childhood toys. She gave her approval of Gray's answer—*The Emperor's New Groove,* the jokes always land—and dove into a monologue on Disney's live-action remakes of classics versus original new content. Having not watched a Disney movie outside of Star Wars and Marvel in the past five years, Gray could hardly keep up.

Just past eleven on Wednesday morning, Gray arrived at a midcity outdoor café that, despite being a few miles from the French Quarter, was still surrounded by discarded beads and plastic hurricane glasses. Gray scoped out the seated customers for the long, straight light-brown hair and big brown eyes she remembered from Carolina's profile. She spotted a woman sitting alone at a table set for two. Her hair looked a bit shorter than the Mercurious photos and she was wearing glasses. Gray supposed her photos could have been a little outdated. She strode over to the table and dropped into the open seat. "Hey, Carolina?"

The woman jumped a little at Gray's voice, her attention pulled from her phone. "Oh, no, I'm not Carolina."

"Oh!" Gray said, her eyes widened with surprise and a touch of embarrassment. "So sorry to disturb you." She smiled apologetically and jumped out of the seat, taking a few steps away to distance herself from Not Carolina.

"Gray?"

She turned and saw the real Carolina seated a few tables away. Trying to gain her bearings, Gray waved and slowly walked to the correct seat. She mustered a semi-confident smile and tried again. "Carolina?"

"Yes! Nice to meet you."

Gray sat down and tucked her aviator sunglasses into her shirt pocket. Her date's long hair, round eyes, and close-lipped smile matched her profile, although she didn't look so different from the woman Gray had mistaken for Carolina. "Hey. You have a doppelgänger over there."

"Huh," Carolina said. "I have one of those faces, I guess. I went ahead and ordered a carafe of mimosas while I waited. They're what I always get when I'm here for brunch."

"Oh. Cool," Gray said, thinking that all she really wanted was a strong coffee. She'd stayed up too late playing a particularly heated game of Risk with Robbie and Cherry, but winning had made the lost sleep worth it in the end. And although she'd been feeling more confident in her first-date conversational skills after her evening with Jackson, the lack of sleep combined with the wrong-table gaffe put Gray right back in awkward territory. "Do you come here often?" she asked, realizing belatedly that she'd picked one of the most overused pickup lines of all time.

"Yeah, it's my go-to brunch spot. Had to get my usual— chocolate chip waffles with a side of hash browns—before I leave town on Friday."

"Where are you headed?" Gray asked.

"Happiest place on Earth."

Gray waited for clarification that didn't come. As the seconds stretched on, Carolina's eyebrows moved higher and higher up her forehead in a look of disbelief—and displeasure. Gray shifted in her seat. "Where's that?" she asked.

"Disney World," Carolina said slowly, as if the answer was entirely obvious.

"Oh, right," Gray said, flipping over the menu to glance at the brunch entrées. "I would ask for business or pleasure, but sounds like pleasure."

Carolina frowned. "It's actually for both. I'm a Disfluencer."

"A what?"

"A Disney influencer," Carolina said, a smidge of annoyance at Gray's naïveté audible in her words. "I have a Disney-focused Instagram account. I have almost forty thousand followers and this trip should push me over that. Dee-dubs trips are great for engagement."

Gray furrowed her brow. "Dee-dubs . . ."

"D.W.," Carolina spelled out. "Disney World?"

"Right." Gray looked over her shoulder for a server, thinking that a mimosa actually sounded pretty nice right now. Seeing none, she turned back to Carolina. "So Disney pays you to promote Disney World on Instagram?"

"Disney doesn't pay Disfluencers," Carolina said. "I get paid through sponsorships and ad spots, sometimes with people who sell officially licensed Disney merch. Mostly I partner with clothing retailers who aren't associated with Disney but are great for bounding." At the blank expression on Gray's face, Carolina sighed and explained. "Disneybounding. When you dress up in stylish, modern outfits inspired by Disney characters. I'm bounding as Vanellope von Schweetz right now." She gestured at her teal hoodie and the pink bandana tied around her ponytail.

"Penelope who?"

Carolina rolled her eyes. "From *Wreck-It Ralph*. What, do you live under a rock?"

"I don't think so? Been a while since I checked in with the mouse, I guess," Gray said, grinning in a way that was usually dashing enough to distract people from her occasional awkwardness. But Carolina's expression remained as cold as a performance of Disney on Ice. Although she was struggling with the subject area, Gray tried to continue the conversation on something Carolina clearly cared about immensely. "Do you ever Disneybound as any Marvel characters? Like She-Hulk or Captain Marvel or something?"

"Definitely not," Carolina said, immediately shutting down Gray's only chance at understanding what she was into. "They're not *really* Disney properties. I mean, technically, yes, but in the spirit of Disney fandom? No."

Gray sank a little in her seat and returned to their previous topic. "I haven't been to Disney World since I was six. What's there to do for . . . you know, adults?"

Clearly she'd said the wrong thing, because Carolina looked at Gray as if she'd magically sprouted a third eyeball. "Everything! Rides, food, shopping, entertainment, all the stuff you loved as a kid. It's all there waiting for you to rediscover your childhood joy. It's magic, pure and simple."

Gray couldn't help but chuckle. "I don't think most people would describe the massive Disney machine as 'pure and simple.'"

Carolina scoffed, then lifted her phone from the table and started typing furiously. Finally, a server interrupted to set down a large carafe of orange juice and sparkling wine. "Mimosas and"—the server placed an empty wineglass in front of Carolina and another in front of Gray—"glasses. I'll be back for your food orders in just a second."

"Actually, she won't be staying," said a voice from behind Gray's back. She turned to see the woman she'd first approached thinking she was Carolina, now storming up to the table.

"Thank god," said Carolina, seemingly unsurprised by the stranger's sudden appearance.

"But I'll be ready to order when you return," said Not Carolina to the server. "I'll be moving my things from that table to this one."

The server took the bizarre interruption in stride. They nodded and walked away while Gray was still struggling to process the words coming out of the woman's mouth. She looked back and forth between Carolina and the interloper.

"You should leave. If you don't respect Carolina's interests, then this date is over," said Not Carolina.

Gray looked at Carolina, who was pointedly ignoring eye contact while pouring a mimosa for herself. "What's going on, Carolina?"

"I'm her sister, Georgia. And I'm pulling the plug on this date." Georgia placed a hand on one hip and stared at Gray expectantly. "You can go."

"Carolina, do you know this woman?" Gray asked, starting to wonder if she was being pranked.

Carolina put down the carafe and looked up at Gray. "Yes, she's my sister. She comes on all my first dates."

Gray looked between the two women, now understanding why they looked so similar, but still not comprehending exactly what was going on. "Do you . . . do you want me to leave?"

Carolina had a smug look on her face as she considered Gray. "Yes. If you don't support me as a Disfluencer, and if Georgia isn't feeling it, then there's no sense in sticking it out. We're obviously not a match."

While Gray had started her dating challenge with some worst-case scenarios in mind, this certainly hadn't been one of them. But this moment didn't feel so much like a terrible outcome as dodging a bullet. Gray pushed back her chair and stood. "All right, then. This has been . . . absurd and bizarre." She nodded at Georgia and again at Carolina, her lips pursed. "Have a nice brunch and, uh, tell Goofy I said hello."

Without further ado, Georgia sat in Gray's still-warm seat, and Gray wandered off in search of brunch alone.

Ten

$\mathcal{A}$T FIRST, GRAY wasn't certain if what she'd just experienced with Carolina counted as a date. Shouldn't that involve more than ten minutes of being talked at about Disney before being summarily dismissed? But after discussing it with Cherry, she decided to check Cancer off her list. Apparently water and fire signs made a poor match, and as both were cardinal signs, Gray was likely to bump heads with any Cancer she met. It wasn't Carolina's fault; she was probably perfectly lovely and destined to find happiness with another sign. If the point of the whole dating project was to discover what signs Gray was and wasn't compatible with, then this was fate saying that Cancers weren't for her. And she was bound to have a bad date at some point, right?

Still, she had to admit she was a bit thrown by the experience. It was hard not to take Carolina's rejection personally. Gray had always thought of herself as fairly desirable. It's what had made the idea of taking on the astrology dating challenge in only six weeks possible. But Gray supposed it wasn't entirely fair that she be the only one doing the rejecting. A pep talk from Cherry, who insisted that the stars had better dates for her ahead, helped put Gray back in good spirits.

For the rest of her day off, Gray helped Robbie organize the garden shed and did a little apartment hunting online. As much as she loved spending so much time at Cherry and Robbie's house, she was starting to feel like a bit of a burden on the small family. Her salary and savings gave her plenty of room to afford a place of her own; she just wasn't sure where or what yet. Her instinct was to find a new place close to Cherry's house so she could still drop by for dinners and spend Thursdays watching River. This whole New Orleans adventure was a departure from Gray's original life plan, and it stung a bit to be looking at apartments for one instead of a family home with kids and pets and a big kitchen table and a mudroom full of dirty sneakers. At least she could stay near to the closest thing she had to a family of her own.

After a five-day weekend, Gray was actually excited to return to work on Thursday morning. She had a fantastic idea for a prospective-parent open house at the middle school that she was dying to pitch. She got so lost in preparing materials to present her plan to Principal Taylor and Superintendent Donovan that 5 P.M. sneaked up on her, and she ended up running late to pick up River from Cherry.

Luckily, Cherry seemed unbothered when Gray showed up ten minutes after she promised. "It's not like we're paying you," she said, handing over River's diaper bag. "And anyway, our movie doesn't start for another hour. I'm just looking forward to sitting down in peace and quiet for a minute without a toddler telling me every 'fact' he knows about unicorns."

Gray slung the diaper bag over her shoulder and lifted River from his high chair. "Well, *I'm* looking forward to some quality time with my main little man! Right, River? Ready to go to the park with Aunt Gay?"

"Aunt Gay!" River squealed.

"You know, he's getting better at *R* sounds," Cherry said, handing over the keys to her sedan, which was already suited up with a car seat and supplies for any toddler-sized emergency. "Can you say 'Aunt *Gray*,' River? Aunt Grrrray."

"Aunt Gay!" he said again, poking a chubby finger into Gray's cheek.

"Honestly, I like it better his way," Gray said, bouncing River on her hip. "Anyway, we'll get out of your hair. Have fun at the movies!"

A short drive later, Gray pushed River's stroller through the park, pointing out trees and bugs and lost shoes along the way to help develop the toddler's vocabulary. Gray had some vague, distant memories of her own mom doing the same thing: teaching her that the flowers on the tree Gray would later learn to climb were *magnolias,* that her mom's signature iced tea was served in a *pitcher,* that they sipped their tea on the front porch under an *awning.* The vocabulary lessons were some of the rare memories of their relationship before it soured as Gray grew into a person her mother didn't recognize. Back when things were as simple as learning a new word from someone she trusted.

They found a small playground and Gray unbuckled River, letting him stretch his short legs on the recycled-rubber ground. At River's request, Gray helped him climb onto a seesaw and settled herself on the other end, then did squats to lift River up and down until her thighs grew tired. River waddled over to an oversized spinning tic-tac-toe set and Gray settled down on a nearby bench, adjusting her Mercurious settings to only show the next sign in the zodiac, Leos.

Glancing back and forth between her phone and River, Gray scrolled through profiles. There were a surprising number of Leos on the dating app, and they all knew their best angles. She was about to message someone who caught her eye when she heard a toddler fight breaking out.

"*Mine!*" squealed River as another kid tried to push him away from the rotating plastic tic-tac-toe set.

Gray was already on her feet, preparing to intervene before tears broke out, when a slightly older child in a firefighter hat and a purple tutu stepped between River and the other kid. "It's okay, park toys are for sharing," the child said, playing the perfect peacemaker. "Tic-tac-toe is for two kids. I'll show you."

Stunned by the kid's emotional intelligence, Gray watched as they began explaining the rules of tic-tac-toe. River and the other toddler, too young to fully understand the rules of play, were attentive to the older kid's lesson, but just as quickly began turning the round pieces without any real sense of order. At least they were doing it together without fighting, Gray noticed.

"I like your unicorn shirt," the kid said kindly to River. Gray could see him puff up with pride at the compliment. "What's your name?"

"River."

The other kid smiled. "I like that name. I'm Karys."

River tilted his head. "Carrots?"

"Almost. It's spelled K-A-R-Y-S, but it sounds like carrots without the T," the kid said, clearly not their first time explaining the name.

A panicked voice sounded through the park. "Karys! Where are you?"

Something about the voice rang a bell, and Gray was still trying to place it when the speaker appeared around the corner of a jungle gym.

"Karys?" The woman had dark hair pulled into a short ponytail and was wearing large sunglasses and a tie-dyed tunic over a long, faded denim skirt. Spotting the child in a firefighter hat near Gray, she trotted over and crouched down. "There you are! What did I tell you about staying within my line of sight?"

"Sorry, Ma," said Karys, turning away from the toddlers. "I didn't mean to."

Seeing the child's contrition, Gray couldn't help but step to Karys's defense.

"Karys was only trying to help!" Gray said, approaching the parent. "River and . . . uh, this other kid were having a tiff over the tic-tac-toe set and Karys helped them learn to play with it together. It was really sweet, actu—"

The woman stood and pushed her sunglasses on top of her head. "This is between me and my child," she said in a stern voice.

As she turned to Gray, they both realized at once who the other was. The woman in front of her was Principal Taylor, hardly recognizable without the usual skirt suit. Gray froze, stunned by the revelation. "Oh. Uh, hi."

"Gray?" said Principal Taylor, seeming equally surprised. "What are you—"

She was interrupted by River, who chose exactly that moment to appear at Gray's side, grasping his tiny hand around her forefinger and pulling her to the tic-tac-toe set. "Play! I show you. Unicorns are X's, mermaids are O's," said River.

"Thanks, River, but why play with boring old me when you have such cool new friends? I think Karys likes unicorns and mermaids too," Gray said, redirecting River to the other children.

"I love mermaids!" Karys called out.

It took River only a minute to forget his insistence on Gray playing with him once he and Karys started talking about imaginary creatures. Gray turned back to Principal Taylor, tucking her hands into her jacket pockets. "Sorry about earlier. I was just so impressed by Karys's peacemaking skills."

"She mastered the 'playing well with others' lesson early," said Principal Taylor, adjusting a tote bag on her shoulder. "And she feels the need to spread her knowledge. I guess she gets the teaching instinct from me." She looked over at Karys and gave her a small smile.

Gray realized it was her first time seeing the stern principal really smile in a way that reached her eyes. It seemed to lighten her whole body just a bit, to relax something around her shoulders. In fact, seeing her in casual clothes, her hair tied back, and her makeup faded from a full day of wear made Gray realize that

she was younger than she appeared in her conservative school administrator wardrobe. "Well, I'm glad she ran into River, then,"
Gray said, pulling her attention away from Principal Taylor's
outfit to the playground. "He could probably use a lesson in
sharing at this age. He won't be two for another month, but I'm
realizing all those rumors about the terrible twos actually have
some basis in fact."

Something akin to a laugh escaped Principal Taylor's lips and
Gray felt like she'd finally cracked some kind of code, seeing her
with Karys like this. Maybe encountering her colleague outside
of her intimidating office was what it would take to truly win her
over. She looked back at Gray, seeming to examine her in a new
light as well. "Definitely not just rumors," Principal Taylor said.
"I worried I was raising a sociopath in those days, but Karys
came through it just fine. River will too, one day."

Hearing his name, River wandered back toward Gray. "River?"

"Yes, River, that's you!" Gray said, ruffling his silky-soft hair.
"And this is my friend, Principal Taylor."

River looked over at the other woman, mumbled something a
couple neighborhoods over from "Principal Taylor," then
wrapped his chubby arms in a hug around her denim-skirted
knees. Gray could see her heart melt at the adorable gesture and
reminded herself to buy River an ice cream on the way home to
thank him for improving her work situation immeasurably.

Karys ran up to Principal Taylor, her firefighter hat askew.
"Ma, can River and I play mermaids on the slide?" She pointed
to a low slide attached to a jungle gym behind the tic-tac-toe set.

Principal Taylor looked over at Gray, who nodded her approval. "Sure, Karys. But please help River and keep an eye on
him. He's smaller than you."

"Okay!" Karys chirped. "Come on, River, let's go!"

The two children wandered off, tiny hand in hand. Gray and

Principal Taylor settled down on a bench under the shade of a sprawling old oak tree within view of the slide. Gray crossed an ankle over her knee and leaned back, still struggling to adapt to seeing her co-worker outside of her office. "So did you *laissez les bons temps rouler* during Mardi Gras break, Principal Taylor?"

"Call me Veronica," she said.

Gray felt as if a window in their relationship had just cracked open, letting in a burst of cool, clean air. "Okay, *Veronica.*" It was a name that suited her, one that seemed only slightly less intimidating than Principal Taylor.

"Karys spent the weekend at her dad's house," Veronica said. "We avoided the French Quarter like the plague for the past few days, but we went to a little family-friendly Mardi Gras celebration. And yesterday we read about some New Orleans history pre-colonization. What about you?"

"Went with River to a G-rated Mardi Gras parade, also far from the French Quarter," Gray replied. "Maybe the same one you and Karys went to? Was it the one in Metairie?"

"Yes! We've been going since she was River's age."

"It was a blast. And I didn't have to explain flashing to a toddler," Gray said. "Then yesterday, I . . . Well, I went on a really terrible date."

Veronica turned to Gray, her thin eyebrows raised. "*Really* terrible?"

Gray laughed. "Like, the worst date I've ever been on. And it only lasted ten minutes." She could feel herself toeing the line between professional relationship and something friendlier, which she knew was risky based on how strictly Principal Taylor—*Veronica,* Gray reminded herself internally—had protected her personal boundaries so far. But on this lovely spring day with the sun peeking through the clouds, the first bits of green beginning to appear on tree branches, Gray couldn't help but feel a little buoyant, a little willing to test the boundaries. Maybe it would even help her project with the middle school succeed, in turn helping her prove her worth in her new job.

She shared the story of her date with Carolina, and Veronica was appropriately horrified, especially once she reached the part about Georgia's interruption. Even better, Veronica shared her own bad date story, one where she'd met a man for drinks and was interrupted by his wife, who furiously threw a full glass of red wine in Veronica's unsuspecting face.

"I hope it was good wine at least," Gray said. "I hear the more expensive the wine, the better for your pores."

Veronica laughed. "I can't speak to what it cost, but some of it landed in my mouth and it tasted all right."

Before they knew it, the sun was setting behind the jungle gym, the air growing chilly. River and Karys walked over while Veronica and Gray were still laughing about dreadful dates gone by. Karys approached Gray and leaned in close. "I think River needs a diaper change." She wrinkled her nose, waving a hand in front of her face.

"Ah. Thanks for telling me," Gray said. Karys responded with a smile and a twirl, her tutu spinning around her. "I guess that's our cue," Gray said to Veronica, lifting River by the armpits and settling him into his stroller. Gray hoped his diaper could hold until they made it to a bathroom a few minutes' walk down the trail. "It was really nice running into you, Princi— Veronica."

Veronica stood, pulling her tote bag onto her shoulder. "Good to see you. We'll talk on Monday?"

Having briefly forgotten about their professional ties, it took Gray a moment to realize Veronica was referring to their weekly meeting. "Right," she said. "Monday. See you then."

"And don't think I'm going to go any easier on you because of your adorable kid," Veronica said, a playful look in her eye.

Gray's mouth hung open as she realized she hadn't clarified

her relationship to River. She knew she should correct the mistake, but something in her brain short-circuited before the words could reach her lips. The look on Veronica's face was so warm, night and day from how she'd looked at Gray across the desk in her office. Would she think Gray had been dishonest with her for not explaining sooner? Would she think less of Gray for not being the competent single parent Veronica had assumed she was? If it meant having a more collegial relationship with her coworker, what could it hurt? She was sure Cherry and Robbie wouldn't mind. And although she wasn't willing to admit it, being mistaken for River's parent was a compliment. Wasn't it a sign of how ready she was for kids of her own?

All of these thoughts ran through her head in one tense second before she managed to smile and reply, "Of course. I'm planning to win you over with my *ideas,* not River's natural charm." She unlocked the wheels on the stroller, trying to ignore the itchy feeling blossoming across her ribs. *I didn't lie,* Gray thought. *I just . . . avoided the truth.* "Have a good night," she said to Veronica. And with that, she set off at a quick pace to address the horrid smell emanating from River's diaper.

Eleven

$\mathcal{T}$HAT EVENING, GRAY returned an exhausted, sleeping River to his parents and focused on her mission of finding a Leo on Mercurious. Well, technically, she first spent a couple of hours procrastinating by playing her newest videogame, one where she played a cat burglar nabbing priceless artifacts from museums to return to their countries of origin. But eventually she did return to her astrological mission. Her first date had almost ruined her chance of working peacefully with St. Charles Collegiate Academy, but now she was a third of the way through the zodiac wheel. And even though her most recent date had been a bewildering bust, it had helped her bond with Veronica. It seemed that the French Quarter psychic was right: Gray was on the path to finding true love and her destiny.

With a cup of tea in hand, Gray settled into her favorite armchair and scrolled through profiles. Madame Nouvelle Lune's website described Leos as the "kings of the jungle," persuasive, born with natural leadership skills and an ability to easily win people over. If Gray were to generalize based on the potential matches on Mercurious, she would describe Leos as hot. It seemed every photo she swiped through was more attractive than the last. And as she started a few conversations with matches (using Cherry's suggested icebreaker "If you could have a superpower, what would it be?"), she found it challenging to pick just one Leo to pursue. Flirting with Leos was entertaining enough to be a lifelong hobby. If she wasn't meant to be with another Aries, maybe she could find her twin flame in another fire sign.

Finally, Gray narrowed the playing field down to one: Aisha, a strikingly beautiful woman whose preferred superpower was teleportation. She traveled a lot for work, so magically popping from place to place would allow her more time at home in New Orleans. Gray pointed out that their dream powers weren't that different; Gray would choose to never need sleep, another way to give herself more time. As they bonded over their shared love of videogames and nineties rock, Gray was grateful her dating project coincided with Aisha's brief time in the city between business trips. By their second day texting, they were already sending suggestively flirty messages. Aisha sent a selfie with a glimpse of the side of her naked breast while Gray was at her desk in St. Charles Collegiate Academy's administrative office and Gray blushed so hard that Superintendent Donovan's secretary asked if she was feeling all right.

She didn't have to wait long for her date. On Saturday morning, Aisha invited Gray to a cocktail lounge on the top floor of a hotel north of the French Quarter. The lounge was known for its sweeping view of the New Orleans skyline, and for having an artsy Tennessee Williams theme that fit the sounds of the streetcars passing below. Hoping to approach something near Aisha's level of attractiveness and still shaken from being so quickly rejected by Carolina, Gray spent a couple of hours trying on different outfits and messing with her hair. She eventually settled on a short-sleeved button-down shirt with a cactus print, jeans that made her ass look fantastic, her favorite brown leather boots, and a tiny gold hoop in her nose piercing. Her hair was styled to one side, emphasizing her undercut.

By the time she hopped out of her rideshare at the old hotel, Gray couldn't deny that the twitchy energy coursing through her veins was caused by nervousness. She was even more anxious than she'd been before her date with Carmen the Aries, the first date she'd been on since she was eighteen years old. It was hard to shake the sense of failure from her terrible date with Carolina, as much as she tried. Traveling up the elevator to the roof, Gray took a series of deep breaths and tried to give herself a silent pep talk. *It's just one date,* she thought. *You've already been on four. You'll go on seven more. At best, you have a great time and meet someone cool. At worst, you go home and forget it ever happened.*

But her jitters weren't soothed when she arrived at the bar, Aisha nowhere in sight, and arranged herself in a velvet booth with a dark wooden table. When Aisha eventually arrived, looking like a lesbian goddess in an emerald-green jumpsuit and voluminous curly hair swept to one side to show her own fashionable undercut, Gray's nerves grew even stronger, causing her to accidentally knock over a glass of water onto the table. Wasn't *she* usually the one attractive enough to make people clumsy? "Sorry about that," Gray said as she wiped up the spill with a wad of napkins. "Can I get you a drink?"

"Sure," said Aisha, her voice as smooth and lush as the velvet seating. "Blanche Bijou, please."

Gray moved toward the bar, trying desperately to stop acting like she'd never seen a beautiful woman before. Aisha's skin seemed to actually glow in the lounge's low lighting. Waiting for the two carefully crafted cocktails gave Gray a moment to collect herself, and by the time she returned to the booth, she was able to look at Aisha's face without turning bright red.

"So," Gray began, taking a sip of a whiskey-based cocktail named The Gentleman Caller. "How long are you in New Orleans?"

"Well, my time is already almost up," Aisha said, draped across the booth with a cocktail glass in hand like she was on the cover of *Vogue*. "I'm mostly here from December through February, which is nice because I get to spend the holidays with my family. I start traveling a lot between here and Orlando in the early spring and then I'm all over the place during the summer and fall." She took a sip of her drink, then smacked her perfectly shaped lips in a way that made Gray almost forget what they were talking about. "I love the travel aspect of my job. I just wish I could have a cat, you know?"

"Yeah, totally." Then, remembering her most recent date going south, she said, "Wait, Orlando . . . You don't work at Disney World, do you?"

"I'd make a great Tiana from *The Princess and the Frog,* but no," Aisha said, batting her eyes.

Gray breathed a sigh of relief. "Probably for the best, what with all the frog kissing. So what is it you do, exactly?" She realized that she had no idea, despite the dozens of messages they'd exchanged on Mercurious.

Aisha rolled her eyes, somehow making the expression look elegant rather than petulant. "Ugh, talking about my job is so dull. Let's talk about something else."

It was hard to imagine anything about Aisha being dull. Gray wondered if Aisha's job was something glamorous, like an actress or model. Or maybe, since she was reticent to talk about it, she did something dangerous and secretive. Was she a spy? Gray could certainly see how anyone could accidentally spill all their secrets in an effort to keep Aisha's lovely gaze on them for a minute longer. Despite the questions running through her mind, Gray followed Aisha's lead and changed the subject. "Got it, no job talk. So . . ." Gray stretched for something Aisha couldn't accuse of being boring. Picking a topic she already knew they could comfortably discuss seemed like the right call. "Have you tried that museum-robbing game I told you about?"

It was the perfect move to put both of them on more comfortable ground. Aisha, also a dedicated videogame lover, excitedly told Gray that she'd already made her way to level five, the Field Museum. The conversation eased into a comfortable back-and-forth, and Gray's feelings of awkwardness faded away.

Videogame talk morphed into board game talk, which turned into a heated game of Scrabble, thanks to a stock of games on a shelf next to the bar. The competitive spirit of the date reminded Gray a bit of pub trivia with Carmen. Cherry had advised her that now that she was dating her second fire sign, she might start to recognize the repeating themes of the elements in the grand wheel of the zodiac. There was more than just the competitive spirit that reminded Gray of her date with Carmen; there was also the touch of heat between them, an escalating connection, the sparkle in Aisha's eye as she flirted with Gray over a triple score on the word "cheeky." Madame Nouvelle Lune had warned that two fire signs could bring too much heated conflict to a relationship, but maybe Gray was learning that the heat was what she craved.

After they tallied up the final Scrabble scores—Aisha won by a narrow three-point margin with the word "nutmeg"—Gray went out on a limb. "Do you want to grab something to eat? I saw a restaurant down the block with an oyster happy hour," she suggested while arranging the game pieces in the box.

"Wow," Aisha said, a mischievous grin on her face. "I see what you're up to."

"What do you mean?"

"Oysters," Aisha said, stretching an arm across the back of the booth. Gray couldn't help but notice the sleek outline of toned triceps ripple as she moved. "An aphrodisiac. Clever."

"Oh, I didn't mean—"

"And I like where you're headed," Aisha said.

Gray felt a warmth rise in her cheeks—among other parts. "Then let's head in the same direction, shall we?" She pulled her wallet from her back pocket. "I'll close the tab."

AS GRAY AND AISHA rode the elevator down to the ground level, Gray's mind raced. Sleeping with Aisha had seemed an impossibility from the start because she seemed so thoroughly out of her league—an unusual power imbalance for Gray. Even more, Gray had already had sex with a fire sign. If she were to go all in with Aisha, it wouldn't be part of the one-of-each-element challenge. But what was Gray if not an overachiever? Now that it seemed like a real option, Gray realized she *really* wanted it. Aisha was more than beautiful. She was smart, funny, magnetic. And maybe if Gray leaned into that magnetic pull, she'd learn more about herself along the way, more about who she was meant to love long term. But mostly, how could she possibly pass up the opportunity to sleep with the coolest person she'd ever met, who just so happened to be into her?

Gray and Aisha made eyes at each other while slurping fresh oysters out of the half shell, swallowing the ice-cold delicacies whole. They made suggestive jokes about the briny taste and smooth mouthfeel, gently poking each other with the tiny forks. When the oyster platter was finished, Aisha paid the check and Gray followed her back onto the sidewalk in front of the restaurant.

"Do you want to walk for a few blocks?" Gray suggested, highly anticipating the night ahead of them but also enjoying the evening air. Just as she finished speaking, a group of drunken tourists walked by, one crying loudly about losing her ID and another shouting at her for getting them kicked out of a bar. Once they passed, Gray said, "I hear the city is lovely this time of year."

Aisha looked toward the tourist group and back at Gray, then laughed. "Yeah, sure." She looped an arm through Gray's elbow and started walking south.

They fell into an easy pace, with Aisha pointing out some of her favorite restaurants and Gray asking questions about spring in the city. After a few blocks, they were stopped by a curvy woman wearing what looked like a fringed, sequined bikini set. "Hello, ladies!" she called from outside of a lounge, the window behind her filled with flashing neon signs. "Queer burlesque starting in fifteen minutes. The gayest, most titillating show in the city!" The woman shimmied her shoulders, setting off a flurry of dancing fringe.

Aisha looked at Gray, her eyes lit up. "Do you want to?"

Gray could tell from the expression on Aisha's face that she wanted to go. "I'm down for a little titillation," Gray said with a grin. They approached the door and Gray reached for her wallet. "What's the cover?"

The woman in the fringed bikini did a double take. "For you?" she said to Aisha. "Free."

"That's sweet of you," Aisha said, grabbing Gray's hand and pulling her toward the door. "Thanks a lot!"

Once inside the dark lounge, Aisha led them toward a stage area with folding chairs arranged in front of it, most of them already full. They were walking toward the back row when someone waved from the front, shouting, "There are two seats here!"

After settling in and thanking the kind stranger, they resumed chatting about the New Orleans Jazz Festival. But after a few minutes, the couple seated to their right asked if Gray could take a picture of them with Aisha.

Aisha looked sheepishly at a confused Gray. "Would you mind? Easiest to just say yes and get it over with," she said quietly.

"Sure?" Gray grabbed the stranger's phone. "Say pasties!" she said, then snapped a photo. Gray handed it back and leaned in to Aisha's ear. "Are you some kind of celebrity on the burlesque circuit?"

Aisha shushed Gray as the lights dimmed.

A moment later, the first burlesque performer started their number. It was a sexy, jazzy version of the chicken dance where she pulled feathers from her outfit and blew them into the audience before stripping down to nothing but two rubber duckies taped to her nipples and one attached to the front of a bright-yellow thong. Gray quickly forgot about Aisha's apparent fan club, instead lost in wondering what ducks had to do with the chicken dance.

Each performer upped the ante. By the finale, when a performer lit their tasseled pasties on fire and swung the flaming tips in circles, the entire audience was on their feet, cheering and stomping in appreciation. Aisha and Gray burst back onto the dark street a few minutes later, adrenaline rushing through their veins from the exhilarating show.

Aisha boldly tucked her hand into Gray's back pocket. "Wanna go back to my place?" Aisha asked. "My apartment's only a half a mile from here."

"Absolutely," Gray said without hesitation, a desire to kiss Aisha coursing through her veins. "But you'll have to forgive me for forgetting my rubber duckie thong at home."

The ten-minute walk toward the river passed in what felt like no time at all, with the sounds of various jazz bands mixing to create a soundtrack to the date. As they strolled, Gray and Aisha's hands found new places to roam on each other's bodies, across the back of a neck, along the side of a thigh, brushing a swinging hip. Aisha led Gray to the elevator of a stately old apartment building that had been luxuriously renovated with modern touches. Gray noticed Aisha fumbling with her key in a rush to open the door into her spare but tastefully decorated studio apartment. But Gray had only a moment to take in her surroundings before Aisha pushed her up against a marble kitchen counter, her fingers pushing through Gray's dark-blond hair. Responding instinctually, Gray reciprocated the kiss and ran her hands down Aisha's thighs. She couldn't help but notice how muscular they were.

The heat between them rose quickly. Aisha pushed Gray's jacket off her shoulders onto the counter and kicked her own fashionable sneakers across the room. Their lips hardly left each other's skin as they stumbled toward Aisha's queen-size bed. Gray almost fell to the ground when she tripped over a set of dumbbells and a yoga mat between the kitchen area and her destination. Before she could regain her balance, Aisha shoved Gray onto the lush duvet and began unbuttoning her jumpsuit.

Gray's pulse beat loudly in her ears as Aisha stripped away her clothes, revealing a stunningly fit body. Literally the most muscular body Gray had ever seen in person. "Holy shit," she said, her jaw dropping. "Are you, like, an underwear model or something?" It made some sense in Gray's head, suddenly remembering the reactions of the woman at the door to the burlesque, and the strangers who'd asked for a picture.

Aisha laughed a short, hoarse chuckle. "No."

"Well, you totally could be," Gray said, her eyes stuck on— was that an *eight*-pack of abs?

"Enough of me," Aisha said, pushing a tuft of curly hair behind her ear. "Your turn." She slinked toward the bed, the muscles in her thighs apparent with each step, and started unbuttoning Gray's shirt.

"I, uh, I'm not . . ." Gray said, the feeling of Aisha's fingers against her sternum burning her skin. "You're, like, really hot. It's kind of intimidating," she finally managed. Although she wasn't as fit as she'd been at the height of her college softball days, Gray was typically happy with her body. But looking at Aisha made Gray unexpectedly self-conscious.

"Easy fix." Aisha paused undressing Gray to clap twice, and the lights in her apartment dimmed to a faint glow.

"That is . . . an incredibly sexy apartment feature," Gray said, breathless as Aisha unhooked the last of her buttons and whipped Gray's shirt off, then turned to peeling off Gray's tight jeans. Within seconds, they were both completely nude, their clothes thrown across the room. Aisha shoved away the duvet and Gray felt the smooth, cool texture of silk sheets on her bare skin. She didn't have long to appreciate the lush fabric, as Aisha was suddenly all over her, moving her hands and mouth quickly between Gray's neck and breasts and untoned abs and between her thighs.

Their sex was frenzied, a sprint to the finish line. This was the passion between two fire signs, Gray was beginning to believe, like gasoline and a match. But while she enjoyed the quick burn of her night with Aisha, Gray found herself also struggling to keep up. The athleticism of Aisha's moves pushed Gray to do more, try harder. Aisha climaxed, her back arching and voice rising in response to Gray's tongue between her legs, then flipped both of their bodies around to reciprocate. As Gray came next, something in her body made a distinct popping noise and she cried out in pleasure and surprise. She was still assessing the situation when Aisha jumped up on her knees over Gray's hips, leisurely stretching her arms high above her head and then running them down the sides of her body. When she reached her knees, Aisha leaned forward and began sliding her fingertips from her own skin to Gray's hips and waist.

"Ready for round two yet?" Aisha asked, the enthusiasm in her voice making it clear that she could do this all night.

"I would love to, but . . . uh . . ." Gray gave an experimental shift of her hips and cringed. "I think I did something to my back."

Aisha rolled off Gray, her slender frame immediately assuming a standing position next to the bed. "Yeah? How bad?"

Afraid to make the situation worse, Gray tried gently to sit up, but only made it a few inches before falling back onto the bed.

"It's like I pulled something? Or cracked something? I can't really turn or move it."

"Where does it hurt? High or low?"

"Somewhere in the middle? Lower middle?" Gray said.

Aisha jumped back onto the bed, the sudden movement causing Gray to take a sharp breath in through her teeth. Straddling Gray's hips again, Aisha grabbed Gray's wrists and pulled her arms above her head. "Keep these up here," Aisha said, pushing Gray's palms to the headboard. Gray nodded, and Aisha ran her hands beneath Gray's body until she reached her hips. Grasping each hip firmly, Aisha pulled up, and Gray's back made a second popping sound. This time, Gray felt a sense of relief instead of pain. She sighed and started to move her hands from the headboard. "Not yet!" Aisha commanded. She slid one hand under the center of Gray's spine and placed the other on Gray's sternum between her breasts, then arched Gray's back by pushing on both spots. A second crack sounded, and Gray was surprised to find herself feeling more limber than she had in several years.

"Can I move my hands?" Gray asked.

Aisha moved from on top of Gray to her side. "Yes."

Gray lowered her arms and sat up, then gave an experimental twist of her spine. "Damn. You're good."

Aisha hopped off the bed and strode over to the kitchen cabinets, her naked ass swaying side to side in the low lighting. She returned to the bed with a full glass of water and two Advil tablets. "Take these. They'll keep you from feeling it worse in the morning."

Gray obeyed, then set the glass on a nightstand. "So about that round two?"

Aisha sighed. "It's less fun once I've had to play chiropractor."

"Oh," Gray said, feeling a hint of disappointment. Aisha holding her hands above her head and bossing her around had

had a surprising effect on Gray's libido. "Not into a little doctor-slash-patient role-play, then?"

"I'm not against it, but your spine is sensitive right now."

Gray's back did feel a bit weak, now that Aisha mentioned it. "I guess you're right."

"And I'm running a marathon in the morning, so it's probably for the best anyway," Aisha said, reclining on one arm.

"Oh, wow. All right, then, I'll leave you and your fully functioning spine to get some rest." Gray rose from the silk sheets, stretching her shoulders before searching for her discarded clothing. Aisha lounged in the bed, looking like a mythical goddess in the moonlight streaming in through the window, as Gray silently dressed. Once she'd slid on her jacket, she returned to the bedside, running a hand over the shaved side of her head. "This was really fun. Thanks for fixing my back and . . . for everything else." She leaned down and pressed a kiss on Aisha's cheek. "And, uh, good luck with your marathon tomorrow. Hope I didn't ruin your prep time or something."

Aisha waved off Gray's words. "I do a handful of marathons a year. I'll be fine."

Gray tried to hide her astonishment at Aisha's abilities. Maybe she was a semi-famous fitness instructor. Or a social media influencer, like Carolina but clearly more popular. "Wow. Well, good luck, even though you don't need it. See you around, maybe?"

"See you around," Aisha said through a yawn, pulling the duvet over her naked body. Gray backed through Aisha's apartment door and closed it behind her, already doubting that such a wild, sexy, weird night could possibly have been real.

Twelve

Y THE NEXT morning, Gray was still somewhat convinced that her date with Aisha had been an elaborate dream. The lingering tension in her lower back offered physical evidence though. And her regular debrief with Cherry cemented it as real.

"This is proof that the challenge is working!" Cherry said as she handed Gray a washed cutting board to dry. River, meanwhile, was happily watching cartoon dinosaurs rap about the alphabet on a tablet, headphones firmly in place over his ears to block Gray detailing her non-PG date. "So Leos definitely make the short list of signs you're compatible with, right?" Cherry asked.

Gray toweled off the cutting board as she considered Cherry's question. "I don't know," she admitted. "Did we have fun? For sure. Was she beautiful and really cool? Absolutely. Was I attracted to her? Duh, who wouldn't be?" She placed the cutting board on the counter and accepted a wet measuring cup from Cherry to dry next. "But she's way out of my league."

Cherry laughed. "I'm not used to modest Gray."

"I'm being realistic!"

"I know that *you* know that you're a total catch," Cherry said. "How many queer women have I seen hit on you when we've gone to gay bars? Like, at least one per night out, whenever McKenzie wasn't on your arm. And sometimes then too."

Gray pulled her phone from her pocket and pulled up Aisha's profile, then turned the screen to show Cherry her photos.

"Holy shit," Cherry said, turning off the water and grabbing the phone from Gray's hand. "She's, like, model-level hot."

"That's what I said!"

Cherry scrolled through pictures, the phone only a few inches from her nose. "She looks kind of familiar. Are you sure she isn't an actor or something?"

"Maybe. She was kind of weird about telling me what she does, but I don't have her last name, so I can't really look her up. I tried googling 'Aisha model' and 'Aisha actress' and couldn't find her." Gray held out her hand for her phone. "Anyway, I had a great time, but I think my ego is too fragile to be with someone that amazing. I can't be the, like, noticeably less hot and interesting one forever."

Cherry shrugged and turned on the faucet to continue her dishes. "At least you're self-aware enough to recognize that, I guess. But maybe you can still keep Leos on the short list."

"Maybe," Gray said. "Anyway, what's Virgo's deal? That's next, right?"

Cherry made a fake gagging sound. "So boring. Earth signs who *love* rules." She handed Gray a whisk to dry. "Sorry, I'm biased as a rule-hating Gemini. You should go in with an open mind."

"My mind is as open as a Waffle House during a minor hurricane," Gray said as she held the wet whisk in one hand and opened her Mercurious settings to filter for Virgos with the other. "What should my Virgo icebreaker question be?"

"How they organize closets or something else no one but a Virgo would ever care about," Cherry grumbled.

"Huh. I think the app is down or something," Gray said. "It says 'No profiles found.'"

"Makes sense. Virgos are very chaos averse. Dating apps are nothing but chaos."

Gray pocketed her phone and returned to her drying duties. "Well, I'll check again this evening."

SUNDAY EVENING BROUGHT no more luck when it came to finding a Virgo. But Gray decided to put it out of mind for the time being. With earth signs on the brain, she instead texted Riley the Taurus. They'd been chatting occasionally as the grand opening of Demitasse Café approached, with Gray offering some marketing ideas and connecting Riley with a few of her contacts at local papers. It was all in service of making a new friend and putting down roots in her new city for Gray, but Riley was so grateful for the free advice that she insisted Gray's coffee was always on the house.

Gray knew better than to stay up late on Sunday night prowling for her next date. Her Monday morning meeting with Principal Taylor—was she allowed to call her Veronica at school?—could easily be ruined if Gray was too distracted by her romantic life. She'd had a good interaction with Veronica the previous week, but she wasn't ready to call their professional relationship healed just yet.

And when she arrived at the St. Charles Collegiate Academy principal's office fifteen minutes before their scheduled meeting time, she found her colleague in a particularly sour mood.

"Two hours is completely unacceptable!" Veronica spoke sharply into her desk phone as Gray poked her head through the cracked-open office door. "Tell them to hold the story until we have ample time to respond. Do *any* of these idiots have any concept of journalistic integrity?"

"Should I come back later?" Gray whispered.

Veronica shook her head and pointed at an empty seat across from her. Gray entered the room and gently lowered herself into the seat, wincing at the pain in her lower spine. "Our PR person is here now. I'll call you back." The principal clicked the phone into its base before whoever was on the other line had a chance to respond.

"What was that about?" Gray asked.

Veronica sighed and smoothed the front of her perfectly ironed burgundy blazer. "*The Times-Picayune* contacted us because they want to run some ridiculous piece about parents protesting our spring festival."

"Yikes." Gray had heard rumblings of approaching drama at the annual spring festival scheduled for mid-April. Based on what she'd gathered from Superintendent Donovan and the rest of the staff in the administrative offices, it sounded like a group of disgruntled parents were planning to disrupt the event with protest signs about Veronica's new curriculum for Louisiana history lessons. The irony of the parents expressing disapproval of a syllabus that included free speech and civil disobedience with an organized protest was not lost on Gray.

"I guess our meeting couldn't come at a better time. They want a statement by 10 A.M. so they can publish tomorrow." Veronica pressed a few buttons on her computer, causing a printer to the left of her desk to light up. It spat out two sheets of paper, which the principal handed across the desk to Gray.

Gray skimmed the article, wincing at a few particularly egregious quotes accusing the principal of everything from "eroding her students' conviction in their state's distinguished past" to "besmirching the esteemed name of Andrew Jackson," as if Veronica could hurt the feelings of someone long dead.

Gray looked up when she reached a paragraph halfway through the article. "Enrollment has dropped by a third? Is that true?"

"No!" Veronica said, her lips pinched. "But it's not out of the realm of possibility that it could drop that much, especially with nonsense like this in the paper."

Flipping to the second page, Gray said, "Do you know who's behind this?"

"Well, the main parent they interviewed has an axe to grind because her son was pulled off the football team for academic probation," Veronica said. "But since some of the information they have in there is confidential, I have a feeling the reporter got wind of the story directly from the school board."

"Geez, do they *want* the school to look bad?" Gray asked.

"They want *me* to look bad," Veronica said, frustration written across her face. "The school is collateral damage."

Gray looked up from the paper, now wrinkled from subconsciously balling her fists. "Aren't they telling on themselves here? Didn't the board *vote* for you?"

"I won by a narrow margin. Plenty of them didn't want me in charge because I'm a woman, half Dominican, and only thirty-six at that," Veronica said. Gray was a bit surprised at the principal's age; her intensity, way of carrying herself, and leadership position had initially led Gray to believe that she was likely a decade older than thirty-six. "At the time, the board thought of me as someone with a 'diversity' platform that was good for optics, but their opinions on it changed entirely when they saw I was actually committed to making real changes instead of just planning a couple of vanity professional-development webinars."

Gray laid the printed article on the chair next to her. "I know it doesn't change much, but I think you're the best person imaginable to run this school. These kids are lucky to have you at the helm, and the board is too, even if they don't realize it."

"I'm not fishing for compliments," Veronica said, although her expression softened. "I need to stop that article from running tomorrow."

"Well, that's something I can help with. I'll call my contact at *The Times-Picayune* to see if we can stall," Gray said, feeling extremely grateful for that lunch she'd grabbed with her new reporter friends. "We'll figure out a game plan, and if we're lucky, we'll still have enough time to review the new design for the recruitment webpage today."

Veronica settled back into her chair, a bit of tension leaving her shoulders. "I knew there was a reason we hired you."

GRAY WAS PLEASED to have a problem she could solve, unlike the baffling mystery of the missing Virgos. She threw herself into the middle of the *Times-Picayune* article drama with the kind of determination only an Aries can muster. The charm that had been so elusive on some of her dates came easily to Gray as she sweet-talked a reporter she'd recently befriended, promising an exclusive scoop on the high school's newly selected commencement speaker, an alum who'd gone on to become a famous author. Gray even hinted that she might be able to get the journalist an interview with the author, beloved for her New Orleans–set historical fantasy series starring a mystery-solving psychic.

It wasn't long before Gray was able to deliver good news to Veronica. While the powerfully connected board member had ensured the paper wouldn't fully drop the protest story, Gray's contact had convinced the journalist writing the article to hold it for a few days to get a more balanced perspective. Gray worked with Veronica to prepare carefully crafted comments, and by the time the piece was on newsstands on Thursday morning, it cast a much more favorable light on the new principal than the earlier draft. When Gray passed along the online article, she received an email response that was positively effusive by Veronica's standards: "Nice work. -VT."

And that evening, with River strapped into his stroller, Gray returned to the neighborhood playground, hoping that she might spot Veronica and Karys where she'd run into them the week before.

"See that water over there? That's Bayou St. John," Gray said, pointing across the parking lot. "Can you say 'bayou'?"

"By-oooo," River singsonged back.

"Very good! It's a body of water, but it's not as deep as a lake or a river."

River looked skeptically at Gray. "I River."

"Right, yes," Gray said quickly, having stumbled into this trap before. "But not *you* River. Watery rivers. Remember how we saw the Mississippi River when we went to the zoo?"

They were still debating the difference between toddler River and waterway rivers when they came within view of the oversized tic-tac-toe toy on the playground. Veronica was on the same bench they'd shared the previous Thursday, now waving Gray over. She was again in much more casual clothes than her office attire, a long plaid tunic over leggings. Gray found she enjoyed seeing Veronica without her principal suit of armor.

"Hey, stranger," Gray said, locking the wheels on River's stroller and unbuckling him.

"I hoped I'd run into you," Veronica said, something Gray was surprised to hear from her previously cold colleague. "Thank you again for intervening on that article. I can't believe how much it changed. I practically looked like the good guy, if you read between the lines."

"Hi, River!" said Karys, running over from a nearby set of monkey bars. She'd left her firefighter hat and tutu at home, and was today sporting a unicorn sweatshirt and rainbow-printed leggings. "Look, I wore my unicorn outfit hoping I'd see you!"

River squealed with excitement, then grabbed Karys in a big hug. "We play unicorns on slide?" He neighed and galloped in a circle, holding a finger out from his forehead.

Karys looked to her mom and Gray. "Can we go play on the slide, please?"

"Sure!" Gray said. "Just don't do anything stupid."

Karys paused, her face growing serious. "We don't use that word. It's not very nice. You should find a better word."

Veronica stepped in as Gray stared at Karys, abashed. "You're right, Karys. Ms. Gray meant don't do anything *unsafe*."

"Okay. Bye, Ma!" Karys waved and the two children skipped toward the play set.

"'Find a better word'?" Gray asked once Karys was out of hearing range.

"She's not wrong," Veronica said, smirking. "'Stupid' isn't very nice. And there's almost always a better word for what you're trying to say."

"Fair point," Gray conceded. "Anyway, I'm glad you were pleased with the final article. It took a bit of convincing, but I think they recognized that it was a better piece in the end."

Veronica pushed her sunglasses on top of her head and Gray noticed a concerned wrinkle between her eyebrows. "Yes, much better in the end. But the protest is still on, last I heard. And we've still got the issue of the board blocking us from buying all the new books I requested for the library. Not to mention trying to get them to fork over the money for new student scholarships."

Gray examined Veronica for a moment. "Geez, you're terrible at kicking back and celebrating a win, huh?"

Veronica laughed. "You know, I've heard that more than once."

"Yeah, me too," Gray admitted. "My friend Cherry tells me it's an Aries thing."

Veronica raised an eyebrow. "Is that so?"

"Yes! Fire sign, reporting for duty!" Gray said. "What do you want me to try next? Learn to play the violin so I can busk for scholarship funds? Drop some hot gossip on the worst board members to my reporter friend? Go to their church disguised as a straight girl to spy on how they're plotting to foil your plans next?"

"You can't do that."

"No words inspire an Aries more," Gray said, lifting her chin defiantly. "I'll have you know I took three weeks of violin lessons in middle school."

"Not the violin," Veronica said, smirking at Gray's backward baseball hat. "The last one."

"The undercover church mission?" Gray made an expression as if mortally offended, then straightened her posture, crossed her legs, pushed out her breasts, and said, "Whyever would you think that, sweetheart?" in a high-pitched Southern accent. "I do declare I love Jesus even more than sweet tea." For good measure, she turned her baseball cap around so it faced front.

"What?" Gray said, slumping back into her natural position as Veronica laughed. "With the right dress and wig, I could totally pull it off."

"Like hell you could."

Gray gasped playfully. "Language! I'm calling Karys over here and telling on you. Karys!"

"Stop! You're exhausting," Veronica said, downright giggling as she grabbed Gray's waving hand from the air before Karys noticed.

Gray and Veronica dropped the topic of business, and by the time the sun had dipped below the horizon, they were in a deep debate about whether octopuses or dolphins were smarter. Just as they'd agreed to disagree, Karys and River returned, looking slightly dirtier and more tired than when they'd arrived. "We're hungry, Ma," Karys said.

Veronica looked at the time on her phone and raised her eyebrows in surprise. "Wow! You're right, K. It's dinnertime." She turned to Gray while grabbing her tote bag from beside the bench. "Do you have dinner plans? We've got plenty of beef stew to share."

Gray tried to mask her surprise at the friendly offer. "Yeah, that sounds great. Thank you. Just . . ." Gray whipped out her phone and texted Cherry to let her know they may be home a little late. "Sure, let's do it."

Veronica gave Gray her address, and fifteen minutes later, she was in a family-friendly neighborhood in the middle of the city named after Bayou St. John, entering the home of *the* Principal Taylor, strict disciplinarian and incredibly intimidating school administrator. But Gray wouldn't have known about Veronica's professional persona based on her home. It was a surprisingly cozy raised cottage, full of warm colors, soft fabrics, and tons and tons of bookshelves, upon which Gray would have expected to find dry academic texts that were instead stacked with children's books, historical fiction, memoirs, and a fair amount of romance novels. The walls were decorated with Karys's many works of art, and toys were collected in baskets in each room. It was a home that instantly put Gray at ease and certainly made her see Veronica in a different light. Karys grabbed Gray's and River's hands as soon as they walked in the door and led them around the house, pointing out her favorite watercolor paintings and creations made of feathers, glitter, and glue.

When Karys's tour concluded, she took charge of setting the table, instructing Gray to follow with silverware. River followed them in circles around the table, too small to help but enjoying the process nonetheless. Gray couldn't help but think of her own family dinnertimes at Karys's age, bossing her little brother around as they set out the napkins and placemats.

Picturing her parents' dining room table hit Gray with an unexpected pang. Shouldn't all those lovely family meals at Cherry and Robbie's house have pushed out the memories of her mother pestering her about her unladylike manners and failed Bible tests over meatloaf? Even so, sometimes Gray still missed her mom's cooking. Or maybe she missed reliving her softball-game-winning runs with her dad, or flicking peas back and forth with her brother when their parents weren't looking. Maybe it was more about the sense of belonging, of being a crucial part of the family table rather than a visitor. In another universe, if things had been different, maybe she'd still be sitting at the Young family table for their Thursday pot roast. But in this universe, she felt pretty lucky to be a guest in Veronica Taylor's dining room.

By the time Karys had helped Gray find her old high seat for River, Veronica was plating their meal. It was a leftover beef stew reheated on the stove, served with a side of rice and sliced avocado. Veronica had invited Gray and River to dinner in order to further discuss their work, but the meal was instead spent watching Karys teach River the Spanish words for their meal and for all the furniture in the room. As Gray and Veronica laughed, cheered, and supported Karys's lesson, Gray's memories of the Young family table faded, and she realized she hadn't enjoyed herself this much in a long time.

Once the meal was finished, Karys and River played with a set of painted wooden animals while Gray and Veronica cleaned up. "Thanks again for inviting us," Gray said, dropping a stack of bowls into the sink. "That stew was delicious. And who knew River would love avocado so much?"

"He does look extra cute with his face smeared with green," Veronica said. "Very Wicked Witch of the West."

Gray laughed. "Very. Was the stew hard to make?"

"Not really," Veronica said as she wiped off the counters. "You pretty much just throw everything in a pot. I could send you the recipe."

"Oh, that's kind of you," Gray said. "But I'm an abysmal

cook. It has to be really simple for me to have a chance of it coming out edible."

"I'm sure you're not that bad."

"Ask River. I can't even get his macaroni and cheese right, and there are only, like, two instructions on the box."

Veronica laughed, a sound Gray decided she could get used to coming from her overly serious co-worker. "It's like any other skill. It just takes practice." She joined Gray at the sink, where she was rinsing their dishes. "For a simple sancocho like we just had, you just marinate the beef and brown it, then add water and simmer for—"

"You lost me at 'marinate the beef,'" Gray said apologetically.

Veronica smiled and gestured at a cutting board and knife on the counter. "Here, hand me those and I'll pass dishes to you to load into the dishwasher." Gray followed the directions as Veronica continued. "So maybe you're not ready for sancocho. Start with something simple, like a basic pasta. Kids love pasta, and you can sneak in all kinds of vegetables. My mom had this chicken pasta she used to make in the microwave. Weird, I know. She didn't really make a lot of pasta before she married my dad, so when he requested it, she kind of made it up as she went along and it somehow worked. I could teach you, if you want."

"Really?" Gray asked.

"Sure," Veronica said, sliding a handful of silverware into the dishwasher. "Karys loves it, so she'll be thrilled. She calls it 'oh yay, it's penne.' How about this time next week? Meet at the park again? You buy groceries, I'll show you how to make it."

Gray grinned. Tonight had been a completely unexpected delight. She'd felt right at home in Veronica's place, and the idea of coming back, of setting the table and watching Karys show River her toys and chatting with Veronica while cleaning dishes, sounded like heaven. "I'm in. Just tell me what to pick up at the store."

Right as Veronica clicked the dishwasher shut, River toddled into the kitchen, rubbing his eyes with tiny fists. He bumped into Gray's legs and mumbled, "Aunt Gay, I want go home."

Gray scooped him up into her arms. "You're right, buddy, it's getting late."

"What did he call you?" Veronica asked, her voice suddenly chillier.

Gray had almost forgotten that Veronica thought River was her kid. Somehow, the evening felt so relaxed, so normal, that it hadn't even really come up. But suddenly, she felt the telltale itchiness creeping up her neck. "What? Nothing! Oh, 'angay'? It's this weird way he says 'okay.' Toddlers, am I right?" Gray babbled.

Unconvinced, Veronica looked at River. "River, where's your mommy?"

River dropped his head onto Gray's shoulder, and for a moment she thought she might get away with the lie. But then he said, "At my house."

"And who's this?" Veronica said, her tone gentle but her eyes burning holes into Gray's forehead.

"Aunt Gay," River replied, enunciating clearly despite his exhaustion.

Veronica made eye contact with Gray for a moment, and whatever door that had opened between them seemed to slam shut. "River's not your kid."

Her face burning, Gray swallowed. "No, he's not. He's my best friend Cherry's son. But I'm his godmother. And roommate, kind of?"

"I invited you into our home," Veronica said, her voice dangerously low. "And you lied to me."

"I didn't really mean to lie," Gray whispered as River cuddled into her chest and his eyes fluttered shut. "I really didn't, I just wanted to—"

"I don't tolerate being lied to." Veronica crossed her arms, and Gray was again flooded with the feeling that she'd been sent to the principal's office. "You should leave."

"I'm so sorry, Veronica, I didn't mean—"

"Now."

Standing her ground, Veronica seemed to tower over Gray, even though Gray was a few inches taller. Gray nodded meekly, then ducked through the kitchen door into the living room to collect their things. Veronica followed her, watching her every move. Gray slipped River's shoes onto his limp feet and grabbed her keys from a table by the front door. Karys watched silently, seeming to have sensed the change in her mother's mood, but waved from her spot on the couch when Veronica wasn't looking her way.

Gray cracked open the door, stepped outside, and turned back once more to Veronica, who was still staring daggers at her. "I really am sorry. I hope we can talk about this another time."

"Good night, Gray," Veronica said, her voice firmer than concrete.

Before Gray could say good night back, Veronica closed the door in her face.

Thirteen

$\mathcal{I}$F GRAY THOUGHT the itching sensation she felt while lying was uncomfortable, it was *nothing* compared to the bone-deep shame of being caught in a lie by Veronica. That night, she lay in bed for hours, her mind replaying on loop the moment when Veronica realized River wasn't her kid. She'd only gotten on friendly terms with the principal in order to make their work relationship easier, but she had actually started to see Veronica as a real friend, someone she enjoyed being around, someone who made her feel seen. But Gray had let Veronica's assumptions about River go unchecked in an effort to get ahead, and it had come back to bite her in the ass.

After a night of restless sleep, Gray was especially grateful that she worked from home on Fridays. She woke up determined to find a way to earn back Veronica's trust—and try to keep her job. Apologies, gifts, and sentimental gestures wouldn't work on Veronica. Instead, what could Gray do to break down some of the barriers standing in the way of Veronica's mission for St. Charles?

Her brainstorming led to the seed of an idea. It was a long shot, but with the superintendent's help, it just might work. After she shot off an email request to Dr. Donovan, Gray looked at the calendar and felt a buzzing sense of urgency. Her twenty-ninth birthday, the moment of Saturn return, was only three weeks away. That also meant she was halfway through the six weeks in which she'd planned to complete her astrology dating challenge, yet she was still stuck in her fruitless search for a Virgo.

She needed to dedicate more attention to her zodiac mission if she wanted to get through all the signs in time, but lately, it felt like the challenge had gone on the back burner between work meetings with Veronica, friendly hanging out with Veronica, and now groveling for Veronica's forgiveness. But no matter how much Gray cared about impressing her colleagues or making new friends, she knew that finding her soulmate and starting a family had to be her priority.

Her Friday morning search on Mercurious finally turned up a couple of Virgo options, but upon further inspection, one turned out to be a couple looking for a third and the other unmatched with Gray after she misused "their" instead of "they're" in the chat. If the planets really wanted her to complete the challenge before Saturn return, couldn't they throw her a bone? It looked like she would have to download another dating app if she wanted to get back on track, maybe even more than one. The idea was daunting, especially without the help of Cherry, who was out all day running errands with River in tow. And anyway, Gray had some work to get through before she could double down on her search for her second earth sign.

Once she'd finished up a few work projects from her laptop at home, Gray took a break to drop by Demitasse Café's midmorning grand opening ceremony. Although Gray had seen a sneak preview, she was impressed by Riley's storefront on its first official day, stylishly decorated and overflowing with customers. She made it in the door just before Riley stepped around the front of the counter and quieted the crowd for remarks. Several reporters from local news outlets were gathered near the front, some Gray was pleased to recognize as contacts she'd recommended to Riley.

When Riley's speech concluded, Gray clapped enthusiastically and joined the line forming in front of the cash register. The reporter who had helped delay the article about Veronica and the spring festival protest stopped by to thank Gray for tipping her off to the café opening, steaming mug in hand, and shared that she was working on a piece about new Black-owned businesses in New Orleans, with Riley as one of the main interviewees.

Gray reached the front of the line and was preparing to order when Riley interrupted. "Give her a large macchiato and two palmiers on the house," she said to the cashier, then came around the counter to give Gray a firm handshake. "Thanks for coming."

"Thank *you*," Gray said, then turned to accept a plate with two small puff pastries, each shaped like a rounded heart and glittering with cinnamon sugar. "These look amazing."

"It was your idea to have a signature pastry," Riley said. "If I play my cards right, one day Demitasse Café will be as well known for our palmiers as Café du Monde is for their beignets."

"I'll certainly do my part to spread the word." Gray placed a hand on Riley's shoulder. "Seriously, I'm so proud of what you've done with this place. I hope it's a huge success. You deserve it."

"Good thing we failed at dating so we could be friends, huh?" Riley held out her knuckles for a fist bump, which Gray returned. "Anyway, got to get back to business. But don't be a stranger!"

Gray shuffled over to the pickup area and collected her macchiato, then turned to look for an open seat in the crowded café. Across the room near the front window, she noticed a woman sitting alone at a table with an empty chair. Gray navigated through the crowd and said, "Mind if I sit here?"

The woman looked up from her phone, at first annoyed, but growing curious as she looked Gray up and down. "Sure."

"Thanks." As Gray lowered herself into the seat, she wondered about the stranger across from her, who was still eyeing Gray indiscreetly over the top of her phone. She wouldn't have guessed it from the woman's conservative pantsuit or long blond hair, but Gray was definitely getting queer vibes from the way the woman was checking her out. She slid the plate of pastries toward the middle of the table. "Care for a palmier?"

The stranger eyed Gray's undercut, nose ring, and noticeably gay faux leather jacket. "Sure." She picked up one of the palmiers and nibbled at the edge of it. "Thanks."

"I'm Gray, by the way. Friend of the owner's."

The woman pocketed her phone, seeming to decide she was interested in a conversation. "Stephanie," she said. "I kind of happened upon this whole grand opening thing. I'm staying at the hotel next door."

"Well, lucky find! The coffee here is fantastic," Gray said, gesturing at the macchiato in front of her. "So are you from out of town?"

Stephanie nodded. "I live in D.C. Here on business."

"What kind of business?"

"Event planning." Stephanie paused to take a sip of her drink. "We have a huge event here next year. I'm scoping out the convention center and other host spaces, coordinating with some vendors. I have to leave in a few minutes for a meeting, actually."

"Ah," Gray said, then paused to watch Stephanie rearrange the tub of sugar packets at the center of the table. Hadn't Cherry said something about Virgos loving to organize things? Now that she thought about it, Gray could see that Stephanie's suit was meticulously ironed, her hair styled without a wisp out of place. Wasn't event planning something that required some serious attention to detail? She wouldn't normally be so bold and wasn't even certain Stephanie was her type, but Gray went out on a limb. "Random question. What's your sign?"

Stephanie's head tilted. "Virgo. You?"

Confetti exploded in Gray's head. She couldn't believe her luck. Just this morning she'd wondered if the planets could throw her a bone, and here Stephanie was, having appeared before her as if sent by Saturn. "That's perfect! I'm an Aries."

"Are Virgo and Aries compatible? I don't really keep up with that stuff," Stephanie said.

If Stephanie was leaving in a few minutes, Gray had limited time to turn on the charm. She grinned and leaned in, expertly arching an eyebrow in an expression she'd tested countless times in the mirror. "I'm not sure, but maybe we could find out. Do you have plans tonight?"

Against all odds, Stephanie leaned in. "I do now," Stephanie said. "Meet me at the hotel bar next door? Say, around seven?"

"Seven is great." Gray felt a rush of relief in her shoulders. This would put her at six dates in three weeks. Finally, she could get back on track.

Stephanie stood, gathering her bag and to-go cup. "I've got to run. See you at seven."

"See you then," Gray said with a wave, then contentedly settled in to eat her palmier. Success tasted sweet.

AFTER FINISHING HER WORK for the day, Gray had some time to kill before her date. She spent it specifically trying not to think about the look on Veronica's face when she'd kicked Gray out last night, and instead updating her search parameters on Mercurious. Gray was relieved to see a sizable list of Libras on the app. She began chatting with a couple of options, eager to keep the astrology challenge moving forward in case another sign proved as tricky to check off her list as Virgo had been.

That evening, she returned to the familiar block of the Warehouse District and wandered into the low-lit hotel bar next door to Demitasse Café. She located Stephanie, who was seated on a stool at the far corner of the bar, looking quite different from when they'd first encountered each other that morning. No longer in her business suit, Stephanie instead had her blond hair in a tight topknot and was wearing baggy, trendy clothes more suited to a skater than a corporate event planner. In this look, Gray would have clocked Stephanie as queer much more easily. She navigated through the bar's many tables and plopped down next to Stephanie. "Fancy meeting you here," Gray said, then winced at her cliché opening. The awkward first-date monster had reawakened.

Stephanie nodded at Gray, then flagged down a bartender. "Two PBR and Beam beer-shot combos." She looked toward Gray out of the side of her eye. "Hope you like your liquor brown and your beer cheap."

"Uh, sure," Gray said, a little thrown by the change in Stephanie's demeanor. "How were your meetings?"

"Productive," Stephanie answered.

Gray waited for a moment before realizing Stephanie didn't plan to elaborate. "So is this your first time in New Orleans, or have you let the good times roll before?"

The bartender returned with two shot glasses full of whiskey and two cans of Pabst Blue Ribbon, both cracked open and covered in a fine sheen of condensation. "Been here a few times," Stephanie said, seeming to relax with the drinks in front of her. "I've been to most major cities in the U.S. for work, either coordinating events or scoping them out as potential sites."

"That's awesome that you get to see so many different places," Gray said. "I used to travel a lot when I worked at a wedding-planning company. Destination weddings. Lots of beaches. But now I work for a school group, so most of my work travel is in the same few square miles, from the administrative office to the school campuses. I don't miss the flight delays, but I do miss the piña coladas."

"Convention centers are pretty much the same wherever you go, but it's cool, I guess." Stephanie picked up her Jim Beam glass. "Shots?"

Gray picked up her own whiskey and clinked it against Stephanie's glass. "Cheers to . . . brown liquor and cheap beer."

Before she finished, Stephanie threw back the shot and swallowed it with a completely straight face. Gray followed, trying her hardest not to wince at the burning sensation making its way down her throat. "So, what do you do for fun? Any hobbies?" Gray said, her voice raspier than before.

Their conversation was a bit forced, but Gray managed to keep it moving. Stephanie shared a little about her love of puzzles and her favorite television shows, and Gray realized that the most interesting thing about her life at the moment was the very dating challenge she couldn't discuss. Instead, she dove into a story about a rodeo she'd attended in Oklahoma that was interrupted by a tornado, but when she remembered it ended with her making out with McKenzie in a spider-filled tornado shelter, she had to improvise a new ending that didn't break Cherry's dating rules. Somewhat luckily, Gray was interrupted by Stephanie chugging the last of her PBR and crushing the can in her hand.

"So are we doing this?" Stephanie said.

"Doing what?" Gray asked, her eyebrows furrowed in confusion.

"Going up to my room."

Gray froze for a moment, surprised by the sudden turn in a date she'd found unimpressive so far. Based on Cherry's musings, Gray had thought earth signs were harder to win over, more methodical, slower moving. She'd expected the date to lead somewhere besides the hotel bar, albeit more in the direction of a local restaurant or tourist attraction. But she wasn't opposed to sleeping with Stephanie, and Stephanie certainly seemed game. Gray hadn't expected things to go so well (or so quickly) with

Carmen or Aisha either. And this would allow her to check an earth sign off her "to-do" list. Gray finished the last of her beer and nodded. "Yeah, let's go."

Stephanie told the bartender to put the tab on her room, then led Gray to an elevator and through the labyrinthian hallways to her door. Once inside, they took off their jackets in silence as Gray debated how to proceed. She'd never had sex that felt so impersonal before. Sex with McKenzie had been *very* personal, having been her first and part of a decade-long relationship. And with Carmen and Aisha, she'd had a chance to get to know them, even if it was brief. There had hardly been time to develop heat with Stephanie, besides the burning of the whiskey shot, which Gray wasn't even sure had fully hit her yet. She hoped when it did it would help her stop thinking about McKenzie. Why, after six dates, had her ex suddenly set up shop in a corner of her brain?

But before Gray could shake the specter of her ex, Stephanie took charge by grabbing Gray's hand and pulling her to the bed. Stephanie sat down first and pulled Gray in for a kiss by the lapels of her button-down shirt. The kiss was clumsy, their noses bumping gracelessly against each other's, but Gray felt a rising tide of desire, more for the fact that she was having such an unexpected encounter than specifically for Stephanie.

After a brief period of making out, Stephanie commanded, "Take off my pants." Gray complied, tugging down Stephanie's baggy cargo pants without unbuttoning them. "I'm going to go down on you."

"Oh," Gray said, a little surprised by Stephanie's domineering shift but not turned off by it. "Okay."

Gray shimmied out of her pants and underwear, and they tumbled heavily onto the bed. As Stephanie placed her head between Gray's legs, Gray tried to relax into the moment, tried to appreciate the feel of Stephanie's tongue against her skin instead of overanalyzing the experience. But she was distracted by something lighting up in her peripheral vision. She turned toward the brightness on instinct and saw Stephanie's phone, tossed against the pillow beside her, the screen awakened by the movement of the mattress. Nothing to worry about. But something on the lock screen grabbed Gray's attention, a familiar face. Not just Stephanie smiling in the photo, appearing a few years younger and her hair a slightly darker shade, but the person she was with—was that Ted Cruz? When Stephanie said she was an event planner from D.C., Gray had assumed she worked at some big consulting firm, or maybe a national nonprofit that hosted a lot of events, but maybe she'd overlooked the obvious political connotations. Now fully distracted from the actions happening below her waist, Gray looked across the room and saw, to her horror, a rolling bag with an RNC logo. *Shit*. Maybe it wasn't *that* RNC. Maybe Stephanie worked for the Researching Nanoparticles Council. Or the Revivifying Narwhals Commission.

"Um, what event did you say you were here to plan again?" Gray asked.

Stephanie paused, licking her lips. "I didn't say."

"Well, what is it?"

Stephanie sighed. "You're gonna be all weird about it, aren't you?"

Gray shifted to lean up on her elbow. "Just tell me."

"The Republican National Convention."

Gray jumped into action, pulling herself out from under Stephanie and fumbling to put on her underwear and jeans. She didn't even have them zipped and buttoned before she was at the door. "I've got to run. Thanks for the drinks."

"Come on, it's not even that big of an event! It's only a midterm convention!" Stephanie said, but Gray was already halfway down the hall by the time she finished the sentence.

"*THIS IS WHY PEOPLE* don't have sex with strangers without getting to know them first," Gray said an hour later, her hair still wet after taking a hot shower in an attempt to wash the whole embarrassing evening down the drain.

"So you almost had sex with a Republican," Robbie said as he handed out game controllers to Gray and Cherry. "It's okay, we've all done it."

"Speak for yourself," Gray grumbled. "I'm usually in denial that Republican lesbians even *exist,* much less that I'll find one licking *my* ballot box."

"It's not like all Republicans are inherently evil, and it definitely doesn't make *you* a Republican," Robbie said, settling down on the opposite end of the couch and navigating through the opening screen of Mario Kart.

"You didn't grow up like we did," Cherry said. "Where the Venn diagram of Republicans and evangelical Christians and homophobes is one giant circle."

"Exactly!" Gray said. "I spent my whole childhood being brainwashed by Republicans in my family, in church, in my school . . . I definitely don't need them in my pants."

Robbie shrugged as he looked at the character-selection screen and scrolled over to pick Wario. "Yeah, I guess it was pretty different in the Bay Area."

"I can't believe you got to grow up in San Francisco, the gayest city ever, and we had to grow up in *Oklahoma,*" Gray complained as she moved her cursor to select Donkey Kong.

"Life really isn't fair," Cherry said, picking Toad as her avatar. "But Robbie's right too. It's not the end of the world. If you don't like her politics and you weren't really feeling it, then don't go on a second date. Done."

"Easy," Gray said. "And I'm still counting this whole kerfuffle as sex with an earth sign. It was close enough."

"That's fine! Your challenge, your call. Libras are definitely going to be more up your alley anyway," Cherry said. "They're fun, peacemakers, great taste in music. Everyone loves Libras."

A cry echoed down the hallway from River's room. Everyone froze for a moment, quietly hoping River would soothe himself back to sleep. When River cried out again, Robbie and Cherry engaged in a silent, gesture-filled debate over whose turn it was to check on him. But then River let out a pitiful call for "Momma" and the argument was decided. Cherry left the couch, and Robbie and Gray settled in to wait for her return.

"So this astrology dating thing," Robbie said, crossing an ankle over his knee. "You really think it's working?"

Gray dropped her game controller on the empty middle cushion. "I guess? I've been able to find someone of each sign so far, and I think I'm making good time."

"No. I mean, like, do you think it will really find your future wife or whatever?"

"That's the goal."

"Just seems like you're putting a lot of faith in some real woo-woo shit, is all I'm saying," Robbie said, not unkindly. "Don't get me wrong. I like reading horoscopes and listening to Cherry talk about sun signs and moon signs as much as the next person. But I don't know that I'd make any major life decisions based on it."

Surprised by Robbie's interest, Gray took a moment to fold her knees up toward her chest and place her socked feet on the couch. "I wouldn't say I'm, like, putting *faith* in it necessarily. But it does feel like . . . something to do? That will maybe work?" Gray clocked the uncertainty in her own voice. Why did she feel so exposed by Robbie's question when pretty much every step in the challenge so far had felt like progress in some way toward her goal of finding out who she was meant to fall in love with? Straightening up, Gray decided to defend herself. "It feels like I'm fighting for what I want. And I can't give up when I'm already halfway through."

Robbie gave a deferential shrug. "That's cool. No judgment here. It's just . . . You know that whole 'you'll find love when you're not looking for it' mantra? I think there's some truth to it. At least there was for me."

"Didn't you meet Cherry on a dating app?" Gray said skeptically.

"Yeah, sure. But I wasn't, you know, *looking for the one*," Robbie said. "I was in Tulsa for a tech conference and didn't want to have dinner alone. Starting a long-distance relationship was the furthest thing from my mind. But it all worked out, even if it seemed unlikely."

Although she hadn't met Robbie on that first night, Gray had heard the whole story from Cherry and watched their relationship blossom. Robbie was a couple years older than Gray, but looking at his lanky frame in a faded old hoodie, tucked into the corner of the couch, game controller in hand, he reminded Gray of her younger brother. Hell, he was more of a brother to Gray now than her own sibling. "I'm glad you met Cherry that night," Gray said. "Y'all are good for each other. And we wouldn't have ended up as friends if you hadn't." She kicked a heel gently against Robbie's knee. "And it's good having you as a friend. Even when you're giving me shit about my romantic life."

"Giving each other shit is what friendship is all about," Robbie said, unbothered by Gray's mushy declaration. "Anyway, I just wanted to say . . . If you believe the universe will lead you to 'the one,' do you really think it would make you jump through all these impossible hoops?"

"I hear you. But I feel like I'm onto something, like the answers are just a few steps away. And if there's even a small chance it might work, then I'm going to see it through." Gray noticed the caring concern on Robbie's face. Her best friend really had married one of the good ones. "But thanks for checking in, dude."

Cherry reentered the room, still looking over her shoulder toward River's door. "I think he's down. Back to the races?"

And before long, thanks to the perfect distraction with her closest friends, Gray decided to consider her latest date a lesson learned and focus instead on her next match.

Fourteen

ALTHOUGH SHE'D WORRIED her long search for a Virgo would throw her off schedule, Gray was pleased to find a Libra who was quite amenable to meeting up as soon as possible. Skylar (she/they, according to Mercurious) was a social media manager for a local tech company, only twenty-three, but seemed mature for their age based on their profile. Gray struck up a chat late on Friday night after her Virgo date and found Skylar to be thoughtful, kind, and engaging. Maybe astrologers were really onto something with their interpretation of the cosmic ages of the signs, Gray thought, realizing she was now meeting signs in the latter half of the zodiac.

"What should my Libra icebreaker question be?" Gray asked once she finished washing the dishes from their Saturday morning breakfast. Cherry, huddled over her laptop at the marble island, didn't respond. Coming closer, Gray looked over Cherry's shoulder at her screen. "What are you working on?"

Cherry jumped at Gray's voice so close to her ear. "Jesus, warn a girl before you sneak up on her like that."

"We've literally been in the same room for the past hour."

Cherry shifted her computer so Gray could see. "Robbie and I have been planning a little update to River's room," she said. "He's about to move into a toddler bed anyway and is old enough now to tell us what kind of stuff he likes. Not that his ideas are all winners. He asked for a real unicorn."

"That sounds a little out of your price range," Gray said.

"Yeah. But I figured I could make some unicorn posters to

print and frame for him. Remember that graphic design class I took in college?"

"I remember you designing the best party invitations ever in college. Remember the ones you did for that Dolly Parton costume night?" Gray leaned in to look at Cherry's laptop. Pictured on the screen was a colorful illustration of a unicorn midleap with glittery text that said IN A WORLD OF ONE-TRICK PONIES, BE A UNICORN. "Cherry! This is adorable! River is going to love it."

"Thanks!" Cherry said, glowing with pride. "I'm making a couple more. I forgot how fun it is to stretch my creative muscles."

Crouching even closer to the computer, Gray examined the details of Cherry's work. "This is some professional-level shit. Like, you could sell these." An idea struck Gray right in the frontal lobe. She'd been working on her plan to win back Veronica's trust, and maybe her best friend could help her level it up. "Hey, could I commission a poster from you this week? It doesn't have to be this intricate. Just a visually impactful quote."

Cherry twisted around on her barstool. "You know I'd do it for you for free."

Gray shook her head adamantly. "In this house, we pay artists for their work."

"I guess we could agree on a reasonable fee," Cherry said. "When would you need it by?"

Gray shared a few more details with Cherry, who seemed to grow a few inches from her design skills being taken so seriously.

A buzz in her pocket reminded Gray what she'd asked Cherry in the first place. "Hey, how do I break the ice with this Libra?" she asked.

"Oh, I've got a perfect one," Cherry said after only a second of thought. "What's the best party they've ever thrown? They love hosting parties."

Once Gray returned to her bedroom and pulled up Mercurious, Cherry's question worked like a charm. Skylar enthusiastically shared details of her twenty-first birthday, when she'd thrown a cocktail party, taken literally. Guests were asked to dress as their favorite cocktails. Skylar had dressed as a Dark and Stormy, constructing a rain cloud out of old pillow stuffing to float above their head. Others had come costumed as a Bloody Mary, Irish Coffee, even a Buttery Nipple, which included a bikini top fashioned out of butter wrappers. Gray found herself liking Skylar more and more, and after chatting throughout the morning, Gray suggested they meet up in person. Skylar invited Gray to a free outdoor performance by a local zydeco band that evening. *Two dates in two days,* Gray realized, feeling especially daring.

Gray arrived right on time at their designated meeting point a block away from the open-air concert venue. Skylar showed up fashionably late—and literally fashionably, wearing a denim jacket, printed button-down shirt, and wide-brim hat that looked effortlessly chic. They spotted Gray and greeted her with a warm hug. "You're even cuter in person!" Skylar said, holding on to Gray's elbows while looking her up and down.

"Oh, thanks," Gray said, warming to Skylar immediately. "You look great too. Like you just walked out of an *Autostraddle* fashion column."

"This old thing?" Skylar said, looking down at her outfit. "I only changed, like, twenty times before coming. You're kind of intimidatingly cool."

"That's definitely not true," Gray said, a smile creeping up on her face. Skylar's honesty was refreshing. "I spent two hours this morning playing a videogame in my pajamas with flamingos on them. Let's forget intimidation and have a good time, yeah?"

"Deal. Speaking of . . ." Skylar dug in their pocket and produced a plastic bag of what looked like candy. "I brought weed gummies! Want some?"

"Oh! Um . . ." Gray paused. She and Cherry had dabbled in smoking and eating edibles in their younger years, but McKenzie had always frowned on it, and Gray had dropped the practice at some point during their relationship.

"They're the best for just, like, vibing and listening to live music," Skylar said.

Remembering her commitment to trying new things, Gray nodded. "Sure. But I haven't had edibles in forever, so my tolerance is probably super low."

"No problem." Skylar pulled an orange gumdrop from the bag and used their thumbnail to tear it in half. "Five milligrams should do it." Gray popped the gummy in her mouth and chewed, surprised that it tasted like normal sour candy instead of the skunky taste of the brownies she and Cherry made in college. Skylar popped the other half of the orange gumdrop and a whole yellow gumdrop in their mouth. "Cool. Let's go."

They started walking toward the outdoor stage, already hearing the syncopated rhythm of an electric guitar and accordion echoing from down the block. "By the way," Gray said as she matched her pace to Skylar's, "your profile said you use she and they pronouns. Do you prefer that I use one or the other or both?"

"Could you mix it up?" they asked. "I like hearing them used interchangeably."

"You got it." That was easy, since it was already what Gray had been doing in her head when thinking about Skylar.

Skylar looped their arm through Gray's and they continued walking. "This is already a great date."

"Yeah, it is," Gray said, relieved to find herself feeling more connected to Skylar after a few minutes than to most of the people she'd met lately.

Once they turned the corner, Gray spotted someone waving from across the street. She saw a familiar bright smile and voluminous curls. It was Aisha, the Leo. Gray smiled warmly and waved back. Her smile faltered a little, wondering if Aisha seeing her with another person on her arm was breaking dating protocol, but Aisha seemed unbothered. She winked at Gray before turning back to a conversation with her own group of friends.

"Holy shit," Skylar said under her breath, looking between Gray and Aisha. "You *know* her?"

"Uh, yeah, a little," Gray said. "Do you?"

"Not, like, personally," Skylar said. Seeing the confused look on Gray's face, she clarified. "That is AJ Carson, the soccer player, right?"

"Oh," Gray said. She suddenly understood why Aisha had looked vaguely familiar, why strangers gave her free admission to shows and asked to take pictures of her. And, if she went by her initials professionally, why she hadn't turned up in Gray's cursory internet searches.

"I mean, she's a celesbian. And an *Olympian*. I can't believe you're on, like, winking terms."

"Yeah, she is pretty cool," Gray said. Skylar's comment did bring up some deep memory about the U.S. women's soccer team at the previous Olympics, something about a gorgeous, queer star player scoring two goals in the last ten minutes of the game. If it was true, if it really was Aisha, then she'd had sex with an Olympic gold medalist. *How's that for trying new things?*

"When I played soccer in high school, she was totally my hero. I had a poster of her on my bedroom wall and everything," Skylar said, craning her neck to catch another glimpse.

Gray was momentarily jarred by the fact that Skylar was young enough to have idolized Aisha in high school. Aisha must have started playing professionally as a teen. "I never kept up with soccer much, to be honest," Gray admitted. "I was too focused on softball. I played through college."

"Really? I played a little of that in middle school too before I focused on soccer. What position?"

"Shortstop. They called me the Home Run Hurricane back in the day," Gray said, some of her university pride showing. It had been a long time since she'd relived her glory days, so she enjoyed reminiscing for a few minutes of their walk.

They arrived at a small city park with a raised stage where the zydeco band was already in full swing. It was a beautiful spring day, with the sunset peeking through freshly green leaves and a promising warmth to the air. Audience members were spread across the park, some picnicking on the grass, some dancing in front of the stage, others chatting or listening on nearby benches. Skylar located a soft, green patch of grass and they both sat down, enjoying the warmth of the sun on their skin. As they swayed along with the beat of the music, Gray asked Skylar about other music venues and festivals in the city.

The band switched to a slower song, and Gray lay all the way back in the grass, her fingers laced under her head and a look of bliss on her face. Skylar leaned back next to her. "Feeling the gummy, huh?"

Gray had almost forgotten about the edible, but as soon as Skylar said it, she noticed a gentle hum in her limbs, a light sensation in her stomach, a calmness in her brain. "Yeah, I think so."

"Me too," Skylar said, then rolled onto her side and snuggled against Gray, throwing an arm over Gray's stomach. It was a moment of physical intimacy that would have surprised Gray on another first date, but with Skylar, it felt nothing but perfect. Gray pulled one hand from under her head and tucked her arm around Skylar's shoulders. "So tell me your story. Start at the beginning. Where were you born?" Skylar asked.

The combination of the weed with the beautiful weather and great music had lowered all of Gray's defenses. She told Skylar about her childhood in Tulsa, some of her fondest memories with Cherry, even shared a brief description of her now-

nonexistent relationship with her family, something she'd fully
avoided discussing on any other date. Skylar kept asking probing
questions, completely captivated by Gray's every word. Gray
talked about coming out and her terrible experience at conversion therapy, all with a kind of distance she'd rarely been able to
achieve in past conversations, and was moments away from talking about how she met McKenzie when she caught herself. *No
talking about your ex,* Cherry's voice said in Gray's head.

Seeming to sense the direction of the story, Skylar asked, "And
then you met someone?"

The idea of talking about McKenzie on this perfect day felt
wrong, and lying felt even worse. Gray could already feel the telltale itchiness creeping up the back of her neck. "I've been talking
your ear off. It's your turn to tell me your story for a while."

Skylar complied, diving into their own tale of growing up in
the panhandle of Florida. Like Gray, Skylar had had a rocky experience coming out first as pansexual and then as gender nonconforming, and ultimately left her parents' home to move in
with an older cousin in Baton Rouge. Gray responded sympathetically and probed Skylar to share more about her cousin,
Louisa, who sounded lovely.

"We've talked a lot about our pasts," Gray said when they hit
a lull. "What about our futures? Where do you want to go next?"

"Everywhere!" Skylar said, their voice dreamy. "I've spent
most of my two-plus decades in Louisiana. I've finally got a sta-
ble job and a salary and vacation time. I want to see the world!"
With their hand tracing an invisible map in the air above them,
Skylar pointed out all the places they wanted to travel. "Some
people dream of having a big house, but I've never wanted that.
I want, like, four tiny apartments in major cities so I can rotate
between them. January in Mexico City, April in Tokyo, August in
Lisbon, the holidays in New Orleans with Louisa." Skylar sighed.
"That's the fantasy, anyway."

"Sounds amazing," Gray said, tightening her arm around Skylar's back. "Your whole life would be an adventure."

"What about you?" Skylar asked, rolling over to rest her chin and interlocked fingers on Gray's stomach.

"I guess I'm one of the boring people who wants a big house," Gray said, laughing to cover her embarrassment.

"Not boring!" Skylar said. "Just different from what I want. So you want to buy a house in NOLA?"

"Maybe." Gray scratched the back of her neck as she thought about how to put the vision she had for her future life into words. The vivid picture of her old softball teammate's two moms at the Tastee-Freez jumped back into her head unbidden. "It's not really so much about the house as the family in it. I want a big, messy, chaotic, but most of all *loving* family. Growing up, we were the classic family of four: mom, dad, brother, sister. But it never felt like a *family*, like the ones you see on TV who love each other fiercely and laugh together and fight a little because they care. At my parents' house, it was all about church, following the rules, and getting in trouble for not being exactly the daughter my mother wanted. If I'm honest, it wasn't all bad all the time. They loved me in their own way. But looking back, it's hard not to let all the bad overshadow the good. My parents said loud and clear that their love comes with conditions."

"And you don't talk to any of them anymore?" Skylar asked. "Not even your brother?"

"I haven't spoken to my mom and dad since a couple of years after I moved out, back when I still tried to occasionally check in to see if they'd gotten cooler about the whole gay thing. It fell apart in 2015 after same-sex marriage was legalized and they completely lost it. If I saw them around town after that, at a restaurant or the grocery store or wherever, I'd hide. My brother and I stayed in touch a little longer. We went to the same college for a couple of years before I graduated, and it felt different for a while after he moved away from home, like we could understand each other, like he might realize how limiting our upbringing was." Gray paused for a moment, pushing down the discomfort of talking about her brother. She missed him the most. Or at least she missed him differently from her parents. It used to feel like they were on the same side against their family's rigid rules. The pain of losing that relationship used to sting; it still hurt now, but more like a distant ache, an echo of what it used to be.

"But he met this girl right after I graduated," Gray continued, "in a Baptist student group. And it was like . . . I don't know, like following what my parents and the church told him he should want in life was just natural. Easier. Whatever. I met her a couple of times, and she was fine. A little boring, but he seemed happy in that everything-in-my-life-is-laid-out-for-me kind of way. He invited me to the wedding at my parents' church, the summer after he graduated. But he wouldn't let me bring . . . a woman as my plus-one." *McKenzie,* Gray filled in internally. They'd been together for six years then, a lifetime in heterosexual dating years. Benjamin had met McKenzie, and Gray thought they liked each other enough. Gray swallowed past the knot in her throat and continued. "And if I couldn't bring someone I loved to his wedding, if I couldn't bring my whole *self* . . . Well, we had a big fight. I skipped the wedding, and we haven't talked since."

Skylar made a sympathetic noise, their eyebrows angling upward. "That sucks, dude. I'm sorry."

"Me too." Gray blew out breath toward the sky. "When I have a family, when I have my own kids, it won't be like that. My love will come with no conditions, just endless support for them to be exactly who they want to be." Gray pictured her old softball teammate's two moms, the private smile they shared over their kids' heads, the way they exchanged bites of ice cream. Wasn't that the kind of love they had? Wasn't that why Alyssa and her brother always seemed so happy, so confident? Because their moms loved them without trying to change them?

"Sounds like your life would be pretty full of adventure too," Skylar said.

"Yeah, I guess so," Gray said. "Anyway, any travel plans soon? Where do you want to go first?"

Skylar dove into a list of places she wanted to visit in the United States before exploring the globe. But as their discussion continued, the itchy sensation continued to creep along the back of Gray's neck. She wasn't even lying about anything, so why wouldn't the itching stop? Gray scratched the offending area and felt something moving on her fingers, then quickly found the answer to her prickly problem: ants. *Lots* of ants, all over the back of her neck, in her hair, down the back of her shirt.

Hearing Gray gasp, Skylar rolled away and sat up to find they were also crawling with the tiny bugs. Both of them jumped up and began swatting at themselves, attempting to brush away the ants, looking a bit like they were moved by the music but had no sense of rhythm.

Recognizing their dance as a lost cause, Skylar said, "My apartment is a mile away. I know it's a little far, but I'd rather walk and shower off to avoid an ant infestation in my car. Want to join me?"

"Absolutely," Gray said, batting at another ant as it emerged from her sleeve.

BY THE TIME they reached Skylar's apartment, they'd gotten so lost in conversation that they almost forgot the reason for their walk. Plenty of the ants had found their way out of sleeves and pant legs, although the memory of the bugs was itchy enough on its own.

As they walked up two flights of stairs, Gray asked, "So what's our best bet for getting the ants off of our bodies without spreading them all over your home?"

"I know this is a first date, and your comfort is more important to me than a few ants," Skylar said. "But I'd recommend we strip down, throw our clothes in the washing machine, and get straight into the shower."

"I'll be most comfortable when I'm not covered in ants, so sounds like a plan," Gray said.

"But," Skylar said, "I only have one bathroom."

"Oh," Gray said, realizing the predicament. But with the bubbly sensation of the edible making her feel like she was floating an inch above the ground, and with the memory of Skylar curled up against Gray's side in the grass, showering together sounded not only acceptable to Gray but like a fantastic idea. "I've already bared my soul to you today, so I guess I'm fine with some bare skin too. If you are, I mean."

They exited the staircase to a small landing area. Skylar dug in a pocket for keys. Gray noticed a hint of a blush on their cheeks. "I'm down for sure. All right, let's do this."

She opened the door and ran inside, Gray right behind. Suddenly, the de-anting mission felt less disgusting and more like a hilarious adventure. Giggling, they stripped off their shoes, socks, and pants. Skylar pulled off their denim jacket and started to unbutton their shirt, then paused. "I should warn you that I, uh, I had top surgery a year ago, so I have some scarring."

Gray shrugged. "No big deal."

"It's just that I've had people be weird about it before."

"I'm so sorry that's happened to you, Skylar," Gray said, stopping with her jeans in hand. "I promise I have absolutely no problem with your scars or your surgery. Actually, I find it really sexy that you don't let other people's expectations control your body, that you do what makes you happy."

A tentative smile crept up on Skylar's face, one that slowly morphed into a confident grin. They finished unbuttoning their shirt and dropped it to reveal a flat chest with two shiny, pink scars along the rib cage.

"You look amazing," Gray said, then pulled off her own long-sleeved shirt and sports bra to even the score.

Skylar stepped closer, her eyes trained on Gray's body, then slowly reached out a finger to trace a line down Gray's sternum. Gray's skin hummed with anticipation. Skylar held up the finger to show a single ant. "Got one."

The ant crawled around the edge of Skylar's nail. Gray laughed, the tension of the moment broken. "God, it's still alive! We've got to get in the shower before one crawls in my ear and takes over my brain." She pulled off her underwear and bundled up her clothing in her arms. "Where's the washing machine?"

After dropping their grass-covered clothes in the washer, Gray and Skylar were left with nothing between them but a few determined ants. Despite their nudity, Gray found herself feeling completely at ease, perhaps because of the edibles, or maybe because of her connection with Skylar.

Skylar led Gray to the bathroom and turned on the shower, luckily big enough to comfortably fit them both. As they waited for the water to heat up, they laughed about what should have been a terribly awkward situation, but somehow still felt funny. After a few minutes, steam rose in the shower, and Gray and Skylar stepped through the glass doors and took turns rinsing ants down the drain.

"Can you check my back?" Gray asked, turning to give Skylar a clear view.

"Ant-free," Skylar announced. But before Gray could turn back around, Skylar ran their fingernails across Gray's shoulders, then started kneading their palms across Gray's tense muscles. Gray relaxed into the steamy air and Skylar's massage, feeling so serene she thought she might turn into water herself and slip right down the drain. She returned the favor, soaping up her hands to rub Skylar's back. What started as a genuine attempt to debug themselves turned into something much more pleasurable. With slick, soapy bubbles coating their skin, Gray and Skylar took their time, both finding immense pleasure before the water went cold.

Fifteen

CHERRY, ROBBIE, AND RIVER were already halfway through their Sunday morning breakfast when Gray waltzed through the door, wearing the same clothes as the day before, freshly laundered.

"Did you just get home?" Cherry asked, her eyes wide.

Gray smiled sheepishly. "Yeah."

"Nice!" Robbie said.

Cherry jumped up, squealing with joy. She grabbed Gray's hands and pulled her in a dance around the kitchen. Even River got in on the excitement, clapping his tiny hands to celebrate an occasion he didn't understand.

"Let's go out on the back patio so you can tell me all the lurid details," Cherry suggested. "Do you want some food?"

"I had a bagel and coffee at Skylar's," Gray said.

Robbie passed Cherry her plate and took over feeding River. "Y'all go talk about your grown-up stuff. I'll clean up in here."

Cherry and Gray found a sunny spot on the patio and settled into two Adirondack chairs. Gray walked Cherry through the date, including the steamy shower sex, the surprisingly restful sleep snuggled up next to Skylar, and another round of fun when they woke in the morning.

"Oh my god, look at you," Cherry said. "You're literally glowing. It must have been that good, huh?"

"Yeah, it really was," Gray said.

"And you slept with an air sign! That's three of the four elements."

Interestingly, Gray hadn't even thought about the astrology challenge once they'd arrived at Skylar's apartment. It was as if removing their clothes had also removed any other motives, anything distracting Gray from enjoying the experience. It was the most relaxed she'd been during a sexual encounter since McKenzie. "I guess so," she said, remembering Cherry's comment. "Only a water sign left."

Cherry waved a hand. "Easy. You've still got Scorpio and Pisces, so solid chance you'll be interested in one of them. So is Skylar going on the short list?" Gray stared at Cherry blankly. "You know, the list of people who you might ask out again once you're done with the dating sprint."

"Right, the list," Gray said. "I don't know that we're really at the same place in our lives. They kept talking about how much they want to travel the world and explore new cultures and stuff, and I'm trying to settle down. But we were definitely compatible in other ways, so yeah, I'd put Skylar on the short list. Or at least Libras more broadly."

"Who else?"

"Jackson, definitely," Gray said. "The Gemini."

Cherry nodded sagely. "Makes sense. Air signs balance fire signs the best. We've known that since the beginning. So Gemini and Libra make the cut. Who else?"

Gray stared off toward the trees in Cherry's backyard, watching the Spanish moss shift in the wind as she thought back through her dates so far. "Carmen was fun—the Aries—but I should have probably learned by now that Aries isn't my one true match."

"She can go on the 'maybe' list," Cherry suggested.

"And I really liked Aisha," Gray continued, "but she's even more out of my league than I realized. Apparently she's an Olympian?"

"Shut the fuck up," Cherry said, clearly living for the gossip.

Gray told Cherry what Skylar had said about Aisha, then googled "AJ Carson" to find it was true. An image popped up immediately of Aisha posing with a gold medal between her teeth.

Once she and Cherry recovered from the realization, Gray reviewed her short list of potential matches. As much as Gray didn't want to dismiss any sign based on a single date, she felt fairly confident that Taurus, Cancer, and Virgo weren't her destiny. Gemini and Libra were at the top of the list, with Leo and Aries right behind. Aisha was amazing, but Gray wasn't sure she could play second fiddle for life to a superstar Leo. Her relationship with McKenzie had been on more equal ground, but every day had still felt like a battle over who was the coolest or hottest or most talented. That wasn't what Gray wanted in the long term. She wanted a love where both partners could shine.

"Next up is Scorpio," said Cherry.

"Yep, and no prospects yet," Gray said. "Any advice for the search?"

"Scorpios are . . ." Cherry paused, weighing her words. "Well, some people say they're the villains of the zodiac. But as another unfairly villainized sign myself, I'd say that's not a fair assessment. They're water signs, so they're fiercely loyal to their loved ones and are emotionally intelligent. But you also don't want to get on their bad side. That's all I'll say about that."

Gray thought that sounded mildly terrifying, but what was she going to do now? Give up? Certainly not. "Any idea for an icebreaker?" she asked.

Cherry thought for a moment, then said, "Let's lean into the villain thing. Ask, 'What famous villain do you think is most misunderstood?' At least you'll get an early warning if they're deeply evil, right?"

"I'll give it a try," Gray said. "But I really don't want to leave this date with a sworn nemesis."

Cherry pulled a pair of sunglasses from her pocket and slid them on. "I would never lead you astray, bestie."

FIRST, GRAY HAD another plan to carry out before she could focus on finding a Scorpio date. She didn't quite have all her ducks in a row for Project Win Back Veronica's Trust in time for their weekly Monday morning meeting. But clearly Veronica wasn't ready to give Gray another chance yet either. Gray awoke to a calendar cancellation. The email from Veronica said only, "Conflicting meeting. -VT."

While it might have been true that she had a conflict, Gray suspected Veronica was avoiding her. No matter; now she had time to make her apology extravaganza just right. After calculating what details she needed to wrap up, Gray shot the principal a text.

> *I have something important to show you. Can I meet you in the school library tomorrow after 5?*

Gray frequently checked her phone for a reply as she got ready to head to her office, but she received nothing from Veronica. She did see three dots appear a few times, a sign that Veronica had seen her message and was trying to craft a response. But it wasn't until hours later, as Gray was grabbing a catfish po' boy from a food truck during her lunch break, that she finally received a text.

Tomorrow, 6 PM.

Gray grinned at Veronica's cold reply. She was clearly still displeased with Gray, but she'd given her a chance. That was all Gray needed.

———

GRAY ARRIVED A couple of hours before their meeting the next day. That way the security guard could let her in before leaving for the day, and it gave her plenty of time to set up. The principal, however, didn't arrive until twenty minutes after six, her high heels tapping brusquely against the linoleum.

"This better actually be important," she said as she rounded the door into the library. "I have a very busy week and—is that *Brown Girl Dreaming*?"

Gray looked up from the child-sized armchair she'd wedged herself into, one ankle crossed over the other knee, book in hand. "Yeah, it is. It's amazing."

"I know it is. That's why I put it on my list of—" Veronica froze, looking over Gray's shoulder at two shelves full of gleaming new books. "Oh," she said, her tone completely changing from irritation to surprise.

Gray stood, the armchair momentarily lifting with her before clattering back to the ground. "Surprise!" she said, gesturing grandly to the shelves Veronica was already inspecting. "I thought about streamers and glitter cannons, but I didn't want to get on the janitorial staff's bad side."

Her mouth hanging open in awe, Veronica ran a finger along the spine of a copy of *The Prince and the Dressmaker*. "This is . . . Is it everything on our library wish list?"

"Plus a few extras recommended by that Diversifying Middle Schools Consortium you're a member of," Gray said.

Veronica slid out one book, *Long Way Down* by Jason Reynolds, and thumbed through it. "There's no way you got the board to approve buying them."

"Hell has not frozen over, no," Gray said. "Besides, I wouldn't go over your head like that."

"Then how did you do this?" Veronica said, her hair hanging

around her face, making it hard for Gray to gauge her reaction. "Did you buy them yourself? That's thousands of dollars. Not to mention the board could still find a way to pull them from the shelves."

Gray rocked on her heels, nervous as a middle schooler trying to impress the principal. "I would have spent thousands of dollars on this if I had it to spare. But I thought of that too. So I came up with something better. You know Gina Byers Kane?"

For the first time, Veronica actually made eye contact with Gray. "The paranormal mystery author?"

"That's the one." Gray stepped closer and put the book she'd been reading back on the shelf by the other copies. "You know we just announced she's the keynote speaker at the high school graduation this year?"

Veronica gave a single nod, clearly waiting for Gray to get to the point.

"After a chat with Dr. Donovan, I convinced him to reach out to Gina and explain the situation—that we were having trouble getting approval for the books you hoped to buy. She's pretty into free speech and access to books, you know. On the board of trustees at PEN America and everything."

"Huh," Veronica said. "That makes me love her books even more."

"Me too," Gray said. "Well, at least it makes me *want* to read them more. But the TV series is fantastic."

Veronica all but rolled her eyes and gestured for Gray to continue with her story.

"Right. Anyway, Dr. Donovan and Gina had a nice chat over the weekend, and she agreed to donate all the books on your list. It's a win-win. You don't have to fight the board for approval. *And* if they try to argue the books should be removed from the shelves, they look like jerks for refusing a gift from one of the school's most notable alums. Who will also be mentioning her opposition to book banning in an interview I arranged with *The Times-Picayune* about her commencement speech in May."

Gray could see that Veronica was racking her brain for a downside. "That's . . . a workable solution, actually," she admitted.

"Dr. Donovan called it 'brilliant,' but I'll take 'workable.'"

Stepping back to take in the wall of books in front of her, Veronica said, "You know, the librarian is going to be mad at you for moving around her organized collection for all of this. And while she'll love all these new additions, it's going to be a lot of work on her end."

Gray waved away the concern. "Ms. Nole and I are tight. She helped me clear out this space for the grand reveal. And besides, I told her I'd come in on Friday to help her catalog them and put on all the protective covers and whatnot."

The principal raised an impressed eyebrow. If she was looking for a critical retort, she came up dry.

Catching sight of her briefcase on a computer table, Gray drew in a sharp breath. "I almost forgot, there's more!" She grabbed her bag and slid out a glossy sheet of paper. "I commissioned my friend Cherry to make these posters with a quote from one of Gina Byers Kane's books."

She held up the page for Veronica to examine the colorful design. At the center was the text WHILE READING A HUNDRED BOOKS, SHE WALKED IN A HUNDRED PAIRS OF SHOES, SAW A HUNDRED DIFFERENT VIEWS, AND LEARNED A HUNDRED UNFORGETTABLE LESSONS. Cherry had worked in a variety of illustrated shoes on the poster. Cowboy boots, high heels, ballerina slippers, soccer cleats, and more tucked between letters and bursts of color.

"Cool, right?" Gray said. "Cherry's really talented. We told Gina that we'd like to hang some of these around the school to thank her for her donation. She absolutely loved it, even wanted a copy to hang in her writing room. And she agreed to sign a poster, along with a full set of her Crescent City Seer series, for the silent auction at the SCCA parent gala in May."

Veronica plucked the poster from Gray's hand and paced the room, then collapsed into a chair behind the librarian's desk. "This is . . . I don't know what to say."

"You don't have to say anything," Gray said. She followed Veronica's path and perched on the edge of the desk. "You dreamed it. You worked incredibly hard to create a plan for this school. You made the list of books, not to mention a strong argument for why they were needed. I just helped you cross the finish line."

"This is a huge weight off my shoulders, Gray," Veronica said, fully dropping the guarded expression she'd worn all evening.

"I'm glad." Gray straightened a stack of lesson plans beside her while gathering her nerve to say what she'd been meaning to convey with this whole shebang. "I know I messed up by not telling you about River. I wish I could take it back. Betraying your trust is the last thing I want to do. All of this—"

"Is enough," Veronica interrupted quietly.

"It . . . It is?"

"I hate apologies," she said, leaning back in the desk chair. "You made a big mistake. And I trust you'll never lie to me like that again. But words never mean as much as actions. And this . . ." Veronica waved a hand toward the full shelves. "I know this wasn't easy to pull off. I've been working toward it for months. This is a win, one you somehow accomplished in under a week. And it gives me hope that maybe there are more wins ahead."

With Veronica's forgiveness, Gray felt like she could finally breathe again for the first time in days. "There are so many more wins ahead for us. I know it," she said, her voice low and earnest.

Veronica examined Gray for a moment, then stood. "I've got

to run. I meant what I said about having a busy week. But Gray?" She grabbed Gray's hand where it rested on the desk. "Thank you."

Gray grinned at Veronica. "For you? My pleasure."

With one last look at the donated books, Veronica turned to the library exit. She stopped just in front of the door and turned back. "Are we still on for our cooking lesson on Thursday?"

Any remaining concern about Veronica holding a grudge faded from Gray's mind. There was no way she would invite Gray into her home if there was an ounce of mistrust. "Absolutely," she said.

Veronica knocked her knuckles against the doorframe twice, then disappeared into the hallway. Gray thought about following her, but decided instead to grab that copy of *Brown Girl Dreaming* and settle back down in the tiny armchair. She'd almost reached the end earlier, and it really was amazing.

Sixteen

By Thursday, Gray was still walking tall from successfully proving her worth to Veronica—and to Dr. Donovan, who was delighted by their newly donated books and the fact that he was now on a first-name basis with a literary celebrity. He'd even given Gray that afternoon off as thanks. Of course, never being one to sit around twiddling her thumbs, she'd immediately filled it by asking her new reporter friends if they wanted to blow off work and meet her somewhere for an early happy hour. They'd ended up sharing beignets at a hotel restaurant in the French Quarter. One journalist had put the tab on the company card, saying that Gray tipping them off to the Republican National Convention potentially taking place in the city the following year counted as work. So at least her date with Stephanie the Virgo hadn't been a total loss.

As she was exiting through the hotel lobby, Gray heard someone call her name. She looked up to see a familiar person with reddish hair waving from the concierge desk. *Jackson.* The Gemini currently sitting at number one on her short list! Was fate telling her to keep that option open? Gray waved, straightened her olive-green blazer, turned to check her teeth in the reflective window, and strode over to her potential soulmate.

"Gray! What a sight for sore eyes!" Jackson walked around the counter and wrapped Gray in a hug.

"Good to see you." Gray's words were muffled by Jackson's shoulder. She pulled back and asked, "How have you been?"

"Good, good. Work has slowed down a little, but it's still festival season, so . . . you know." Jackson shrugged. "You?"

"Great! Also busy, but settling into the city more every day." Gray paused, running her fingers through the buzzed side of her hair. Jackson looked exactly as beautiful and ethereal as she remembered in a flowing floral top and with their auburn waves pinned back from their smiling face. It was early yet to think about what would happen after her birthday when the challenge was over, but Gray felt like she had to take advantage of this moment. "Things should slow down for me in a few weeks, and I was hoping we could see each other again then. If you want to."

Jackson's eyes went a little soft, their smile bordering on pitying. Gray could tell instantly that the answer wouldn't be what she hoped. "Oh, Gray. That's so sweet of you. But I . . . Well . . ." Jackson looked down at their feet, then back up at Gray. "I've been seeing someone else."

"Oh." Gray felt an invisible punch to her gut, sensed the air being sucked out of the room.

"Céline, actually. That ghost tour guide?"

"Wow. That's great." Gray tried to smile supportively, but she felt the corners of her lips wobble. "She seemed really cool."

"She is," Jackson said, their face lighting up. "I don't want to jinx it or anything, but it's going so well. Like, it legit feels like the stars aligned and the universe pushed us together. Being with her, it's just right, you know?" Jackson saw Gray's expression and their glow dimmed slightly. "I'm sorry, Gray. You're lovely, it's not—"

"No, no, I get it," Gray said, shooting for blasé instead of devastated. "I'm really happy for you."

Gray knew her words didn't match her tone, but Jackson seemed heartened by her response. "Thank you. I'm really happy too," they said.

Still reeling from the new information, Gray quickly wound

up the conversation, said her goodbyes, and stepped out into the sunlight, wishing desperately that the stars would align for her like they had for Jackson.

GRAY WAS STILL in a bit of a daze as she picked up River for their dinner at Veronica's house. Even River seemed to notice her mood. As Gray buckled him into his car seat for their run to the grocery store, he reached out a chubby hand and poked Gray's cheek. "Aunt Gay sad? Why Aunt Gay sad?"

Putting on a big smile, Gray deflected. "I'm not sad, River! How can I be sad when we're going to the park and to dinner with your friend Karys?"

"Carrots!" River said.

That brought a little more authenticity to Gray's smile. "Pretty close, buddy. All right, let's go to the store."

After picking up the ingredients from Veronica's list, Gray and River arrived right on time at the small neighborhood park. Gray found Veronica on their regular bench and settled in next to her as they watched River and Karys run off toward the swing set.

All it took were brief hellos for Veronica to ask, "Is something wrong?"

Was Gray's dour disposition that obvious? Was she pouting like the child across the playground who'd been told to wait his turn for the slide? "I'm fine," she said shortly.

Veronica examined Gray over the top of her boxy sunglasses, a wry grin on her lips. "Do you want to tell me about it?"

"About what?"

"About whatever has you walking around like you're in a tragic silent film."

Gray sighed. "Do I have 'loser who will never find love' tattooed on my forehead?"

Veronica looked away to watch Karys and River galloping after each other, giving Gray a moment of privacy after her outburst. "Another bad date?" she asked.

"Not exactly," Gray admitted. "It was a great date, actually, a few weeks ago. I really liked this person. I thought it might turn into something down the line, but I waited too long and now they're with someone else."

"Why did you wait?" Veronica asked.

Gray looked at Veronica out of the corner of her eye, then back across the playground to where the kids were playing unicorns. "It's kind of a long story."

"I've got time. Especially since the meal I'm teaching you to make only takes about fifteen minutes, start to finish."

"Really? Wow." Gray wasn't sure if sharing her dating mission with Veronica was a good idea. For starters, Veronica was a coworker. Even more, she could be quite rigid and traditional, at least in her professional role. Astrology—and Gray's very queer and sometimes steamy dating experiences—could prove offputting. But thanks to the *Fight Club*-style rule about talking about her challenge to dates, Gray hadn't spoken to anyone about her romantic adventures besides Cherry and Robbie. Sharing her struggles with someone else was appealing. And weren't she and Veronica more than just work acquaintances at this point? Didn't the curious and open look on Veronica's face seem more like that of a friend? "Well, it all started with a visit to my friend's astrologer."

Gray went on to explain how she'd hoped to leave with a simple answer of which sign would be her best match, only to end up with a mission to date all twelve signs. She'd never heard the principal laugh so hard or gasp with such delighted surprise. Even better, Gray was pleased to see that Veronica didn't bat an eye when she used she/her or they/them pronouns to reference her dates. Because she came from a conservative family and home-town, it was a rare treat to find a straight person with whom Gray could comfortably discuss her queer dating life.

"So you're doing this whole thing because of . . . Saturn retro-grade?" Veronica asked once Gray had finished brief summaries of each date she'd had so far. Minus the R-rated content, at least. That seemed a bridge too far for discussion with a co-worker.

"Saturn return," Gray corrected. "It's the thing that happens every twenty-nine years when Saturn is in the exact same place in the sky as when you were born. When you're, like, pushed onto the right path by the planets or whatever. Expect big life changes, or so says Madame Nouvelle Lune."

Veronica stared off into the middle distance thoughtfully. "I guess that makes sense. I had Karys when I was twenty-nine. *And* I decided to start taking on some administrative duties in addi-tion to teaching."

"Well, now you'll be more prepared for your next Saturn re-turn when you're . . . fifty-eight," Gray said, doing some quick mental math.

"What is it you said Saturn return is urging you to do? Find your true love?"

"That, and settle down, start building the family I've always wanted, have kids," Gray said, staring out at River as he spun down a spiral slide. She may have told herself that she'd let Ve-ronica believe he was her kid for business reasons, but Gray knew that deep down, she enjoyed playing at parenting on her Thurs-day evenings.

"So you *thought* the Gemini might be your perfect match, but now they're seeing someone else," Veronica said.

"Exactly." Gray's spirit had previously been lifted by sharing the story of her last few weeks, but remembering what started the conversation brought her right back down to Earth. "So now

I'm wondering, was it really meant to be and I missed my chance? Or maybe it's a sign I'm meant to be with the Libra. Or one of the fire signs?"

"Or maybe you're meant to be with a Gemini, just not that one," Veronica said. "You're learning about the signs, right? Not limiting yourself to these exact twelve people you meet on Mercurious? Or maybe you're destined to end up with one of the signs you haven't gotten to yet. There's no point drawing conclusions before you've finished your experiment and analyzed the data. That's just basic scientific method."

Gray laughed. "I'm not sure the scientific method is applicable here. Do you even believe in astrology?"

"Do you?"

Gray leaned back against the bench and felt Veronica's fingertips press against her shoulder. Despite her sometimes frosty behavior, Veronica was surprisingly tactile once someone was on her good side, punctuating her sentences with a hand on an arm or smoothing a lapel. "I think so?" Gray answered. "I mean, my best friend, Cherry, does, and she can point out all these ways it makes my life make sense. And they say fire signs and air signs are compatible, and earth and water signs are compatible, and that appears to be bearing out in my love life. The more I learn about astrology, the more helpful answers I seem to find in it."

"It's just like any other framework from which to view the world, right?" Veronica said. "A way to understand and relate to other people, even if they're different from you. And unlike many other frameworks, it doesn't discriminate based on race, gender, sexuality, class, religion, what have you."

"So you *do* believe it?"

"Oh, definitely not," Veronica said. "It's got the same ability to inspire and create empathy as any other faith system, and the same dangers of unquestioning belief, right? But it's fun to explore."

Gray felt her brain twitch at that comment. She'd never really thought of astrology as a religion, and she wasn't sure how it sat with her. But that set off her subconscious religious-trauma warning bell, which tended to send Gray running in the opposite direction to avoid getting lost in memories, the good ones sometimes even more dangerous than the bad. She checked her watch. "Whoops, I think my story blew us way past River's dinnertime."

"Perhaps we should continue this conversation at my house," Veronica said, taking the hint. "We've got a cooking lesson to attend to."

VERONICA AND GRAY buckled Karys and River into separate cars and drove to Veronica's redbrick house. Gray carried in an insulated bag of groceries and unloaded it on the counter while Veronica set the children up with a puzzle. Once the kids were distracted, Gray's lesson began.

Veronica rinsed a plastic clamshell container of cherry tomatoes and then set them on the counter next to a cutting board and a long, thin knife. "Your first task: slice those in half."

"Sounds easy enough," Gray said, picking up the knife.

"You'll need this." Veronica slipped a green apron over Gray's head.

As Veronica tied the apron strings behind her back, Gray looked down to see a screen-printed alligator wearing a chef hat on the apron, along with the words YOU CAN THANK ME GATOR. "If you say so, Chef." She pulled a handful of cherry tomatoes from the clamshell and set them on the cutting board, chasing down a few as they threatened to roll off the counter. Targeting one, she brought down the knife. But instead of cutting the tomato, it sent it rolling across the counter. Gray grabbed it and brought it back, then made another attempt that ended up slicing off a tiny bit of the tomato's skin. On her third attempt, the blade hit the middle of the tomato, but at an angle that managed to squish the tomato instead of cutting it, sending a stream of red juice flying straight at Gray's apron. "Agh!" Gray grunted as it splashed her.

Veronica looked over at the mess. "See, that's why you always wear an apron."

"I thought it was just because I looked so good in it," Gray said. She turned around and struck a model-like pose with her hands resting on the counter and her face looking seriously off into the distance.

Veronica laughed, a full, warm sound Gray was grateful to hear again after their rocky past week. It seemed all was really forgiven. "That too." She pulled a dinner plate from a cabinet and handed it to Gray. "Use this."

"Now you want me to slice tomatoes and spin plates at the same time?"

"No, goofball, like this." Veronica took the plate from Gray's hand and placed it on top of the tomatoes so that the circular rim on the bottom of the plate held them in place. She took Gray's hand and splayed it across the top of the plate, then came around behind Gray and placed her own right hand over Gray's hand, both gripping the knife. "Hold the plate with gentle pressure," Veronica instructed. She guided Gray's wrist to hold the knife parallel to the counter, aiming between the plate and the cutting board. "Try to keep the blade flat like this, and evenly between the board and the plate, then . . ." They both pushed the knife through the tomatoes, then Veronica let go of Gray's hand and pulled back.

Gray lifted the plate to see the tomatoes cleanly sliced in half, with only a small amount of juice splattered around them. "Damn. A teacher, a school administrator, an amazing mom, a chef, and a magician? You keep surprising me, Veronica Taylor."

Although Veronica turned at that moment to locate a stone-ware baking dish, Gray spotted a grin on her face.

Their conversation was interrupted by River, who toddled into the kitchen with a distraught look on his face, saying, "Aunt Gay! Aunt Gay!"

Gray wiped her hands on her apron and scooped River up in her arms. "What is it, Riv?"

He held out a tiny thumb, his lower lip pushed out in a pout. "Gotta ouchie."

"He squished his thumb playing with my Wonder Woman toy," Karys said, following River into the kitchen.

River quieted as Gray examined his thumb. "No blood, no swelling, no bruising. Can you wiggle it for me?" Gray asked.

"No," River said, still pouting.

"How about a thumb war?" Gray asked. She grasped River's tiny finger in hers and moved her thumb back and forth. River mirrored the movement, seemingly without pain, and giggled as Gray let him trap her thumb under his. "So strong! Well, it appears to be in working order to me." Gray spun River around in a circle before setting him back on the floor. "Why don't you go back and play with Karys? And tell Wonder Woman to be a little gentler with your thumbs."

The kids zoomed out of the room, River's injury seemingly forgotten. Gray turned to Veronica, who was looking at her with an unreadable expression. "Anyway, what's next in the recipe?"

Veronica pointed at the cutting board in front of Gray. "Gotta finish that step before we can move forward."

"Right, of course." Gray sliced the rest of the tomatoes using the plate method, then followed Veronica's instructions to toss them in the dish with a little seasoning, olive oil, garlic, and roasted red peppers from a jar. Veronica placed a lid on the dish and put it in the microwave for five minutes. While it cooked,

Veronica chopped up some grilled chicken from her refrigerator and Gray grated a block of Parmesan cheese. The microwave dinged, and they added some broth and a box of penne pasta.

"Back in the microwave for twelve minutes," Veronica said, setting the timer accordingly. She rinsed her hands in the sink and turned back to Gray. "So for this dating thing, what made you realize it was time to find your soulmate? Why did you go to that astrologer now?"

Gray sat down at a barstool and pushed her hair out of her face. "That story's almost as long as the dating challenge itself."

Veronica looked at the microwave. "We have eleven and a half minutes. That long enough?"

Although she hesitated at first, Gray reminded herself that this wasn't a date with one of the signs. She could talk about McKenzie all she wanted. "The most concise explanation is, a tough breakup," Gray said. "When my ex and I got together, we were so young. Neither of us knew what we wanted out of life, what we wanted a family to look like. Well, to be fair, *I* knew what kind of family I wanted. It just seemed so far in the future, and I figured McKenzie needed some time before she came around to the idea of kids. Took another decade for me to realize she was *not* coming around to anything just because I willed it so, and our visions for the future didn't really work together anymore."

"A decade," Veronica said. "That's a lot of your life to just move on from like that."

Gray gulped, recognizing that Veronica had immediately gotten right to the heart of her recent struggles with only a little information. "Yeah. Sometimes I feel like I don't know who I am anymore without McKenzie, like I'm only half of a person walking around, lost."

"If it helps, you seem like a fully realized person to me," Veronica said, leaning on the island across from Gray. "With that whole 'I laugh in the face of danger and will overcome any challenge with pure gall' thing you've got going on, I'd say you've got the energy and drive of a person and a half, at least."

Gray laughed. "Thanks, but the 'laugh in the face of danger' bit is all an act. I saw a garden snake in Cherry and Robbie's backyard last week and screamed so loud the neighbors came over to check on me." She shrugged. "What about you? How long were you with Karys's dad?"

"Not nearly as long as you were with your ex, but I guess having a kid really accelerates all those realizations about different visions for the future you were talking about." Veronica peered around the corner to check on Karys and River, then returned, her voice a little lower than before. "We were only together for less than a year when I got pregnant. But I'd always wanted kids, and I was almost thirty and figured this was my shot. Dylan seemed like he'd make a great dad, and he is. Just not a great husband. To me, at least."

Gray nodded thoughtfully. She figured seeing the tough-shelled Veronica open up like this wasn't something many people got to witness, and she didn't want to blow it like she had the previous Thursday.

"We were married for about two years before we admitted we were both miserable," Veronica said. "It was mutual and about as peaceful as a divorce can be, I suppose. Especially after we separated. We could put the clash between us aside and focus on being good parents instead. Karys hated the divorce at first. A lot of acting out, tantrums. Therapy helped, but it was realizing she now gets two bedrooms and two sets of toys that finally made her see the light."

Gray smiled. "Hard to imagine Karys acting out. She seems so mature."

"Did I mention therapy?" Veronica came around the kitchen island and sat on the barstool next to Gray. "Her dad and I have reached a good place for co-parenting. Karys stays with him Monday and Tuesday nights, then she's here Wednesday and Thursday nights, and we alternate weekends. Sometimes we get our wires crossed, but Dylan and I are on good terms these days, so it mostly works."

The heart-to-heart was interrupted by a beep from the microwave. When Gray pulled out the stoneware dish and removed the lid, she was hit with a wave of fragrant steam, bursting with garlic, roasted red pepper, and herbs. Veronica nudged her out of the way and stirred in the chicken, Parmesan, and some fresh basil. "Wait, this legitimately looks like delicious pasta," she said, looking over Veronica's shoulder.

"What did you expect, sushi?" Veronica said as she walked toward the island.

"Okay, sassafras," Gray said. "It just seems too easy to be true, is all."

Veronica pulled two ceramic bowls and two kid-friendly plastic bowls from a cabinet. "I told you I'd show you something even an abysmal cook can make, didn't I?" Veronica bumped an elbow against Gray's ribs with a smile, then strode to the kitchen doorway. "Karys, time to set the table!"

THE PASTA HAD indeed turned out to be an impressive meal, one Gray couldn't wait to make for Cherry and Robbie to show off her new skills. River had loved it just as much as Karys, partially because she'd taught him the "oh yay, it's penne" song she'd made up to accompany the dish. But even better than the food was the company. Sitting down to dinner with Veronica and Karys felt different than having dinner with Cherry and Robbie. Gray felt more like an equal than the pitiable, brokenhearted third wheel they'd brought in like a lost dog, although Gray knew that dynamic was all in her head. Not to mention how much Gray enjoyed watching Veronica and Karys together. Karys was smart as a whip, and Gray could see all the ways Veronica nurtured her imaginative instincts.

Even though dinner and the board game they played afterward had pushed Gray over an hour past the time she usually brought River home to his parents, she still felt like the evening had ended too soon. As they said their goodbyes, River gave Karys a big hug, and in high spirits from the lovely evening, Gray mirrored River's move and gave Veronica a hug too. Although Gray could tell she was a bit surprised at first from the tension in her body, Veronica quickly relaxed and returned the gesture. It was a rare gift, Gray understood, to see the softer side of Veronica.

The short drive home was long enough to rock River to sleep. He was completely knocked out by the time Gray pulled into the driveway, and he didn't even stir while Gray carried him into the house, changed him into pajamas, and tucked him into bed. She gently closed his door just as Cherry exited her own room in pink bunny slippers and a silky robe.

"Asleep?" Cherry asked at a barely audible volume. Gray nodded silently, and they both tiptoed down the hall to the kitchen. "I'm going to make some mint tea. Want some?"

"Sure," Gray said. "Sorry I got him home so late."

Cherry waved off the apology as she filled an electric kettle with water from the faucet. "You warned me ahead of time, so no big. It actually worked out for"—Cherry wiggled her eyebrows suggestively—"personal reasons."

Gray faked a gag. "Gross, Mom."

"Hey, you tell me all the juicy details of your sex life. It's only fair." Cherry placed the kettle on its stand. "Besides, it's hard to make banging fun when you're doing it with an objective."

"Doesn't sex always have an objective?"

"Fair point," Cherry said. "But spontaneity is half of the

thrill, and once you start talking about schedules and hormone levels and whatnot—"

"Wait, are you trying to get pregnant again?" Gray interrupted.

Cherry turned around, her expression a bit sheepish. "Yeah, I've been meaning to tell you."

"But I thought you were going to wait until River was a little older," Gray said, thrown by the news.

"He *is* a little older," Cherry said. "He's about to turn two. He'll probably be close to three by the time the next baby is born, if Robbie and I can hurry up and get it cooking."

Gray massaged the back of her neck with one hand. "It just feels so soon. I . . . I don't know what to say."

"Life comes at you fast." Cherry pulled two mugs out of a cabinet and two tea bags from a drawer. "And you could say 'congratulations.' Or 'good luck.' Something, you know, supportive?" Her tone was cagey, a noted change from her usual nonchalance.

"I'm happy for you!" Gray said quickly. "It's just . . ." She rubbed her face and tried to collect her thoughts, tried to understand why Cherry's proclamation had sent her into a panic. "I'm so close to figuring out who my soulmate should be, you know? If things go well, I could maybe get married in the next year, have a baby a year after that. And I guess I always pictured our kids being best friends and growing up together like we did. Can't you wait just a little longer? So we can do it together? Like our moms but way cooler?"

With a heavy sigh, Cherry lifted the kettle to pour water into the mugs. "Let's sit down." She carried the mugs to the table and sat, Gray taking the chair across from her. "Gray, you know you're my best friend in the whole world."

"Same," Gray said.

"And I would rather dive into a pit of scorpions than do anything to intentionally hurt you."

"That's a little dramatic, but same, I guess."

"But you can see why what you said—asking me to wait to get pregnant—hurts me, right?" Cherry said gently. "Asking me to choose between what I want, what I've agreed on with Robbie, and what you want?"

Something in Gray's brain immediately clicked into position, replacing what she could now recognize as jealousy with shame. "I'm sorry, Cherry. You're totally right, I shouldn't have said that."

"I know, I know." Cherry reached out a hand and put it on top of Gray's. "I get it, I know Saturn has you in a weird place right now. But as much as I love you, Robbie and I can't make our family-planning decisions based on your schedule."

"Of course you can't. Forget I said anything," Gray said, her cheeks burning.

"I want our kids to grow up together too," Cherry said, ignoring Gray's request. "But there's no way to guarantee they'll be as close as we are. It's way more important to me that they have their aunt Gay in their lives."

"One hundred percent. They couldn't keep me out of their lives if they tried," Gray said, still feeling deeply embarrassed by her earlier response. She gathered her mug in her hands and blew across the steamy surface of the tea. "Really, I'm sorry about what I said. What I meant was, I'm so fucking happy for you and Robbie and River. And I'm here to support you, whatever you need. Do you need someone to run your ovulation calendar? I'm great at schedule management."

"Absolutely not, but thanks, G." Cherry smiled, a true grin that made Gray know all was forgiven. "And don't think this 2 Fast 2 Pregnant: The Sequel business is going to get me off your nuts about your astrology project. You locked down a date with a Scorpio, yeah?"

"Tomorrow for lunch!" Gray said, grateful for a change of subject. "I told him it wasn't exactly an ideal time for me, but he apparently already had a reservation at this restaurant that's hard to get into or something."

"He?" Cherry asked.

"Niko. Trans man."

"Cool," Cherry said. "Did you use the icebreaker I suggested? The one about misunderstood villains?"

Gray nodded. "Captain Hook. He said if a bunch of obnoxious kids who refused to mature at all wouldn't leave him alone, he'd be pretty annoyed by it too."

Cherry hummed in agreement. "What was your answer?"

"Wicked Witch of the West. I didn't have to make much of an argument. He's seen *Wicked,* so he gets it," Gray said.

"Sounds like a winner. Let me know how it goes!"

"You know I will!" Gray said. Relieved that a tough conversation had still managed to end on a good note, she took her tea upstairs to her apartment to start planning her outfit for her next date.

Seventeen

AFTER SPENDING THE MORNING helping the SCCA middle school librarian organize all the newly donated books, Gray arrived right on time for Niko's lunch reservation at a seafood restaurant on the outskirts of the French Quarter. It took only a moment to spot her date looking at his phone on the other side of the waiting area. He had short dark hair in a carefully styled high fade and was wearing a burgundy suit that was a tad formal for a Friday lunch, but it looked nice on him. Seeing Niko's outfit, Gray was grateful she'd opted at the last minute for navy slacks instead of jeans, even if they'd picked up a little dust while moving bookshelves.

"Niko, right?" Gray said as she approached him.

Niko looked up and his brow seemed to release some tension. "Great, you made it."

Influenced by the formal attire, she offered a handshake and Niko returned it. "Nice to meet you. Shall we?"

A hostess seated them at a table for two along a side wall, then placed two menus on the white tablecloth in front of them. Gray lifted the menu and glanced over the offerings. "Do you have any favorites?" she asked.

"Favorite what?" Niko replied. Gray looked up. He hadn't touched the menu, but was instead staring over Gray's shoulder in the direction of the door. She glanced behind her. There was nothing to see but a few more customers entering and servers attending to seated diners.

"Dishes here," Gray prompted, sensing Niko's unease. She

certainly couldn't judge Niko for letting his nerves get the best of him. At least the awkward tension wasn't her doing this time.

"Oh," Niko said. "No, I've never been here before."

Gray was a little surprised, given how set Niko had been on coming here. Returning her attention to the menu, she said, "I've never eaten alligator. Have you?"

"Yeah," Niko said. "Tastes like chicken, but chewier. Anything is good when you deep-fry it."

"A ringing endorsement," Gray said. "Maybe they should call it chicken of the bayou." Gray thought the joke was at least a B-plus, but Niko offered only a weak smile.

After a server dropped by to take their order, they were again left in uncomfortable silence. Gray racked her brain for any details in Niko's Mercurious profile that might kick-start their conversation. "So, you're into poker?"

That earned a bit of Niko's attention. "Yeah, I am," he said, leaning back in his chair. "Started out as a hobby and now it's more of a side hustle. I'm currently ranked twenty-sixth in the state."

"Wow," Gray said. She knew very little about the game, but that sounded impressive. "So you must have a really good poker face, huh?"

"I'm a Scorpio. Comes with the territory."

"I've heard Scorpios get a bad rap," Gray said, happy to wade into the more familiar topic of astrology. "Are the rumors true?"

Niko started to talk about the symbol of the scorpion hurting their image, but seemed to lose the thread halfway through, watching a young queer couple settle in at a table across the room. Gray wondered if he felt the same relief she did, now that they weren't the only queer people in the restaurant. Being the token gay wasn't as common in New Orleans as in Tulsa, but it was always nice to be in good company. After a moment, she prompted him with, "You were saying? About scorpions?"

"Right," Niko said, sitting up a little straighter and smoothing the lapels of his suit jacket. "When you've got a symbol like the scorpion, you're destined to be a villain. But scorpions aren't so bad, you know? They only hurt you if you mess with them first. Scorpios are the same."

A server dropped off the appetizer, and Gray picked up a piece and popped it into her mouth. "You're right," she said after swallowing it. "Tastes like chewy chicken."

Niko plucked a piece from the basket and dipped it in a cup of creamy sauce on the side. "Better with ranch."

But rather than take a bite himself, he reached across the table, and as the ranch-dipped alligator approached in what felt like slow motion, Gray realized with intense embarrassment that he intended to feed it to her. Before she could decide how to say no without being rude, politeness overruled, and she opened her mouth to accept the bite. "I guess that is tastier," Gray said awkwardly, then quickly grabbed another piece, dipped it in some ranch, and stuffed it in her mouth to try to signal that she was not about to reciprocate. Niko laughed loudly and, with a glance at the other couple's table, said, "You're hilarious!"

Gray raised her eyebrows. After some stilted conversation about favorite spots in New Orleans, their meals arrived, and Gray busied herself with her catfish po' boy. An awkward silence stretched between them. When Gray chanced a glance at Niko, he was smiling and nodding at her as if she'd just said something particularly fascinating.

Gray couldn't help but remember another date that had gone poorly: her date with a Cancer. While she'd been thrown off by Carolina and her sister ending the date so abruptly, she ultimately appreciated the honesty. They really hadn't been compatible, and it was a relief to stop pretending things might turn out differently. Gray signaled a passing server. "Could I please get a to-go box for this? Thanks so much." She wiped her mouth with her cloth napkin and looked up at Niko resolutely. "It's clear that we're not really connecting. So I appreciate the lunch invite, but I'm going to head out."

"What?" Niko said, seeming to turn his full attention to the words coming out of Gray's mouth for the first time all afternoon. "Why?"

"I've been trying to get to know you, but you seem more interested in their date than in ours," Gray said, nodding toward the queer couple. "And I've got to get back to work, anyway."

A look of desperation reached Niko's eyes as he put a hand on top of Gray's. "Wait, wait, please stay!"

"Not unless you tell me what's going on," Gray said.

"Okay, fine," Niko said. Gray settled back in her chair, one eyebrow raised. "That woman over there? In the buffalo plaid?" Gray nodded. "That's my ex and her new partner, who happens to be my former friend. They met through me. Before we broke up."

Gray's scolding expression softened. "Oh. Wow."

"Yeah, wow." Niko took a deep breath. "That's what I said too when I found out, but, you know, angrier."

"This reservation," Gray said, all now becoming clear. "You knew they would be here, didn't you?"

"Our online calendars are still linked," Niko said under his breath. "I saw when she scheduled it."

"And you invited me because . . ."

Niko scratched his forehead. "Do I have to say it?" Gray nodded, and Niko looked down at the table, embarrassed. "Because you're hot and I wanted to make them jealous."

Despite the unusual situation, Gray couldn't help but warm to Niko from the honesty. And the compliment. "Well, you should have said that from the beginning." Having recently been through her own breakup, although not nearly as messy as the one Niko described, she could sympathize. Gray reached across the table and smoothed a tuft of Niko's dark hair. "So I could help you instead of sitting here thinking you were a weirdo."

A look of delight crossed Niko's face as he realized Gray was on his side. He grabbed her hand and brushed a theatrical kiss on her knuckles. "You're my hero."

Gray glanced across the restaurant, then looked at Niko with a lovesick expression on her face. "Quick, they're looking this way. Feed me another gator bite."

Niko complied. "You're right, this is much more fun."

Gray chewed and swallowed the appetizer like it was sexier than a chocolate-dipped strawberry. "Mmm. Nothing tastes better than making your ex jealous, right?" If McKenzie had cheated on Gray, she would have wanted someone to do the same thing for her. Still feeling the weight of the other couple's eyes on them, Gray had an idea. "Kiss me."

"Really?" Niko said, looking like Gray had just told him he'd won the lottery. "You don't mind?"

"Consider it a good deed from one recently single queer to another," Gray said. She'd promised Cherry she wouldn't bring up McKenzie, but this felt like a special exception. Puckering her lips, Gray leaned across the small table. Niko met her halfway, and Gray was pleased to find that the kiss wasn't bad. It was surprisingly steamy, actually, although the fire between them definitely felt more like sweet revenge than real chemistry. Losing themselves in the heat of the moment, Gray and Niko started full-on making out, and Gray's hand was creeping around the back of Niko's neck to draw him even closer when an exasperated grunt interrupted them. They peeled apart to see Niko's ex standing at their table, hands on her hips and a look of outrage on her face.

"What the fuck, Niko!" the ex yelled. Several tables stopped their conversations and turned their heads toward the evolving scene.

"Oh, hey, Jenn," Niko said, his delight barely concealed under a calm gaze. "Didn't realize you were here."

"Like hell you didn't!" she shrieked. "I'm supposed to believe you just happened to be making out in the same restaurant where Gabe and I are having lunch? Please."

The server returned at just that moment with the to-go box Gray had requested. "Everything all right over here?" the server asked, eyeing Jenn.

"All good!" Gray said, her voice higher pitched than usual.

The server backed away and Jenn resumed yelling at Niko about ruining her date. Gray pretended she couldn't hear a thing as she loaded the last half of her po' boy into the box. When she'd decided to voluntarily support Niko's efforts, she hadn't intended to cause a scene.

"If you're so in *love* with Gabe, why are you worried about me?" Niko yelled back, no longer able to play it cool. "You cheated on me with *my* friend, you have *no* right to tell me who I can and can't make out with."

A few people at nearby tables gasped at that revelation, and others started whispering among themselves.

"Oh, that's a nice moral high ground you've got there considering you're the one who *cheated first*," Jenn said scathingly, eliciting more gasps from their audience of diners.

"Maybe I should go," Gray whispered.

"No, sugar muffin," Niko said, grabbing Gray's hand again. "Stay. She's all bark and no bite."

"You gave her the *same* nickname you gave me?" Jenn said, her voice cracking with emotion. "How's this for no bite?" Jenn picked up Niko's pasta and Gray watched in what felt like slow motion as she dumped the creamy linguini and shrimp on his head. The people at the tables around them gasped and stared at Niko as he sat in stunned silence, noodles strung over his head and one piece of shrimp curled halfway into his jacket pocket.

Gray wiped a stray splash of Alfredo sauce from her cheek and licked her finger; she had to admit it was pretty tasty. But Gray was starting to get what Cherry meant about not getting on a Scorpio's bad side. As Niko and Jenn continued their stare-off, Gray pulled two twenty-dollar bills from her wallet and slapped them on the table. "Well, that's my cue. Good luck, Niko. I hear vinegar is best for dairy-based stains."

And before Niko could reply, Gray strode out of the restaurant with her to-go box in hand, wondering if her final date with a water sign would make such a splash.

Eighteen

GRAY HAD BEEN willing to help Niko taunt Jenn because she was intrigued by the drama, but once things turned messy, she'd realized the fun of the moment wasn't worth it. Jenn had seemed genuinely upset, and clearly Niko's troubles were too complex for Gray to unwittingly insert herself into them. With four dates left, one of each element, Gray was determined to finish the challenge without instigating any more food fights. And since sexy times weren't in the cards with Scorpio, that meant Pisces would be Gray's last chance to sleep with a water sign before the end of the challenge. Gray could cross that bridge when she came to it. She had three more dates to find first.

A knock on her door interrupted Gray's scrolling through Sagittarius profiles on Mercurious. She opened it to find Robbie balancing a stack of boxes and plastic bins.

"Morning, Gray," Robbie said, his elbow resting on a box that, according to the outside, held a crib. "Sorry to bother you, but Cherry and I are switching out a bunch of River's baby stuff for toddler stuff and I was wondering if you had any spare room to store some of this."

Gray rubbed the back of her neck, eyeing the teetering pile. "I'm not sure. It's a little tight up here, but maybe I can move some things around. Isn't there space in the garage?"

"Yeah, but it's not temperature controlled," Robbie said. "And since we're hoping to use this stuff again, we don't want it to get damaged."

"Right, right," Gray said. "Yeah, of course. I'll make it work."

After helping Robbie stack the boxes against the wall outside her door, Gray entered her apartment and looked around, trying to decide how she could rearrange her things to make room for storage. But as she thought about squeezing the remnants of her Tulsa life into an even smaller footprint, a realization dawned on her: It was time to get her own place.

Living with Cherry and Robbie had been perfect for relocating to a new city on a short timeline. And since she'd moved directly from her parents' house to college dorms to her home with McKenzie, Gray wasn't sure she knew how to live alone. Having her friends just down a flight of stairs kept her loneliness at bay. Gray's hope that finding her soulmate and starting a family was right around the corner had made it easy to justify living off Cherry and Robbie's generosity. But her savings combined with her new salary was plenty to afford a place of her own. And with River growing up and another baby potentially coming soon, Cherry and Robbie needed their house back.

After shifting around the furniture in her room to clear a corner for River's things, Gray switched lanes from searching for a Sagittarius to searching for the perfect apartment. Her dating adventures had taken her to several interesting neighborhoods around town, historic and modern, trendy downtown and family neighborhoods. But Gray couldn't imagine living too far from her chosen family. She found several good options in neighborhoods near Cherry and Robbie's house, a few of which offered tours that very afternoon. After making a short list, she still had some questions about the local housing market and rental process. Her friends were busy setting up River's new toddler furniture. And in any case, Gray didn't want to make them feel like they had pushed her out, especially after she'd already responded poorly to Cherry's news that they were trying to get pregnant. So instead, she called her next-closest friend in the city.

Veronica picked up after only one ring. "Gray! I was just thinking about you."

"You were?" Gray said.

"I'm preparing some materials for next week's board meeting," Veronica said. "I was trying to figure out how to present the current student registration numbers and new state testing protocols without the whole meeting descending into chaos. I was wishing I could do that thing you do where you make problems sound like opportunities."

Gray laughed and settled into her favorite armchair. "Classic PR trick. Being a glass-half-full person is practically a job requirement. I can take a look at whatever you're working on, if you'd like."

"That would be helpful," Veronica said. "But hey, why did you call?"

"Well, I could use a little perspective from a New Orleans person. A New Orleander? A New Orleandickan?"

"A New Orleanian," Veronica said, a smile audible through the phone.

"New Orleanian, right," Gray said, smiling back. "I'm doing a little apartment hunting this morning and was wondering if you had any recommendations. Neighborhoods, apartment complexes, management companies, realtors. Any advice would be great, since finding a home in the Big Easy seems to be big hard."

"Gray," Veronica said, her voice serious. "I've been training for this moment my whole life. I scroll through Zillow to help me fall asleep at night. I'm literally watching HGTV right now."

"Really?"

"Really!" Veronica said. "Tell me what you're looking for."

With Veronica's enthusiastic support, Gray felt her stress melt away, the exact opposite response to their first conversation when Veronica nearly had her fired. They talked for a while about Gray's must-haves, budget, and ideal local amenities. When Gray mentioned some of the apartments she was eyeing, Veronica demanded that she send her the links, and soon they were flipping through online listings together, comparing pros and cons. Gray listed the units she was planning to tour that afternoon.

"Can I come with you?" Veronica asked.

"Oh my god, are you serious? That would be amazing," Gray said. "To be honest, I've never toured homes alone before. I was always looking with my ex."

"I hadn't either before my divorce," Veronica said. "It's definitely better to have a second set of eyes. And since Karys is with her dad this weekend, I'd love to have something else to do with my Saturday afternoon besides work."

"So it's a win-win," Gray said, suddenly looking forward to her search for a new home instead of dreading it. "I'll pick you up in an hour."

IT WAS HARD for Gray to believe how quickly things had moved once Veronica was involved in the apartment hunt. She'd come to understand Principal Veronica, Mom Veronica, and a bit of Friend Veronica, but Gray was surprised to find that Real Estate Veronica was a different persona entirely. She was optimistic, visionary, delighted by the tiniest details. Gray had never seen Veronica more amped up than when she was espousing the benefits of a good ceiling fan.

The decision to start looking for a new place in earnest had only struck Gray that morning, and by dinnertime, she'd signed a yearlong lease on a two-bedroom apartment with hardwood floors, exposed brick, and lots of windows in the Lower Garden District. The tastefully maintained historic building was on a shady oak-lined street tucked between an artsy antiques store and a vegan café. Veronica had somehow managed to negotiate the monthly rent down by two hundred dollars.

Later, as Gray and Veronica were enjoying banh mi at a small Vietnamese restaurant down the block from her new place, Gray was still marveling at the pictures she'd taken of the apartment during the tour. "Can you believe the breakfast bar?" Gray said, zooming in on a photo of the kitchen and showing it to Veronica.

"All the beautiful architecture of the French Quarter at half the price," Veronica said. "I told you we should look upriver. And it's only a ten-minute drive from my house."

Gray glowed, pleased that Veronica wanted her nearby. Having such a meaningful friendship after only a couple of months made Gray feel like New Orleans really could be her new home.

"So how'd that date go yesterday?" Veronica asked. "Scorpio, right?"

Gray took a bite of her banh mi and chewed over Veronica's question. "I think 'bizarre' is the only word to describe it. Or maybe 'farcical.'"

As Gray told her the full story of her lunch with Niko, Veronica was surprised and delighted in equal measure. "I'm sorry for the wild ride, but I've got to say I'm enjoying living vicariously through you," she said when Gray finished. "All of the excitement without any of the personal drama."

"I'm glad someone's enjoying it, because I don't know that I'm much closer to finding my soulmate than when I started," Gray confessed. "I thought the answer would be clearer than this."

"Well, you're not done yet, right?" Veronica said. "What sign is next?"

"Sagittarius."

"Do you have a date with a Sagittarius lined up?"

Gray nodded. "Meeting tomorrow for coffee and a walk through Crescent Park around ten. Arielle. She's an interpreter, speaks like four languages or something. And she has a cute cat named Pistachio."

"Cute cats are always a good sign." Veronica looked at some of the jalapeños Gray had removed from her sandwich and left on her plate. "Can I have those?"

Gray nodded and slid her plate closer to Veronica, who swept them onto her own dish and popped one into her mouth. Gray flinched. "Wait, you're eating raw jalapeños just, like, by themselves?"

"Yes, they're delicious," Veronica said, her face entirely calm.

Gray knew if she'd bitten into a slice of raw jalapeño, she'd be crying in pain. "Just like that? Seeds and all?"

Veronica swallowed, shrugged, and tossed another slice onto her tongue. "I like the tingly sensation on my taste buds. What, you don't eat spicy peppers?"

"Sure I do," Gray said, immediately defensive. "Just, like, not on its own like that. Mixed into a stir-fry or on a pizza or something."

"Yet you pulled them off of your sandwich just now," Veronica said.

"Yeah, well, I don't look as cute as you when I eat them," Gray said. "You're practically glowing with Scovilles. I get all red and blotchy and teary-eyed."

"They're the best-kept secret of my beauty routine," Veronica said, striking a pose with her chin resting on her hand. At the uncharacteristic gesture, Gray wondered if her own goofiness was starting to rub off on Veronica. "Anyway, the dating challenge. I don't think I know anything about Sagittarius. What's their deal?"

"From what I've gathered, they like to go off the beaten path. Enjoy rooting for the underdog. Appreciate unique experiences and travel." Gray paused to take a sip of her smoothie. "And they're fire signs, like me. I've liked the first two fire signs I met, so I guess I'm expecting it to go well." She stopped short of explaining to Veronica that she'd had exhilarating sexual encounters with both fire signs, deciding it was a bit much for her straight friend.

"So maybe your third fire sign will provide some of the clarity you're looking for," Veronica said. "What's your sign again?"

"Aries."

Veronica nodded. "And what are Aries supposed to be like?"

"Go-getters. Competitive. Enthusiastic. Passionate."

"That sounds like you," Veronica said.

Gray sat up a little straighter, pleased. "What's your sign?" she asked. They'd talked plenty about astrology but not about where Veronica fell in the zodiac. "No, wait. Let me guess. Gemini?"

"What makes you think that?" Veronica asked, a playful look on her face.

"You're so different at work than you are now that I've gotten to know you outside of the school," Gray said. "Geminis are 'the twins' because they're . . . What's a nice way of saying two-faced?"

Veronica laughed. "Multilayered? Full of surprises?" she offered.

"Exactly. Not that it's a bad thing! My best friend, Cherry, is a Gemini, and I obviously love the shit out of her," Gray said. "So am I right? You're a Gemini?"

Suspense built while Veronica drank from her Vietnamese coffee. Finally, she finished and shook her head. "Guess again."

"Damn." Gray thought for a moment before landing on a second hunch. "Are you an Aries like me?" Veronica didn't answer, instead gesturing for Gray to continue with her reasoning. "You're obviously a go-getter, considering you were made principal at such a young age. And I feel like we, you know, get each other. We have similarities."

A small smile curled Veronica's lips. "I agree that we 'get each other.' But I'm not an Aries."

"Okay, okay, one more try." Gray reflected on the dates she'd been on so far. None of the people she'd met seemed much like the woman sitting across from her. Maybe she was one of the signs Gray hadn't yet dated or learned much about. "Capricorn? You could be an earth sign because you're so grounded, and I'm pretty sure Capricorns are also passionate about their careers."

"Nope," Veronica said.

Gray huffed out a frustrated breath. "All right, then, I give up. What are you?"

"Aquarius."

"Oh! I haven't gotten to Aquarius yet," Gray said. "But aren't they, like, hippies and free spirits or whatever?"

Veronica assumed a mock-offended expression. "Is my spirit not free enough for you?"

"I guess you were wearing tie-dye that first time I saw you in the park. Anyway, most of what I know about Aquariuses I learned from *Hair*." She sang a few lines about the dawning of the age of Aquarius until Veronica stopped her, laughing.

"You'll have to tell me what you learn about Aquariuses after your date," Veronica said. "Maybe they'll win the whole thing. Is it weird if I'm rooting for them?"

"Not weird," Gray said. "You've got to root for the home team. I'd be rooting for Aries if I hadn't already learned my lesson with McKenzie."

Veronica slurped the last of her coffee. "So when are you going to move into the new place?"

"The lease technically starts on March thirty-first, so I guess I'll try to move everything before my birthday on April fourth so I can wake up in my new digs," Gray said, mapping out the timeline in her head.

"Do you need movers?" Veronica asked. "One of the dads in

the PTA owns a moving company. I bet I could get him to give you a discount."

"For real? That would be amazing," Gray said. "I thought I could make it to thirty before being too old to move my own stuff, but last time I pulled something in my shoulder carrying my dresser up the stairs."

"Save that energy for packing and unpacking." Veronica looked down at her watch. "You should probably get started now, since you've only got a little over a week. Mind dropping me off on your way home?"

Gray agreed, although she felt a smidge disappointed that her day with Veronica was coming to an end. They said goodbye with a hug once they reached Veronica's house, and Gray promised to update her on her Sagittarius date during their next meeting at the middle school. Somehow Gray seemed to actually look forward to Monday mornings now.

Nineteen

GRAY ARRIVED AT the French Quarter the next morning in a pair of comfortable sneakers with a sense of optimism for the date ahead. Her conversations with Arielle on Mercurious had been brief but promising. Cherry's suggested icebreaker—most exciting place you've ever traveled—hadn't helped get the conversation going. But Arielle, who apparently hated chatting via text, promised to think it over and have an answer by the time she met up with Gray in person.

Upon entering the coffee shop where they'd agreed to meet, Gray searched for the wavy brown shoulder-length hair and big smile she'd seen on Arielle's profile. After a few minutes of searching and waiting, Gray's desire for caffeine won out and she ordered a latte. She was seated and well into her drink by the time Arielle actually arrived, almost twenty minutes late, enough to take the shine off Gray's enthusiasm.

"Gray! Hey!" Arielle said, spotting her date from the door. She walked over to Gray's table and dropped her messenger bag on an empty chair. "Sorry I'm late. I don't believe in clocks. Let me get coffee and we can get moving."

"Nice to meet you too," Gray said grumpily to Arielle's back, already halfway to the cashier.

But once they set off on the walking path along the Mississippi River, Gray couldn't help but be charmed by the urban park, city views, and Arielle's laissez-faire attitude. Although there were plenty of plaques and maps directing their attention to the park's architecture and history, Arielle pointed out things Gray never would have noticed. She directed Gray's attention to a rusted old railcar half overtaken by ivy, a colorful mural visible across the river, and a cluster of bees peacefully enjoying the flowers on the sunny spring day. It was a delightful reminder that even after exploring New Orleans for almost two months, there was so much more to see.

Coming upon a fenced dog park, Arielle and Gray sat on a bench to watch the pups play. They laughed about the power dynamics between an enormous Great Dane and a tiny fluff ball of a dog who appeared to be bossing him around. Settling into an easy conversation, Gray asked Arielle if she'd had some time to think about the most exciting place she'd visited.

Arielle chewed her lip. "It's a tough question. I travel a ton for translating jobs and for fun, so much I sometimes wonder why I bother paying rent at all." She paused and took a sip from her cold brew. "What's your answer?"

"I haven't traveled extensively, probably not as much as you," Gray said. "But I used to work for a queer-wedding-planning company and occasionally got to travel for some of the bigger destination weddings."

Arielle sat up straighter, intrigued. "Really? Didn't you say you moved here from Oklahoma?"

"Yeah. Kind of a surprising place for a bunch of queer weddings, right?" Gray said. "But I think it's even more important in a red state to have a business like that. To make sure you won't encounter any negativity when working with vendors and whatnot."

Arielle nodded. "I guess that makes sense."

"Anyway, I went to this one wedding in Bangkok and it was completely magical. The grooms rode in on elephants through a waterfall. I mean, it doesn't get better than that. But everything about Thailand was amazing. The beaches, the food, the architecture, the history, it's all fantastic. I even went out to this gay island with . . . a friend." Gray had narrowly caught herself before mentioning her ex. It had been a romantic and passionate side trip during their time in Thailand. But remembering what happened when she bent the rules about sharing her relationship history on her date with Niko, she pulled back on the more personal details. "It's basically just a whole island of the most beautiful beaches you've ever seen and really fun queer clubs. Gay heaven, basically."

"Wow," Arielle said. "I've heard Thailand is gay friendly, but I've never been."

"Definitely worth a trip," Gray said. "So what's your answer?"

"I've been to plenty of the places that are supposed to be the most exciting. You know, Paris, Sydney, Tokyo, London, São Paulo." Arielle gazed out at the water, the sun glowing on her golden skin. "But the place I remember most fondly, the one that surprised me the most, it's a lot closer. Have you heard of Avery Island?"

Gray shook her head.

"It's not far from here, but it feels like its own cool little world," Arielle said, a dreamy look on her face. "It's in the middle of the bayou and the whole thing is made of salt and—"

"*Made* of salt? How does that even work?" Gray asked.

"It's this huge dome of salt deposits from the Mississippi," Arielle said. "They mine it and everything. And you know Tabasco, the hot sauce? It was invented on Avery Island and they have this whole museum and factory you can tour and a tasting room and everything. When I was there, they let me taste the pepper mash straight from the aging barrels and I still dream of it. I pity people who don't eat hot sauce. They'll never understand the thrill. Do you like spicy food?"

"Sure," Gray said, remembering her conversation about jalapeños with Veronica the previous day. "That all sounds amazing. Gotta admit I'm still struggling to picture an island made of salt though. Is it, like, a giant Himalayan salt lamp?" Gray tried to picture a glowing rocky pink island akin to the birthday gift she'd bought McKenzie a few years back.

"No, it doesn't really look like salt." Arielle contemplated how to explain it. "The island is super lush and green and has a bunch of wildlife. But it's still . . . different. I guess you have to see it to understand it." Arielle looked at Gray, then down at her watch. "Do you have afternoon plans, by chance?"

Gray had planned to get a jump start on packing, but that didn't sound as fun as seeing what surprises Arielle had in store. "You know, my calendar just opened up."

"Then let's go!"

"Go where?" Gray asked, looking away from a corgi she'd been watching chase a schnauzer.

"Avery Island!" Arielle said, sitting up straighter on the bench. "It's only a couple hours' drive, and we can visit the Tabasco factory and look around a little." Turning to Gray, Arielle assumed a similar puppy-eyed expression to the dogs in the park across from them. "What's more fun than a spur-of-the-moment Sunday road trip? I'll drive if you'll pitch in for gas."

Although she knew getting into a car with a stranger to travel across the state was objectively a bad idea, Gray was intrigued. She'd been wanting to see more of her new home state anyway, right? After thinking it over for a minute, Gray shrugged. "Let's do it!"

It didn't take long for them to walk back through the park to Arielle's SUV. Gray waited patiently as Arielle collected an armful of detritus from the passenger seat and shoved it into the trunk. They buckled in, and between Arielle's special playlist for impromptu road trips, chatting about past favorite spur-of-the-moment adventures, and a highly competitive game of spotting wildlife within view of the car, the two-hour journey was over before they knew it.

As their entire drive had been through the vibrant green bay-
ous of southern Louisiana, Gray was disappointed to find that
Avery Island didn't appear any different from the surrounding
areas. She wasn't quite sure what she was expecting—sandy salt
shores or maybe visible mounds of minerals. But she was still
happy to be along for the ride. Arielle navigated to a group of
redbrick buildings tucked among the gnarled oaks draped in
Spanish moss. It was the Tabasco headquarters, marked with
large pepper-shaped signs and colorful statues.

Gray paid for their tickets and they set off on a self-guided
tour of the museum, reading about Avery Island's history and
the founding of the hot sauce brand. The next stop after the museum was a small greenhouse filled with pepper plants like those
cultivated to make the sauce. Gray was enchanted by the bright,
colorful peppers that looked almost like Christmas lights strung
on the bushes. Meanwhile, Arielle only had eyes for the giant
warehouse where the peppers were mashed, preserved with Avery
Island salt, and aged in giant wooden barrels.

"God, I wish I could steal a whole barrel in the back of my
car," Arielle said dreamily. "Think of all the good stuff in those
barrels. Pure spicy deliciousness, none of the vinegar watering it
down. Hope your taste buds are ready."

"I'm a fire sign, you know I can take the heat," Gray quipped.
It was big talk for someone who'd been known to cry from a little too much horseradish.

After seeing the barrels, they got a peek at what Gray had
hoped to see upon arrival on the island: towering walls of salt. A
special room on the tour was designed to imitate the salt mines
beneath Avery Island's surface. Gray gaped at the layered, coarse
texture of the room and stopped to read every sign about the
salt's uses, as well as the mastodon and mammoth fossils found
preserved in it.

Gray and Arielle got a glimpse of the bottling process and

then headed to the gift shop and tasting table. Arielle pulled up a stool and asked for two full tasting experiences, rubbing her hands together in anticipation. An employee provided them with cups of oyster crackers and pointed out the suggested order, from least spicy to most spicy.

"Scared?" Arielle asked, watching Gray uncap the first bottle.

"I'm not afraid of anything," Gray said, her palms beginning to sweat with fear.

It started off easy with a sweet-and-spicy sauce, one that even Gray could eat without flinching. The next three sauces, a mild green jalapeño, tangy buffalo, and cayenne garlic, brought a pinkish blush to Gray's cheeks, but she was mostly able to cover her discomfort. Tabasco's take on sriracha was the first sauce to leave a lingering heat in her mouth, although Arielle seemed to not mind at all, mounding a terrifying amount of sauce onto her cracker. The smoky chipotle sauce caused Gray to suck in a breath of cool air, which she hid by gushing about how delicious it would be with barbecue. By the time they hit the classic red Tabasco Sauce, Gray felt a tingle of sweat emerging along her hairline.

"Finally, we're getting to the good stuff," Arielle said. She glanced over at Gray, who was fanning herself with a sheet of tasting notes. "Wait, is the basic sauce too hot for you?"

"What? No! It's hot sauce for babies," Gray said, trying to control the rush of saliva in her mouth.

"You sure? Your face is looking a little red."

Gray wiped her forehead with the back of her hand. "Just warm in here, is all."

Arielle looked skeptical but didn't push the issue. Next up was a habanero sauce. Gray gently tilted the bottle to get the smallest drop possible on her cracker, but it was still enough to scorch her taste buds. "Yum," she said, although it was hard to get out, as her tongue was beginning to go numb.

"Your neck is kinda blotchy," Arielle said. "Do you want to stop?"

"I'm fine!" Gray said. "Eyes on your own cracker!"

Arielle looked pleased by Gray's refusal to give up. "We have one sauce left, but if we're going by the Scoville scale, we should try the mash first, because the Scorpion Sauce is hotter," she said. Arielle pulled a jar of roughly mashed peppers and salt toward them along with two tiny spoons. "Ready? This is where the magic happens." Gray nodded, and Arielle went first, filling her spoon with the red paste. She popped the mash into her mouth, savoring it like a fine cheese. "God, it's even better than I remembered. Oh! Got some heat too."

If Arielle was commenting on the heat after seeming unbothered so far, Gray knew this one was going to leave her breathing smoke. But she couldn't walk away now. This was the main draw for the entire trip. Gray dipped the tip of her spoon into the mash and pulled out a tiny dot. After a steadying breath, she tasted it. The first moment was delicious, sweet and ripe and flavorful, but the fire came in only a second behind, flooding her cheeks, her sinuses, her whole head with a tingly burning sensation.

"What do you think?" Arielle asked, still smacking her lips.

"Dewiciouth!" Gray said, her voice hoarse, tears streaming down her cheeks.

Seeing the expression Gray couldn't hide, Arielle burst out laughing. "Too spicy for you."

"No!" Gray said, refusing to admit defeat. "I love it. Too bad I can't have seconds without double-dipping." She picked up a napkin and wiped the tears from her face, then blew her nose.

"Should I ask them for another spoon?" Arielle tested Gray's commitment by starting to raise her hand for the employee's attention.

Gray grabbed Arielle's hand and pushed it back down. "No! I, uh, don't want to be greedy."

Arielle slid over the final bottle, one with an ominous black label. "Then I hope you're ready for the big finale."

Her mouth and throat still stinging, Gray hesitated, looking at the bottle with wide eyes.

"We drove all this way for you to quit now?" Arielle looked at Gray expectantly, then shrugged. "I thought you could handle the heat, but I guess you're too scared."

"I'm not scared!" Gray said, unable to back down from a challenge.

"That's my girl!" Arielle pounded Gray on the back, then uncapped the bottle and handed it to her. "You've got this."

Gray shook a dash of the sauce onto a cracker and downed it before she could have any second thoughts. With this bite, the fire hit in no time at all. Her vision seeming to cloud, Gray coughed and jumped up from her stool. "Water," she croaked.

Still chewing on her own cracker covered in Scorpion Sauce, Arielle patted Gray's back sympathetically. "Water will only make it worse. Have another cracker or two."

Gray followed Arielle's directions, and eventually, the burning faded away. She sat back down and mopped the sweat and tears from her face with a fresh napkin.

"What a champ," Arielle said, an amused expression on her face. She seemed unfazed by the spiciest sauce the brand had to offer. "But you've got to work on that tolerance if you're going to make it in New Orleans, you know. I've never seen anyone get so flushed over a little hot sauce."

" 'A little hot sauce,' she says," Gray grumbled. "As if I didn't just try nine hot sauces and some weird mash delivered straight from hell."

Arielle patted Gray's shoulder, laughing. "You were very brave."

Gray let her saliva do the rest of the work of clearing the burning sensation from her mouth while she and Arielle wandered the gift shop. Remembering the satisfied look on Veronica's face as she snacked on raw jalapeños the previous day, Gray picked up a variety pack of limited-edition hot sauces to bring her as a souvenir, along with adult- and kid-sized aprons with the Tabasco logo for Veronica and Karys. It wasn't until she was in line at the cash register that she realized she should probably pick up souvenirs for Cherry, Robbie, and River too. She grabbed a couple of adult T-shirts and a Tabasco-branded teddy bear and checked out.

After grabbing sandwiches at the on-site restaurant, Arielle and Gray hit the road to return home. As they neared the city, jamming out to Arielle's playlist, Gray wondered where Sagittarius might rank on her short list. She'd really enjoyed their adventure, and she liked Arielle's curiosity, enthusiasm, and competitive spirit. But she also felt no desire to pursue Arielle romantically. Remembering how relieved she'd been by Riley's honesty on her second astrology date at the unopened café, Gray decided to make a similar move.

"Today was a blast," Gray said, looking at the sun setting over the bayou. "Thanks for showing me Avery Island. I totally loved it."

"It was fun, wasn't it?" Arielle said.

"Yeah." Gray ran a hand along the side of her head. "And I feel like we have this awesome connection, but maybe more . . . as friends?"

"Obviously," Arielle said.

"Oh," Gray said, surprised, relieved, and a tiny bit disappointed. It was hard not to feel a sting of rejection, even if she'd started it.

Arielle's eyes left the road long enough to glance at Gray, and the smile on her face showed no ill will. "I knew when you started sweating at the classic Tabasco that we weren't meant to be," she said. "How can there be a spark between us when you're scared of the burn?"

Gray couldn't help but laugh. "So you aren't attracted to me because I can't handle hot sauce?"

"Exactly," Arielle said, now laughing at her own gustatory standards. "But I'm down to be friends."

Gray breathed a sigh of relief. "Cool. Well, on our next hot sauce tour, maybe I'll take a pass on the hottest one."

"If we're going to be friends, you should know that I'll always goad you into trying the hottest sauce," Arielle said.

"And I'll probably always fall for it," Gray admitted. As the last bit of daylight cast a glow across the car, Gray smiled at the thought that her astrology experiment might help her keep exploring new things long past her final first date.

Twenty

GRAY DROPPED A gift bag on Veronica's desk the moment she arrived at St. Charles Collegiate Academy for her Monday morning meeting, an anticipatory smile on her face.

"What's this?" Veronica asked.

"Just a little something that reminded me of you."

Veronica arched an eyebrow curiously, then dug in and found the set of hot sauces. After a brief pause, she said, "Tabasco sauce reminded you of me? I'm the 'spicy Latina,' is that all you think of me?"

Gray's panic was immediately apparent on her face. "No! No, not at all, I was just thinking of the jalapeño—"

Veronica cackled, her face breaking into a satisfied grin. "Wow, I really got you with that one."

Gray buried her face in her hands, embarrassed. "Oh my god. I was halfway to planning another massive book donation."

"You'd have to find someone to fund a library expansion first." Veronica looked closer at the gift in her hand. "Cranberry serrano sounds delicious. Thank you."

"I went to the Tabasco factory!" Gray said, still feeling the need to apologize. "I didn't just, like, see hot sauce and think of you."

Digging back into the bag, Veronica pulled out the two aprons.

"For you and Karys," Gray said as Veronica unfolded them. "Since real chefs always wear an apron."

"My mom and I always used to wear matching aprons when I was a kid and she was teaching me how to cook," Veronica said, her expression softer than before. "They're wonderful. Karys will love them."

Gray mentally patted herself on the back. "I'm glad. And I've got another gift. This one's less for you personally, but I think you'll like it all the same." She went on to tell Veronica that, after a few very persuasive phone calls, a local bank was planning to sponsor five scholarships for promising students from high-need families in each grade of the middle school for at least the next three years.

Veronica blinked. "Now you're the one pranking me."

"Am not!" Gray said. "I heard they were looking to raise their philanthropic profile, and I found out the CEO has a set of twins that just started kindergarten on the elementary campus. He has zero ties to the parents and board members giving you grief. I checked." The tip-off had come from Robbie, who worked in the bank's IT department. It was good to have friends in high places—or at least places full of cash. "The bank will give you total control over the student selection and retention process," Gray continued. "And they're thinking of those three years as a trial period. If it goes well, they'll hopefully make a more permanent commitment."

"What about when those kids move on to the high school?" Veronica asked, clearly looking for a downside.

"They're open to adding scholarships at the high school level too."

A slight frown displayed Veronica's skepticism. "That's a lot of money. Why would they do all that?"

"Plenty of reasons," Gray said. "Tax breaks, good PR, fulfilling the promises for their own DEI initiatives. They've grown significantly in recent years, so they had some extra charitable dollars to spread around." She crossed an ankle over her knee and leaned closer. "Now you just need to meet with them sometime this week to get them to sign on the dotted line."

"This week? Is that enough time for me to do the research to be appropriately convincing?"

Gray pulled a file folder from the bag she'd placed by her chair, then dropped it on the desk in front of Veronica. "I already did the research for you. I've got talking points and background on each of the executives so you know what's most likely to move them. And besides, they've already verbally committed. You just have to be yourself, tell them why this matters to you."

"You make it sound so easy," Veronica said, her expression a mix of apprehension and hope.

"It is. They'll recognize your expertise and passion as quickly as I did when I first met you," Gray said, grinning. "But maybe don't threaten to kick them out of your office if they're running a few minutes late."

THE WEEK SEEMED to fly by without a second to think about her next date. Gray ran into Veronica on campus every day while running a series of focus groups with students, parents, and alumni to help craft their new marketing plans. Even so, she felt a rush of joy upon spotting Veronica on their usual park bench on Thursday afternoon, waving as she pushed her sunglasses on top of her dark hair. Gray wanted to hear all about Veronica's Thursday morning meeting with the bank executives, which had gone perfectly according to plan. But even more, she wanted to relax and chat with her friend while River and Karys played. Before parting ways, Karys talked Gray into joining her on the monkey bars, and although her upper-body strength wasn't as robust as when she was a child, she managed to make it from one side to the other as Veronica and River cheered from the ground.

But when Gray woke up on Friday and looked at her work calendar, she realized with a jolt that time to find her soulmate was running out. Her birthday was in one week. One week to go on three more dates before Saturn return was officially aligned. It felt like a total reversal from the start of the challenge, when her thrilling date with Carmen had distracted her so much she'd almost ruined her chance at impressing Veronica with her public relations prowess. Now work was getting in the way of her romantic goals.

So Gray turned her attention to finding a Capricorn, the final earth sign in the zodiac. An ambitious young law student named Tara stood out from the start. Cherry's suggested icebreaker— "As a kid, what did you want to be when you grew up?"—had led Tara to reveal her lifelong dream of becoming mayor of New Orleans. And she appreciated Gray's ambitious childhood goal of splitting her time between professional softball and rocket science. (She'd dropped the latter career plan when she realized how many science classes were required to become a scientist.)

Conveniently, Tara was quick to bring up meeting in person. That may have been for less than romantic purposes, since she seemed primarily interested in recruiting Gray to volunteer at a small-business market the following morning. But considering her sense of urgency to complete her challenge, Gray decided that was close enough to a date. Even if it meant she had to wake up at the crack of dawn to participate.

Gray dressed in the shadowy predawn hours, sneaked out of her apartment before the rest of the house was awake, and drove to a spot near the river she recognized from her walk through the park with Arielle the previous weekend. But this time, instead of a few bikers, joggers, or dog walkers, Gray found herself walking among a crowd of vendors setting up tents and unloading items for sale.

"Gray!" a voice yelled from her right. Gray looked over to see Tara seated behind a folding table with a clipboard in hand, her glossy black hair in a thick braid down her back. As soon as Gray arrived at the table, Tara wrapped her in a hug. Tara's soft curves and warm welcome made their embrace feel familiar, not like they were meeting for the first time. "Thanks for coming! What shirt size do you wear?"

"Medium." Gray noticed the breathable material of Tara's bright-blue polo with a New Orleans Chamber of Commerce logo on the breast. "Oh, that's nice. Do I get one?"

"You only get a polo after a hundred hours of volunteer service," Tara said, then ducked under the table and returned with an unflattering neon-yellow T-shirt. "But until then, you get this very fashionable tee!" She held it up and turned it around to show VOLUNTEER printed across the back over a larger image of the same logo from the polo.

Gray pulled off her sweatshirt and pulled the T-shirt over her tank, then struck a pose with her hands on her hips. Even though she'd mostly gotten over the awkwardness of starting a first date, she was grateful for another activity to jump right into, like her first date at pub trivia. Having a task to do always seemed to make things run a little smoother when meeting someone new. It put her more in PR get-the-job-done mode, which apparently some people found charming. "All right, put me to work."

Tara handed Gray a clipboard with a numbered map of booths and explained how it coordinated with a list of vendors on the backside, then showed Gray where to check in sellers as they arrived. When a vendor approached the table, Gray watched as Tara cheerily marked them off the list and pointed them to their designated area.

"Here comes Kayvone from Light Me Up Candles," Tara said as a woman with a rolling cart full of boxes came toward them. "Why don't you check her in?"

Gray referenced the list of booths and looked up just in time as Kayvone reached the table. "Good morning! Light Me Up Candles, right? Your booth is number twenty-seven, down there on the right next to the red tent for"—she paused to look at her clipboard—"Pretty Paws Pet Supply."

"What's your name?" Kayvone asked.

"Oh. Gray. Sorry, forgot to say that bit. You're Kayvone, right?"

"Thanks, Gray," Kayvone said, then turned to Tara. "She's cute. Another dating app find?"

Tara blushed slightly, but put on an easy smile for Kayvone. "Better get set up, the first shoppers will be here in about twenty minutes."

Kayvone winked at Tara before walking away toward her booth. Her comment stuck in Gray's head as she checked in the next wave of vendors. When they hit a lull, she had to ask. "So you bring a lot of your dates here?"

Tara gave Gray an embarrassed grin. "Hey, I'm a busy person, but I'm still looking for love," she said. "I can two-birds-one-stone my dating life and volunteer recruitment. Saves time and helps the city! Some people even come back. Suneetha, down there handing out water bottles? She's only a handful of events away from earning her own polo. And see that booth selling pralines down there? That's Tiffany. She signed up as a vendor after our date."

"No judgment," Gray said, knowing she certainly couldn't criticize anyone trying to fulfill unique personal goals while on Mercurious. "I admire your dedication. Is all this volunteer management part of your path to becoming mayor of New Orleans?"

"My whole life has been part of that path," Tara said, her eyes lighting up. "New Orleans is the best city in the whole world, and growing up here has been an incredible gift. I want to give back to the city and guide it into the future."

"You've already got your campaign speech ready, I see."

Tara laughed. "I've been workshopping it since my valedictorian speech at high school graduation."

Between checking in vendors, Gray picked Tara's brain about her plans for getting into politics. Once the booths were all claimed, Tara explained how their duties would shift to helping shoppers navigate the market and advising them on the closest ATM and public bathrooms.

The first couple of hours of the small-business market whizzed by in a flurry of customers and small problems to solve. Gray and Tara took turns managing the information table while the other walked through the booths, Gray shopping for a few things to decorate her new apartment, Tara mostly interested in chatting with the sellers. Before Gray realized it, the market was winding down and the vendors were packing up their displays, most carrying considerably lighter boxes than they'd brought.

As Gray helped load the volunteer table into Tara's SUV, she realized they'd hardly had any time to chat about anything besides the market and Tara's future mayorship. "I'm starving. Want to grab an early lunch somewhere? My treat," Gray offered.

"That sounds lovely, but I've got"—Tara pulled out her phone and scrolled through her calendar—"a lot going on this afternoon. I have a study group for my class on land use law, then I'm knocking on doors for a friend running for city council, going to a fundraising dinner for the food bank, and I promised to help my mom with her taxes tonight."

"Wow. That *is* a lot," Gray said, her head spinning. "Do you ever sleep?"

"I'll sleep when I'm dead." Tara shrugged. "Speaking of, I could actually use some coffee. Care to join me for a cup?"

"Sounds great," Gray said. Seeing Tara's enthusiasm and hardworking attitude brought someone else to mind. "And I know just the place. Have you been to Demitasse Café?"

"Oh, I saw that interview with the owner in *The Times-Picayune* and have been meaning to go!" Tara said. "It's all fair-trade and organic, right?"

Gray felt a burst of joy knowing she'd helped facilitate that very article. "Yes, and delicious. You're going to love it." She told Tara the cross streets of the shop, and they both hopped into their separate cars, agreeing to meet once they arrived.

When they found each other on the sidewalk outside the café, Gray was surprised to see that Tara had somehow managed to change clothes during the short drive. Instead of her volunteer polo, Tara was now wearing a stylish trench coat over a cream top, and she'd swapped her sneakers for a pair of chunky tan boots. It made sense that Tara would have wardrobe changes ready in her car with such a packed schedule, Gray realized.

Gray pulled the door open and gestured for Tara to enter. "After you."

Tara nodded her thanks and joined the line to order. Gray pointed out some of her favorite features of the coffee shop, and Tara listened eagerly. Just before they made it to the register, Riley seemed to appear out of nowhere to wrap an arm around Gray's shoulders.

"One of my favorite customers!" Riley pointed to a series of framed vintage photos of celebrities and public figures drinking coffee hung along the wall. "How do you like the new decorations? Your idea."

"They look so glamorous!" Gray said. "It may have been my idea, but you executed it much better than I could have."

"I can't even tell you how many positive comments we've gotten on them." Riley paused, catching sight of Tara. "Who's this?"

"My friend Tara," Gray said, moving aside to allow Tara and Riley to shake hands.

Something in the air seemed to change when their hands connected. There was a new energy pulsing around them, one Gray hadn't noticed in the time she'd spent with either of them before.

"Tara Ortega." Tara looked at Riley's outfit, impeccably styled as always. "I love that jacket. McQueen?"

"Of course," Riley said, her hand still lingering in Tara's. "And your boots are fantastic. Jimmy Choos?"

"My favorite!"

Riley and Tara stared into each other's eyes and Gray felt the distinct discomfort of being a third wheel. Finally, Riley cleared her throat and pulled her hand back from Tara's. "What can I get for you ladies? On the house."

Tara asked for a macchiato, and then shared another charged moment with Riley talking about how it was both of their favorite espresso drinks. Gray interjected eventually to say she'd like one as well, and Riley insisted that she would make them herself. As they watched Riley prepare their drinks on the state-of-the-art espresso maker, Tara complimented Riley's taste in designing the café and menu. Once she mentioned her volunteer role at the chamber of commerce, Riley insisted on sitting down with them to talk about resources she could utilize as a small-business owner. Conversation flowed easily between the two of them as Gray sat back, sipping her macchiato and watching their chemistry sparkle. Eventually, she stood up and excused herself for a made-up appointment. Riley and Tara hardly seemed to notice, as they were so deep in discussion of how Riley might sell coffee at the monthly small-business market. Gray made her exit while mentally patting herself on the back for playing such an adept matchmaker. The planets may not have guided her to dates with Riley and Tara for her own romantic purposes, but Gray was happy to be a tool in the universe's plans for the Taurus and Capricorn.

Twenty-one

WHAT HAD GRAY been thinking when she decided to sign a lease that started the week of her birthday? The same week she was due to complete her dating challenge, and in the midst of a busy semester at St. Charles Collegiate Academy? It seemed Saturn return really was pushing her toward big life changes.

When she'd told Cherry and Robbie about her new apartment, they'd been nothing but supportive. In fact, between oohing and aahing over the pictures she'd taken during her tour, they'd even seemed a little sad Gray wouldn't be under the same roof. Maybe it was their bittersweet reaction that had Gray feeling glum about the big move. Or perhaps it was because Gray wasn't sure she felt "grown-up" enough to move into her own space for the first time. So she made a plan to show her friends—and herself—just how ready she was to live alone. Gray would make dinner for Cherry, Robbie, and River using the pasta recipe she'd learned from Veronica. It was the perfect way to prove she'd learned to be a little more self-reliant in the kitchen. Or at least she was capable of learning. And it would provide the perfect going-away dinner to celebrate her last night in the garage apartment.

By 6 P.M., everything was going to plan. Cherry, Robbie, and River were out for a walk. The chicken was grilled and the tomatoes were perfectly sliced, although Veronica's plate method somehow still ended with a little juice splashed on Gray's T-shirt. Maybe she should have gotten herself one of those Tabasco aprons too. Gray found a heavy, lidded casserole dish and loaded it with olive oil, tomatoes, roasted red peppers, and seasoning. She set the microwave for five minutes, then ran upstairs to her apartment to change her shirt.

The first hint that something had gone wrong was the bright flash of purple light Gray saw when she entered the kitchen. Then there was the smell, something bitter and smoky instead of garlicky and delicious. But it wasn't until she saw the flames lighting up the inside of the microwave that she realized exactly how wrong her plans had gone. She turned off the microwave immediately and waited for the flames to die down before opening the door and fanning away the smoke. It appeared the dish, one she'd assumed was microwave safe, had metal screws attaching the handles. Those had somehow managed to catch the oil on fire, which in turn cracked the ceramic dish into pieces, leaving the microwave a scorched mess and dinner inedible. Cherry, Robbie, and River returned just in time to find Gray cursing at the catastrophe and burning her fingers on the rubble.

Cherry told Robbie to entertain River in the living room and jumped into action. She somehow managed to calm Gray, clean up the mess, and create an impromptu pasta dish from the remaining ingredients plus a little butter and Parmesan cheese in under half an hour. But while Cherry had saved dinner, her joking comment about how she should buy a kitchen fire extinguisher as a housewarming gift left Gray feeling even more apprehensive than before. How could she possibly live by herself when she couldn't even figure out how to use a microwave without threatening to burn the house down? How could she ever raise kids when she was still so childish herself?

But with a lease signed and movers coming the next day, it was too late for Gray to chicken out on her new apartment. After buying Cherry and Robbie a new microwave and casserole dish, she spent Sunday evening hiding out in the garage apartment to finish packing her things, which was admittedly pretty easy since she'd only moved in less than two months prior. She was packing up the last of her clothes when she heard a knock on the door.

"It's me!" Gray heard Cherry's voice say through the door. "Just wanted to see if you needed any help."

Gray opened the door, revealing the stacks of boxes and deconstructed furniture behind her. Gray rubbed the back of her neck and looked down at her feet. "Hey, Cher."

"Hey, G." Cherry looked around at the stacks of boxes and empty walls. "Oh. Looks like you've got it under control up here."

Gray grunted noncommittally, turning back to packing a drawer of sweaters.

Sensing Gray's mood, Cherry walked over and leaned against the top of the dresser. "What's wrong? Aren't you excited about your new place? It's gorgeous."

"Excited, sure," Gray said in an unconvincing monotone. "Also stressed. And terrified. And maybe a little disappointed."

"Disappointed?" Cherry said, trying to read Gray's face as she focused on folding a striped maroon sweater. "You don't regret leaving Tulsa, do you?"

"What? No!" Gray said, looking up from the task at hand. "Why would you think that?"

Cherry looked sheepish as she wiped a bit of dust from the edge of the dresser. "When you first told us you were moving, for a moment . . . Well, I thought you might be moving back to get together with McKenzie again."

Gray couldn't help but laugh with surprise. "Seriously?"

"You've been kinda distant lately," Cherry said. "Like you've been sharing all your highs and lows with someone else, someone besides me and Robbie. And with all the dating, I was afraid you'd decided you'd seen enough of the single world and wanted to go back to your comfort zone."

"No way," Gray said. "I mean, yeah, breaking up with McKenzie and moving away from Oklahoma was rough. But being here with you and Robbie has been the only thing keeping me upright. You've been my friend, my family, my landlord, my therapist, everything. I don't know how I can ever repay you."

"Do you have any idea how expensive good babysitters are these days? We're even," Cherry said, a gentle smile on her face. "And having you here has made New Orleans finally really feel like home for me too."

"Same," Gray said. "There's no way I'm going back to McKenzie. If anything, the dates I've been on have shown me that there's more for me out there than I realized. Like, if you'd told me when I first moved here that I'd go on ten dates in less than six weeks, that I'd see cool places and meet new friends and have sex with four new people in that time, I'd have laughed in your face. But I've done all that. I've discovered all these cool hidden corners of the city. I've got this amazing friendship with Veronica after only a month. I think you'll really like her, by the way. And I've realized that love *is* out there for me, with someone who wants a family like I want, someone on the same path. Maybe the stars have been less than crystal clear about who that person is or if I've found them yet. But I'm definitely not going back to Tulsa. Maybe I'll reconnect with McKenzie at some point as friends, but I'm on a path forward now, and I'm not turning back." As soon as she said it, Gray knew it was true.

Cherry faux-sniffled and wiped an invisible tear from her cheek. "You've blossomed from my little fuzzy caterpillar into a beautiful butterfly. You're totally different now from the sad, pitiful Gray who pulled into our driveway in February."

"Pitiful, but still devastatingly handsome, right?"

"Always." Cherry dropped onto the foot of Gray's bed. "So if it's not about McKenzie or Oklahoma, why are you disappointed?"

Gray sat down next to Cherry and crossed her legs. The moment reminded Gray of their childhood sleepovers, of all the years they'd spent whispering secrets in blanket forts and figuring out what they wanted out of life. "Maybe this is my Saturn return talking, but I'm scared to live alone. I know I'm almost twenty-nine years old, a grown-ass adult, but I've never done it before and I'm terrified. What if I suck at being on my own? What if I hate the silence, or lose my keys, or can't figure out what painting to hang on the bedroom wall?"

"You won't suck at being on your own," Cherry said. "If it's too quiet, you'll turn on some music. Give me a spare key in case yours goes missing. And you know I will always provide commentary on your interior decorating, whether or not you ask for it."

"That helps," Gray said. "But what if this apartment isn't what I want? All I've ever dreamed of is a cute house with a garage and a backyard and a wife who loves me and a bunch of kids and a Saint Bernard or whatever. And instead I'm getting this sad little bachelor pad."

Cherry held out her palm. "Show me the pictures again."

Gray pulled out her phone, navigated to the photos of the apartment, and handed it to Cherry.

"First of all, this place is *way* too classy to be a bachelor pad," Cherry said, flipping through the pictures and zooming in for emphasis. "It's got 'wife material' written all over it. And there's nothing sad about this breakfast bar. I can already picture you and your future soulmate having pancakes and mimosas right here."

"As soon as I figure out how to make pancakes," Gray said, feeling a little lighter already.

"Hold on," Cherry said when she reached a picture of the built-in bookshelves in the living room. "Is that Veronica?"

"Yeah, that's her." Gray looked at the candid shot of Veronica checking out the view from the windows.

"But she's hot!" Cherry said. "I thought she was, like, fifty with schoolmarm vibes!"

"She's thirty-six."

Cherry looked between the phone and Gray, who was staring at the photo of Veronica. "Hold on, are y'all a thing? Romantically?"

"What? No!" Gray said forcefully. "She's straight. And my co-worker."

"Your straight co-worker who went apartment hunting with you? Who you've been hanging out with regularly?" Cherry said skeptically.

"It's not like that."

"Okay, just had to make sure." Cherry shrugged and tucked a loose lock of red hair behind her ear. "My point is, this apartment is a total gem. And even if it's not the five-bedroom, three-and-a-half-bathroom family home with a game room and a reading nook and a two-car garage you want, it can still be a great place to live right now. That's why you rented this place instead of buying it, right?" Cherry threw an arm over Gray's shoulders and tilted her closer. "I know it doesn't feel like it right now, but you've got time. You can still have that cute house with all those kids and that Saint Bernard. Think of this apartment as a step toward that, not a change in the plans."

Gray stared at Cherry for a moment before her face broke into a smile.

"What? What are you looking at me like that for?"

"You're gonna be so good at mom pep talks when River gets older," Gray said. "You've always been smart, but this whole life coach thing? It's new."

Cherry let go of Gray's shoulders and leaned back on the bed.

"Well, you're not the only one getting a new perspective on life from Saturn return."

"Oh yeah, you're turning twenty-nine too," Gray said. It was obvious, now that she thought about it, but ever since Cherry and Robbie got married, she'd seemed to have her shit more together than Gray. It was hard to picture her going through the same existential discomfort Madame Nouvelle Lune had pointed out as a symptom of Saturn's movements. "What's come to light for you?"

"For one, I've decided I can't be a stay-at-home mom forever," Cherry said, running her hand along the edge of Gray's quilt. "I love River and want more kids. But I think I want to find something I can do part-time from home too. I've been considering taking a course on graphic design. For, like, branding and advertising and whatnot."

"Oh, Cherry, you'd be great at that!" Gray said earnestly.

"You think so?" Cherry said, clearly pleased with Gray's response.

"Absolutely! People would definitely pay money for those posters you designed for River's room, and you know everyone at my work is still obsessed with that design you made with the Gina Byers Kane quote. You've got a great eye. And I even think I could connect you with some folks who may be interested," Gray said, her mind on Riley's coffee shop and some of the small-business owners from the market with Tara.

"Someday I'll take you up on that," Cherry said. "And I also think Saturn return has something to do with this feeling that it's time for another baby."

"Huh. I guess that makes sense," Gray said. "It's got me wanting, like, five kids. Maybe six. Maybe more. Enough for a family softball team."

Cherry chewed a nail, seeming to contemplate something. "On that topic—and you understand that this is just a random thing I'm telling you, it's not a big announcement—my period is late."

Gray gasped and jumped up from the bed, her hands clasped over her mouth.

"*And* if it's what your face is implying, I will obviously take a test and find out and tell Robbie, who should be the first to know."

Gray lowered her hands and gathered her cool. "Right, of course."

"But you're the first person I've told I'm late, so that's special too," Cherry added.

Gray clapped her hands and bounced on her heels. "Can we do a happy dance?"

"A happy-slash-hopeful dance," Cherry said, standing up from the bed. "Sure."

They grabbed each other's arms and danced around in a circle, giggling like they were back in one of their childhood bedrooms talking about a crush. Once they finished, Cherry stood with her hands on her hips. "Speaking of Saturn return, don't you still have two dates left? And only, what, five days until your birthday?"

Gray ruffled her bangs. "Yeah. I know, it's a little tight."

"You've got this!" Cherry said, jumping right back into pep talk mode. "Aquarius next, right?"

Gray nodded. "Aquarius and Pisces."

"You're going to love Aquarius." Cherry walked over to an open box of books and started rearranging them to make more room. "You've gotten along with both of the other air signs. And Aquariuses are so cool. They're completely themselves, no matter what anyone else thinks, and they see the world through this lens of, like, we can fix this, we can make things better. I have a good feeling about this one."

"I'm mostly just concerned about getting one to agree to go

on a date with me ASAP," Gray said. "Oh, I still need an ice-breaker. Do you have one?"

Cherry thought for a moment while she finished filling the box and folded down the top to close it. "How about 'What's your weirdest hobby?'"

"I can work with that."

"Great." Cherry brushed the dust from her hands onto her leggings. "Well, thank you for the wonderful heart-to-heart, but I better get to bed. Need any help before the movers come in the morning? You know I'll be up early with River anyway."

"I think I'm good. The movers Veronica recommended seem great," Gray said. She wrapped Cherry in a big hug, holding on a couple beats longer than usual. "Thanks for being my bestie, Cherry."

Cherry gave her an extra squeeze before letting go. "Thanks for being *my* bestie, Gray. I can't wait to see your apartment in person."

Once Cherry was gone, Gray collapsed onto her bed, exhausted but feeling far more confident in her new place than an hour before. Remembering Cherry's enthusiasm about Aquariuses, Gray pulled out her phone and updated her search parameters on Mercurious. As she waited for her potential matches to load, she grinned, thinking about how Cherry might be pregnant. It felt good being happy for her friend. Somehow, it made her feel happier for herself about her own next steps. They were both going places, and even if they weren't living at the same address, they were still doing it together.

Twenty-two

*A*S GRAY HAD so recently been reminded, moving is a nightmare. Packing up all the trappings of a life into a series of boxes, debating what memories to keep and what to throw away, unearthing mysteries and mostly unpleasant surprises, only to unload it all again shortly afterward is an exercise in emotional and physical torture.

The challenge had been all the more harrowing a few months earlier, when Gray had to separate her life in Tulsa from her partner's, one item at a time, wondering, Who paid for this decorative basket? Had she chosen that candle scent? When had their important documents gotten shuffled together like a stack of cards? Each drawer held an existential crisis of what belonged to Gray and what belonged to McKenzie, which parts of their life had been shaped by whom. How could she separate a decade of shared decisions, ten years of gluing their lives together a piece at a time? And even more, how could she do it alone over a couple of evenings while McKenzie was out working weddings with all of Gray's friends?

Ultimately, Gray had erred on the side of minimalism, taking the things she absolutely needed or that were hers from before they met. The rest she left so that McKenzie could keep living her normal life in their once-shared home without searching for the scissors or the hand towels or the extension cords only to find they had disappeared along with Gray. Leaving the house mostly intact felt a bit like an apology for blowing up the life they'd created. Sometimes, though, she did wonder if leaving McKenzie in a house full of their nostalgia-laden belongings was its own form of torture. That wasn't how she'd intended it, at least.

But as she moved out of Cherry and Robbie's garage apartment, it was a bit shocking to see that her almost thirty years of life had amounted to only a small pile of boxes and furniture, hardly even justification for hiring the two-person moving crew and truck. She'd taken the whole day off work to move, but the movers were in and out in under two hours, leaving her the rest of the day to unpack. Most of that time was spent shuffling the same few pieces of furniture back and forth as the afternoon light shifted across the wooden floors. It was a novelty to organize and decorate her space without caring what anyone else thought.

Of course, the novelty quickly morphed into frustrated indecision. Should the bed go under the window for optimal sun? Or across from the door to create more open space? Overwhelmed, Gray decided to take a break and check her work inbox on her phone. She was halfway through writing a response to an email from Veronica when she decided she could kill two birds with one stone—or rather, one phone call.

"This is your last warning before I contact your parents *again*, Ian," Gray heard Veronica's voice saying distantly on the other line once the call went through. "I don't want to hear anything more from Mrs. Sanderson about you causing disruptions in class, *especially* regarding hidden mason jars. Do I make myself clear?"

"Yes, Principal Taylor," a tiny voice said.

"Good. Close the door on your way out, please." Gray heard a click, then Veronica's voice sounded loud and clear. "Gray. Hi."

"Mason jars?" Gray asked immediately.

Veronica sighed. "The fifth-grade American history class just learned about Prohibition and seems to have developed a fascination with moonshine. One student has been trying to convince his classmates that his concoction of Dr Pepper, grape juice, and old ketchup will get them drunk."

Gray burst into laughter. "Sounds like you might have inspired the next Jim Beam."

"It would be funnier if his friend hadn't vomited all over the gym after trying it," Veronica said grimly, although Gray could also hear her smile through the phone.

Gray got back to business, answering a few questions Veronica had emailed her about how to announce the bank-sponsored scholarships to the board, now that they were officially in the works. "I'll write a draft memo for you, maybe some FAQs," Gray offered once they'd agreed on a plan. "I can have them on your desk in a couple of days. It can be first order of business once I finish my move."

"The move!" Veronica said. "How's it going? Oh, you shouldn't have called me while you're supposed to be off work."

"No problem. Talking to you hardly feels like work," Gray said. "And it's going pretty well. The movers you recommended were fantastic and superfast. Now it's just me, begging my furniture to tell me where it's supposed to go. The bed is being particularly tight-lipped."

"Against the wall across from the door, obviously," Veronica said.

"Whoa, I've been staring at this room for an hour but you just *know* like that?"

"It makes sense. It gives you more space for a bedside table, and it won't block your access to opening the window. More floor space too."

Gray snapped her fingers. "I thought about the floor space part, but the rest didn't even occur to me. You know, if you ever get tired of this principal thing, you might have a future in interior design."

"I think interior design takes a little more skill than knowing where to put a bed." Gray heard Veronica's desk chair squeak like she was leaning back. "Anyway, your birthday's sneaking up on us. When's your Aquarius date?"

"Tonight at five," Gray said, plopping down in her armchair and imagining she was sitting across from Veronica in her office. "At the art museum in City Park. Kristen. She's working on a PhD in anthropology at Tulane. Seems pretty cool."

"Oh, an academic," Veronica said in a singsongy voice. "I was already rooting for Aquarius, but she sounds like a real winner. I better let you go so you can get your apartment together. If things go well, you may want to invite her back for a nightcap."

"Don't you put that pressure on me, Veronica Taylor!" Gray said in a faux chiding voice. "But I probably should run. Thanks for the design advice. I'll see you soon."

"Good luck tonight!" Veronica said before ending the call.

BUOYED BY VERONICA'S Aquarian enthusiasm, Gray got her furniture settled and a few pieces of art on the walls. She wouldn't want a messy apartment to get in the way of astrological magic, if this really was her destiny. And even with all the unpacking she accomplished that afternoon, Gray still managed to pick an outfit—a simple but flattering maroon Henley, jeans, and the same boots she'd worn to visit Madame Nouvelle Lune—and arrive at the art museum five minutes early. Gray settled down on a bench beside the front doors and arranged herself in a casual pose that boldly declared "eligible lesbian bachelor."

Five minutes ticked by as Gray smiled at anyone who looked even a bit like Kristen's profile picture on Mercurious. Then ten minutes. At fifteen minutes after their designated meeting time, Gray double-checked her chat history with Kristen to make sure she was at the right spot, then messaged her to ask if they were still on for the date. It wasn't until another ten minutes after that missive that Gray started to feel the dull burn of being stood up.

Gray was pacing the sidewalk in front of the museum, wondering how long she should wait before giving up, when her phone buzzed. She pulled it out of her pocket eagerly expecting a note from Kristen saying she would be there any moment, but instead found a text from Veronica.

*How's it going? Is your Aquarius
living up to my high expectations?*

Gray typed out a response, a bit embarrassed of her truthful answer.

> *She didn't show and isn't answering
> my messages, so either she got
> abducted by aliens and the spaceship
> doesn't have wifi or I got ghosted.*

*Oh no! And with only four days until
your birthday!*

*Doesn't she know you're on a
deadline here?*

> *I don't tell my dates about the
> astrology thing, so no, she doesn't.*

The dots indicating Veronica was typing appeared and disappeared a few times. Gray assumed she was struggling to come up with sympathetic words, or perhaps laughing at her misfortune. After another minute, a text came through.

*Are you still at City Park? I happen
to know an Aquarius without plans
this evening.*

Really? I'm still here!

Okay, sit tight.

Gray's disappointment rocketed right back up to eager anticipation. Maybe her birthday deadline wasn't impossible after all. Who was Veronica sending her way? Would it be weird for Gray to go on a date with one of Veronica's friends? Did Veronica even *have* other queer friends besides Gray? And how was she going to know who her date was when she saw them?

After another fifteen minutes of anxiously waiting, Gray saw a beautiful woman in the distance and hoped it was whoever Veronica contacted. The woman was wearing a green sundress that billowed dramatically in the wind, sunglasses, and a wide-brimmed hat that partially blocked her face. Her dark hair swung loose above her shoulders and she had a casual swish to her walk that kept Gray's eyes on her as she drew closer. Something about her gave off the vibe that she could be friends with Veronica. In fact, she kind of looked like she could be Veronica's sister. Actually . . . Wait. *Was* that Veronica?

"Gray!" She said as she approached, waving.

Shit. And also, *thank god.* It was Veronica.

Gray stood, and Veronica's hat brushed her cheek as she leaned in for a hug. Her nerves dissipated in Veronica's embrace.

"Sorry you got ghosted," Veronica said once she pulled back, grabbing Gray by the elbows. "Have you been stood up before?"

"Nope, first time."

Veronica tilted her head. "You're kidding! Well, I guess dating when you're gorgeous really is different. I've been ghosted on at least half the app dates I've ever tried to go on."

Warmth rushed to Gray's cheeks. "Anyone who ever skipped out on a date with you is a nitwit who should regret their decision for eternity."

"Good thing you didn't make the same mistake," Veronica said with a grin.

"I didn't realize the Aquarius with no plans was *you*," Gray said, still surprised but not disappointed.

"Well, I figured you were in a pinch," Veronica said, readjusting a tote bag on her shoulder. "Karys is at her dad's tonight, so I'm free to help you out. Since you're racing the clock and all."

"That's very kind of you," Gray said cautiously. "But does it even count as a date? I'm supposed to find, you know, someone who could actually potentially be a romantic match. Someone available and queer."

"Last I checked, I'm exceedingly single and bisexual."

Gray's jaw dropped.

Veronica, taking in Gray's shock, laughed. "Be careful or you'll catch flies."

Gray snapped her mouth shut and tried to mask the fact that her brain was actively exploding. "I'm sorry. I mean, good for you. I mean, fuck. I'm just . . . surprised, I guess. You never told me."

"You never asked."

"You're right. I've just been over here, relearning what happens when you assume." Gray offered her arm to Veronica. "Shall we check out the museum while I remove my foot from my mouth?"

Veronica took Gray's arm, luckily looking more amused than offended by Gray's discombobulation. "Let's skip the museum for now. I have a better idea."

They took off in the opposite direction of the museum, Veronica pointing them toward a calm lake surrounded by gnarled old trees and a few eye-catching sculptures. While Gray's mind reeled, rethinking every encounter they'd had and trying to figure out how she had missed Veronica's queerness, her date seemed completely at ease.

"Wow, this is beautiful!" Gray said, trying to ground herself in the moment. The early evening light was beginning to fade, illuminating the surface of the lake with reflections of the pastel-painted sky. Gray pointed toward a few empty picnic tables. "Are we going to sit down and enjoy the view for a while?"

"Yes, but not here."

They stopped for a moment to watch a duck and her trail of tiny yellow ducklings floating across the surface of the lake, then continued around the curving path until they came upon an old oak tree, its branches spread wide and dotted with freshly emerged green leaves. As Veronica guided Gray off the path toward the tree, Gray heard a mesmerizing, ghostly kind of music. It was all-enveloping, so enchanting that at first she couldn't tell if the sound was coming from somewhere or emanating from her own body. The closer they got to the trunk of the oak, the louder the sound got, as if the tree were calling to her.

"What's that sound?" Gray asked.

Veronica pointed to the branches of the tree, where Gray could now see clusters of black metal tubes hanging and drifting in the wind. "Wind chimes," Veronica said, her soft voice blending into the strange music. "Dozens of them. Installed by some local artist, all selected to ring in the same scale."

Gray stood wordlessly in the majesty of the tree for a moment, Veronica still holding her arm as she absorbed the echoing clangs of the wind chimes. "It's remarkable," she said finally, feeling the sound ring through every cell of her being.

"It's called the Singing Oak." Veronica dropped her head onto

Gray's shoulder and closed her eyes. "It's one of my favorite places in the city. It's no secret—plenty of people know about it—but it still feels like it's all mine, in a way. At least the music it makes when I'm here is always unique."

"I see why you like it," Gray said, her hair rustled by the same wind playing the chimes. "I could sit here and listen to it for hours."

"Lucky for you, I brought a blanket." Veronica pulled out a sheet of blue-striped fabric from her tote bag. Gray helped her spread it on a patch of grass under the farthest-reaching branches of the tree. "City Park closes at sunset, but we've got a little while before then. Almost an hour, I'd guess," Veronica said.

They settled down on the blanket, side by side, looking out at the lake. The sound of the wind chimes grew and faded with the shifting breeze, mixing with the songs of the crickets and katydids. "It feels like a movie score," Gray said after listening for a minute. "Like we have our own theme music."

"And with the sky like that?" Veronica leaned toward Gray, her finger tracing a tuft of peach-colored clouds floating across the lavender sky. "Definitely a movie moment."

"You sure know how to impress a date." As soon as the words left her mouth, Gray froze, her shoulder bumping against Veronica's. "*Is* this a date? Or a friend date? Or a . . . something else?"

"You've got a challenge to complete, so it's definitely a date," Veronica said. "And we're also friends, right? So I guess it's a date between friends."

"A date between friends, of course." Gray didn't feel like that had answered her question in the slightest, but she didn't ask for clarification. Looking at Veronica now, with the sunset giving her a soft, warm glow, Gray liked the idea of leaving the door open to something more.

Veronica sat up and reached for the tote. "Are you hungry? I picked up dinner on the way." She pulled out two sandwiches wrapped in paper. "Muffaletta from the deli around the corner from my place."

"I'm starving," Gray said, accepting one of the parcels from Veronica. "Thank you for thinking of everything."

Between bites, they chatted more about Gray's new apartment and Veronica's plans to renovate her back patio. Gray was still confused about the nature of their date, but she was more at ease than she had been with any other sign so far, even when she'd had the help of an edible with the Libra.

When they finished their sandwiches, Veronica pulled out two plastic containers and handed one to Gray. She opened it to find a cinnamon-scented slice of a sweet roll, topped with a glaze and dusting of purple, green, and yellow sugar. "Is this king cake?" Gray asked.

"Yes, homemade," Veronica said as she handed Gray a plastic fork.

"Wow! Thank you. But, uh . . . Wasn't Mardi Gras, like, almost a month ago?" Gray asked, cautiously poking at the cake.

Veronica laughed. "Don't worry, it's fresh. Like a true New Orleans kid, Karys absolutely adores it. She made a whole Power-Point presentation last year about why king cake shouldn't only be for Mardi Gras. She said it's basically cinnamon rolls, and I couldn't really think of a good argument against that, so I make it pretty often."

"A slideshow and everything? Wow." Gray took a bite, relishing the perfect combination of soft doughy bread, warmly spiced filling, sweet glaze, and crunchy coarse sugar. "You know, I think Karys is onto something," Gray said. "I could eat this every day."

"She is a pretty smart kid, huh?"

Gray couldn't help but smile at the proud look on Veronica's face as she cut a bite of her dessert. "She's the best," Gray agreed. "I feel really lucky to know her. And especially to get to watch you with her. How you create a safe, loving environment for her to explore the world and flex her creativity and build empathy. It's incredible, really. I hope I can be a fraction as good at parenting as you are someday."

"You will be," Veronica said, lifting the brim of her sun hat to look directly at Gray. "I see you with River. I mean, I even believed he was your kid for a minute. He obviously loves you and trusts you and looks to you for help when things go wrong, and that's not easy with a toddler." She paused to take a bite of cake. "So you really want kids? Even after living with one almost in his terrible twos? And after seeing what a nightmare dealing with schools and other parents can be?"

"I really do." Gray set her cake aside and leaned back on her elbows. "More than anything else, really. I know life with kids is messy and unpredictable and challenging, but it's exactly the challenge I've always wanted. To introduce them to the world, and encourage them to be exactly themselves, and love them through whatever challenges they face." Like a good luck talisman, her old softball teammate's moms appeared in her head. "And a partner who wants that too. Someone I can love fiercely and grow alongside and share big important events and tiny inconsequential moments with. Someone to help our kids develop into thoughtful, empathetic adults, even if they like different things or make different choices than we would. As long as our kids are kind and openhearted, they'll be perfect to us. That dream has kept me going through the darkest days."

She could feel Veronica's gaze on her, waiting for her to continue, but Gray sensed it was more of a patient, open presence, ready to listen to whatever she wanted to share, not at all judgmental. With the ringing of the wind chimes drowning out the rest of the park, Gray felt like they'd found their own private corner of the world.

"My parents wanted perfect children too, but their idea of

perfect came with a lot more conditions," Gray said after a moment. "They wanted kids who looked like them, spoke like them, acted like them, believed what they believed. I never could follow all of their rules or be who they wanted me to be, even when I was hardly older than River. The more I pushed at the borders of what they thought was 'normal,' the more they tightened the rules, and the smaller my world got. Thank god I had Cherry. There were some days I felt like she was the only person who got me, you know?"

"Cherry sounds wonderful, from what you've said about her," Veronica said, lying down on her side next to Gray and resting her head on her fist. "I'd love to meet her someday."

Gray pictured Cherry's fire-engine-red hair and chaotic energy next to the Veronica she'd met that first day at the middle school, stern and rule following. It was a strange combination. But then she looked at the Veronica in front of her today, lounging in her sundress, relaxed, open, easygoing. Veronica had proved over and over again that there were more layers to her than Gray ever expected. "Yeah, I think you'd like her," Gray said. "Anyway, growing up in my family was tough, to say the least. My brother, he got into plenty of trouble, but he was into the whole church thing. And the rules were a little easier to follow as a boy. He was always their pride and joy, and I was always the disappointment. I don't think my parents were intentionally cruel. They cared about me. But they thought loving me meant fixing me. And if I wouldn't let them fix me . . . Well, when I came out in high school, they made it clear that I couldn't be gay and their daughter. It was one or the other."

Veronica made a sympathetic sound, but Gray couldn't meet her eye.

"They sent me to conversion therapy, which was exactly as terrible as it sounds. At least what I saw of it. I spent most of the time sneaking out with Cherry's help. It was actually a little fun for a while, lying to make my parents think the therapy was working while really Cherry and I were gallivanting around town. There was one time in June before senior year when I was supposed to be at therapy but actually went to Tulsa Pride and kissed *four* different girls. That was a good day." Gray sighed, the memory still bittersweet on her tongue. "But six months later I had a blowout fight with my mother and told her the truth. I'm gay, and no amount of church or counseling or rule enforcing was going to change it. She sobbed. I'd never seen her cry so hard, like I'd ruined her whole life, just by being me. 'Now you'll never give me grandchildren,' she said." Gray scoffed. "Like being a lesbian makes me infertile or incapable of adopting or something."

A particularly strong burst of wind set the chimes above them into motion, and Gray took a moment to readjust onto her hip, mirroring Veronica's position and looking directly at her big brown eyes.

"Well, I'm going to have kids," Gray said. "A ton of them. The coolest, weirdest, most amazing, wrapped-in-love kids you've ever seen. But she had something right—they'll *never* be her grandchildren. *My* children will know that family means love without conditions, support for whoever they are or choose to be, as long as they're also putting kindness into the world instead of hate. I'm going to have the most amazing family, each kid perfect in their own way, and I won't give her the opportunity to dim their shine like she tried to do to me."

Veronica stared into Gray's eyes for a moment, an emotional expression on her face, then reached out to tuck a stray lock of Gray's dirty-blond hair behind her ear. "Gray, I'm so sorry your family ever made you feel like you were anything less than wonderful. They didn't deserve all of the magic that you are."

Gray swallowed what could have turned into a sob, instead

focusing on the way the vibrant sunset was turning Veronica's face into a watercolor painting. "Thank you, Veronica. I think you're pretty magical yourself. I hope your family saw that."

"Oh, I was lucky in the family department." Veronica pulled her sun hat from her head and tucked it under the tote bag, then continued. "My mother's family is super close, even though most of them still live in the DR. My brother and sister and I try to get down there to see them at least once a year or so. My dad, though, I think his family experience was closer to yours. His parents didn't approve of him marrying a Dominican woman. I think he shielded us kids and my ma from the worst of them though, and Ma has enough family to make up for them not being in our lives."

"Your parents . . . Do they know you're bi?" Gray asked.

"Oh yeah, they know," Veronica said. "I came out to them in grad school, when I had a pretty serious girlfriend. They were really supportive, having some experience themselves with being in a relationship outside of societal norms." Veronica shifted her hips, moving even closer to Gray. "I think me being a lesbian might have been a little easier for them to understand though. They didn't get the whole bisexual thing, thought it was more transitional, especially when I was bringing a woman home for the holidays. When I met Dylan a few years later, they were really thrown for a loop. But I think they've done some self-educating since then, and they're the first to speak up now whenever they hear someone say something biphobic."

"So they're still together?"

"They had their fortieth anniversary last year. I caught them making out in a closet like a couple of teenagers when I was visiting for Christmas."

Gray laughed, Veronica's story clearing any lingering sadness from her mind. "They sound amazing."

"They are. The way they raised me and my siblings, it kind of sounds like what you were talking about. You would probably thrive in the chaos of our DR reunions. Do you speak Spanish?"

Gray shook her head with an apologetic expression.

"Well, you and my dad could sit in a corner together trying to piece together what's going on while we're all talking over each other," Veronica said with a teasing grin.

"You'd have to give me a little warning so I could do a crash course in Spanish first," Gray said, delighted by the very idea of seeing what version of Veronica appeared with her family. Another burst of wind shifted the chimes in the oak branches above them. Gray looked up to see the sun approaching the horizon, reflecting its rays across the rippled surface of the lake as a few people walked or jogged around the perimeter. "I'm pretty sure this is the most perfect sunset I've ever seen," she said. "The colors are so vibrant, the way they're lighting up all these old oaks. And oh my god, do you see all these fireflies?" Little bursts of glowing golden light floated around them, one only a few inches behind Veronica's head.

"I'm enjoying the view from here," Veronica said.

Gray looked back to see Veronica was now less than a foot from her face, staring intensely into Gray's green eyes, her dark hair rustling in the wind like the leaves above them. Something had evolved between them as the sun moved lower in the sky. Gray wondered if the wind chimes had hypnotized her somehow, if the colorful sky and scent of spring blossoms were playing tricks on her.

"Maybe you were onto something about Aquariuses," Gray said, her voice hardly raised above a whisper. "This is the best date I've been on."

Veronica reached out and ran her fingertips from Gray's shoulder down her sleeve, across her wrist, tracing the crevices of her palm. "Since this is your chance to test astrological compatibility . . . could I kiss you?"

Gray's knee bent forward, bridging the gap between them and brushing Veronica's thigh. "It *is* a learning opportunity," she said. "Yes, I think we should. Academically speaking."

They both leaned in ever so slowly, Gray brushing Veronica's hair delicately aside and Veronica's hand resting on Gray's hip. Neither blinked as their faces came within six inches of each other, then four, then two. Their eyelashes fluttered shut just before their lips met, gentle, tentative, questioning. As softly as they'd started the kiss, they each pulled back the tiniest amount and opened their eyes, examining the other for a sign that they'd crossed a line and wanted to stop. But instead of finding resistance, they found matching expressions of longing. Every cell of Gray's body was telling her to lean in, to kiss Veronica again, to hold her tight and never let go. And based on the way Veronica pulled Gray forward for a kiss more heated and passionate than the first, her body must have been telling her the same thing. Had this chemistry been here all along, building between them, just waiting for the tiniest spark to catch flame?

As their bodies met, chest against chest, Veronica's knee tucked between Gray's, their lips locked together, the sound of the wind chimes swelled around them in a particularly strong breeze. The oak branches shuddered, dropping a few verdant leaves on the couple below. Their kiss could have lasted for minutes or hours or days, even years, their bodies becoming one with the tree roots beneath them. Nothing mattered but the feeling of Veronica in Gray's arms, the shared heat between their skin, the cinnamon-sugar taste of king cake on Veronica's tongue.

But the world *did* exist outside of their embrace, as they were eventually reminded by a park employee driving by on a golf cart. "City Park closes at sunset. Please make your way to the park exits," they announced over a loudspeaker attached to the vehicle.

Veronica and Gray carefully extricated their limbs, a bit

stunned to find how lost they'd gotten in each other. They sat up wordlessly, straightening their clothes and adjusting their hair.

"That was the best science experiment I've ever done," Gray said, breaking the silence.

Veronica laughed. "Even better than baking soda volcanoes. And that's a high bar."

Together, they packed up the remains of their picnic into the tote bag, then shook off the blanket and folded it. Feeling a bit like her body was full of helium and she might float away, Gray offered Veronica her arm. "Shall we?"

Veronica looped her hand through Gray's elbow and they set off back around the lake toward the gravel parking lot. Although they'd walked the same way when they first arrived, something about their body language and tension was different now, more intimate. They walked slowly, silently, both unready to see the last sliver of sun disappear into the dark. When they reached Gray's car, they came to a stop and turned to face each other, Veronica's hand clinging to Gray's. Their gaze said something in a language their ears couldn't understand.

Finally, Gray found the courage to speak. "Do you want to come to my apartment? Perhaps help me figure out the layout for the living room? I could use some advice from a . . ." Gray gulped. "A friend." The word felt richer now on Gray's tongue.

"I'd love to," Veronica said, her shoulders relaxing down an inch. "It's what friends are for, right?" She squeezed Gray's fingers before releasing her hand. "I'm parked over there. See you at your place?"

Gray agreed, then watched Veronica's retreating frame as she walked across the lot. Once she reached her car, Veronica turned back and waved when she saw that Gray was still looking at her. In a daze, Gray waved back, then ducked into her driver's seat, wondering how a walk through the park had turned her entire world upside down.

Twenty-three

*A*S GRAY STOOD on the stoop of her apartment building, waiting for Veronica to arrive, she worried at first that things would be different between them without the mesmerizing chimes of the Singing Oak. Had it created a special otherworldly place just for them? She'd never even dreamed she'd kiss Veronica, but now that she had, Gray might spontaneously combust if it didn't happen again as soon as possible.

Her worries were quickly assuaged when Veronica appeared around the corner of the brick building, her face lighting up when she spotted Gray waiting with her hands in her pockets. Veronica strode right up to Gray, kissed her on the cheek, and tucked her arm back through Gray's as if nothing had changed since they left City Park.

Gray led Veronica up the stairs to her third-floor unit and unlocked the door. "Ta-da! Not that different from when you last saw it, I guess. But now I have"—she gestured to the boxes and furniture organized in the corners of the room—"a single armchair, a bookshelf, and a throw blanket without a couch to put it on. Oh, and exactly two paintings." She nodded toward a colorful canvas with an impression of the Tulsa skyline and a boxy modernist work she'd picked up at the small-business fair the previous week.

Before Gray finished, Veronica had already left her side to pace around the kitchen and living space. She paused in front of the picture windows facing a row of historic buildings and, if you found exactly the right angle, a slice of the Mississippi River.

"The view is even more beautiful at night," Veronica said. She turned around and scanned the apartment from her new angle. "Although the sunlight is nice too. Either way, it's a gorgeous place. A very talented apartment hunter must have helped you find it."

Gray laughed, then joined Veronica by the window, wrapping her arms around Veronica's waist from behind. "The absolute best apartment hunter in town," she said, her voice low.

Veronica twisted them around to both face the room, with Gray still holding her around the middle. "You're going to need more furniture to fill all this space," Veronica said, then began pointing out different areas. "Another bookshelf or maybe a chest over there, on that empty wall. You'll need a couch or at least a sizable love seat there, and a coffee table. What do you think about a big piece of art here? Something colorful. Maybe a hanging tapestry? Or a decorative mirror to reflect the sunlight?"

Gray and Veronica stood like that for a while, using interior design as an excuse to hold each other close. When they ran out of ideas, Gray begrudgingly let go of Veronica's waist and meandered toward the refrigerator. "You were so well prepared for our picnic. I wish I had some food or something to offer you like a good Southerner." Gray dug into the tote bag of cold items she'd shoved onto a shelf without bothering to unpack it. "I've got . . . half a pint of strawberries and a couple cans of LaCroix?"

"Hostess extraordinaire," Veronica said. "Bring them over. I'll spread out this throw blanket and we'll have a picnic part two."

Before Gray joined Veronica on the floor, she located a Bluetooth speaker in a partially unpacked box and hit play on an album by a local jazz band she'd heard playing on the streets of the French Quarter. With the mood set, Gray and Veronica dug into the strawberries—only slightly past their prime, sweeter for it—and got back to their conversation about decorating Gray's new digs.

Gray froze midway through a sentence about antiques shopping for barstools when Veronica took a bite of a particularly juicy strawberry, leaving a distracting trail of juice dripping from the corner of her lips. Veronica looked at her expectantly and Gray stuttered out, "You've got . . . uh . . . s-some strawberry . . ."

The arch in Veronica's right eyebrow made it clear that she was fully aware of the upper hand she held in the moment. "Where?" She ran her tongue slowly along the opposite side of her lips, then swallowed in a way that made Gray gulp too. "Did I get it?"

"No, it's . . . the other . . ." Gray's brain was betraying her, mixing all of her words into a jumbled mess. Or perhaps it wasn't her brain at fault so much as other parts of her body.

Veronica leaned in across their now-empty LaCroix cans, looking intensely into Gray's eyes. "Why don't you get it for me?"

Gray didn't need to be asked twice. She closed the gap between them and licked the sweet and sticky strawberry juice from the corner of Veronica's mouth, then took Veronica's plump bottom lip between her teeth. Veronica responded immediately by pushing aside the remains of their second picnic and climbing into Gray's lap, wrapping her legs around Gray's torso. Their kiss seemed to pick up where their intimate moment under the old oak tree had stopped, bursting into a passionate heat that Gray felt might set her whole apartment aflame.

In her time spent befriending Veronica, Gray had often found herself trying to reconcile the different ways Veronica presented herself to the world: a buttoned-up school principal, a warm and creative mother, an advocate for social change, a skilled chef and cooking teacher, a tenacious apartment hunter. Of all the Veronicas she'd met, the one now tangled up in Gray's limbs, the one sliding a hand up the skin of Gray's lower back beneath her shirt, the one that smelled like strawberries and spring air—she was without a doubt Gray's favorite. The unguarded desire in Veronica's every move seemed to merge all the other Veronicas into a single being, one person who *wanted* things so desperately, *wanted* the world to make sense and become a better place, who, above all, at this moment, *wanted* Gray. And Gray had never wanted someone else so badly. Every other thought and distraction in Gray's head melted away when Veronica kissed the soft skin under the curve of Gray's jaw. Every self-conscious concern or nagging wonder if she was on the right track evaporated when Veronica let out a little moan at Gray's hands tangling into her hair.

Veronica used her legs to tighten her hold on Gray, pressing her hips against the gap of skin between Gray's shirt and jeans, which had somehow in the past few minutes come unbuttoned. Gray could feel the warmth of Veronica against her stomach, a heat that she thought might melt her completely. Was this really happening? Gray tried to pinch her left forearm, but Veronica jumped slightly and said, "Ouch!"

"Sorry," Gray said, her voice husky. "I was trying to see if I was dreaming. I must have pinched you on accident."

Veronica pushed the longer part of Gray's hair back from her forehead and, their faces still only a few inches apart, looked back and forth between Gray's two green eyes. "I'm very much awake. You are too."

A hint of Gray's self-awareness returned in the break from making out. "Should we . . ." she started, then paused to clear her throat. "Is this a good idea?"

"Based on what my body is telling me right now," Veronica said, her eyelids heavy with desire, "it's a phenomenal idea. And if I ask my brain"—she pulled an arm from Gray's lower back to tick off reasons on her fingers—"we're both adults interested in a consensual good time, yes?"

"Yes," Gray said immediately.

"You could use a good housewarming to celebrate your new place."

Gray nodded, her eyes traveling from Veronica's face to her sternum to her heaving chest. "Since you're trying to figure out your chemistry with Aquariuses, it's an important experiment. For scientific purposes."

Gray had completely forgotten about the astrology challenge. It seemed irrelevant to whatever was going on between them at the moment, but she was happy to admit it as evidence in Veronica's growing case. "I love science," she growled.

Veronica raised a fourth finger. "And it's the friendly thing to do. You know, for friendship."

"For friendship!" Gray cheered. With a list of reasons she couldn't possibly refute, Gray dove back into kissing Veronica with even more passion. As her lips strayed from Veronica's mouth to her neck, then her shoulder, then her collarbone, Gray began fumbling with the buttons at the top of Veronica's green sundress. They were tiny and numerous, stretching from the neck of the dress to the bottom hem, and releasing them one by one was an act of incredibly seductive torture for both of them.

Once Gray had unbuttoned enough of Veronica's dress to reveal her silky emerald bra, she froze for a moment, admiring how the glossy fabric shined against the smooth golden skin of Veronica's breasts, rising and falling with each intake of air. "Holy shit," she breathed. "You're a goddess."

"I'm not," Veronica said, breathing roughly through her mouth. "I'm a human being who very much wants you to get this dress off of me as quickly as possible."

"That's too bad," Gray said with a wicked grin. "Because I'm going to take my time." She pushed Veronica down against the blanket by the shoulders, and Veronica let out a pleased gasp. She continued unbuttoning Veronica's dress as she laid a trail of kisses from Veronica's throat down her sternum, then across the swelling landscape of her cleavage. As Gray reached the waist and then approached the hem of the garment, she parted it to reveal Veronica's smooth stomach, the soft curve of her hips, the pearlescent waves of stretch marks that turned her skin into a living work of art. The slowness of Gray's touch and heat of her kisses were making Veronica squirm with desire beneath her. Finally, the dress was opened from top to bottom, and the silky green panties that perfectly matched Veronica's bra were on display. Gray wondered for a moment if Veronica's matching lingerie meant she was expecting their date to take this turn—at least more so than Gray.

"My god, you're stunning," Gray said, leaning back to wonder at the magic of Veronica's mostly naked form on her living room floor, the streetlights from outside casting shadows across her torso.

After a moment, Veronica sat up and gripped the bottom hem of Gray's shirt. "Haven't you made me wait long enough?" Gray's grin was hidden by her Henley as Veronica pulled it up and over her head. Once the shirt was off, Veronica immediately set to work on pulling off Gray's jeans. But it was a difficult task with Veronica between Gray's knees and Gray kneeling over her. "Please, get these off as soon as possible," Veronica said after a moment of struggling.

Gray twisted away from Veronica and stood, then pulled off her jeans and threw them across the room. Now it was Veronica's turn to rest back on her elbows, taking in the expanse of Gray's skin not hidden by her pale-blue jersey bra or black boy-shorts underwear. Veronica's gaze felt almost as physical on Gray's body as her hands and lips had been moments before. Not able to withstand the heat of the tension between them, Gray dropped back to the ground on top of Veronica and kissed her, running her hands down Veronica's sides until they met the elastic of her panties. Veronica unclasped Gray's bra with a flick of her fingers, and it dropped down between them. As Gray shifted to untangle it from her arms, her knee slipped on the blanket against the hardwood floor, and Gray fell onto her hip to Veronica's side.

"Ouch," she said, wincing. Remembering her hopeful preparations for the evening, Gray said, "You know, I did put the good sheets on my bed. Should we move somewhere a little more comfortable?"

Veronica pushed herself up from the ground with one hand on Gray's leg. "The *good* sheets, you say?" She raised an eyebrow and smirked seductively, then took a few steps backward toward the door to Gray's bedroom. Along the way, Veronica reached behind her back and unclasped her bra, letting the straps slide down her shoulders and the cups pull away from her breasts. But before Gray could see any new skin, Veronica disappeared into the bedroom, then tossed the bra around the doorframe so it landed near Gray's feet. Gray was still staring at it, stunned by her luck, when Veronica's green silky panties landed next to them.

Leaping up from the blanket, Gray shed her own underwear and raced to join Veronica in her bedroom. She found Veronica sprawled across her bed, completely naked, Gray's quilt thrown aside so she could luxuriate in the soft sheets. Gray wanted to spend a moment, a day, a week, taking in the picture of Veronica on her bed, but her desire to touch every square inch of bare skin on Veronica's body won out. Gray climbed onto the mattress above Veronica, pressing one thigh against the heat between Veronica's legs, and took one of Veronica's pert nipples in her mouth. Veronica's sharp intake of breath was the most erotic thing Gray had heard in her entire life. The way she arched her back and pressed her body against Gray's was a revelation. The bed felt like a raft adrift on a vast ocean, the rest of the world

melting away to leave only this, only the static electricity spark-
ing between their skin, only the salty taste of Veronica on Gray's
tongue.

SOMEWHERE BETWEEN GETTING in bed and Gray's third (or was it
fourth?) orgasm of the evening, she'd completely lost track of
time, place, even her own name. Once her brain had reorganized
itself, Gray and Veronica were clutching each other, limbs tangled in a nest of wrinkled sheets and pillows. Their breathing
slowed into a matching rhythm, and Veronica turned her head to
look at Gray, a look of bliss on her face as she traced the outline
of Gray's lower lip with her thumb.

"So," Veronica said, her light touch roaming to the outer curve
of Gray's ear. "I think we can conclude that Aries and Aquarius
have sexual chemistry."

"Thank god for the scientific method," Gray said.

Veronica's pupils shifted between Gray's lips, forehead,
cheeks, and chin before settling on her eyes. "It's late. I should
probably head out."

"Do you have to?" Gray breathed.

"I wish I didn't," Veronica said. "But I've got to be at school
before the buses. It's my morning to greet the students as they
arrive."

"Right." The rest of the world and their responsibilities slowly
took shape around Gray. "It's good for morale."

Veronica lifted her hand from Gray's head, and Gray felt an
empty coldness immediately take its place. The mattress shifted
as Veronica stood, and Gray watched her naked form retreat to
the living room and return shortly afterward, her underwear and
bra back on and her dress hanging open in the front. "These buttons really are difficult. I usually just pull the dress on and off

over my head without dealing with them." Veronica walked around the bed, fiddling with the buttons at her neck. "Can I get a hand?"

Gray sat up on the edge of the mattress and started closing the buttons at the bottom hem. "Do you think we might do this again sometime?" she ventured lightly, secretly dreading their night together coming to an end.

"I suppose we should," Veronica said. "See if the experiment is replicable, if we get the same satisfactory results?" She bent her leg to bump her knee against Gray's hands.

Gray's heart lightened at the idea that this might not be the last time she held Veronica in her arms. "It does seem like the responsible thing to do."

They worked at Veronica's buttons in silence for a few minutes until their hands met around the level of her hips, only a small slice of skin peeking between the fabric. Unable to watch Veronica's midriff disappear so quickly, Gray grabbed Veronica's wrists to stop their movement, then placed a tender kiss below Veronica's belly button, right above the top of her underwear. She pulled back ever so slowly, and Veronica leaned down to press her lips to Gray's. They held each other for one more beat, Gray feeling Veronica's pulse under her thumbs. When they separated, their eyes both seemed to say that they wished time could stop and they could stay in this room forever. But they wordlessly nodded at each other to communicate that they understood life had to go on as normal.

Gray followed Veronica into the main room of her apartment, then pulled on her underwear and Henley. She walked Veronica to the door and grabbed her hand before she could reach for the handle, lacing their fingers together. "You know, I'm glad I got ghosted by that other Aquarius," she said. "This was so perfect, I can't imagine the universe wanted it any other way."

Veronica rolled her eyes playfully. "You and your universe talk," she said, her voice soft as the Singing Oak's chimes.

Gray lifted Veronica's hand to her lips and left a kiss on her knuckles. "Good night, Principal Taylor," she said.

Veronica's mouth twitched as she looked down at their intertwined hands, then back at Gray's face. "Good night, Ms. Young." And with that, she swept through Gray's door, leaving Gray to spend the remainder of her first night in her apartment alone.

Twenty-four

*A*FTER A WEEK of psyching herself up about living alone in her very grown-up apartment, Gray had expected to spend the evening after her date leisurely unpacking and celebrating her big step. But instead, she spent it with Veronica. Remembering her evening with Veronica. Wondering what Veronica was doing now. Noticing the smell of Veronica on her sheets. Imagining Veronica's kisses still lingering on her skin.

At first, Gray was floating on air. Her? Having *this* erotic dream of an evening with *that* Veronica? When she'd had no idea Veronica was even queer a mere six hours ago? Who'd have guessed?

Slowly, that elation drifted into a few heavier questions. *Why* had Veronica decided to go on a date with Gray? And what was up with that whole "just friends" thing? Was it simply a congenial good time, and nothing between them would change? Was that even possible? Would it really happen again? Would Gray survive if it didn't?

Lying in bed, bewildered, Gray eventually looked at her phone to see it was almost 1 A.M. Her calendar app had flipped over to Tuesday, April 1. She wondered for a moment if it had all been some kind of elaborate April Fool's Day joke. Well, if it was, she couldn't be too upset about a joke that made her climax multiple times. That was the kind of punch line she could appreciate.

Then she realized: April. Gray's birthday was only three days away. The end of her zodiac dating project was looming, and she'd essentially forgotten about it since she first set eyes on Veronica at City Park. Even when she'd joked about Aquariuses, it hadn't fully connected in Gray's head that the challenge was almost over. She was now only one date away from Saturn return, from realizing her romantic destiny.

Wait. Was *this* her romantic destiny? Had Saturn return been guiding Gray toward Veronica all along? It made sense, in a way. She'd met Veronica the day after her first date. They'd planted the seeds of friendship over Gray's dating hijinks. It had blossomed into something more at the exact moment of her Aquarius date. Their connection had been undeniable. And Veronica was what Gray wanted in a partner: brilliant, funny, *gorgeous,* passionate, responsible, and a great parent.

Did Gray even really need to go on that last date with a Pisces? Hadn't she found what she was looking for already? This was the happily ever after the planets wanted her to find, wasn't it? She'd come to Madame Nouvelle Lune with a question, and she'd finally found her answer, just days short of her birthday. Gray grabbed her phone and deleted the Mercurious app. *There.* Goodbye forever, dating apps. She'd gone on her last first date.

For a moment, right as she drifted off to sleep, she could almost believe that the pillow tucked behind her back was Veronica, still holding on to Gray as they breathed in rhythm.

THE NEXT MORNING dawned overcast and damp. Gray wondered for a moment as she dressed how the Singing Oak's chimes sounded in the rain.

Despite the weather and a pronounced lack of sleep, Gray had a bounce in her step when she arrived at the SCCA administrative office building, ready to focus on an enrollment campaign for the elementary school. The middle school board drama had taken up most of Gray's time since starting her new job. It was refreshing to redirect her focus for a little while. She pushed aside her rolling chair in favor of her large blue balance ball and settled in at her desk, bouncing softly from left to right. Sunlight from the window behind Gray usually made her small office feel larger, cramped as it was with file cabinets and bookshelves that apparently couldn't be stored anywhere else in the building. But today, nothing could bring Gray down, not the gray sky or her full inbox or the decades' worth of the historical school documents cluttering her space.

The morning went by in a pleasant haze. Gray had almost forgotten about the threatening clouds by the time she made it to the building's front door to pick up dumplings from her favorite food truck. She had to turn back for her umbrella.

"Gray!" said Dr. Donovan's assistant, Patty, when she spotted Gray coming down the hallway. "There you are. Dr. Donovan needs to see you."

"I'm headed out to lunch," Gray said breezily as she pulled her umbrella from a hook on her office door. "Can I catch him later?"

It wasn't until Gray was closer that she noticed the tense look on Patty's face. "Your lunch will have to wait," Patty said.

"Oh." Gray dropped her umbrella on the floor and backed out of her doorway. "All right, then. Thanks, Patty." As she walked to the opposite corner of the building, Gray's mood darkened, wondering what had gone wrong with the board or the parents' group or alumni this time. She wished the spring festival were over with so they could stop talking about who was and wasn't protesting which parts of it and how they planned to respond. Then again, Gray knew that's why she'd been hired in the first place: to be a voice of calm in the storm.

As she reached the end of the hall and the door to Dr. Donovan's corner office, Gray put on her most competent and relaxed facial expression, ready to save the day. "Hi, Dr. Donovan, Patty said you wanted to see— Oh. Hello, Ver— Principal Taylor."

Gray's smile faltered for only a moment upon seeing Veronica already seated across the desk from the superintendent. Veronica barely looked at her before turning back toward Dr. Donovan. Although the way Gray smoothly dropped into the chair next to her seemed completely normal, she could feel the temperature of her skin rise a couple of degrees simply being in the same room as Veronica. She mentally swatted aside images of Veronica's bare skin between the buttons of that green dress, trying with all her might to focus on whatever it was Dr. Donovan had already started to say.

". . . highly inadvisable, the timing couldn't be worse. I have no problem with it, of course, but the optics are difficult to manage, wouldn't you say?" he said, fiddling with the end of his tie.

Gray noticed as she looked at Dr. Donovan, trying to catch up to whatever conversation was already midstream, that she'd never seen him look so uncomfortable before. And that was saying something, as "uncomfortable" seemed to be his resting state.

"Sorry, what are we talking about here?" Gray asked when she realized he was staring at her and waiting for a response.

Dr. Donovan cleared his throat and swallowed, then gestured between Gray and Veronica with an open palm. "Your relationship."

Gray's heart pounded in her ears for a brief moment, thinking the superintendent was talking about their newly discovered romance. Reason quickly took over. There was no way he could know about that, unless he was having them tailed. "Our professional relationship? Couldn't be better, I'd say. We're on the same page and have been making great progress with getting the website and advertising copy in line with the new curriculum goals—"

"Gray," Veronica said quietly. Gray looked to her right to see Veronica give her one swift shake of the head.

Dr. Donovan sighed heavily, then turned his computer monitor so Gray and Veronica could both see the screen. The first thing Gray noticed was the beautiful sunset, the leafy green oaks, the bright colors like a scene in a movie. But then she noticed the couple kissing on the picnic blanket at the bottom of the image. Not just kissing, but *making out*. And not just any couple, but . . . *Veronica and Gray*.

"Where did you get this?" Veronica asked, her voice carefully controlled.

"A parent of a student at the high school," Dr. Donovan said. "They emailed it to me and the board president. Said they saw the two of you at City Park yesterday evening and found the situation highly unprofessional."

"First of all," Veronica said, a fiery edge to her voice, "it's a complete invasion of privacy to take a picture of *anyone* in an intimate moment like this, and even more inappropriate to email it around with wild accusations. And second, there's no way to prove that's us." Veronica pointed toward the figures at the bottom of the screen. "You can't even see their faces."

Dr. Donovan hit a button and a second image appeared. It seemed the photographer had moved slightly farther down the walking path around the pond, now aiming the camera from closer to Gray's and Veronica's feet. From this angle, you could clearly see the shaved side of Gray's head and her nose ring, and while Veronica's face was partially obscured by her hair, it was clearer than in the first photo. Even more damning was the St. Charles Collegiate Academy tote bag at her feet. And even worse than that, Veronica had her knee pressed between Gray's legs, giving a shadowy view under her sundress.

"For god's sake, take that away," said Veronica, turning from the computer screen.

Dr. Donovan's face showed that he didn't want to be having this conversation any more than the two of them. "I believe it will be rather challenging to refute that the two of you are in these images," he said as he clicked out of the window and shifted his computer monitor back to its normal position. "Especially seeing as the parent who took the photos says she recognized both of you, Principal Taylor from when her child was in your history class in middle school, Ms. Young from the focus groups last week."

Veronica and Gray sat in tense silence, neither making eye contact with the other. Gray could feel her cheeks burning. The branches of the oak hanging over them had made the moment feel so private. Gray had never envisioned the consequences of their actions coming to such a terrible head.

"While there's technically nothing stopping you from pursuing a romantic relationship," Dr. Donovan said slowly, "it does create an opportunity for criticism. Some might call it—or rather, already are calling it—a conflict of interest. Inappropriate. Not to mention . . . other more political comments."

"Because we're two women," Veronica said, saving Dr. Donovan from having to admit this point of contention himself.

Gray closed her eyes and dropped her head even farther toward her chest. She caught herself before saying "Fuck," instead releasing air on the *F* sound and then going silent.

"Well, there's quite an easy solution for this, then," Veronica said after a moment, sitting up straighter in her wooden chair. Gray and Dr. Donovan both turned to look at her, surprised. "It never happens again. We tell everyone what it was—a shortsighted mistake. We apologize, and eventually it goes away."

Gray turned to Veronica, feeling a bit like she'd just been slapped upside the head. *A shortsighted mistake?*

"That's one option," Dr. Donovan said. "However, I think you might be underestimating the board's memory. At least the memory of certain members, who I don't see letting this go so easily. The pictures have already been making the rounds among the board members and parents and alumni who are . . . less than supportive of your mission, Principal Taylor. I've heard rumors there's already a petition for your removal being circulated."

Veronica's shoulders fell, and Gray saw a look of shock cross her face. They all sat in silence for a moment, letting Dr. Donovan's statement wash over them. All of those people had seen photos of Gray and Veronica's passionate moment. It felt only slightly less invasive than if someone had managed to catch a snapshot of them later in Gray's apartment.

After a moment, Gray felt a sense of calm wash over her as the answer became clear. "I'll be right back," she said before dashing out of the office, leaving the confused faces of Veronica and Dr. Donovan behind her.

It took less than ten minutes for Gray to sweep back in, interrupting the principal and superintendent's discussion of potential options, which seemed fruitless so far. Gray dropped a sheet of paper, still warm from the printer, onto Dr. Donovan's desk.

Dr. Donovan pulled a pair of bifocals from the inner pocket of his suit jacket and put them on to inspect the few sentences in the letter.

"What is that?" Veronica asked.

Finishing reading the statement, Dr. Donovan nodded. "Well, this is probably the cleanest solution, although I regret it had to come to this," he said, then stood up from his desk and tucked the sheet of paper into a file folder. "I'll take this to HR immediately and proceed with next steps." He offered his large palm to Gray, and she shook it firmly. "It's been a pleasure, Ms. Young. Up until now, of course."

"Thank you for the opportunity, Dr. Donovan," Gray said, her voice lighter and more confident than she expected it could be in a moment like this.

"Wait," Veronica said, realization dawning. "What's going on? You're not—"

Dr. Donovan had already reached his doorway. "I trust you know what to do, Ms. Young."

"Yes, I'll be out before the end of the hour," Gray said. "I hope I can count on you for a reference?"

"A glowing one," Dr. Donovan said with a small smile and nod, clearly pleased to have a troublesome problem so quickly solved.

Once his shadow cleared from the door, Gray started to follow him, but Veronica grabbed her sleeve and stood to block the door. "Gray, what was that? Please don't tell me—"

"My resignation letter," Gray said simply, then tried to step around Veronica. "If you'll excuse me, I need to go pack up my office."

Veronica placed a hand on each side of the doorframe, trying to make her petite body as much of an impediment to Gray's exit as possible. "No. You can't do this."

"I already did." Gray lifted one of Veronica's arms and slid past her.

Veronica chased after her down the hall, taking two quick steps in her heels for each of Gray's confident strides. "Gray, stop. There must be another answer! Take a moment to think about this."

"I did," Gray said. "And I made my decision." She pushed open the door to her office, and Veronica followed her inside.

"Gray, you can't just quit like this. You can't let them win," Veronica said, more ruffled than Gray had ever seen her before. In a professional context, at least.

Gray found an SCCA-branded backpack she'd been given at orientation in the bottom drawer of a filing cabinet. She unzipped it and began collecting her personal items, but Veronica kept trying to get between Gray and her desk.

"There must be something else we can do, something that will let you keep doing your job. We tell them it's photoshopped, it's a deepfake. Or we tell them the truth. It's not a relationship, it was a momentary lapse in judgment."

Gray felt a jab in the ribs at that, knowing a relationship was exactly what she was hoping would come next. Calling it a lapse in judgment was a massive oversimplification of a night that Gray felt certain would change the course of her life. In fact, it already had. "It's the only way, Veronica," Gray said, shifting past her to collect her framed diploma from the University of Tulsa from the back wall. "You *know* how set some of these board members and parents are against you. There's no way they'd just let it go. At this point, how many people have already seen the photos? Do you want to have to go in front of the entire SCCA community to argue for our right to be together?"

Veronica moved to block Gray's path away from the back wall. "You can't make this decision for the both of us. At least give us a *minute* to think through alternatives."

"The faster we put an end to the speculation, the sooner you'll be able to get back to doing your job," Gray said. "You're the principal. You're the visionary for this whole school. Those kids *need* you to keep doing what you're doing. And me, us, *this* . . ." Gray pointed from her chest to Veronica's. "I can't let it ruin your credibility. You're too important to me."

"But you're doing the work too," Veronica said urgently. "You're making a difference for those kids too."

"Without me, you find another PR person, and I find some other job, and SCCA goes on," Gray said, placing the framed diploma on the ground. "Without you, the board replaces you with some puppet principal they control. All the curriculum changes you've fought for, all the scholarships and initiatives to bring in new students and teachers, all the updates to the mission to make it more inclusive and equitable, it all just disappears." She moved around her desk and grabbed Veronica's hands between them. "And besides. If I don't work with you anymore, there's nothing to stop us from being together."

"Together," Veronica said, staring down at Gray's fingers wrapped around her own.

"Yes. We can go on another date. A hundred dates. Don't you see? This is what Madame Nouvelle Lune said, this is what Saturn return was leading me—"

"Stop talking about fucking astrology," Veronica said abruptly. "All you can think about is your horoscope and your frivolous dates and your theoretical future kids. The work you're doing here *actually* matters, but you only care about your imaginary family that's too perfect to ever really exist. You're giving up on SCCA for an unrealistic dream."

Gray scoffed, trying to hide the hurt she felt from Veronica's stab. "Of course I'm not giving up. If you know me at all, you know I don't just give up on things when the going gets tough."

"Maybe I *don't* know you at all," Veronica said. "And maybe you don't know me either. We've both just blown up our lives and you've quit your job for someone you slept with one time."

Gray whipped around to face Veronica, her packing forgotten. "How can you say I don't know you at all? Sure, I may not know your every secret, but after last night, surely you can see we've got a connection. And I'm doing this because of that, because being together is our destiny."

"Don't," Veronica said, her voice heavy with emotion. "Don't do that, don't make this your big romantic gesture. I want to do my *job,* and I need you as my colleague to do it."

"But you care about this job, and I care about you, and I can't let you get pushed out or fired from something that means so much to you. You matter to me, way more than SCCA, way more than a paycheck, even though I . . . God, I just signed a lease. But I'll figure it out, because you're what matters. You matter more to me than anyone I've met since I moved here, more than—"

"It's too much!" Veronica said. "This is exactly what I don't want, this responsibility and guilt hanging over my head because you *care* about me too much."

Gray was caught off guard by Veronica's reaction. "I'm not trying to make you feel *guilty*, I'm trying to fix this mess we've gotten ourselves into," she said defensively.

Veronica backed away toward the door. "This was all such a huge mistake," she said, sounding as if she was talking more to herself than to Gray. "I've got a daughter to raise, a school to manage, so many students who count on me. I can't believe I let myself get so wrapped up in this, in one night of regrets."

Gray followed her, touching Veronica's cheek tenderly. "I don't regret a thing, Veronica," she said softly. "I wouldn't take back last night for anything."

"Yeah, well, I would," Veronica said, twitching her head away from Gray's hand. "You've got this whole happy ending mapped out, but it's not *my* happy ending. I don't want a new spouse and a ton of kids and a white picket fence. I want to help navigate this school into the future, and I can't do that while living out some little fairy tale you made up."

A curl of hurt twisted in Gray's chest. "We can have both," she said, trying to ignore Veronica's argument. "I'll find some other PR job, you'll keep doing amazing work with the students. It will blow over in no time, and we'll still—"

"*We'll* do nothing," Veronica said. She grabbed the doorknob, determined, cold in her classic professional way. "You're quitting, so it's all up to me now. You'll go off on your frothy little dating adventure, living your fancy-free sitcom life, and I'll be here picking up the pieces."

"Veronica, stop," Gray said. "You know there's more to it than that. And I want to help you!"

"You've done enough," Veronica said over her shoulder before slamming Gray's office door behind her.

Twenty-five

THE WHIPLASH FROM feeling so confident in her choice to resign to feeling like she'd ruined everything was confounding. The idea that she'd destroyed her friendship, her relationship, her potential future with Veronica was even worse. Once Gray had finished packing her things—a task that felt all too familiar after just moving—she sat behind the wheel of her car and tried to decide where to go. Going back to her new apartment, filled only with memories of Veronica, seemed terrible. But going crying back to Cherry and Robbie after a single day of living alone felt too pitiful to endure. She could go to Demitasse Café and mope over an Americano, but begging Riley for a job at the coffee shop until she found something else seemed like one of her only viable options at the moment, and it wouldn't help her case to show up still in shock. She'd paid two months' rent up front, but she'd need to find a new way to get paid soon.

Gray noticed that her hands were shaking on the wheel, and she knew driving in her current state of mind was a bad idea. She locked her things in the trunk and instead started walking with no destination in mind, letting her feet hit the pavement one in front of the other as she turned the past twenty-four hours over and over again in her brain to examine it from every angle. No matter how difficult the situation, Gray had always been able to find a silver lining somewhere. Surely she could find one in her current predicament.

The problem was that Veronica had become Gray's silver lining. Annoyed with obstructionist school board members? Commiserate with Veronica. Bad date? Laugh about it with Veronica. Stressed out by the housing market? Ask Veronica for help. Who was she supposed to turn to when things got rocky with Veronica?

Perhaps if Gray could fix her bad mood, she could find the bright side. She started by adjusting her walk. If she could *look* like she was in good spirits, maybe that would translate into something more internal. Gray straightened her posture, lifted her chin, tried to find a light, casual pace. The act of looking up at the city around her helped. She hadn't been paying much attention to where she was headed when she set out from the SCCA administrative offices, not even fully noticing the drizzly rain falling on her head. But the skies had begun to clear, and Gray had found her way to the Mississippi River, where the gentle lapping sounds of the water and birdcalls brought her back into her body.

Gray's gaze scanned from the river back to the path ahead, and she spotted someone curiously eyeing her from down the sidewalk. Nothing put her in better spirits than being checked out by a stranger. As they approached each other, Gray gave the stranger a flirtatious grin, and she saw their cheeks go pink.

The moment helped Gray stumble into the silver lining she'd been searching for. *Finish the astrology dating challenge.* The whole purpose in moving to New Orleans, in visiting Madame Nouvelle Lune, in all of her romantic escapades, was to find her true love and start the family she'd always wanted. She'd thought she'd found that in Veronica. But maybe the whole SCCA kerfuffle was the universe pushing her to finish what she started and find that Pisces.

The sounds of a jazz band a few streets over drew Gray's attention, and she followed the music into the French Quarter. That was one thing she loved about New Orleans: Even on a dreary old Tuesday afternoon, there was still a party going on somewhere. Gray located the band and stood on the sidewalk to watch for a couple of songs. When they took a break, she turned around and realized this particular stretch of Royal Street looked familiar. In fact, she was standing right in front of Cat O'Connor's Pub, the same bar where she'd gone on her first date with Carmen, the Aries. Seeing this as another sign from fate, Gray ducked inside.

The pub was considerably less crowded than the last time Gray had seen it, but there were still a few groups of patrons catching an early happy hour. Gray settled down at the corner of the bar and ordered an Alligator Tears Punch, leaning into the nostalgia for a very different time, even if it was only six weeks prior. Visions of pub trivia and sex in the restroom danced in her head as she took her first syrupy sip. It only took her a few seconds to spot Carmen's ram tiki glass among the Pub Club memorabilia decorating the walls.

Her mind still reeling from the last twenty-four hours, Gray re-downloaded Mercurious. Once she signed in, it opened to her messages with Kristen, the Aquarius who had ghosted her. Getting stood up was the first domino to fall in the unpredictable chain of events. She'd actually thought Aquarius was her destiny for a moment there, that all of this was meant to lead her to Veronica. But, as Veronica had so clearly told her, their happy ending wasn't meant to be. Was another Aquarius her destiny? Or could they only lead to confusion and disaster?

No matter; it was Pisces time. Maybe it was the sign she'd *really* been meant to find all along. If Aries was the baby of the zodiac, Pisces was the oldest sign with the most worldly wisdom. Someone with some intrinsic knowledge of the universe sounded fantastic right about then, when Gray felt so hopelessly lost.

As Gray browsed the handful of Pisces profiles her search turned up, the memory of having sex in this very establishment still fresh in her mind, she remembered another aspect of the challenge. She'd told Cherry that she would try to have sex with at least one person from each element. It had sounded impossible when Cherry first suggested it, but she'd found it a lot easier than expected. She'd hit it out of the ballpark with fire signs, having a great time with Carmen the Aries and Aisha the Leo. Things hadn't gone great with Stephanie the Virgo, but it counted toward sex with an earth sign. Gray had a much better time with Skylar the Libra, an air sign. Actually, Gray realized, she'd slept with two air signs if she counted Veronica. It was uncomfortable to think of Veronica as "the Aquarius," just another date. But maybe that's all they were meant to be: former co-workers who went on one ill-advised date.

Gray hadn't slept with a water sign yet, but she still had one more chance. And she liked her prospects. From their profiles, the Pisces on Mercurious seemed gentle, kind, thoughtful. They were teachers and nurses and caretakers. Their profile pictures featured cute animals, flowers, and reassuring smiles. One person caught Gray's interest: Molly (she/her), age thirty-four, an artist from Arkansas, pictured with an overweight gray tabby cat. Molly had wavy brown hair with a few streaks dyed teal, a scattering of freckles across her cheeks, and big brown eyes with dark lashes. Her smile was close-lipped, tentative but warm. Something about her looked vaguely familiar, but Gray couldn't quite put her finger on it. Gray starred Molly's profile and immediately got a notification that they'd matched. Molly must have been actively cruising Mercurious at the same moment as Gray. Could the planets be more aligned?

When Gray opened a chat window with Molly she realized that, for the first time, she didn't have an icebreaker from Cherry. She was on her own for this one.

GRAY: Hey Molly! Hope your Tuesday is going better than mine. What's your cat's name? It's adorable.

MOLLY: Thanks! Her name is Marmalade. And I'm not sure how bad your Tuesday is, but mine is pretty terrible.
GRAY: I'm sorry to hear that. Want to talk about it? Maybe both of our days can still turn around.

They chatted for a while, Molly sharing that she'd had a contract for a custom art piece fall through, Gray staying vague about her "work troubles." Their bad days seemed to be great for bonding, but Gray didn't really want to relive all the lurid details that led her to quit. Once she'd finished her punch and a pint of beer, Gray grew bold enough to invite Molly to join her for a drink. Molly quickly agreed, and she must have been nearby, because Gray had only taken a couple sips of her next beer when Molly arrived.

Spotting Gray at the bar, Molly walked over and plopped onto the stool next to her. She was wearing dark eye makeup and a baggy sleeveless shirt that showed off numerous tattoos running up and down both arms. "Well, I already feel better just being here," Molly said. "I couldn't stare at the inside of my studio for another second. What are you drinking?"

"The pilsner," Gray said. Molly felt so immediately familiar to Gray that it seemed more like she was catching up with an old friend than meeting someone for the first time. "Thanks for meeting me here. I'm already a couple drinks in, fair warning."

"I can catch up," Molly said, flipping her brown-and-teal hair over her shoulder. "I've been here a couple of times before, I think. Do they do trivia?"

"On Sundays," Gray confirmed, feeling more like a local than she had in New Orleans at any point so far.

"Right." Molly flagged down a bartender and ordered the same beer Gray was drinking and a shot of tequila. After throwing back the shot, she paused to really look at Gray for the first time. Her eyebrows furrowed, and she said, "You look super familiar to me. Do I know you from somewhere?"

"Well, I'm on this little app called Mercurious," Gray said. The two drinks had brought about a constant buzzing in Gray's brain, enough to distract her from the existential terror she was experiencing from losing her job and her potential soulmate in one afternoon.

Molly waved away the comment, flashing a few colorful rings. "Other than that. Are you, like, an actor or something? Are you on commercials?"

"Nope, I work in PR," Gray said. She examined Molly's face a little more closely. "You know, I feel like I recognize you too. Maybe we've met before. But I just moved here a couple months ago."

Molly took a sip of her beer as she contemplated. "Where did you move here from?" she asked.

"Tulsa, Oklahoma."

"Never been." Molly pulled her hair up into a messy bun on top of her head and secured it with an elastic band on her wrist. "I did work with this one company from Oklahoma, but it was a long time ago, maybe eight or nine years. It was a—"

"—wedding company," Gray finished, finally realizing where she'd seen Molly before now that her hair was pulled back. "I worked your wedding, right?"

"Oh my god," Molly said, an invisible light bulb clicking on above her head.

Gray nodded, the memory sharpening as she spoke. Molly hadn't had teal hair or as many tattoos back then, but Gray could picture her in her wedding dress. "The one in Arkansas, in the mountains at that inn, right?" The day came rushing back to Gray's mind. She was still in college, working part-time as a manual laborer / tech troubleshooter / bartender / errand boi for the company, which was started by some of McKenzie's friends. McKenzie coordinated vendors, baked cakes, and helped with marketing. It was an all-hands-on-deck kind of business, and at that particular wedding, Gray's hands had touched every inch of the deck. It was a perfect spring day at a quaint little bed-and-breakfast tucked in the Ozarks. Everything was going according to plan—until it started to pour rain. Gray and McKenzie had been tasked with running all of the gifts, flowers, and electrical equipment under awnings while the guests were swept inside to dry off by the fireplace and snack on hors d'oeuvres until the storm passed. It had been a mess, but worth it in the end, when the happy couple was able to finish their vows with a stunning rainbow backdrop.

Molly winced. "Yeah, the Hummingbird Inn."

"Oh," Gray said, noticing Molly's reaction. "Sorry. Based on the fact that we're here now, having met on a dating app, I'm guessing things didn't quite work out."

Molly took a hearty chug of beer, then shook her head sharply. "You'd guess right." Looking at Gray, Molly tilted her head as if she too was thinking back on her wedding day. "But you . . . You were dating that other bartender, weren't you? The pretty one with the dark hair who decorated the cake?"

"McKenzie," Gray said, now her turn to grimace. "Yeah."

"And based on the fact that *you're* here, I'm guessing that . . ."

"Didn't work out either," Gray said. After a brief moment of silence, Gray clinked her pint glass against Molly's. "Well, cheers to both being single again," she said wryly.

"Cheers," Molly said. They both took a drink, loosening the awkward tension from the realization.

"You owned that bed-and-breakfast, right? When did you move away?" Gray asked.

"About the same time my wife left," Molly said, fiddling with her many rings. "Six years ago now. Been moving around wherever I can find customers for my artwork since then. Mostly stained glass, some metal sculptures. New Orleans is a great place for weird art. I feel like I end up here at least once a year.

But it makes dating pretty tough, all of that moving around. How long have you been on the hunt?"

"Couple of months. Same time I moved to Louisiana," Gray said. "McKenzie and I were together for a *decade*. Almost all of my twenties. Trying to learn to date now makes me feel like an adult in a baby swimming class. Just splashing around, blowing bubbles, and feeling too old to be here." Catching herself, Gray slapped her palm against her forehead. "Shit, I'm not supposed to talk about my ex."

"It's fine, I started it," Molly said. "Who told you it's off-limits? Does Emily Post offer lesbian dating etiquette?"

"No. My best friend, Cherry," Gray said, her tongue loosened by her earlier drinks. "She set these dating rules for me. No talking about my ex, no immediately falling in love, no talking about the astrology challenge— Dammit, I did it again," Gray said, catching herself a second too late.

"Astrology challenge?" Molly said, sitting up straighter on her barstool. "Now that's something I'd love to hear about. What's the challenge? Guessing your date's sun, moon, and rising signs? Acting like a different sign on every date? Trying to prove it's all meaningless?"

Gray dropped her head into her hands. "God, I've already let this one go off the rails and you've only been here for, like, ten minutes."

Molly placed a hand on Gray's shoulder. "My day is already way better than it was before you messaged me, if that helps."

Gray looked up at Molly and bit her lip. She wasn't supposed to talk about her ex, but even briefly chatting about McKenzie had made her feel better about the clusterfuck that was currently her life. Maybe talking about her dating experiment wasn't such a bad idea either, if Molly was genuinely interested. "You really want to hear about it?"

"I might die of curiosity if I don't."

Giving Molly a brief overview of her past six weeks of dates was surprisingly cathartic. Molly was obsessed with astrology herself and begged Gray for details about her dates. It was all fun and games for a while, as Molly had her own stories to add about dates with various signs. But after Gray talked about playing matchmaker with her Capricorn and Taurus dates, and Molly praised the pairing's compatibility, Gray clammed up.

"So what about Aquarius? That was your last date before me, right?" Molly asked.

Gray waved to a bartender and asked for another round before replying. "It was good. And then it was fucking amazing. And then it was terrible." Molly waited silently for Gray to continue, and eventually she found the words to explain her history with Veronica before the date.

"So you went on a date with your friend?" Molly asked, leaning in with an elbow on the bar.

"Well, it wasn't *supposed* to be her. I got ghosted and Veronica volunteered to step in." Gray ran her fingertips along the shaved side of her undercut, still perplexed by how things had escalated so quickly. "It was *her* idea, *her* choice to show up looking completely gorgeous and date-ready, *her* plan to go to this ridiculously perfect location with this magical wind chime tree—"

"The Singing Oak?" Molly said, her eyes wide. "Wow. That's romantic as hell for a *friend* date."

"Right?" Gray said. "I mean, in a place like that, with the sun setting and the fireflies and everything, how could we *not* end up making out? And then when the making out was so fun, how could we *not* end up going back to my place and seeing how much more fun we could have?"

"Naturally. So that's when things got bad, when you went back to your place?"

"No, that part was great," Gray said, staring dreamily at the shelves of liquor bottles against the wall behind the bar. "Like, once-in-a-lifetime-stars-aligned-best-sex-of-my-life wonderful. I genuinely felt like I found my soulmate. This was the answer I'd been looking for."

Molly tilted her head. "Then I guess I'm missing the downside."

Gray swirled her pint glass in a puddle of condensation. "Remember how I mentioned that terrible workday today? Some parent saw us in the park, got pictures—uncomfortably intimate pictures—of us kissing, and by lunchtime, they'd already made their rounds to every parent, alumnus, teacher, janitor, school nurse, and classroom gerbil."

Molly gasped. "That's even more terrible than I expected."

"Yeah, me too." Gray rubbed her palms across her slacks, a bit disoriented by the fact that they were the same pair she'd put on this morning while she was still walking on air. "Anyway, I quit. I mean, what else could I do? There was no way it was going to just blow over, and Veronica couldn't quit. She's too important to the school, to those kids, to every life she's ever touched. If we wanted to be together, it was the only option."

"Sure," Molly said. "I'd have done the same thing."

"But Veronica was furious," Gray said, feeling the flood of dread return. "She somehow managed to make me feel like I'd given up and abandoned her by resigning while also saying it was all a big mistake and shouldn't have happened. Like, talk about mixed signals. Does she want me to stick around or does she never want to see me again? Pick a side, right?"

Molly eyed Gray sympathetically. "If it's any consolation, I think you officially won the worst-day contest," she said.

Gray cracked a smile. "Thanks. I do love winning."

"Of course. You're an Aries."

"The *best* of all Aries," Gray said with a wink. "Anyway, I guess Veronica was right. Looking back, it could only have ended in some kind of disaster. I'd already broken the dating project rules with her, like I now have with you. I'd told her plenty about my ex. She knew all about the astrology challenge. Hell, I fell head over heels right then, just like Cherry told me not to. I thought the stars had given me the answer to my soulmate question, but she wasn't really my soulmate and now I'm back at square one."

"So you're giving up on Veronica just like that?" Molly asked.

Gray scoffed. "No. I mean, yes. I mean . . . What do you mean?"

"Look, I'm a tattooed lesbian artist with teal hair, I know enough astrology to understand it's far more complex than checking your horoscope," Molly said. "Expecting a sun sign alone to give you a no-questions-asked soulmate without any problems or hurdles to overcome seems a little unrealistic. Love isn't that easy. Just because you have some shit to work through doesn't mean it isn't written in the stars. I'm surprised you would give up on Veronica when you've clearly been falling in love with her for a while."

Gray nearly fell off her barstool. "I . . . I have?"

"It's obvious, isn't it?" Molly said gently. "You just didn't realize it because you thought she was straight. The way you talk about first meeting her, the look on your face when you're thinking about her, the sexual chemistry from the first moment y'all opened yourselves up to it . . . I mean, Jesus, you quit your *job* for her."

Gray's vision blurred at the edges as Molly's words hit her. She thought about how happy she felt in Veronica's presence, how delighted she was by every new layer of Veronica she uncovered, how painful it was to hear Veronica say their date was a mistake. "Fuck," Gray finally said, her voice cracking. "I've *been* in love with her."

"Well, don't look so horrified by it," Molly said, patting Gray's elbow. "It's good news, right? It's what you wanted. But it's not the end. What's her moon sign? How about her rising sign? What house is her Venus in, which rules passion and love? What about her Mars, for conflict and aggression? Or Mercury, for communication? You've still got a lot more compatibility to figure out, some aspects the stars can tell you, some they can't. Most importantly, you've got to find out if she's open to loving you back."

"But she doesn't love me back." Thinking back on the previous night, Gray's stomach seemed to fall through the bottom of her barstool, down through the concrete floor, deep into the earth beneath them. "She said we were just friends, that it was just a fun little exploit. And when I quit my job, she said she regretted the whole thing and acted like she never wanted to see me again."

Molly shrugged, then drank the last dregs of her beer. "I know a fair amount about astrology, a little about you after this chat, and nothing about Veronica, so I'm not sure I have the answers for you here," she said. "But I *do* know that love is messy and complicated and confusing and sometimes wonderful, but it's rarely straightforward. Maybe the stars are speaking to you in ways you don't know how to interpret."

Gray chewed on her bottom lip. "Maybe," she conceded. If only she could drag Veronica to Madame Nouvelle Lune to get the answers she sought.

"It's getting late, and I've got to run." Molly signaled the bartender and handed over her credit card to pay for both of their drinks.

"You don't have to do that," Gray said. "I just talked your ear off about all my personal problems. I should be paying *you* for the advice."

"Don't worry about it. I had a great time talking with you." Molly stood from the barstool and gave Gray a firm pat on the back. "And besides, you're unemployed now."

"Oh," Gray said with a dark laugh. "Right."

Molly leaned in and kissed Gray on the cheek, kindly but not romantically. "Good luck, Gray," she said. "I hope you find what you're looking for."

"Thanks," Gray said with a crooked smile. "I hope you do too."

With a nod, Molly left Gray, alone at the bar, finishing her astrology dating challenge in the same place it began.

Twenty-six

ABOUT FIFTEEN MINUTES LATER, Gray exited Cat O'Connor's Pub and climbed into the passenger seat of Cherry's Subaru.

"Aunt Gay!" River greeted her from his car seat behind her. "Look, new unicorn!" He proudly displayed a sparkly green-and-blue plush toy.

"Hi, River!" Gray said. "Very cool. What's its name?"

"Doggie!" River replied. Gray was halfway to asking why he'd named a unicorn Doggie before she realized he'd been distracted by someone walking their German shepherd on the sidewalk. Ah, to have the enthusiastically short attention span of a toddler.

Gray turned to Cherry, who was merging back into traffic. "Thanks for being my DD, Cher."

"No prob," Cherry said, checking her blind spot over her shoulder. "With any luck, I'll be sober and ready for your DD needs for the next nine months. And anyway, I've been dying to see your apartment."

It was a short drive to Gray's new building. In truth, Gray probably could have walked, but after her heart-to-heart with a near stranger, it was apparent Gray could use some advice from someone who actually knew her. After giving Cherry a short tour of her place, Gray settled River down with a box of plastic mixing bowls, wooden spoons, and Tupperware, the closest things she had to toys on hand. Meanwhile, she caught Cherry up on what had gone down with Veronica and SCCA—using some

careful metaphors to protect River's tiny ears from the more sa-
lacious details.

"I *knew* there was something going on between you and Veronica," Cherry said when Gray was finished. "Sorry, I know
that's not helpful in this moment. But your date was right. You
get that ooey-gooey look on your face when you talk about her.
You did even before things got . . . R-rated."

Gray crossed her ankle over her knee, trying to make herself
comfortable on the hearth of the fireplace, while Cherry sat in
the magenta armchair. "Sucks that I was the last person to figure
it out," Gray said. "And now I'm even more confused than when
I started this whole thing. Is Veronica my soulmate? Or another
Aquarius? Or, who knows, maybe I was supposed to end up with
a Pisces but I messed that up too. Molly seemed great, but there
was no hope for something happening between us when I was
talking all about my ex and my dating challenge and all the other
chaos of my romantic life."

Cherry leaned back into the chair and sighed. "I love astrology,
but sometimes I wish the stars would just spit it out, you know?
Give us clear guidance instead of confusingly vague messages."

"For real!" Gray said. "I thought the point of this dating thing
was to find clarity about who I was compatible with, but now
I've got more questions than answers. If only I could go back to
see Madame Nouvelle Lune again and ask what I was supposed
to learn from this whole thing."

At that moment, River toddled over to Cherry, banging a
wooden spoon against a red-lidded container. "Momma! Hold
dis," he said, placing the container in Cherry's lap before wan-
dering back toward his box of goodies.

"Like, I guess I've got a short list," Gray continued, "but it's
still, what, four signs? That's a third of all people! What am I
supposed to do with that?"

"Speak of the devil," Cherry said, examining the Tupperware River had dropped in her lap. "Is this . . . Is this Madame Nouvelle Lune's? From the gumbo?"

"Oh yeah," Gray said. "I guess it is. I totally forgot about that."

Cherry looked up sharply at Gray. "Maybe this is the universe telling us it's time we returned it," she said, a familiar mischievous gleam in her eye, one Gray recognized from years of disobeying their parents.

A LITTLE OVER an hour later, after calling ahead to make sure an impromptu visit was okay, Gray directed Cherry down the gravel road toward Madame Nouvelle Lune's farmhouse. They parked by the familiar chicken coop. As soon as River was unbuckled from his car seat, he ran over to greet the chatty birds.

The astrologer appeared in a faded purple caftan and cowboy boots, waving at them from the front door of the house. "Hello there!" she said, her familiar Cajun accent like a warm hug for Gray's ears. "Mighty nice of y'all to make the drive just to return a piece of Tupperware. Why don't you come on in and rest for a spell?"

Cherry turned to look at Gray, her expression exactly like River's might be upon seeing a real unicorn.

"Thanks, Dori," Gray yelled over the sound of River talking to the chickens. "We'd love to, if it isn't a bother."

"Not at all," Dori said.

As they wandered into the foyer, Cherry couldn't take her eyes off Dori. Gray had never seen her more starstruck, not even when they'd sweet-talked their way backstage after a Demi Lovato concert in high school. Cherry kept staring at Dori's wild blond hair, her weathered hands, her long necklaces with mystic crystal charms.

"Thanks again for letting us drop by," Gray said, handing over the clean plastic container. "And for the gumbo. It was delicious."

"My pleasure, dear," Dori said. River, seeming to take in the astrologer for the first time, approached her legs and grabbed the hem of her caftan. "And who are you?" she asked.

River and Cherry seemed to clam up at Dori's attention, so Gray stepped in. "This is River. He'll be two in a couple weeks. Say hi, buddy."

River let go of Dori's dress to shyly move his fingers up and down in a wave.

"Well, it's mighty nice to meet you, River," Dori said, her voice warm. "I think I've got a few critters that you might like to see as well. You like goats?"

River stared at her with wide eyes, having never seen a goat before outside of his illustrated barnyard animals book.

Dori led them toward the back door, then down the patio stairs to an enclosure. Two nearly full-sized goats ran up to the fence, looking curiously at the newcomers. "Now, Gray, I do believe you met Disco and Cha Cha once before, *non*?"

"I can't believe how big they've gotten," Gray said, stunned by the size of the goats she'd held in her arms and bottle-fed just six weeks prior.

"Gos!" River said, delightedly sticking his hand through the fencing.

"Be careful, River!" Cherry said, finally finding her voice in front of her astrology hero.

Dori walked over next to River and rested her elbows on top of the barrier. "That's right, *cher*, watch your fingers. They'll be expecting a snack round abouts now." After a moment of watching River wave at the goats, she said, "You know, they sure do love yellow dandelions. Like that little patch right out there. Why don't you go pick some of those flowers and we can feed them to our friends Disco and Cha Cha?"

"Gos eat flowers?" River said, his mind blown.

"Goats'll eat just about anything you offer to them," Dori said. After sending River on his dandelion-picking mission, Dori turned back to Gray and Cherry.

Cherry gathered her courage and said, "Madame Nouvelle Lune, I'm such a huge fan. Your horoscopes and all of your astrology content have changed my life. I look to it for everything, every major and minor decision. You're incredible."

"That's mighty kind. And please, call me Dori," she said, then paused to look Cherry over. "Are you expecting another little one?"

Cherry gasped, her face going pale. "I . . . I mean, I hope so, I've been trying, but it's too early to tell."

"May the stars be on your side with this one," Dori said. "You're a Gemini sun, *oui*?"

"Oh my god, you truly know everything," Cherry said, unable to contain her excitement.

Dori laughed. "Not everything. I looked you up in my subscriber list after Gray called."

"Right," Cherry said, looking a little embarrassed. "That makes sense."

Dori looked at Cherry again, then closed her eyes and took a deep breath. "The baby'll be a Sagittarius, I expect. Good pairing for you, although they might bump heads with our little Aries over there." She nodded toward River, who was working at pulling up a dandelion with particularly strong roots.

"I . . . I don't know what to say. Thank you, Dori. I hope you're right."

Gray looked over to see that Cherry had glistening tears in her eyes. She smiled reassuringly at her best friend, pleased she could witness this moment.

"And you," Dori said, turning her attention to Gray. "How's Saturn return treating you?"

"Um, well, it's pretty confusing at the moment," Gray said, swatting at a mosquito on her arm. "I thought I'd have that existential clarity or however you described it by now, but I finished the dating experiment you suggested and it didn't really give me the results I was hoping for."

Dori furrowed her eyebrows. "Now what dating experiment was that?"

"Dating one person of every sign?" Gray said, surprised that it didn't seem to ring a bell for the astrologer. "You know, to get a glimpse into the wisdom of the zodiac wheel and figure out my perfect match before Saturn return happens on my birthday?"

"*Mon cher,*" Dori said with a sigh, "I don't believe I recommended such a thing."

"You didn't?" Gray and Cherry said in unison. They turned to look at each other and, at the same moment, remembered that they'd in fact gotten carried away with Madame Nouvelle Lune's mystical commentary and snowballed it into the dating challenge themselves. It wasn't the first time they'd had collective amnesia about the genesis of their wild ideas, but they'd truly both forgotten how exactly Gray had found herself in this romantic conundrum.

Gray turned back to Dori, looking a bit embarrassed. "My bad. I guess we thought about what you said about the karmic wheel and what I can learn from each sign, and then we came up with the experiment ourselves. It just felt like the quickest way to find out which sign is my soulmate."

"Saturn return isn't just about a birthday. It's a wide window of change around your twenty-ninth year," Dori said, looking sympathetic to Gray's plight. "Astrology is no Magic 8 Ball, and it's no lab test either."

"But didn't you just use astrology to guess that Cherry was pregnant? How else could you have known that?" Gray asked.

"That? Well, the stars give me some intuition about people,

but that's something already done, not seeing the future." Dori shifted her weight to lean her back against the fence, and Disco sniffed her hand through a gap in the wooden planks. "The zodiac can help us understand ourselves and others, figure out what forces and priorities might be shaping their perspectives," she said. "It can show us what energies are at play based on the planetary positions. But it ain't a fortune-telling device. It can't tell us what to do or what will happen. That's all up to *us*, the decisions we make, our actions. As for a perfect soulmate . . . Well, I don't know that finding love is so easy as stumbling across that one person you're destined to meet. Too many factors at play for that. And as much as I wish astrology could give you the name of your true love written out clearly in the sky, that's simply not how the stars speak to us."

Gray's shoulders slumped. "Oh. I guess I didn't walk away with that impression after we met."

"I'm sorry, *pauvre bête*," Dori said gently. "Sometimes I wish it could be that easy too. The stars haven't led me right to true love's door either." She gestured toward the house behind them. "But the planets have guided me to finding all kinds of good things, people I care about, critters to keep me company. And anyway, I got my own second Saturn return coming round the corner next year, so I'm about to be reminded how tough it can be."

Gray took that to mean Dori was approaching fifty-eight years old. She seemed at once younger and older than that. Something about her seemed timeless, ageless. "So what do I do, then?" Gray asked. "I understand more about the signs now, about what I like and don't like in a partner, how to date, even. But how do I know who I should be with when I feel like time is running out?"

"You may feel like time is running out," Dori said sagely, "but the universe rarely runs according to your schedule. All you can do is listen to your own heart, what the planets might be whispering in your ear, and figure out what feels right to you. And sometimes that means taking your time."

At that moment, River came toddling back over, his fists full of yellow dandelions and their green leaves. "I got flowers!" he said proudly.

As Dori showed River and Cherry how to offer the treats to the goats without losing any fingers, Gray let Dori's words settle into her chest. She knew the astrologer had offered her insightful advice, but she wasn't yet sure what to do with it.

AFTER THE GOATS had eaten all of their offerings, Gray, Cherry, and River headed back to the car with a couple of bags of home-made pralines Dori insisted they needed for the trip. As it was now well past River's usual bedtime, it didn't take long for him to nod off in his car seat. Meanwhile, Cherry followed her phone's GPS directions while Gray stared moodily out the window at the night sky.

Once they hit the highway, Cherry glanced away from the windshield over at Gray. "Penny for your thoughts?"

Gray jumped a little at Cherry's voice, having almost forgotten where she was. "These thoughts? They're very heavy, complex, deep. Worth at least a quarter."

"How about your thoughts in exchange for not charging you for gas on this little excursion?"

"Deal." Gray rubbed her face, then smoothed her hair as she prepared to venture into the rocky terrain of her current mental state. "Do you remember back when we were kids in Sunday school? Back before we turned into moody little teenagers and started doubting all the religious beliefs we'd been taught? When we didn't realize that *not* believing was an option?"

"Sure."

"There's something about those beliefs that I missed when we left them behind," Gray said slowly, weighing her words as she spoke. "It faded after a while, but maybe I'd still been hanging on to it without realizing it. It was that evangelical faith that the big, difficult parts of life weren't in our hands. There was no point in worrying too hard about what we should do or how things would turn out or if we were on the right track, because some magical dude in the sky had it under control. And as long as I said my prayers and tried to follow the rules in this little book, it would all turn out okay for me in the end."

"The end being heaven?" Cherry said.

"Right. But also, like, that vague belief that God will take care of you and give you nice things in this life too. I don't think that's *totally* the message the Bible sends, but it's pretty much how it gets boiled down for Sunday school." Gray stared out the window for another moment before continuing. "I'm wondering if I threw myself so hard into astrology because I wanted it to give me back those simple answers, that trust that everything will be all right. Maybe when I broke up with McKenzie and my whole life was upended, I tried to fall back on that 'Jesus, take the wheel' mentality, except it was more like 'Cosmos, take the wheel.'"

"You know that I love astrology and do see truth in it," Cherry said. "Or at least, as a Gemini, I half believe it and half don't, since I'm a flip-flopper at heart. But I think you're right that it can be easy to substitute it in as this all-knowing higher power when that's not really what it promises to be." Cherry drummed her thumbs on the steering wheel, contemplating. "I think I owe you an apology for getting all wound up in this dating challenge with you, since apparently that's not what Madame Nouvelle Lune meant at all."

"Hey, I'm the one who was begging for some mission I could complete like Dora the Explorer," Gray said. "Like astrology was my singing map, and I just had to go through the horoscope forest, climb rising sign hill, and cross Mercury retrograde river to find my perfect match. You helped me iron out the details and cheered me on, but *I'm* the dummy who thought I could *win* at love if I could cross the astrology challenge finish line." Gray rubbed the heel of her palm against her forehead. "I just want the perfect wife and family in my head to be *real* already."

"But no spouse or family can be both *perfect* and *real*," Cherry said. "You know that, right?"

"Yeah, yeah, of course," Gray said, although she hadn't thought of it in such clear terms. Cherry had a point. "It's just . . . Do you remember Alyssa, our teammate on the Twisters?"

"First base, braces, obsessed with My Little Pony?"

"That's the one."

"What about her?" Cherry asked as she looked over her shoulder to change lanes.

Gray leaned her head against the cool glass of the passenger-side window and told Cherry about her memory of that day at the Tastee-Freez. It was one of the only significant moments in her life she had neither experienced with Cherry nor told Cherry about after the fact. Gray supposed she'd kept the moment to herself out of some superstitious fear of ruining it. "I still picture that afternoon a lot when I think about what I want my future to be like," Gray admitted when she'd finished telling the story. "Alyssa's moms had it right, you know?"

Cherry looked away from the road to search Gray's face for a moment, then burst out laughing. It took her a moment to catch her breath, but when she did, she said, "How well did you know Alyssa's moms, Gray?"

"Not super well," Gray said, feeling a little defensive for baring her soul and getting laughed at. "My parents wouldn't let me go to their house, remember? But I know a good thing when I see it."

Seeming to recognize that her reaction had been insensitive,

Cherry said more gently, "Maybe you saw a good *day*. But that didn't make their *relationship* good. I went to a party for the softball team at Alyssa's house once, and her moms had this huge screaming match about giving us soda. It was in the kitchen, but we could hear every word from the living room. Super awkward. I thought Alyssa was going to die of embarrassment."

Gray couldn't match Cherry's story to the image of Alyssa's moms in her head. "Couples fight," she reasoned. "Just because you saw one disagreement doesn't mean their marriage wasn't aspirational."

"Remember how Alyssa left the team in sixth grade because she moved to Ohio?" Cherry asked.

Gray nodded.

"That's because her moms got divorced," Cherry said. "One of them, Misty, took the kids with her to live with their grandparents." She checked Gray's expression before breaking the even worse news. "A couple years later, I heard a rumor her other mom cheated with a rival softball team's coach."

Gray's beloved mental picture at the Tastee-Freez shattered like a broken mirror. "No way," she said, pulling at the seat belt she suddenly felt was choking her. "How did I miss that? Why didn't you tell me?"

Cherry shrugged. "I don't know. I didn't realize they meant so much to you, I guess."

"But at least they were good parents, right?" said Gray, grasping at straws to keep her picture of the perfect family alive. "Alyssa and her brother always seemed so well adjusted."

Looking sorry for what she was about to disclose, Cherry said, "Well, uh . . . I actually heard last year that Alyssa's brother was involved in some crypto scam targeting the elderly. I thought I told you about that."

"Fuck. That was *him*?" Gray vaguely remembered Cherry telling her about some article she'd read on a con artist from Tulsa, but she hadn't put the pieces together. Most of her attention had been focused on playing Elden Ring on her PC.

"Yeah. I think the trial is going on now." Cherry glanced at River over her shoulder, then turned back to the road. "Look, I'm not saying that you won't have a wife you love or amazing kids. I want those things for you too. But if you're looking for *perfect,* and especially for the perfect family to just fall into your lap, through astrology or religion or whatever means, you're setting yourself up for disappointment."

"God, I'm such an idiot," Gray said, dropping her head into her hands. "I'm almost thirty. I should know nothing about life is that simple. Everything is messy and no one has the answers."

Cherry reached across the console to pat Gray's knee. "You know, maybe Saturn return hasn't helped you find your soulmate. But perhaps this is part of something else it's trying to teach you," she suggested.

"Like what? 'Life is an endlessly confusing quagmire, try not to die'?"

"Maybe," Cherry said. "But in, like, a nice way. Despite what our parents tried to tell us, there are no right or wrong answers. There's no prewritten script or cheat sheets or dude in the sky telling you what choices to make. So that means it can be whatever you want it to be. You get to pick your own priorities and goals and dreams and act accordingly. And people can tell you they disagree with what you choose, but it's still ultimately your decisions that matter, not theirs."

Gray gulped. "Sounds kind of terrifying, doesn't it?"

"Sure. But kind of awesome too. Like an open-world videogame. No levels or quests you're tasked with beating. You get out of it whatever you put into it."

"Huh," Gray said, considering. "You're quite the modern philosopher, Cher."

"Thanks. It's probably because my Uranus is in Aquarius."

Cherry reached for the radio dial. "How about an old-fashioned Dolly Parton sing-along to make us feel better?"

"Won't it wake River?"

Cherry peeked over her shoulder. "Nah, he's fully passed out. He'd sleep through a whole hoedown at this point."

Gray grinned. "All right then. But only if we start with 'Backwoods Barbie.'"

"Deal." Cherry handed Gray her phone to find her song request, and before long, Gray's inner turmoil faded into the familiar twanging tunes of countless best-friend road trips gone by.

Twenty-seven

$\mathcal{I}$T WAS A truly gorgeous Thursday evening, the kind of spring weather that made Gray feel like anything, no matter how seemingly dead and hopeless, could suddenly burst into lively color. The past two days had been as transformative for her as they had been for the newly bloomed flowers. Retrospection on her conversations with Molly, Madame Nouvelle Lune, and Cherry, along with some soul-cleansing apartment decorating, had transformed Gray's confused dread of the future into optimism. As she walked into her usual neighborhood park with River's stroller, she felt she couldn't still be the same person she'd been the last time she'd walked on these sidewalks.

As she approached the park, Gray felt a sense of anticipation buzzing across her skin. She wanted at once to sprint to her regular bench and to delay, dragging her feet in case the person she hoped to see wasn't there. Despite her reservations, River's excited chatter about the swing set meant Gray couldn't stall. She held her breath as they rounded the corner within view of the jungle gym.

But her bench was empty. Gray's eyes searched hopefully for dark, shining hair in a long bob, or a precocious kid in an eclectic outfit. But as River pleaded to be released from his stroller, Gray had to accept that the face she was looking for wasn't there.

With all the soul-searching Gray had undergone in the past few days, she knew she shouldn't be so easily crushed. She still had so much work to do to straighten out her priorities. Maybe it was a sign that she was trying to reach out too soon—or maybe she needed to stop looking for omniscient signs in everything that happened to her. That thought didn't protect her from feeling a little glum as she pushed the swing higher and higher. But River's squeals of delight slowly lightened Gray's mood, and by the time she set him back on the ground to run toward the slide, she'd decided to not let her unfulfilled expectations ruin her evening with her favorite godson.

Once River had come barreling down the twisty slide into Gray's waiting arms five times, he turned his attention to the oversized tic-tac-toe set, and Gray settled down on her usual bench. *This is fine*, she thought. *I can focus on me. And River. This is not a disappointment. The universe doesn't work on my timeline.*

Just when she'd almost convinced herself it was true, she heard a familiar high-pitched voice calling, "River!"

It was Karys, running from the direction of a different pathway into the park. She was wearing a pair of rainbow-striped leggings, a Wonder Woman shirt and cape, and a cowboy hat. The completely Karys outfit put a huge grin on Gray's face.

Karys and River hugged, and then Karys spotted Gray. She climbed onto the bench next to Gray and wrapped her arms around her neck for a hug, her hat nearly falling off when it collided with Gray's head. "Hi, Miss Gray," Karys said. "I got a new bracelet from my dad. Wanna see?"

"I'd love to," Gray said, her anticipation ratcheting immediately back up.

Gray was complimenting the tiny paintbrush and palette charms dangling from Karys's bracelet when she heard the voice she'd been hoping would reach her ears.

"Karys! Where did you— Oh." Veronica rounded the jungle gym, her hair ruffled by the breeze and eyes hidden by chunky sunglasses. She was wearing the same tie-dyed tunic she'd worn the first time Gray encountered her at this very park, hitting Gray with a rush of nostalgia. After hesitating for a moment, Veronica walked over to the bench and sat down at the far edge. She gave Karys a soft pat on the back and encouraged her to go play with River by the tic-tac-toe set.

Veronica and Gray sat wordlessly without making eye contact, staring out at the playground, both waiting for the other to break the silence. Although Gray had spent a lot of time imagining what she would say in this moment, it was surprisingly cleansing to sit together quietly, letting some of the pain of their last encounter lose its sting.

After what felt like a day but was probably closer to ten minutes, Veronica spoke. "I hoped you would be here," she said so quietly that it took Gray a moment to comprehend her words.

"You did?" Gray asked, turning to look at Veronica's profile.

"And now that you are, I don't know what to say."

Recognizing this as her chance to make things right, Gray jumped. "I do," she said. "I've been thinking about all of the things I want to say to you since the moment you walked out of my office. And I want to start by saying I'm sorry. For a lot of things, some of which were in my control, and some that weren't, but that I'm still sorry happened to you. To us."

Being someone who lived by a better-to-ask-for-forgiveness-than-permission motto, Gray was experienced with apologies. But this one felt like the most important apology of her life, and she wanted to get it right. "First of all," Gray said, "since you probably won't get much regret or sympathy from the source, I'm sorry that parent took those incredibly personal and invasive pictures, and I'm sorry that the board president felt entitled to share them widely. You have a right to privacy, even if you're something of a public figure. That's completely inappropriate. I hate that it's something you'll likely have to deal with the consequences of for a long time, and something you'll have in the back of your head whenever you're outside of your house in the future. That should never have happened to you."

Veronica didn't say anything or even turn her head to look at Gray, but her lips tightened in a way that made Gray know she was listening.

"And while I'm not sorry about what happened between us that night, I *am* sorry that it started in such a public space that exposed you to this kind of difficult situation." Gray looked to make sure River and Karys weren't within hearing range and then continued. "I was . . . I was so wrapped up in kissing you that I didn't think about where we were or who might see. I wish in retrospect that I'd been more cautious in that moment. But I could never regret what it led to between us later that night, because it was one of the best nights of my life. Even knowing what happened afterward. And it honestly hurts me a lot to know you wish it never happened."

Gray angled her body toward Veronica, wishing she would give her some kind of sign of how she felt about Gray's words, but seeing none, she carried on.

"I'm also sorry that I quit like that without giving you a chance to weigh in, without taking the time for us to consider options. It was rash, which I know is one of my bad habits. But I don't regret the decision I made, because I made it out of care and concern for you and your students. I promise you that I wasn't walking away because I didn't care about your goals. In fact"—Gray swiveled to pull a binder out of a bag hanging from River's stroller—"over the past few days, I've worked on some of the projects I left unfinished. Updates to the school's mission statement, a letter to parents about the curriculum changes for next school year, suggested language for advertising those new sponsored scholarships, some talking points for various potential situations with the board, including the, um, rather tricky one we found ourselves in a few days ago. Take or leave whatever you want from it. I just wanted to save you some late nights drafting or waiting for the next PR specialist to be hired."

Gray placed the binder gently between them, a kind of peace offering to Veronica. Veronica's gaze shifted from the playground to the binder, although she didn't pick it up.

"I know that things got complicated between us really quickly," Gray said, "and I know that was because, as soon as I realized I had feelings for you, I put a lot of unnecessary weight on it. I've been in a weird place lately. I felt like I was falling behind, like I wanted to suddenly level up ten steps without doing the work, or even figuring out if those are the steps I wanted and needed. I'm still working on breaking that mindset. But what I'm trying to say with all of this is that you're the best thing that's happened to me since I moved to New Orleans. Since I broke up with my ex, even. And I don't want this to be the end of us. However you'll have me—playground acquaintance, friend, something more, to be determined—I'll take it. I won't force it into some box. I'm here to figure out, with you, what we are. I've seen all of these wonderful aspects of you that you don't always show the rest of the world, and I know there are still so many sides of you I haven't seen yet. You're brilliant and fierce and compassionate and fascinating, and I'd do anything to be even a footnote in your story."

Gray didn't have anything else to say after that big finish, so she sat quietly, hoping Veronica wouldn't suggest she fall into a hole and leave her alone forever. Her eyes still locked on the binder between them, Veronica ever so slowly reached out her left hand to pick it up, then began thumbing through the thirty-ish pages included. "You did all of this in the past few days?" Veronica said, her voice hoarse.

"Well, some of it I'd started before I left and put on a thumb drive when I was packing up," Gray said, feeling a rush of relief that Veronica was engaging in the conversation. "Don't tell Dr. Donovan, I'm pretty sure that's against the rules."

Veronica carefully closed the binder and set it on the other end of the bench, scooting a few inches closer to Gray. "I'm . . . I'm incredibly grateful that you did all of this work for me," Veronica said, seeming to find her voice. "That you quit your *job* for me, that you still want to be around me when *I* should be the one apologizing to *you*. You said all of those kind and thoughtful words, and I'm still at a loss."

"You don't have anything to apologize for," Gray said.

"Of course I do." Veronica pushed her sunglasses on top of her head and angled herself toward Gray. "Those things I said on Tuesday . . . They were horrible, Gray. I'm sorry, truly. I was obviously furious about those pictures, panicking that they were already making the rounds, and scared, so scared of what it meant. And they've been a nightmare since, although things are starting to turn around."

Gray felt a little tension release from between her shoulders. "They are?"

"Yes, but that's not what matters right now," Veronica said. "What matters is that I had no right to yell at you for sacrificing your source of income to save me. That was a life-altering gift you gave me, resigning, and I didn't know how to accept it. And all of this . . ." She gestured to the binder Gray had brought her, then shook her head, stunned. "What am I going to do with you, Gray? You're this wild fireball of optimism and determination and no-mountain-we-can't-climb attitude, not to mention the best kisser I've ever met."

Gray felt her cheeks go pink. "So you don't regret our date?" she asked hopefully.

"Of *course* I don't regret our date," Veronica said immediately. "I regret that parent thinking they could invade our privacy like that. Maybe I regret letting myself become so unaware of our surroundings. But kissing you, going home with you? I wouldn't change it for the world."

"Me neither." Gray reached out to place her fingers over Veronica's hand where it rested on the bench. "But if you felt that way, why didn't you reach out afterward?"

Veronica laced her fingers through Gray's. "I still don't have all the words I want to say to you straightened out in my head," she said carefully. "I always know what to say, but something about you ties my tongue in knots. I haven't been able to get you out of my mind since you walked into my office that first day, late and disheveled and brimming with tenacity. I was glad you gave me a compelling reason not to ask Donovan to fire you, because I wanted to see you again before you'd even walked out the door."

Gray squeezed Veronica's fingers gently, her heart soaring, wondering how she'd been the last to notice what had been going on between them.

"And the more I got to know you, the more intrigued I was, the more I wanted to spend every moment together. But I'm cautious. I have to be. At my age, with my job, with Karys, I *have* to be careful." Veronica looked off toward the kids, who were still fully engaged in their play, unaware of the intense conversation happening on the bench. "You told me how you wanted to get married quickly, start a family as soon as possible . . . Gray, I like you so much it scares me. And in the midst of all that stress and anxiety when you quit, you saying that us being together was our *destiny* . . . Well, it sent me into this wild panic. This terror that things were moving too quickly for me to be thoughtful and deliberate. But underneath that fear was a tiny glimmer of hope, of wanting that for myself, for us." Veronica paused, her lip barely trembling. "As much as I care about you, jumping into the deep end with you is completely terrifying. If that's what you still want, a wife and kids as soon as possible . . . I don't think I can be that for you. I need time. To figure out what that means for my life right now. To figure out if it's the right thing for Karys."

Gray followed Veronica's gaze to where Karys was helping a smaller child onto the seesaw in front of her. She smiled fondly, then turned back to Veronica. "Well, I've been doing some thinking about that," Gray said. "I went to see that astrologer I told you about, Madame Nouvelle Lune, and had a bit of a realization that I was looking for answers she couldn't give me, and neither could the stars."

Veronica turned to look at Gray, her head tilted to the side curiously.

"It feels obvious now," Gray said, looking down at her shoes against the recycled-rubber ground. "But so much of this recent quarter-life crisis or whatever you want to call it was a reaction to how my parents raised me. The way I threw myself into astrology looking for answers, feeling like I was running behind in life, even the image I have in my head of the family I want—I think it was all part of this need to prove myself as worthy and successful and happy without them. But if I'm happy without them, why am I still measuring myself against their yardsticks, you know?"

Gray had forgotten they were still holding hands until Veronica squeezed her fingers a little tighter. "So getting married and having kids . . . You don't want that anymore?" Veronica asked.

"I think I do," Gray said. "I love kids. I want a partner who loves me to be my co-parent. I think those desires are mine, not forced on me by my parents. But the rush is off. I don't have anything to prove to anyone but myself. If those things are right for me, I'll find them in my own time."

"Oh, Gray," Veronica said, moving even closer so their hips were touching and their joined hands rested on Veronica's knee. "That's a lot to figure out all on your own."

"Yeah, I know," Gray said. "Which is why I talked some of it out with Cherry. And I set up an appointment with a queer-friendly therapist for next week. I've got to stop looking to astrology for answers and start looking inside of myself, and I think I could use a professional's help for that. And as soon as I get a new job and new health insurance, I'm going to freeze my eggs so I have that option when I'm truly ready. I actually have an interview lined up for a PR job with the city council, thanks to the Capricorn I went on a date with, and I've got a good feeling about it."

"You seem two years wiser after only two days," Veronica said. "So does this mean you don't believe in astrology anymore?"

" 'Believe' is a complicated word," Gray said, considering. "It's still kind of interesting, right? I might check my horoscope sometimes. But when it comes to life's big questions, I'm going to look inward for the answers instead of to the planets."

Veronica nodded. "That sounds like a reasonable approach."

Gray looked down at their intertwined hands and swallowed. "So does all of this change anything for you? About feeling like I'm asking you to dive into the deep end? Do you think we could take our time and figure out what we want together?"

Veronica closed her eyes for a moment, seeming to contemplate Gray's question as the spring breeze ruffled her hair. "I would like that. Taking our time. Together," she said.

Gray's heart soared. She'd had no idea where this conversation might go when she'd arrived at the park; her main priority was simply seeing Veronica's face again. But now she knew what she wanted, more than anything, was to figure out what was next in her life with Veronica by her side. No pressure to hurry their relationship along. No rush to take things to the next level. Just the two of them, and sweet Karys, taking things one day at a time. "Oh, Veronica," Gray said, her voice heavy, while the rest of her felt light as air. "I would like that too."

They sat in companionable silence for a few minutes, enjoying the feeling of their fingers intertwined.

"So what happened with the board and those pictures?" Gray asked eventually. "You said things were looking up?"

Veronica settled in closer to Gray's side with a sigh. "Well, your resignation must have lit some kind of fire under Dr. Donovan," she said. "You know he's always been a little standoffish when it comes to conflict with the board. But he went all in this time. He called an emergency meeting to demand they stop circulating the pictures, pushed the president to resign for sharing them so widely. He even used some scary legal threats about revenge porn, since you could kind of see up my dress in that one picture. Turns out Dr. Donovan and I had more allies on the board than we realized. They just weren't as vocal as the other side, until now. They forced the board president to step down early, and the president-elect took over with a demand that the photos never be shared or discussed again, since you'd already quit." Veronica crossed her legs so her foot brushed against Gray's knee. "And Dr. Donovan told me that he's planning to retire in a couple of years and wants to position me to take over as superintendent when he does."

Gray's eyes went wide. "For all three schools? Veronica! That's incredible!" She reached her arm around Veronica's shoulders in a side hug.

"And I realized," Veronica said, resting her head against Gray, "that the first person I wanted to tell—about the stressful board stuff, about the good news when they chose to defend me, about Dr. Donovan's plan, the good and the bad and the hopeful stuff for the future—was you."

The sun was making its descent over the playground, lighting up the sky with pastel colors reminiscent of their date at City Park. Gray looked down at Veronica, and Veronica glanced up. Their eyes said more in that moment than all the words they'd shared. They inched closer, eyes drifting toward each other's lips, a kiss feeling wonderfully inevitable, until they were interrupted by a small voice.

"Aunt Gay, I hungy."

Gray and Veronica looked at River as one, blinking away the intimacy of the moment. "You're right, River," Gray said, looking at her watch with surprise. "It's past dinnertime, huh? I'll take you home to your mom and dad."

Karys approached them right behind River. "Ma, can Miss Gray and River come over for dinner again?"

"Sorry, Karys, but River has to go home for dinner with his parents," Gray said.

"Okay," Karys said. "What about you? Can you come over for dinner?"

Gray looked to Veronica, who nodded encouragingly. "Sure, I can come to dinner," Gray said, barely trying to conceal her joy at how the evening had turned around. "Thanks for inviting me, Karys."

"You know, I think we can do better than that," Veronica said, her foot nudging Gray's knee. "What if Miss Gray has a sleepover at our house?"

Karys's face lit up. "On a school night?" she asked, delighted and scandalized.

"Well, it is a special occasion." Veronica looked at Gray, a familiar mischief dancing in her eyes. "What do you think, Miss Gray?"

Never breaking eye contact with Veronica, Gray grinned. "I love sleepovers. I'm in."

THE NEXT MORNING, Gray awakened to the mattress shifting with someone else's weight. She cracked her eyes open, realizing first, that she wasn't in her own bed, second, that she was completely naked, and third, that she was incredibly happy with how the previous day had ended. Vignettes flashed through her head of Veronica revealing the smooth golden skin beneath her tie-dyed tunic, Veronica's lips against Gray's collarbone, Veronica's finger tracing a pattern along Gray's inner thigh, Veronica's tongue on . . . Suffice it to say, it had been a fantastic night. Gray opened her eyes to see Veronica sitting on the edge of the bed. "Good morning," Gray said, her voice cracking.

Veronica leaned over to plant a kiss on Gray's lips. "Good morning, sunshine."

"What time is it?" Gray asked, still squinting at the sun beaming in through Veronica's gauzy curtains.

"Almost seven." Veronica stood up and tossed Gray a pair of sweatpants and an LSU hoodie. "Better put these on. Karys has something she wants to show you before she leaves for school."

Before Gray could ask any questions, Veronica disappeared through her bedroom door. Gray rolled out of bed, threw on Veronica's clothes, and brushed her teeth in the en suite bathroom, then wandered toward the living room. As soon as she rounded the corner of the hall, Veronica and Karys, decked out in party hats and the matching aprons Gray had brought them from the Tabasco factory, started singing "Happy Birthday." It appeared they'd been up for a while. They had decorated the dining table with a construction paper banner, balloons, and Gray's favorite part, a crayon drawing of what appeared to be Gray, Veronica, Karys, and a dinosaur, rendered in a style Gray recognized from Karys's artwork framed around the house.

"Thank you! What a wonderful surprise," Gray said when the song ended. "I'd honestly forgotten today was my birthday."

"How could you forget your birthday?" Karys asked. She grabbed Gray's hand and pulled her to a chair at the head of the table. "Sit here, I'll be right back."

Gray gave Veronica a joyful and surprised smile as Karys ran into the kitchen.

"I told her it was your birthday, but the rest was her idea," Veronica said.

Karys reappeared at the door of the kitchen, a plate of pancakes topped with whipped cream and sprinkles in her hands. She carefully placed the plate in front of Gray, then pulled a blue birthday candle from her apron pocket and stuck it in the middle of the pancakes. "Ma, fire please."

Veronica walked over to Gray's side and lit the candle with a match. "Make a wish," she said.

Gray squeezed her eyes shut, trying to come up with a wish. She'd spent so much time contemplating the future, worrying she was falling behind, wanting more than what she currently had. But sitting between Veronica and Karys, in this beautiful moment, she couldn't dream of anything more perfect. She thought, *I wish for more of this,* then blew out the candle.

Karys and Veronica joined Gray at the table to eat their pancakes over a conversation about the best birthday cake flavors. When they were done, Veronica sent Karys to finish getting ready for school. Despite Veronica's protestations, Gray helped clear the table and wash dishes in the kitchen.

"Do you have Karys tonight?" Gray asked while organizing plates in the dishwasher.

"I do," Veronica said, passing over a handful of forks.

"Do you have plans?" Gray closed the washer and straightened up. "I'm having a little housewarming-slash-birthday party at my apartment. Nothing big, just a few people I've met since I moved. I know River would love having a friend to play with. And, you know, I'd love having *you* there."

"To play with?" Veronica smiled mischievously.

Gray tucked a hand into Veronica's back pocket. "That's for the after-party."

———

FOR ALL HER WORRIES about living alone in her new apartment, Gray was delighted to realize how much it already felt like home. Part of that was because she'd hit a sale at the antiques store down the block and gotten a great deal on a lot of gently used and refurbished furniture. The walls were still a bit empty, but for now, Gray had dotted them with streamers and balloons.

But what really transformed the space was filling it with new and old friends. Once the party was under way, she took a moment to watch her worlds pleasantly colliding. Cherry was asking for feedback on the punch she'd made from Jackson the Gemini and their partner, Céline. Riley the Taurus and Tara the Capricorn were lounging on the new couch, telling a couple of Gray's local journalist acquaintances the story of how Gray had introduced them. Robbie was helping Molly the Pisces hang a small work of stained glass she'd brought as a housewarming gift. Arielle the Sagittarius was checking out the cheese and veggie trays on the breakfast bar, trying to goad one of Gray's new downstairs neighbors into tasting the hot sauce she'd given Gray upon arrival. Here they all were, beautiful and bright and charming, showing Gray that she'd found exactly where she was supposed to be.

Gray's moment of reflection was interrupted by a knock at the door. She opened it to find the two people that made her party complete. Veronica greeted her with a warm hug, while Karys peeked in the door looking for River.

"Carrots!" River said, toddling over to his friend. "Wanna play unicorns?"

Karys held a pointed finger against her forehead and galloped into the living room, River close on her heels. "Hey, what if we played narwhals?" she suggested. Seeing River's confused expression, she said, "They're like unicorns, but in the *ocean*."

River's eyes went wider than Gray had ever seen them. "Water unicorns? Whoa!" They disappeared into a play space Gray had set up in her office.

Gray turned her attention back to Veronica. "Can I get you a drink? Beer, wine, seltzer? Cherry's signature pink lemonade punch? Warning, it's potent."

"Seltzer sounds great."

Gray walked to the kitchen and came back with Veronica's drink. Although she knew the polite thing to do was to start introducing Veronica to the rest of her guests, she couldn't help but steal one more private moment first. Tugging Veronica's belt loop, she led her around the corner into her bedroom and wrapped her in a short but passionate kiss. By the time they reentered the living room area, they were giggling like teenagers.

"See those two over there?" Gray pointed toward the fireplace. "Local journalists. The woman on the right is the one who helped us fix that hit piece in *The Times-Picayune*."

"I'll have to thank her," Veronica said. "Are any of your astrology dates here?"

Gray blushed. "Um, yeah. A few." She discreetly identified Jackson, Riley, Tara, Arielle, and Molly as they walked toward the kitchen. "I guess with you, that makes six. Half of the zodiac."

Cherry appeared before them, her face lit up with excitement. "Oh my god, you must be Veronica." She started to hold out a hand, then instead grabbed Veronica in a hug. "I've heard so much about you."

"And I you," Veronica said, seeming unfazed by the hug from a stranger.

"Don't believe everything Gray says," Cherry stage-whispered. "*She's* the one who stole the Beanie Baby from *me* in second grade."

"Noted," Veronica said with a laugh. "Thank you for designing those posters with the Gina Byers Kane quote. They light up my day every time I see them in the school library."

Cherry seemed to glow at the compliment. "You're too kind."

"Now, there's something I don't hear often," Veronica said.

Cherry laughed heartily. "Well, I like you already. But I'm also an air sign, so we're meant to be friends." Cherry turned to Gray, who was watching the interaction play out with immense delight. "She knows about the whole astrology thing, right?"

"She does," Gray said, "but maybe we shouldn't talk—"

"Wait, is the Leo here?" Veronica said in a conspiratorial tone. "I've always wanted to meet an Olympian."

"No, she's out of town," Gray said. "And don't you think it's weird to—"

"I knew Gray would be compatible with an Aquarius," Cherry interrupted. "I was rooting for that or Gemini. Isn't the Gemini here?"

"I'm a Gemini!" Jackson said, catching the word from across the room. "Why? What's up?"

Molly jumped in, connecting the dots. "Oh my god! You're the Gemini Gray went on a date with? I'm the Pisces!"

"We also both went on dates with Gray. Right, babe?" Tara said, turning to Riley.

"Are all twelve of your astrology dates here?" Molly asked loudly.

"Astrology dates?" Arielle said. "Was I part of this too?" Fortunately, she seemed more intrigued than betrayed.

Gray looked between Cherry and Veronica, who, like everyone else in the room, were staring at her expectantly.

"I think it's time you told them," Veronica suggested.

Cherry nodded emphatically.

Gray cleared her throat, a little nervous to come clean about the experiment in which several people in the room had been unknowingly involved.

Seeing Gray's uncertainty, Veronica placed a hand on her lower back and gave her an affirming nod. "It's a good story," she whispered. "They'll enjoy it."

Gray gave Veronica a private smile, then turned her attention to the room at large. "Well," she said, "it all started when I went to see this astrologer."

Acknowledgments

I know you just read a whole-ass novel I wrote, but allow me, if you will, one more story.

Years ago, before I'd gone so deep into the astrology rabbit hole, six months ahead of my twenty-ninth birthday but before I knew anything about Saturn return, I decided on a whim to write a book. When it was finished, I put it away, never planning to do anything with it. Then I broke my leg. With nothing to do but sit on the couch and feel sorry for myself, I dusted off that manuscript and tried to see what I could do with it. A few months later, a couple of weeks before my Saturn return, I met Katy Nishimoto. Katy went on to become my editor, and that manuscript went on to become my debut novel, *Queerly Beloved*.

As I look back, it's hard not to see that sequence of events as the hand of the universe pushing me toward where I was meant to be. My first thanks, for as long as we can make books together, goes to Katy. Thank you, Katy, for being a brilliant editor, inspiring creative partner, and champion of my work from the beginning. Whether or not our meeting was written in the stars, I'm incredibly honored that you saw something in my writing and decided to join me on this grand bookish adventure.

I'm also grateful to Katy for introducing me to my magnificent agent, Jamie Carr. Jamie, thank you for your creative vision, your enthusiasm, your patience, and your unwavering support. I can't imagine doing any of this without you. Gemini twin power for life!

Thank you to all of the good folks at The Dial Press and Random House who supported this book: the visionary leadership of Whitney Frick, Andy Ward, and Avideh Bashirrad; the publicity and marketing brilliance of Debbie Aroff, Maria Braeckel, Madison Dettlinger, and Melissa Folds; and the thoughtful design, editing, and support of Diane Hobbing, Donna Cheng, Cassie Gonzales, Cara DuBois, and Rose Fox. Thanks also to the team at The Book Group, and to Berni Barta and Michelle Weiner at CAA for championing my writing for film and TV. Y'all are rock stars.

Writing for *Book Riot* has been instrumental for building my bookish community and finding the courage to write my own books. Thanks to Liberty Hardy, Annika Barranti Klein, Jess Pryde, Jamie Canavés, Rachel Brittain, P.N. Hinton, and all the other Rioters who have cheered me on and helped me find my place in the big literary world.

Booksellers are some of my favorite people on Earth. Thank you to all the booksellers who have put my books in the hands of readers. Extra special thanks to Hannah, Christine, Malik, Char, and the whole team at Loyalty Bookstores in D.C. and Silver Spring; Laurie, Laynie Rose, Amy, Destinee, and everyone at East City Bookshop in D.C.; Pat & co. at Magic City Books in Tulsa; and Lynne and the folks at WordsWorth Books in Little Rock. Thanks also to the magical and wonderful librarians who fight to keep queer books on the shelves, and a special shout-out to Ellen at the Tulsa Library and Darryl at D.C.'s Petworth Library for celebrating *Queerly Beloved* with your patrons. I'm also grateful to the wonderful book bloggers, reviewers, Bookstagrammers, and BookTokers who spread the reading love.

Something I have now that I didn't have my first go-round is friendship with other authors. Thank you to all the authors who have commiserated and celebrated with me, including Ginny Myers Sain, Tirzah Price, TJ Alexander, Courtney Kae, Timothy Janovsky, Elissa Sussman, Alison Cochrun, Ashley Herring Blake, and the many others who have welcomed me into their hearts and DMs.

Thank you to the friends and family who have supported me in ways large and small while working on this book: Trey Johnston (Leo legend), André Sanabia Johnston (Libra lovebug), Jordan Gates (Aries angel), Sinovia Mayfield (Gemini gem), Diane Britton (Virgo . . . vivant? Okay, I'll stop), Anne Jessup, Donald Jessup, Britton Gildersleeve, Paige Robnett, Eric Barnes, Megan Zorch, Catherine Roberts, Meredith Nelson, Heidi Demuynck, Noura Hemady, Katie Yeilding, Ari Johnson, Sarah Pradhan Johnson, and the many others I wish I had infinite pages to thank.

My mom, April Dumond, is the first Aries I ever met, and like Gray, she's an Aries to her core: passionate, driven, courageous, and hardheaded in the best way. Thank you, Mom, for showing me how to fight for what I want. Thanks also to my dad, Ralph Dumond, for taking me to the library as often as I wanted as a kid and not doubting me too hard when I told him I was quitting my day job to write. I also owe him and all the wonderful Cancers in my life an apology for the bad rap they got in Carolina. But y'all have to admit you're not always great at opening up to strangers!

Finally, my eternal gratitude goes to my wife, Mary Jessup. Way back in 2010, I went to a space-themed house party. I cut stars out of yellow construction paper, wrote

the names of the stars in the Big Dipper on them, and
pinned them to myself as a last-minute costume. In my very
first words to Mary, who hadn't worn a costume, I offered
her one of my construction paper stars to wear. So in a way,
the stars really did have something to do with bringing us
together. Mary, thank you for believing in my writing before I did, for talking through my bookish bumps in the
road, for cheering with me and crying with me and riding
ill-advised 3 A.M. Greyhound buses to book events with me,
and for loving me always. I'm so goddamn lucky to spend
my life at your side.

LOOKING
for a SIGN

Susie Dumond

Dial Delights

*Love Stories
for the
Open-Hearted*

Madame Nouvelle Lune's
Celestial Circle Newsletter
The Life Cycle of the Zodiac Wheel

Bonjour, beautiful stardust beings! And if you're a new Celestial Circle member, welcome! You can expect weekly newsletters from yours truly covering timely astrological events and deep dives into what the planets can tell us about ourselves and our world.

I trust that you're all setting your intentions for the next four weeks just in time for tonight's new moon in Aries. Find my tips for working with the energy of the moon phases on my <u>website</u>.

Now that the moon is making its own fresh start in the first sign of the zodiac, it's the perfect time to discuss the life cycle of astrology. This is one of my favorite windows into understanding the stars and the flavor each sign brings to the great gumbo pot of humanity.

Each sign is associated with its own age—not of the body, but of the soul. Starting with newborn Aries, the ages run in order through Pisces at the end of life. Now, I trust y'all astro darlings know that there are people of all ages in each sun sign. But perhaps you've met a child that seems too wise for their years or a senior citizen with spry, child-like energy. That magic spark inside each of us has an age that doesn't necessarily match our driver's license.

Let's take a look at the spiritual age of each of the signs, shall we?

Aries

Aries are the infants of the zodiac, opening their eyes to find a whole new world to explore. They take on any challenge with a sense of wonder and joy, wiggling toward what they want and grasping at it with their chubby little baby hands. Even when they're rushing headlong into a bad decision, you can't help but find them adorable.

Taurus

Tauruses are one-year-olds, learning to crawl and then walk, determined to figure out how to get around on their own. Home and family are their safe place to explore. They're discovering what they like—and what they don't like. Don't rush them, because if they fall, they'll scream.

Gemini

Geminis bring all the charm and frustrations of a child in their terrible twos. Curious and difficult to control, they seem to have their hands in everything, so much so that you wonder if there's secretly two of them. But their wit and creativity make it tough to stay mad at them for long.

Cancer

Elementary-school-aged Cancers are just beginning to understand the big outside world. They're most comfortable at home around family, and they can have an emotional reaction to being taken out of their safe zone. But they've also got a playground energy full of childlike joy.

Leo

Just like teenagers, Leos are bold, audacious, and sometimes a bit self-centered. Confidence comes naturally to them, so don't you dare try telling them what to do. They

spend a lot of time styling their hair and selecting their outfits, but they're not all vanity. They also make loyal friends
and are quick to defend their loved ones.

Virgo

Conscientious Virgos are in their early twenties, writing
their own rules for existing in the world. They don't look to
others to take care of their problems; the power to find so-
lutions is inside themselves. But also like a twentysome-
thing, they struggle to accept help when it's offered.

Libra

Libras represent maturation into adulthood with all its at-
tendant responsibilities and pressures. Like their symbol of
the scales, Libras seek fairness and balance. Some may perceive these tendencies as people-pleasing. But really, Libras
know it helps to have friends on your side.

Scorpio

Falling in the midthirties, Scorpios have grown a bit of a
shell that can be hard to crack. They've been around long
enough to have higher standards for themselves and the
people around them, and they don't forgive easily. But once
you get past that scorpion exoskeleton, they're secretly
softies on the inside.

Sagittarius

Sagittariuses inhabit a just-over-the-hill middle age. They
know life is short, and it's time to start checking things off
their bucket list. That's why the archer loves seeing the
sights and traveling off the beaten path. They're straight
shooters who don't coddle anyone, but you know you'll always get their honest opinion.

Capricorn

Nearing their sixties, Capricorns put career front and center, feeling they have limited time to reach their goals and build a legacy. They're driven by status and want others to recognize their success. When not working, Capricorns prioritize family above all else. Mess with their loved ones and you'll get the sea goat horns.

Aquarius

Aquariuses are the recent retirees of the zodiac, no longer concerned with being taken seriously and more interested in living their best lives. That's not to say they don't care about others; they truly want to make the world a better place. But they certainly don't care what society considers "cool" and prefer being lovable weirdos.

Pisces

Like people at the end of a long life, Pisces know what really matters. They are the most emotionally intelligent of the signs. They're also prone to nostalgia and can write a birthday card message that will bring you to tears. If you want sage advice on life's biggest questions, try asking a Pisces to join you for a cup of tea.

That's all for this week, starbits! Until next time, you can find me on my website, www.madamenouvelleluneastro.com.

Best wishes from the bayou,

MNL

The Signs as Iconic New Orleans Food and Drinks

ARIES (MARCH 21–APRIL 19)
Eggs Sardou & Creole Bloody Mary
Ambitious, flashy, and a little bit spicy

TAURUS (APRIL 20–MAY 20)
Red Beans and Rice & Sazerac
No-frills, reliable, and classic

GEMINI (MAY 21–JUNE 20)
Bananas Foster & Absinthe Frappé
Hot and cold, intriguing, with a dash of chaos

CANCER (JUNE 21–JULY 22)
Beignets & Chicory Coffee
Soothing, nostalgic, and a bit of a softie

LEO (JULY 23–AUGUST 22)
King Cake & Hurricane
Iconic, celebratory, at the center of the action

VIRGO (AUGUST 23–SEPTEMBER 22)
Gumbo & Vieux Carré
Sensible, detail oriented, always hits the spot

LIBRA (SEPTEMBER 23–OCTOBER 22)
Jambalaya & Pimm's Cup
Balanced, refreshing, beloved crowd-pleaser

SCORPIO (OCTOBER 23–NOVEMBER 21)
Muffaletta & Abita Root Beer
Complex, layered, salty, and sweet

SAGITTARIUS (NOVEMBER 22–DECEMBER 21)
Crawfish Étoufée & Café Brûlot Diabolique
Adventurous, authentic, laughs in the face of danger

CAPRICORN (DECEMBER 22–JANUARY 19)
Oysters Rockefeller & Ramos Gin Fizz
Ambitious, luxurious, always a little extra

AQUARIUS (JANUARY 20–FEBRUARY 18)
Turtle Soup & Grasshopper
Original, bold, and full of surprises

PISCES (FEBRUARY 19–MARCH 20)
Pralines & Brandy Milk Punch
Comforting, warm, just a little nutty

Veronica's
"Oh Yay, It's Penne" Chicken Pasta

Ingredients:
- 1 tbsp olive oil
- 3 cloves garlic, thinly sliced
- 1 pint cherry tomatoes, halved
- 12 oz roasted red peppers, chopped
- 2 tsp Italian seasoning
- ½ tsp salt
- ¼ tsp black pepper
- 2 cups chicken broth
- ⅓ cup dry white wine (or additional chicken broth)
- 3 cups uncooked penne pasta
- 2 cups diced cooked chicken
- ⅓ cup grated Parmesan cheese
- 1 cup fresh basil, thinly sliced
- Additional Parmesan cheese and basil for garnish (optional)

Directions:
1. In a heavy, microwave-safe covered dish (like stoneware, ceramic, or glass), combine olive oil, garlic, cherry tomatoes, roasted red peppers, Italian seasoning, salt, and pepper. Stir and microwave on high, covered, for 4–5 minutes.
2. Add chicken broth, white wine, and penne pasta to dish. Stir and microwave on high, covered, for 7 minutes. Stir and microwave for an additional 5 minutes. If pasta is not tender, microwave for 2–3 minutes at a time until al dente.
3. Mix in diced chicken, ⅓ cup grated Parmesan, and 1 cup sliced basil. Serve topped with additional cheese and basil, if desired.

Veronica's Anytime King Cake

Dough Ingredients:
- ⅔ cup whole milk, warmed to 100°–115° F
- 2 tbsp granulated sugar
- 1 envelope instant yeast (2 ¼ tsp)
- 3 cups bread flour, plus extra for kneading
- ¾ tsp salt
- 2 large eggs, lightly beaten
- 8 tbsp butter (1 stick), room temperature
- 1 tbsp vegetable oil

Filling Ingredients:
- 4 tbsp butter (½ stick), softened
- ¾ cup brown sugar
- 2 tsp ground cinnamon
- ½ tsp ground nutmeg
- Zest of 1 orange

Icing Ingredients and Decoration:
- Miniature plastic baby (optional)
- 1 cup powdered sugar
- 2 tsp milk
- 2 tsp orange juice
- Green, purple, and yellow sugar

Directions:
1. Combine the warm milk, 2 tbsp sugar, and instant yeast in a small bowl and mix thoroughly with a fork. Let stand until frothy and fragrant, about 10 minutes.
2. In the bowl of a stand mixer fitted with a dough hook,

combine 3 cups bread flour, yeast mixture, and salt. Stir with spatula to begin combining. Add lightly beaten eggs and continue stirring until a shaggy dough forms.

3. Turn mixer on low. Once the flour is fully incorporated, add the butter one tablespoon at a time, giving each pat time to absorb into the dough. Once butter is incorporated, continue mixing dough on low for 5 minutes until smooth and elastic, pulling away from the sides of the bowl. (If you don't have a stand mixer, you can knead by hand for about 10–15 minutes.)

4. Move dough to a lightly floured surface and knead a few times by hand, then shape it into a ball and place in a large bowl coated with 1 tbsp oil. Cover with a damp dish towel and store in a warm place to rise until doubled in size, about 60–75 minutes.

5. While dough is rising, in a small bowl, using a rubber spatula, mix together 4 tbsp softened butter, brown sugar, cinnamon, nutmeg, and orange zest for filling.

6. When risen, transfer the dough to a lightly floured surface and punch down any large air pockets. Cut into three equal pieces. Roll each piece into a rope about 20 inches long, then use a rolling pin to flatten each rope into a long, skinny rectangle, about 20 inches by 3 inches.

7. Sprinkle a third of the filling onto each strip of dough, then spread evenly across dough with an offset spatula. Roll each strip back into a long rope, pinching the edges of the dough to seal in the filling. Braid the three ropes of dough together, lightly stretch braid to reach 20 inches in length, and form into a circle, pressing and tucking the ends together.

8. Place the braided ring on a baking sheet greased or lined with parchment paper, cover with dish towel, and allow to rise for about 45 minutes.

9. Preheat the oven to 350° F during second rise. When dough

is doubled and lightly puffy, bake until golden brown, 25–35 minutes. Remove from the oven and let the cake cool completely. If using, tuck the plastic baby figurine into a fold in the bottom of the cake.

10.   In a small bowl, using a rubber spatula, mix together the powdered sugar, milk, and orange juice for the icing. Drizzle over top of cake. Before icing sets, alternately sprinkle the purple, green, and yellow sugar across different sections of the cake.

Notes:

- *Whoever finds the plastic baby in their slice of cake is said to have good luck! You can also use a clay ball or dried bean. This token is traditionally called "*la fève.*"*

- *The filling for this cake is versatile. Leave out the orange in the filling and icing if you prefer. You can also add chopped nuts or dried fruits.*

- *Instead of braiding the dough, you can roll the dough into a single rectangle measuring about 20 by 10 inches, spread the filling, roll it up like a jelly roll, and connect the ends to form a circle.*

SUSIE DUMOND is a queer writer originally from Little Rock, Arkansas. She is the author of *Queerly Beloved* and *Looking for a Sign*, and is a senior contributor at *Book Riot*. Susie lives in Washington, D.C., with her wife, Mary, and her cat, Maple. When she's not writing or reading, you can find her baking cupcakes or belting karaoke at the nearest gay bar.

susiedumond.com
Instagram: @susiedoom

About the Type

This book was set in Sabon, a typeface designed by the well-known German typographer Jan Tschichold (1902–74). Sabon's design is based upon the original letterforms of sixteenth-century French type designer Claude Garamond and was created specifically to be used for three sources: foundry type for hand composition, Linotype, and Monotype. Tschichold named his typeface for the famous Frankfurt typefounder Jacques Sabon (c. 1520–80).

Books Driven by the Heart

Sign up for our newsletter and find more you'll love:

thedialpress.com

:camera: @THEDIALPRESS

:arrow_forward: @THEDIALPRESS